THE MIRRORMAKER

60 YEARS IN CANADA
1933
1993
HarperCollins

THE MIRRORMAKER

Intrigue, treachery, and murder in Venice

DAVID THOMPSON

HarperCollins*PublishersLtd*

THE MIRRORMAKER

For information address HarperCollins Publishers Ltd, Suite 2900, Hazelton Lanes, 55 Avenue Road, Toronto, Canada M5R 3L2.

First Edition

Endpapers illustration: *Bird's-Eye View of Venice* (detail, upper central portion). Woodcut, 1500, 67.5 x 100.4 cm. Jacopo de Barbari, Italian, ca. 1460/70-before 1516.

Canadian Cataloguing in Publication Data

Thompson, David, 1953-
The mirrormaker

ISBN 0-00-224009-2

I. Title.

PS8589.H478M57 1993 C813'.54 C93-093744-9
PR9199.3.T57M57 1993

---

93 94 95 96 97 98 99 ❖ RRD 10 9 8 7 6 5 4 3 2 1

For L & L

Homo homini aut deus aut lupus.

Man is to man either a god or a wolf.

ERASMUS

Piave
Taglia
mento
Brescia
Venice
HUNGARY
Nice
(ITALY)
THE GULF
(ADRIATIC SEA)
Ragusa
(CORSICA)
Rome
Naples
(SARDINIA)
TYRRHENIAN
SEA
CORF
IONIAN
SEA
(SICILY)
Messina
MALTA
MEDITERRAN

THE TURKISH EMPIRE
Constantinople
AEGEAN SEA
EECE)
Athens
ca
N
W
E
S
Rhodes
RHODES
Candia
CRETE
CYPRUS
A N S E A

Part One

I

Lazaro turned the corner and saw, in the faint light of a torch far off down the cobbled street, the finely made mask of a wolf, covered in hair. The wolf head tilted up and seemed to howl at the moon. He was drawn toward it, but, before he could move, it disappeared around a corner. Somewhere a bell tolled. He hurried down the narrow *calle*, turned the corner, and mounted a small humped bridge, pausing alone in the center. The water in the canal was dark and seemed to suck the light out of the air. There was a movement in the faint reflection on the water's surface, and he looked up to see another bridge further along the canal. The man with the wolf mask was there, crossing. Lazaro hurried on, holding his arm, feeling the warmth of the recent wound, wondering if the assassins were following. He crossed the second bridge and entered a larger but deserted *calle*. The mask was there again, then gone. He turned another corner to follow, but it seemed to vanish into the air, lost in the whirlwind of the streets.

He stumbled toward an exceptionally boisterous crowd gathered at a corner. A woman in the crowd noticed him and turned, hoisting her skirt high. She wore a small mask tied to her pubic hair. The crowd erupted in laughter. A thin man in a rooster mask urinating on the wall turned to see what had occasioned the laughter, continuing to urinate, wetting the leg of the man next to him who also sported a rooster headdress. The two began to shove each other, and all attention turned from Lazaro to the cockfight in progress. He moved on.

At the corner to another darker and still more narrow *calle* he saw, far off, a woman leaning against the wall, half seated on the lip of a shuttered window, her dress pulled up and tucked into her belt and her bodice opened, revealing large breasts. A man leaned against her, holding her legs up around his waist, his stockings about his ankles, his bare buttocks thrusting. A second man sat beside them, pouring wine from a flask into his mouth. They didn't seem to notice Lazaro as he passed. At the end of the *calle* he stopped and leaned against the side rail of a small bridge, looking into the canal.

Wisps of mist came up from the canal and danced about the paving stones. A dim light grew in the alley, and he looked up to see that the moon was now above him. Lazaro reached for the flask of wine slung over his shoulder and tipped it, burning, into his throat. Almost immediately the wine turned in its descent. He fell to his knees and saw, briefly, his reflection on the surface of the water, then shut his eyes and vomited into the canal. When he was finished he stumbled off into Carnevale, not quite sure who he was or where he had been. The memory of the fight earlier that night was dimming now, mixing with many similar memories.

He felt very tired, and, thinking now only of his bed, he turned and made his way through the mad streets to his lodgings. He tumbled up the stairs, past sleeping dogs and small men, past moaning women, groaning under the weight of their lives, past men straining to spend themselves in some fury which made it impossible for them to think of death, if only for a moment.

The door slammed behind him and he was safe. With his good arm he pushed open the window and ignored the unpleasant smell in favor of the cool night breeze which came in from the sea, twisting its way through the watery labyrinth. The moon was now clear of the clouds and painted a ghostly hue across the rooftops, illuminating the odd chimneys and the platforms on which the young women sunned themselves by day in aid of blonde beauty. For a moment he recalled the girl he had watched secretly since arriving but then pushed her image from his mind. With bloodied fingers he undid the studded leather coat, removed his weapon, his tunic and pants. Standing naked before the moon, he was seized with but resisted a distant pagan urge to spring naked through the window and run about the rooftops with the cats that hunted here and there for rats and pigeons.

There was a rustle, and the cat whose visits marked a rhythm known only to itself, came to his window, paused to be stroked, and then was gone.

He watched thin strands of cloud cut across the face of the moon, then turned to examine his arm. The cobwebs he had applied soon after the fight had clotted the blood, and the piece of cloth he had wrapped around it would do until morning. He tried to remember if he had played the fool, but he could find nothing but glimpses of things he knew had occurred too long ago to have been this night. The bed creaked as he sat down then fell back, his arm throbbing dully, his mind searching for some thoughts to lull him away from dread of mortality. Somehow he found a long-forgotten prayer: "My Lord and God, do not abandon me; remember my need, for many evil thoughts and horrid fears trouble my mind and terrify my soul."

Sleep came to him but gave him little solace. He dreamed of a shimmering angel, her long hair billowing in a moonlit breeze, and of a mirror in which he saw foreign, murderous eyes in his own face. He screamed, but his mouth was full of sand.

II

Lazaro awoke naked, spread across the bed, his legs curled up into his stomach like a child, his wounded arm cupped to his chest, his good arm folded under his head. For a few moments he did not move, just lay there, feeling the sun on his body, smelling the fish from the market at the corner, hearing the bustling sounds of the day. It put him in mind of waking as a boy with the warm sun of Rhodes bathing his room. He knew it was Rhodes, for in his memory he heard his mother singing as she prepared bread and his father's deep voice telling a story to his brother. Then he felt the brush of air coming in through the open window: it was the first of March, the beginning of a new year, and Venice was cool.

The door opened before he could get up and close the window, and in walked Renata, the innkeeper's daughter. After a weak attempt to pull his bedclothes over him he gave up and resigned himself to what he knew would come. Naked men did not surprise her.

She slammed a pitcher of water on the rough table beside the window then turned. "You were quiet when you came in last night," she said as she bent to pick up his clothes.

He said nothing, preferring to watch the play of the canal-reflected sunlight on the ceiling.

She flung his pants at him and hung the rest over the foot of the bed. "You dress like a barbarian and smell just as bad. Do you want a bath?"

He had had a bath under her hands before, and, though it had been pleasing enough, today he had neither the money nor the inclination.

As if she could read his mind she forced her lips into a friendly pout, brushed her long bleached hair from her face, and offered, "You won't have to pay for the extras."

He thought for a moment, then swung his legs over the edge of the bed and stood to pull on his pants. "No thanks," he said, shaking his head, "I have other business to . . ."

"Business!" she said, and headed for the door in a huff. She paused and pointed at his arm. "And don't get any blood on the sheets or Papa will have to charge you extra." She slammed the door, and he heard her marching down the stairs.

Lazaro shook his head then sat down on the bed again. A growling stomach and a painful head from last evening's drinking were the least of his worries. His left arm throbbed. It had been some time since he had thought in terms of his sword arm and his dagger arm, but the habit had returned in those few moments in the dark *calle* last night. His stay in Venice had allowed him to drift away from the life he knew, and he had grown accustomed to the many pleasures which this city offered. But most pleasures required money, and he had not made any in some time.

As he had stumbled along in Carnevale last night, from somewhere had come his name, a voice crying out to him from the past, from the battlefields of Brescia, and elsewhere. From another life it had called to him, that voice, and had wakened him. The call to action had been brief, fierce, painful, and strangely satisfying, frighteningly satisfying.

He glanced at the cloth wrapped around his arm and untied it. The wound seemed healthy; he was thankful the blade had been sharp and clean. The blood which was showing through was mainly from the night before, although there was some evidence of fresh bleeding, probably from rolling on it in the night. It would leave a straight scar, an addition to the collection which decorated his body. Not all the scars came from battle. Many, particularly those on his back, had resulted from beatings by teachers, as they had tried to teach him obedience. It had been a lesson he could not learn.

The old man's face came to his mind: Angelo, the glassmaker. Angelo would be at the furnaces, Carnevale or no. And this morning Lazaro missed the odd comfort he found when he visited Angelo and watched the mystery. The sound and feel of the heat of the furnace, the weight of the metal gathered white-hot on the end of the *punti*, the soft hiss of the master's breath, the glow of the shape as it grew, swung in the air, achieved balance, and ended, annealing, as a fragile object, light frozen. And if only he could find some way to spirit Angelo and his skill out of Venice and north, his fortune would be made. That pleased him as well.

Lazaro stood again and finished tying his pants, then stumbled to the table. There was a metal mirror hung behind the water pitcher and Lazaro stared into it. Unlike the precise and honest mirrors fashioned by Angelo, this mirror was dark and imperfect, with a pitted reflective surface which allowed him only a glimpse of a portion of his face or body at a time. But Lazaro preferred this. Though he was fascinated by the beauty of true mirrors, he had never been comfortable looking into them. Angelo had commented on it and Lazaro had replied, with attempted wit, that man was supposed to be created in the image of God, and that he couldn't bear to see that God was so ugly. But it was more truthful than he had wished to be. Either God was so much less than what the Church said, or man's fall from grace had left him horribly scarred and twisted. In either case, Lazaro didn't appreciate the reminder. Most of all, a good mirror seemed to allow Lazaro to see too far into himself, past what he could display to others, past even what he could display to himself. Deep within him there was something which defined him, and a mirror allowed him to catch a glimpse. It wasn't an image of God.

Even this metal mirror seemed too precise this morning and he turned away. Grasping the pitcher he held it to his lips and quaffed nearly half of it, water streaming down his chest. He took some of it and bathed the wound, then hung his head out the window and poured the rest over his dark hair. Setting the pitcher down on the table, he ran his fingers through his hair, drew his wet hands over his face, then leaned on the window sill, looking out over the city.

For him, it was a city which was defined by the darkness it contained — that was the Venice he knew. But by light of day it was a different place: civilized, formed of human hands, almost home. The labyrinth gave way to streets and canals, the *calli* and *rii* of Venice. Somewhere below he heard the cry of the water merchant, "*Acqua fresca, acqua fresca,*" as she wandered through the *calli*, two water jugs balanced on a yoke over her shoulders. Above the *calle* there was not one continuous roof now but many. And the blue-black had given way to sienna tiles. Reflective surfaces diffused the light so that his eyes ached in their sockets. In the distance he could just see the Campanile stretch above the city and he knew that at its roots lay the Piazza, and beyond, the Grand Canal, and, further still, the Lagoon and the Gulf. Here and there on poles jutting out from second- and third-floor windows hung the washing of the city. And everywhere there were chimneys rising to a fat, swollen cluster above the roof tiles. But what struck him most was the light which shone up from below — sunlight reflecting off the surface of the canal below and playing out on the ceilings of the rooms along the *rio* — *la vecchia* they called it — like the lines on the face of an old lady squinting. Water and light were everywhere. And when the light was right the city glowed with some power, some energy which seemed to flow within the very water itself.

Then he lifted his eyes to the platform where his vision appeared almost every day. It was nearly time and he had no doubt that she would be there. Even though there was still a chill in the air he was sure she would come out, wearing her wide-brimmed crownless hat so that her golden tresses would catch the bleaching rays of the sun but her gentle face would be spared. He had found out her name by following her home and inquiring, and it sang in his mind: Marzia Zorzi.

As if by incantation, she appeared. She was accompanied by a servant who helped her to sit on the chair firmly attached to the *altana*, then began arranging her hair so that the golden tresses fell about the hat's brim and every strand was evenly exposed. She was beautiful, more beautiful than all the painted angels he had ever seen.

His stomach growled again, and the pain in his head returned. Much as he wanted to watch Marzia for a while longer, he knew that if he did not get some meat and drink soon he would be useless for the entire day, and he could not afford to be so. He had thought he might visit Angelo, to be warmed by his company and by the furnaces, and to see as well if he had any odd pieces which he wanted Lazaro to sell outside regular channels, but the events of the past evening had given him a more immediate task. He had to locate Béres.

Seeing him had raised many questions. There were the simple questions — What was Béres doing in Venice again? What sort of trouble was he in? Then there were the more difficult questions, those which Béres would ask. And it would start with Béres asking him why he was still in Venice.

Lazaro knew that the answers he had would not satisfy Béres; they barely satisfied him. He had grown weary of the life of the mercenary and even contracted intrigues were somehow less palatable. As he dressed and thought of his answers, his lodgings paled in the new light — a small room on the fourth floor of a building with a tavern — the Dancing Mouse — on the ground floor, a room which was often noisome, usually noisy, and always itchy. What kept him there wasn't the hospitality of the owner, a fat woman who had a timid stickman for a husband, or desire for their daughter, a girl with comfortable beauty and little virtue. The place was cheap and it afforded a view of Marzia's *casa*, but then Marzia didn't keep him in Venice either. The view was an added bonus but it was not in itself enough.

Was it the glass?

In some ways, yes. Glass manufacture was a carefully guarded secret in Venice. The wealth of the city depended on holding a monopoly on the manufacture of the best glass pieces, particularly mirrors, and the Secretariat spared little energy in protecting its resource. Glassmakers were unable to leave Venice without permission of the Secretariat, and that permission was seldom, if ever, granted. And unless one was admitted to the glassmaking guild, one was not allowed to learn of its secrets. It had been over a year since he had met the old mirrormaker Angelo, and from their first meeting Lazaro had felt an affinity for the old man. Angelo seemed to hold these laws in disdain and had the talent which allowed him to do so. He had allowed Lazaro to act as an occasional and unlicensed glass merchant. There had been profit there and, surprisingly, no interference from the Secretariat. Lately Angelo had taken to inviting Lazaro to his factory and Lazaro had found this fascinating. However, he was not confident that the Secretariat would allow this to continue long without interference. Lazaro was sure the profit and the interference would be greatly magnified if Angelo could ever be enticed to leave Venice to set up a shop in Augsburg or Paris. Yet, the more Lazaro got to know Angelo, the more he worried that he might never leave. Anyone else would have given up long ago, found some more willing, if less talented, glassmaker. Béres would remind him that it wasn't natural to spend a year waiting for the right moment.

Perhaps most of all, though he sensed this as a possible truth only when it came to him stealthily, it was his past which beckoned him and enticed him to stay just a little bit longer. Lazaro had found something comforting in the smell and the heat of the furnace, and in the glass itself. There were memories of his father imbedded in the glass. He had been a glass merchant and had entertained his sons and his wife with the beauty of glass and sunlight. But, although Lazaro's mother had been Venetian, his parentage had made it impossible for him to ever be considered a citizen of Venice. As quickly as these thoughts entered his mind he began to dismiss them, and the images they conjured. It mattered little to him now, and there was really nothing here which might teach him of his mother; she had spent most of her life in Crete. And Rhodes. The mirage faded from his mind and in its place once more was the mirror of Venice; not just the old man's manufactured object, but the mirror which Venice held up to life — a cruel and true mirror it was.

There was no more time to watch Marzia on her *altana*. He had to locate Béres. And his stomach was growling regularly now. He would have to eat something. Even the mean cooking of Renata's mother would do.

The fish stew was heavy in Lazaro's stomach as he headed down the *calli* and across the squares to the Piazza. Some of these streets he had crossed the night before in his search for the man who had called his name. Finally Lazaro had spotted him —Béres — being dragged along by the *bravi* of the Signori di Notte, the Lords of the Night, the civil guard of Venice. They seldom bothered the ruffians who were Venetian born and bred, but the ruffians who had been in the service of Venice and now came to call on their mistress, these ruffians they were on the lookout for. So he had come to the rescue of his old comrade-in-arms and had nearly lost his life. He had been partaking of the joys of Carnevale, the beauties and the beasts, not expecting a fight, and when the fight had presented itself he had had little time to consider his involvement or choose his ground. It had been a pitched battle, a street fight with sword and stiletto in a narrow alley. He had knocked out one assassin but another had attacked him and had sliced his arm. That man had sustained a more meaningful wound and would not be troubling anyone for a while. In the aftermath of the mêlée Béres had disappeared, but Lazaro knew he had not imagined him.

On Béres's last night in Venice they had drunk in a small inn kept by Peter Pander, located just outside the Fondaco dei Tedeschi — the business hall of the Germans — and that's where he expected to find Béres today. The place was frequented by the northern barbarians and the Venetians stayed away. Though they loved wine, women, and the occasional song, the Venetians felt threatened by the barbarians' power when they turned to these vices. In fact, Lazaro thought to himself, he had seen little to verify the claims of the Venetians regarding the character of these barbarians. For the most part they were dour businessmen, likely to get you drunk and laid in order to conclude a business transaction. But Béres was different. He was more Venetian in his enjoyment of pleasure, though even in the depths (or heights, Béres would have said) occasioned by the wine or the women or the song, his head was still clear. And by the cruel light of day the battle or the business deal would be found to favor him.

As Lazaro approached the tavern, he heard a scuffle within, some curses in Hungarian, then a table overturning and the sound of fighting. He entered and as his eyes grew accustomed to the brown light he saw a bear of a man in his mid-fifties, strong and hearty, holding a struggling dwarf upside down. It was Béres. He was banging the dwarf's head on the floor, and the dwarf was trying to shield his head with the cap he held in his hands, thus leaving his pockets free to empty.

Béres was surrounded by other merchants who, although clothed in some of the fineries of Venice, either wore some articles of clothing which set them apart or simply seemed different in their bearing or in the shapes of their faces and heads. Lazaro did not know the men but he recognized the dwarf. It was Sebastiano, a pickpocket who normally worked the crowded Rialto Market across the bridge from the Fondaco. Poor Sebastiano had chosen the wrong mark.

A reddish-brown purse struck the floor, and Béres smiled and ceased banging Sebastiano's head but would not let him down. "Now my little mouse, it is time for a bath," he said, and carried him to the window. Sebastiano pulled his cap over his eyes, choosing not to see what he knew would next occur. With his free fist, Béres smashed open the shutters and leaned out over the small *rio*. He looked about to be sure that no boats were passing, then dropped Sebastiano. As the dwarf hit the water the merchants inside the tavern burst into laughter. Béres walked back to the pile of treasure and took his purse, then gathered the rest and gave it to the barman. "Make sure the little fellow gets this, all of it. He works hard to steal it and I don't want him to lose any." The barman nodded.

Béres turned and, seeing Lazaro, grabbed a flask of wine, shouting to the merchants that he would join them later. "*Kedves baratam*," he said as he crashed into Lazaro and pulled him close in a rough hug. "You survived the night after all." Lazaro winced as Béres squeezed his wounded arm. Béres released his grip a bit, then squeezed even harder. "No point in coddling it, my young Moor, you've seen worse than that." They walked to a table and sat down.

It had been at the second battle of Brescia that Lazaro had met Béres, a Magyar baron who had come to fight and join in the spoils. They had a common acquaintance in Augsburg, the merchant-banker Fugger, and that, coupled with their love of the wonderful Hungarian wine, Tokay, had been enough to begin the bond. Béres had brought some men with him, but they had all been killed, except for a young German named Vom Scheidt, who loved good wine and married women. The three had worked well together and, surprisingly, they had survived. They had profited from the battles, and Venice had benefited from their involvement.

But, the fate of all mercenaries, when the wars finished they were not very welcome in Venice. The Secretariat saw the value of having battle-hardened men close at hand and humored them, allowing them to visit so long as they did not become too disruptive. And when they did become too disruptive, the Secretariat dealt with them silently and quickly.

There would be other battles soon, no doubt. Although there was relative peace with the rest of Europe, Suleiman, the Great Turk, was flexing his muscles in Hungary with his irregular cavalry, the Akinji, and sending shivers through the west. Selim, his father, had attacked the Knights of St. John at Rhodes and had invaded Hungary, but in both exploits he had failed. It seemed natural that the son would try to succeed where the father had failed.

It struck Lazaro as odd that Béres was not fighting in Hungary.

"Transylvania is crawling with the Akinji," Béres explained, "and soon I'll have to return and deal with those lice, but, for the moment, I am needed here. And I have brought a business proposition."

Lazaro recognized the hushed tone which Béres now took. It had led him into danger too often in the past. He smiled and clapped his hands over his ears. "Don't talk to me. Look what happened last night."

Béres pulled his hands off his ears. "You look foolish," he said with a grin and handed him the flask, motioning for him to take a drink. It was Tokay. Lazaro knew it meant trouble. Béres hunched his shoulders and the hairs in his fur collar turned up like the hackles of a wolf. "You've been near the glass furnaces too long and it's melted your brains."

Lazaro had expected him to bring up Angelo, and his own inaction now made him defensive. "There's no point rushing something this delicate. Extracting a glassmaker from this pit is no small task." He had considered carefully the manner in which a mirrormaker could be escorted from Venice, and in doing so he had come to know more of the assassins and their master. The assassins were the secret police of Venice, *bravi* controlled by the Grand Chancellor and under the direct supervision of one Giambattista Beccaria. They were seldom seen, though their presence was always felt; they wandered about in disguise, something easily done in a city which lurched from one festival to another and had a dizzying penchant for masks and costumes. Apart from being expert swordsmen they carried a cold weapon as their trademark, a razor-sharp glass stiletto to shove into the belly then break off and leave to work its magic among the intestines. "Any member of the guild who slips away from Murano is sentenced to death. And no one will buy a glassmaker who won't survive long, even if I could deliver him in one piece."

"You've developed a respect for law," Béres sighed, pulling off his wool cap to stroke his bald head.

Lazaro shook his head, "I'd rather not be declared a Barbarian." Just seven years before, the statute governing outlaws had been reaffirmed and strengthened. It provided that anyone declared a Barbarian could be killed by anyone else for a bounty. And any outlaw who had been sentenced with a crime could have that sentence erased by bringing in the head of someone convicted of a greater crime. It appealed to what Machiavelli considered to be a man's better qualities. "We'd have every outlaw in Europe after our asses . . ."

Béres smiled and raised his bushy eyebrows. "No profit without risk."

". . . and the assassins as well."

"I wouldn't give much for the swordplay we faced last night," Béres said in a voice which taunted.

"We?" Lazaro rolled his eyes.

Béres just shrugged and smiled again.

Lazaro shook his head. "It's not their swordplay. They're madmen. They don't stop."

"Are you finished?" Béres asked.

Lazaro smiled and grabbed the flask. "Yes."

"I'm not interested in your glassmaker at the moment." Béres said, shrugging his shoulders. "You think everybody wants to drink out of those little transparent curlicues with dragons on them? Well, they don't. There are more important things than glass. Not that we couldn't make a handsome profit at it, mind, but no, that's not what I'm here for this time."

Lazaro passed the flask back and leaned forward. "So what is it then?"

"Fugger."

Lazaro sat back. He should have known. "Here in Venice?"

Béres nodded. "He sent word that he wanted me to escort him, so I came. And he wanted me to find you, so I did."

Lazaro nodded, and they got up, Béres leading the way.

As they headed for the Fondaco, Lazaro thought of the time almost two years ago when Fugger had last called on him. It was cold, mid-March, 1520. Fugger had had a problem. One of the Pope's bankers, Chigi, had a squeeze on Venice and Fugger needed it broken. It was Fugger's own fault. He had lent Emperor Maximilian the money to wage war on Venice and so Venice had been forced to borrow from Chigi. But Chigi didn't like to charge overt interest; that would have been usury. Instead, he had extracted from Venice a monopoly on the lucrative alum trade which flowed through its port, and took the Jewels of St. Mark as collateral. Things went from bad to worse: the wars over, Chigi still held Venice by its jewels; Fugger had a plan to make a great deal of money in the alum trade and he would have shared it but Chigi would not hear of it. The Pope was on Chigi's side, as were a few influential citizens of Venice. Fugger didn't care much about the old men of Venice — most of them would have a price, but he couldn't be seen to be taking any extraordinary action because, as the Pope reminded him, he had been favored with a papal monopoly for collecting the money paid out for indulgences in Germany.

If this delicate business matter was to be resolved in Fugger's favor, a practiced, dependable, and discreet hand was required. Fugger asked Lazaro to take care of it. The records showed that Chigi had died of a sudden illness on the sixth of April. Pleased, Fugger had offered Lazaro an appointment in Augsburg, but Lazaro had just wanted to be left alone, and so Fugger had given him a generous payment, only recently depleted.

Now Fugger was back, and he hadn't come to take the waters. Perhaps he would be interested in investing in a mirrormaker. This might be just the opportunity he had been waiting for, Lazaro thought as they passed through the inner courtyard of the Fondaco, filled with German merchants busy with their goods. They entered the dark hallway at the back, then walked to the end. Conscious of the echoing cadence of their footfalls, Lazaro tried to break stride, but Béres grabbed his arm and pulled him on. They paused at the door and Béres looked deep into Lazaro's eyes. Lazaro had seen that look before, at moments of great danger in battle when Béres was about to try something daring and profitable. There was the time the Swiss Landsknechts had held a particularly well-appointed *casa*, and Béres had been sure of the riches contained therein. There had been a roof nearby and some rope . . .

Béres opened the door, and they entered a smallish chamber, window closed and shuttered. The light entered in small golden streams about the cracks in the shutters and caught the dust floating. One beam of light cut across a guard standing on one side of the table at the far end of the room. There was a guard in the shadow at the other end and a man seated behind the table, fat and furred, with his back to them. In front of the table were two chairs. As their eyes became accustomed to the light Lazaro noticed another man with a red cap standing beside the seated man, pointing over his shoulder to a book which the seated man held in his lap. Above them was a mirror which showed most of the room. Lazaro noticed the reflection of himself standing beside Béres, and he averted his eyes.

The red-capped man looked up, then came toward them and led them to the chairs as the two guards left the room, pulling the doors closed. Lazaro listened and heard them walk down the hall, though he was aware that they stopped before they had gone the entire length. He also noticed that there was no other door and that the window was securely bolted.

Suddenly the furred man turned and rose from behind the table and walked into the light. It was Jakob Fugger.

"Lazaro, it's been too long," he said with a smile, hugged him, and then held him at arm's length and looked deeply into his face. "You haven't changed, has he, Janos?" he said, turning to Béres, then signaling them both to sit, waved for his bodyguard to bring a chair around for him.

Lazaro saw that Fugger hadn't changed either, except that his teeth were even browner than they had been. Otherwise, he was still the same short, stout, bulbous-nosed German merchant he had always been. Fugger now turned to Lazaro and Lazaro was struck by the power in the man's eyes.

"When I have placed my trust in a man's ability once, I expect never to be disappointed. And that is doubly true when that ability includes loyalty. I just want to warn you that I haven't changed." A smile returned to his face and he spread his hands like an old street merchant. "But I don't need to say that to you. I wouldn't have come all this way to see you if I didn't believe in you."

Béres smiled at Lazaro, but Lazaro knew that a warning was meant.

Fugger sat back in his chair and wiped his brow with a white handkerchief. Lazaro could smell perfume, and it seemed out of place with this German. Fugger cleared his throat and swallowed whatever it was that had been troubling him. "There is a man, Lazaro, a merchant here in Venice, who has become a boil on my ass. He opposed me two years ago in that alum matter and he cost me a lot of money then. I might have forgiven him for that, but he keeps it up." Fugger almost banged his hand on the desk but stopped himself before the hand hit and coughed into the handkerchief. He paused for a moment then continued. "You see — I only have to think of him and he disrupts my equilibrium. If I believed in witches, I would think that he has had *una strega* cast a spell on me." Fugger paused again and smiled. "If I believed in witches I wouldn't have had to come all the way here, would I?" He laughed, and Béres and Lazaro smiled. Then Fugger's face became grim again. "He has hurt me in business a little, and I can handle that. That's business. After all, we're not in a guild. I don't expect friendship. But his political position in Venice at the moment is . . ." Fugger searched for the word, "troublesome. He stands in the way of some major profits I intend to reap, and some deposits I intend to protect." Fugger smiled at them again. "I am a patient man, but his interference continues to cost me. I have lost profits and now I have lost my patience. I wish that money could buy me what I need, but some men just have no sensible price."

Béres looked at Lazaro and Lazaro nodded to him. "Is there anything to drink in this barn?" Béres asked.

Fugger nodded to his bodyguard, standing quietly by the door, and the man left. "I need the matter resolved. I can't touch him, and no one associated with me can be implicated. Things are very sensitive at the moment. Not just here in *La Serenissima*, as these Venetians like to call their bug-infested swamp, but in Rome as well. The Pope still allows me a good percentage on the indulgences."

"I thought it was the other way around," Béres said with a grin.

"Brother Luther must be cutting into your business," Lazaro remarked.

"Brother Luther still understands our way of life. I have nothing against free enterprise but I will not countenance competition, at least not competition against me." A small chuckle bubbled in his mouth. "Anyway, all I need is a bit of breathing space, some living room. That's why I have come to you, my friend," he said, looking at Lazaro.

Lazaro had known what his answer would be even while Béres was leading him to the Fondaco. It wasn't wise to say no to Fugger. "For you, Jakob," was Lazaro's reply.

Fugger smiled and clapped his hands together. "Janos will give you the necessary details regarding this *zentilhomeni*. He told me you had designs on an alchemist, some mirrormaker. Perhaps we'll talk of it some time. They do good work here." He pulled out a small mirror and held it up for Lazaro to see. It was a common enough mirror but Lazaro had noticed that the demand for them from the various shops in Venice had increased. Between the glass and the reflective amalgam of tin and mercury the mirrormaker had painted a faint death's head. "It adds a certain quality which I appreciate," Fugger said as he looked at his image in the glass. "There is such beauty in that metal, such deception."

Fugger's man returned with a flask of wine and a purse. Fugger handed the purse to Lazaro and the wine to Béres. "I'm sorry that I can't visit longer but I have some urgent business details to attend to, and I will be out of the city for a few days. Then I will be back here only to gather my guards and head back to Augsburg." He clasped Lazaro's hand. "We'll speak again then. In the meantime, be humble around this god," he said poking Béres in the belly. Then he was gone.

Béres waited until the footsteps died away in the hallway, then slapped Lazaro on the shoulder. "Let's get some fresh air." They came out of the Fondaco and strolled along the Mercerie toward the Piazza San Marco. All along the Mercerie were the shops of a hundred nations, all trading in the atmosphere of Venice, an atmosphere which, for centuries, had been conducive to doing profitable business.

"You don't seem happy with your good fortune," Béres said as they passed a shop run by Turks.

Lazaro paused to look at some of the goods displayed but dismissed the merchant with a few phrases in Turkish. He had been bothered that he had not had an opportunity to discuss the exportation of Angelo with Fugger, but once this assignment was completed there would be another chance. "I was getting used to the idea of being out of the business," he said, stopping to buy some dates.

Béres put his arm around Lazaro's shoulders and hugged him. "And if you pray really hard, you'll become a virgin again, too."

Lazaro spit a date pit at him. "What's your cut?"

Béres shook his head. "Such a head for business, and from someone so reluctant to do business. Don't worry, he's already taken care of me handsomely." They walked on down the street in silence, looking from side to side at the goods displayed in the various shops. "No one's forcing you," Béres said finally.

Béres was right, Lazaro thought. No one was forcing him. He had grown accustomed to a more peaceful life, a life with boundaries, clear, defined. Yet there was something in what they had said today, done last night, and would probably do later which excited him. He felt the pull. "Fugger is getting fat. And old."

"He's the same age as me. But you're right, not nearly as handsome," Béres said, grinning, "though considerably wealthier."

"What's the plan?"

"I have people working on some information. We'll know by tonight perhaps." Béres looked at Lazaro as they walked along. "It'll be like a wolf hunting a child in a village street."

Lazaro smiled and wanted to say it was nothing he hadn't done before, but he knew what Béres was getting at. Chigi had been an easier matter. There had been more time for planning. This promised to be faster, darker. And he had been slow last night, as his arm reminded him. "It'll be fine," was all Lazaro could manage.

Béres chuckled. "And I was worried that you were turning into a glass merchant."

They emerged at the gate under the Torre dell'Orologio and entered the Piazza San Marco. The day was well under way. Lazaro could smell the cheese hanging in the shops and, as well, the fish. To his left were shops selling vegetables, and everywhere about the Piazza lesser merchants wandered, peasants selling everything imaginable, anything that might bring a price. Those who had no wares to sell sold themselves. Here and there an armless beggar, perhaps a veteran of the campaigns, a cripple, or one so disfigured by disease that it was impossible to tell which sex was represented. There were merchants of health who sold potions for a variety of afflictions from headaches and impotence to the French pox.

Lazaro had seen much of this plague lately, especially among the prostitutes who accounted for a high percentage of the street population of Venice. He had heard it discussed as a pestilence brought from the newly invaded Hispanola by Columbus and spread by the soldiers, though others argued that it was a well-known disease, recorded in the Bible in many places and brought to Europe either by Jews or Turks. Wherever it had come from, its effects were clear. The pox afflicted the face and body of the person and left horrible scars. If it didn't kill you, it would leave you mad. It seemed a weaker but still unwelcome cousin of that great plague which came and went with impunity. If one believed in a wrathful God, it did appear to be God's punishment for lechery.

Lazaro found himself standing alone, watching the people mill about. Béres was nowhere to be seen. He wandered for a few moments more, then bought some bread and cheese and sat down in a sunny spot in the arcades of the Ducal Palace, near where the notaries had their stalls. It was a pleasant day, the height of Carnevale. People went to and fro gathering the requirements for their feasts. There would be parties galore this night, and even more drunkenness in the streets than there had been the past few nights. The entire city was building to a crescendo. Tonight in Venice the vanities would shine in all their glory.

During the wars, the Signoria — the ruling council of Venice — had installed *Provveditori sopra le pompe*, magistrates whose duty was to enforce the sumptuary laws. Inspectors ranged through the city, measuring ruffles which appeared too long, checking kitchens to see that oysters were not being served if the dinner party exceeded twenty guests, citing women whose dresses were too ornate or who had too many pearls in their hair. Through these laws it was hoped that God's anger might be placated and that people would not engage in immoderate expenditure but rather would fund the state in its campaigns. Even then, the laws were honored more in their breach. And with the wars over, pomp had again become unbridled fashion.

And then she was there, the vanity of vanities, walking past him with a maidservant in tow. Marzia Zorzi. He almost choked on his cheese. He was accustomed to seeing her at a distance, sunning herself on her balcony, or ahead of him in a crowd as he followed her home. She walked right past him, and then she stopped, and he was sure that she looked at him. But no — she had merely stumbled and turned to see the offending stone which had almost turned her ankle. The maid bent to check Marzia's *zoccoli*, the platform shoes worn by the best-dressed women to keep their feet out of the wet refuse of the *calli* and to give them height.

Marzia stood serene, the sun shining through her *filio d'oro*, her golden hair, caught in that crimped and tied mass. The light of the gracious sun then trickled down her face, catching in the corners of her up-turned lips, settling in her dimples. Some of that most fortunate light trickled still further, past the golden pendant which hung about her neck with the small screened flea trap, and ran along the curve of her breasts showing above the rich brocade of her dress. Though it seemed that a halo shone about her, it was only the golden tresses, filled with the light of Phoebus. The rest of the Piazza was crowded with lesser beings, mere shards of flesh, lacking the eternal and blinding light of soul. Her eyes seemed to catch his for an instant and her lips parted in a warm embracing smile. She raised her arm gently in the beginning of a wave.

At that same moment a young man coming out of the Ducal Palace behind where Lazaro sat, walked past Lazaro's shoulder toward her. Her smile was for him. They met and touched their hands in friendship then spoke. He was a young noble, Lazaro could tell that by his dress. His hair was dyed blond and on his stockings was embroidered the colored badge of his club — most young nobles were involved in *della calze* — this one showed a sword piercing a fiery heart. His shoes were particularly wondrous, being slashed here and there and ribboned to excess. Lazaro questioned for a moment Marzia's taste, but then thought that perhaps this young man was simply a friend. Their lips were moving in conversation but Lazaro was not close enough to hear what they were saying to each other, though he tried, and he prayed to God to be blessed for a moment with the ears of an ass. But God must not have been listening, or Himself lacked large enough ears. The conversation ended and she continued on, the young man accompanying her, the maid still in tow, and was soon lost in the crowd.

Béres gave Lazaro a kick. "Hey, young captain, here you sit, cheese in hand, dreaming of the fine flesh of fresh Venetian virgins. Well, forget it. We have some work yet to do before this day is through."

Lazaro reached up and pulled Béres quickly to the ground beside him. "Listen, old man, for your sake I hope you have some of that wine left, for I am thirsty after my lunching, and I have been too wrapped in my thoughts of young virgins to get anything to drink."

"You're returning to your senses then, Lazaro," Béres said with a beaming smile and handed the wine flask to him. "Perhaps the sight of these young women is raising you" — Béres took back the wine flask — "from the dead." He took a draft and his voice took on a quiet, serious tone. "I've been worried about you. I feared the long rest in this pest-ridden town might have softened you. Without the flames of Mars or of Venus to temper your metal you might have dulled, grown insensitive to the finer things in life. Your actions last night weren't up to scratch, but still I keep faith. And faith is always rewarded," he added, turning his eyes to the sky.

They spent the day lounging about the Piazza, eating, drinking, watching the performers on stilts and on tightropes, listening to the plays. From time to time Béres would leave and Lazaro would have time to himself. When he was alone, it seemed, he was more able to notice details of the festival taking place around him. And of the people. One man in particular he had noticed throughout the afternoon, a beggar, apparently mad. His clothing was made of some rough brown cloth and torn in many places, but his skin was so brown or dirty that it was hard to tell where the tears were. Long, unkempt hair hung down over the top half of his face. The lower portion was covered with a scraggly beard. He was tormented by a group of children for a little while, but for the better part of the afternoon, the man had simply stood in a corner and talked to himself, yelling every once in a while and, from time to time, growling like a wolf. This wolfman had a begging cup in front of him and Lazaro noticed that it contained very few coins. He reached into his purse and pulled out a *scudi*, dropping it into the cup. It seemed as if, for a moment, the wolfman became lucid and through his hair his eyes shone. But Lazaro saw quickly enough that they were the blue eyes of a mad dog, and they sent a small chill though his body. He turned and walked across the Piazzetta to the base of the Campanile where some street gamblers were confusing fools in the gathering dusk.

He was startled when Béres nudged him without warning. "I have a surprise for you. Something to blow those cobwebs out of your wintry mind. Those Moors up there," he said, pointing to the bronze Moors on the Torre dell'Orologio whose testicles were ceremoniously, if secretly, rubbed by barren women, "have had more action than you. Well, it's time to doff the hair shirt. You know the Turk, Mustapha?"

"I know that you know him."

Béres waved his hand, dismissing the answer. "I just hope you don't think the way you speak. You know the man I mean. He is having a little party on his cog." With a jerk of his thumb Béres indicated the lagoon where a few ships were moored, ships which had braved the bad winds of the gulf during this season in order to reap the highest profits. "Away from prying eyes."

"What about Fugger's job?"

"In good time." Béres smiled. "We just may have some useful news regarding our quarry while we sup there. Are you up to it?"

Lazaro nodded. "I suppose I can be talked into it."

Béres walked toward the *traghetto* and a waiting gondola, rubbing Lazaro's head, "That's the spirit." The comment brought a smile to Lazaro, until Béres squeezed his wounded arm again.

III

Béres and Lazaro sat back in the cushioned comfort of the gaily decorated gondola as it headed out from the Molo and toward a cog moored halfway between the Piazzetta and the Giudecca. On those islands they could see lights of fine houses built by the rich men of Venice. The gondolier, a man wedded to the ill-formed beliefs he spouted, saw fit to educate Lazaro and Béres about the original inhabitants, and he droned on about how the islands had been inhabited by the Jews, but the land had been taken over because it offered cool breezes to soothe the Christians in the summer heat. He added, as he strained against the strong current of the Giudecca Canal, that the Jews had been treated quite well in Venice, and that the city had displayed its kindness six years ago by giving the Jews a place of their own, an island in the Cannaregio district where they could be safe, shut in at night from marauding Christians. And they were allowed the privilege of paying the Christians who guarded the gates and the canal surrounding the island. It had been a foundry, a *getto*, though the Jews seemed to prefer pronouncing it with a hard *g* — ghetto — perhaps due to the accents of their German cousins who had begun to settle there with them. They liked it, he assured them. And it was better for them than making them all move over to the mainland to Mestre. The other nationalities had *fondachi* of their own, though they were not obliged to wear a yellow cap as were the Jews. However, this precaution was necessary because otherwise it would be too easy for the Jews to pass as Italians, they looked so similar, at least those who did not wear the robes of their eastern origins.

Lazaro grew tired of the lesson and told the gondolier to row more quietly, but the request only made him change the subject to the recent excesses of Carnevale he had witnessed, some, it seemed, on the very cushions on which Béres and Lazaro now sat.

The gondola touched to the *camel*, the wooden platform attached to either side of cogs to float them higher in the shallow waters and to give them stability as they were unloaded. Béres paid the garrulous gondolier, who continued to talk as he rowed away, and he and Lazaro climbed up the ladder which had been fastened to the side of the cog.

Mustapha was a merchant well respected in Venice, and though Venice had been at war with the Turks as the century turned — and given the recent actions of Suleiman, might soon be again — there had been relative peace for the last few years. Not that the Turks didn't gobble up some of Venice's territory from time to time or impose heavier duties on the goods flowing in and out of Islamdom, which, added to the trouble caused by the sea exploration of the Atlantic powers, had weighed heavily on the city. The trade routes opened by Columbus and da Gama challenged the hold which Venice had managed to have on all trade between Europe and the Orient. The wars had made matters even worse. But now a new year was dawning and new hope as well. Business would be better. Business was never good in a war unless one was supplying the warring sides. There would be profit to be made, as long as Venice did not go to war with the Turks.

"My dear Baron," Mustapha said, bowing low as Béres and Lazaro touched the deck. He was a tall and handsome Turk, young and bearded.

Béres smiled at Lazaro, then turned back and slapped his hand into Mustapha's and pulled him into a close hug. "You old son of countless dogs and despoiler of immature cabbages, how are you?"

Mustapha grinned and turned to Lazaro. "He is so irreverent, Allah should strike him dead but Allah wastes no time with such infidels." He moved closer to Lazaro and glanced at Béres. "You have brought a friend with you. The young warrior?"

"Lazaro," Béres said by way of introduction, "but don't let the name fool you. He's more than Italian."

"I would hope so," Mustapha said, and greeted Lazaro in Turkish. They exchanged pleasantries and Mustapha smiled, then put his arms around both men and led them forward across the deck. "I have decided that this evening should be dedicated to the memory of your recent Pope Adrian, and I have arranged suitable entertainment. But first, come in and relax."

The ship was a trading cog, masts, and ropes everywhere and "broader in the beam than a fishwife," Béres mumbled to Lazaro, but Lazaro knew that Béres was afraid of the water. He had sailed on such vessels before, and, though they were seaworthy, he preferred the smaller vessels used by the Christian and Turkish corsairs or the Venetian galleys, powered by oars and trading all through the Mediterranean with ease.

Mustapha led them below deck and through a passageway to a room which had its floor, ceiling, and walls covered with silk. After the sights above deck, Lazaro found this sleight of ship truly marvelous. Mustapha had transformed his vessel into a hall as sumptuous as any to be found in Constantinople. Around the walls, large cushions and low tables were spread about. There were many people there already: Turks, Venetians, Africans, Tedeschi. And there was the blue haze of hashish. Lazaro had not smelled that since the wars.

"Lazarus!" a voice called. It was Vom Scheidt.

"You've avoided the husbands, then," Béres called to him. "Take care of our friend," he added, pointing to Lazaro, then whispered, "I have some business to attend to with Mustapha, but I will let you know if any important news arrives. I expect nothing 'til well past midnight."

Vom Scheidt pulled Lazaro down onto the cushion beside him and hugged him. They had not seen each other in over a year but they were not the sort to notice passage of time and it melted away so quickly that it was as if they had parted only the day before. Vom Scheidt handed Lazaro a hose attached to the hookah which sat on a low table in front of them. "Turks may not know how to drink wine, but they do know how to enjoy themselves, especially when they are away from Suleiman the Lawmaker." He took a long pull on the hose, held his breath for a few seconds, then expelled a cloud of aromatic blue smoke. "Mustapha has the best of everything."

Lazaro tried the hashish and in a very short space of time he agreed wholeheartedly with Vom Scheidt. The smoke had often relaxed them following battles, and more than once preceding, but he could not remember it having been as subtle as this.

"Khef," Vom Scheidt said, reading his mind and pointing to the bowl. Lazaro looked and watched it glow. He noticed that more musicians had appeared and large drums were being pulled up. Suddenly the music changed, and it was as if the air changed with it, thicker, warmer, filled with musk.

A curtain was pulled to one side and a blonde Circassian woman moved in, to the throb of the drums. She was followed by a Moorish girl who, though different in coloring and features, complemented her so completely in looks and in dance that the two were as twins in the blue haze. They were clothed in pure white cotton, slit here and there to free their legs. As they turned, it swirled, parted, tantalized. As they bent, it billowed and revealed. The heat of a room filled with people and the energy of their own dancing soon drew out a sweat on both women. The cotton became damp, and as it did so it became transparent. Lazaro noticed that except for the music the room was silent, not filled with the usual howls from an audience watching such a display. They were entranced. The curtains parted and two more dancers emerged. The spell was broken and the cheering and rhythmic clapping began. More dancers followed, all of whose sexuality was clear, many whose gender was not.

The deep drumming continued, and the sound found its way into Lazaro's mind. He could think no thought, he could only see, hear, feel, smell, and taste. There was no longer an ability to reflect. His mind played no tricks, it simply saw and reacted. As the dancers moved, their veils fell, and, with the veils, their clothes as well. Breasts, bellies, thighs, all flashed past Lazaro as he watched, and his mind swelled. He found his amorousness growing, especially when he caught sight of the Moorish girl who had originally danced opposite the Circassian.

As if his mind had somehow willed it, the Circassian and the Moor approached and, with a last burst of energy, finished their dance and fell beside the men, the Circassian to Vom Scheidt and the Moor to Lazaro. Had he found the energy to raise his head he would have seen that everyone was equally occupied, according to their individual choice; while there had not been a sufficient number of female dancers, many of the Venetians were happy with the ratio.

Time seemed to stretch, and he was lost for a while in a cloud of flesh and music. He had no energy to partake but sufficient to watch. Then, though he was sure it was not as suddenly as it seemed, many of the dancers were gone. He was glad to see that the Moor and the Circassian remained tangled among his and Vom Scheidt's limbs. He saw Mustapha enter the hall and only at that moment did he remember that he was on board a cog, for the ship tilted ever so slightly, and Mustapha made a small joke about a drunken helmsman. Béres moved past Mustapha, smiled and nodded to Lazaro, then sat beside some Tedeschi.

"I hope you have not had your appetite sated," Mustapha began in a loud voice and walked to the center of the floor as people laughed, "for the games are about to begin. As this is the time for Christians to enjoy themselves before they fast as the Holy Father directs, I thought it would be an appropriate gesture to celebrate, not as Adrian would have, but as his predecessor Alexander VI celebrated on the occasion of the betrothal of his beloved daughter Lucrezia."

As Mustapha spoke, servants were clearing the dance floor and setting up lighted candelabra. They then set themselves to strewing chestnuts over the entire floor. Here and there men and women sat up and clapped their hands in anticipation.

"I see some of you are well-versed in church ritual and recognize the preparations for the Dance of the Chestnuts." Mustapha clapped his hands, and at least thirty beautiful Venetian courtesans appeared from various entrances, clad flimsily at best. The musicians began to play again and though it was not as hot-blooded as the music which had been performed previously, it held promise.

Vom Scheidt leaned forward, squeezing the Circassian and the Moorish girl together. "What is this chestnut ritual?"

Lazaro smiled. "Pope Alexander gave a party for Lucrezia when she married the Duke of Ferrara. *Cortigiane* danced until their clothes came off, then wriggled about the floor on the chestnuts, picking them up as ingeniously as possible. If Mustapha follows the full menu, he will offer prizes to those in the audience who can have sex the greatest number of times with the widest selection of whores."

"My God," Vom Scheidt said, settling back with a grin, "I should have been a priest."

"You might be yet." Lazaro leaned back, then noticed that Béres had risen and was waving for him to follow. Untangling himself from his companions, Lazaro moved so as not to block anyone's view of the festivities, though he was sure no one would notice his departure. Reflecting on Béres's choice of this particular time, he decided that the moment must have come for him to set out on the hunt. When he met Béres on deck he found that this was the case.

"There is to be an important late-night meeting in the Ducal Palace. I don't know what it's about, but it provides us with an unexpected opportunity. The Doge and his entourage will soon leave his barge and return to the Palace. As they dock they will send a messenger to bring our quarry to that meeting. Just follow the messenger and do what you must do."

"This messenger — a bodyguard?"

Béres nodded. "Probably, but I've seen you fight. A job like this must be done alone. Don't worry, there is no one but us who knows what is about to take place. The signal from the barge is intended for one of the courtesans here who is a favorite of the Doge, although I don't know what the Doge can do with her. She will return by another gondola later. Even your gondolier thinks he is taking a Turk in to experience the joys of Christian Carnevale. And if you can't carry out the job, no one will know either, except for me and I am an understanding father to you. Even Fugger won't be expecting action this quickly, but this situation has presented itself, and, in the nights of Carnevale, all is possible."

"That gondola," Béres said, pointing to a boat tied to a rope ladder draped over the dark side of the ship, "will take you to the Piazzetta in advance of the Doge and the Chancellor. We await only a signal from the barge over there" — Béres squinted — "somewhere.

Damn this *farkas sötet* — this wolf-darkness. It lets me see the terror by night, but I can't see a goddamn light."

"What about the pestilence that walks in darkness?"

Béres smiled. "I haven't seen him in years. Just watch that barge for a light signaling in this direction — three flashes."

Béres pointed toward what was, to Lazaro's eyes, a bright and noisy hulk sitting in mid-channel. It was the custom of many of the wealthier citizens of Venice, who could not be seen in the company of Turks, to take their courtesans and catamites out to barges whose only purpose was to support their gluttony. As they watched, a light flickered three times.

"There's the signal," Lazaro reported.

Béres smiled. "When I gamble my luck is never this good." Béres pulled Lazaro close to him for a bear hug, then handed him some black lace to tie over his face as a mask. "Go."

As the gondola moved silently toward the quay which ran along the Piazzetta and the Doge's palace, Lazaro, behind the black lace mask, wondered how understanding a father Béres would be if he had the ability to look into Lazaro's heart. For there a struggle waged. He would have no trouble killing the bodyguard, but he wondered if he could offer truthfully the same assurances about the man he was being sent to kill. He thought now of Marzia sunning herself on her *altana* and of his dreams of being with her.

His mission presented an unwelcome complication. Just before he climbed down to the gondola, Béres had given him the name of his target. It was the father of Marzia Zorzi.

IV

As the gondola approached the Piazzetta, the small plaza which led to the more formal Piazza San Marco, the noise of the people reverberated in the cool air. Normally the Piazza would be deserted at this hour, but it was aflame with torches and thronged with people, celebrating. Lazaro passed a coin to the gondolier, stepped onto the *traghetto* and headed to the Piazzetta, moving slowly to the two granite columns between which the public executions were held. The column to his left was topped with a statue of Saint Theodore. He leaned against the other, on which was perched the winged lion of Saint Mark, patron Saint of Venice, and adjusted his black lace mask. Across the Piazza, past the Basilica San Marco, the bronze Moors on the top of the Torre dell'Orologio hammered the bells and the face of the clock showed two. He and Béres had passed through that opening earlier in the day but it seemed different now. Lazaro saw, as if struck for the first time, the Torre with the life-sized Moors at the top, a winged lion below, a Madonna and Child below that, and beneath all, a huge clock face which told not only the time but, more relevant to the fortunes of Venice, the phases of the moon. But it would be the light of the sun on the morrow that would bring a sobering breeze to Venice. And judging by the condition of the people in the streets, she would need it.

The city was alive with masked revelers in capes, lighting their way with torches. Everyone celebrated the end to the death which was winter. Music came up through the warren of streets and as Lazaro turned to look about him he saw the state gondola reach the Molo. Attendants tied it to its berth while the gondoliers scrambled to assist the Doge and the Grand Chancellor up the steps. Normally the gondola would have moved along the Rio de Palazzo to the Doge's *riva*, but the Doge and the Grand Chancellor were making an appearance for Carnevale. They were followed by three men. One was richly robed and was apparently one of the Secretaries to the Chancellory, a tall, powerful man with dark features, young in comparison to the Doge and the Chancellor who appeared to be in their eighties. There was a young man, a *bravo* like so many others in Venice, clean-shaven, unmasked. The third wore a white mask that covered the top half of his face, a black scarf wrapped around his head and neck topped with a black hat, and was dressed in a rich black fabric, with a short black cape around his shoulders. Many men wore similar costumes, but it was as if it was made for this man — Giambattista Beccaria, the Master of the Assassins.

Lazaro recognized him immediately and tossed off a silent prayer to any saint capable of interceding that this would not be the bodyguard sent to fetch Zorzi; he could only assume that such a task would be left to a less-important personage. His answer came quickly. The Doge and the Grand Chancellor walked off toward the Ducal Palace while the Secretary, Beccaria, and the *bravo* spoke for a moment. The Secretary headed off after the Doge while Beccaria stayed a moment longer, apparently giving some last-minute instructions to the *bravo*, then moved after the Secretary, resembling more a shadow than a man. The young man who had been given the role of messenger stood by himself as if taking his bearings, then was off into the crowd. It was almost too fast, and Lazaro had to scramble to follow at a quick pace for fear of losing his quarry.

They wandered through the winding streets of Venice, mounting small humps of bridges, descending and ascending stairs, moving through the throngs of men and women celebrating in the streets. It mattered little to the revelers what it was that they were celebrating: everyone celebrated in Venice. The city was rich in trade and tradition. Festivals consumed half the year, and the other half was spent in recuperating. It was a time for drunkards, whores, and thieves to assemble in the streets and enjoy themselves, and those common folk who were less accomplished could at least masquerade with a pretence to scandalousness.

Turning a corner and heading down a narrow alley he saw two young men in white masks and black hats round a corner ahead of him and race down the alley in the direction he was heading. At their side ran a large dog with a studded collar and chain leash. They let the chain drag, sparking over the cobblestones as they ran, and the drunken people in the alley tried to leap over it as it approached them. Many fell, but none were harmed as the young nobles disappeared around another corner. They were followed by the curses of those who had tumbled and the laughter of those who had leapt high.

As he passed the people trying to help their friends to their feet, a particularly attractive girl held out a flask of wine to him. Although she was beautiful, the mask which covered the top half of her face was fashioned to display an old, pock-marked hag. He glanced at her broad smile, then took the flask and drank from it. She retrieved the flask and immediately bared her breast.

"Care for another drink, *signore*?"

Lazaro shook his head and the alley exploded in laughter as he bowed his way out and turned a corner. It never ceased to amaze him, the power that masks had to free people from their normal inhibitions.

He was now in front of the Dancing Mouse, where he could watch on each clear warm day as Marzia sunned herself in the Venetian fashion, as she had this morning. He remembered the first day he had seen her, in the autumn of the previous year. He had been struck by her clear-skinned and silent beauty. In all his travels, during all of the fighting and even while in the arms of the women who loved the troops, he had dreamed of skin such as that. He had dreamed of much more. It would not have been enough merely to topple her. One woman had been the same as any other to him, but his dream of Marzia sometimes included a desire to live with her the life which she knew; a life of wealth and status, a life with a home. And yet his past, and his mother's, made that all but impossible. By his birth, he could never be a Venetian. Yet birth was not always required. Even the lowest apprentice in Angelo's glass factory was entitled, if his skill allowed him to ascend in the guild, to be considered a citizen of high rank in Venice. Lazaro's skill propelled him in the opposite direction. Tonight he would do what he did best. Tonight he was answering to his true calling. He knew now that he could kill the father of Marzia Zorzi.

The messenger stopped at the gate which opened into the garden of Ca' Zorzi, an impressive *casa* of three floors. Columns flanked the door and supported an iron gate, closed and locked to the night. Lazaro watched as the messenger reached for the bell rope and pulled. It was a very short wait until a servant opened the door and approached with a lamp.

"What's your business?"

The messenger held a roll of parchment at his chest so that the servant could see the Ducal seal. The servant hurriedly unlocked the gate and waved the messenger through then locked it again and led him inside, bolting the door behind them. Lazaro watched through the windows of the *casa* as they walked into the elegant foyer. Grasping the iron spikes atop the wall, he pulled himself up to the top and, peering over, could see the dark marble floor reflecting the grand staircase which led to the second floor. Beautiful paintings and richly framed mirrors hung on the walls, rich drapes added warmth and a magnificent chandelier lit the room with a warm glow. To the side of the staircase was a large double door which opened on the interior courtyard of the *casa*. He saw the servant point and the messenger walked into the courtyard to wait.

Lazaro dropped quietly to the ground and raced along the wall to the next *calle* which ran past the other side of the house. There was a tall wall, covered in vines. He pulled himself up to the top, avoiding the iron spikes placed there for security. The messenger was seated not far from Lazaro's vantage point, beside a small fountain. Lazaro moved into the cover of a sweet-smelling shrub and waited.

Through the limbs of the shrub he could see the stars in full bloom. The night air was pleasing and calm. The fountain gurgled and pathways meandered through the ornamental shrubs and flowers. In the pool, fish flashed in the moonlight. To him the city had disappeared and in its place was an enchanted garden, the garden of Ca'Zorzi. It sounded, as he rolled it about in his mind, like the title to some ancient fable of love and honor. But quickly Lazaro's thoughts returned to the real world in which he lived and the code which governed him. He was under contract and he would see that contract satisfied.

Someone approached — a young woman in a white dress with golden ringlets flowing over her shoulders. Marzia.

"My father will be with you shortly, *signore*," she said as she stopped beside the messenger. He nodded his head politely.

Lazaro could smell her perfume. She was close enough for him to see that skin, soft in the orange light which spilled from the *casa*, not pocked and powdered like so many he had seen but pure, fair.

"Marzia," a voiced boomed from the *casa*. Lazaro watched as a portly man in a splendid robe walked to the fountain. Marzia took her cue and excused herself. Signor Zorzi sat on a bench by the pool and reached his hand for the parchment. The messenger handed it to him and remained standing as he broke the seal and read the message. Zorzi finished and paused for a moment, sighing, then looked up. "You know the contents of this?"

"No, *signore*."

"It is important that I meet tonight with the Doge and you are to provide me with safe conduct to the Palace. Apparently, someone may be lying in wait for my gondola and so we are to take the streets." He paused and looked at the parchment again, then crumpled it and stood. "You're ready to use that thing," he said, pointing at the *bravo*'s blade.

"Yes, *signore*."

Zorzi barely waited for a response. "Wait here. I'll be right back."

Lazaro watched as he walked into the *casa*, throwing the ball of parchment into a brazier and calling for his servant. A fish splashed in the pool, and Lazaro saw the moon's reflection in the rippling water. Its soft hue reminded him of Marzia, and he turned to see if she was about, but he could not see her either through the doors or on the balcony above. She was more beautiful than he had imagined, and her voice . . .

Zorzi returned abruptly to the courtyard, wearing a long black cape, with a sword at his side, and carrying two black hats and two white masks. He walked past the messenger, thrusting a mask and hat into his hand and signaling him to follow. They crossed the courtyard and stopped at a small barred door in the wall not far from where Lazaro perched. Suddenly Zorzi stopped and spoke in a whisper. "I don't know from where the danger is coming. Stand by me tonight and it will be worth more to you than anyone else might have paid." The messenger was about to protest, but Zorzi held up his hand. "The offer is intended as a prudent precaution and as payment for a job well done, not an insult. The money will be paid out to you at the successful completion of your task. Put on your mask." Zorzi's servant appeared and opened the gate for them, then closed and locked it behind them.

In the *calle* the mist was starting to gather in the corners, seeping up from the *rii* and rolling slowly down to the lower spots in the streets. Zorzi and his bodyguard slipped off and Lazaro waited for a moment then followed at a discreet distance. Walking briskly in the darkness without torches, they entered the Calle della Testa which was crowded with masked men and women celebrating Carnevale. Zorzi was silent, walking slightly ahead while the messenger was ever watchful, ready to react to an odd movement in the crowd.

Lazaro was troubled by hunts such as this. Battle was different. There the enemy was discernible, and there was a clear demarcation as to when to fight and when to rest, when to kill and when to save life. In these winding streets those simple truths were muddled. But that muddling brought with it a strange excitement, and Lazaro could feel the flush of it within him as he followed Zorzi.

They now crossed the Rio della Panada then the Rio di San Marino, passed through the Campo San Marino and headed in the direction of the Campo San Maria Formosa. In the Campo a crowd had gathered to watch as men with shaven heads butted cats tied to a plank, trying to crush them and avoid, as much as possible, their sharp claws. The air was filled with the howling and hissing of the cats and the crowd.

As they continued past the street sport, Lazaro wondered what the response to the murder would be. Signor Zorzi was a well-respected businessman and *Ene Aca*, the *Nobili Homini* of Venice. People would think he had been involved in some political intrigue. Such intrigues were part of the everyday life of Venice, and with the various wars and shifting allegiances, things had become even more complicated as the apparent enemy evaporated. It troubled him that this man was being summoned by the Doge and the Grand Chancellor. The Secretariat of the Council of Ten had many eyes and ears, as those unfortunates within the cool, damp dungeons well knew.

They came from either side almost before Lazaro could react. From a crowded street, he had followed Zorzi and the messenger into a dim alley to cut across to the bridge over the Rio di San Guiliano. He had felt a sense of uneasiness wash over him as they entered the alley — he knew that if he was going to take Zorzi, it would be there. Suddenly he saw two men approaching, both wrapped in black capes, both wearing hats, both masked in a fashion most similar to that of the assassins. He wondered for one moment whether perhaps Beccaria had sent men to assist Zorzi. Then he saw the glint of a glass stiletto in each man's hand, drawn and at the ready, the weapon of the assassin.

In that moment he moved not to kill Zorzi but to save him. There was not enough time for Lazaro to know why. It might have been Marzia; it might just as well have been a proprietary interest in Signor Zorzi. But Lazaro left his thoughts behind and depended on his instinct.

As Lazaro raced forward he saw Zorzi spot the danger and draw his sword. The two attackers drew theirs as well, holding their stilettos in their left hands. In this narrow alley it would not be difficult for them to parry and thrust quickly with fatal results. The messenger took his position in front of Zorzi and was ready to defend him valiantly by his posture. He never got the chance. With expert skill the first assassin impaled him, then withdrew his sword and dropped him to the ground. The young boy clutched his stomach with reddening hands, eyes wide, face caught in an incredulous expression of pain. He uttered not one sound. Lazaro seized the moment, ripped the black lace from his face, drew his sword, and leapt in front of Zorzi. One attacker engaged him while the other slipped past and attacked Zorzi.

Lazaro heard the clash of steel behind him but he was too busy to turn. Mindful of the stiletto he parried the opening thrust, then exposed himself in order to slam the man's left hand into the wall. The shard of glass broke from the handle and smashed on the paving stones at their feet. However, his opponent brought his sword down in a masterful stroke and left a gash on Lazaro's right arm. Too close for a thrust, Lazaro threw his fist into the man's chest and drove him back a few paces. He wanted to check on Zorzi but there was no time. It was sufficient that he could still hear them fighting. His opponent had been caught off guard by the maneuver but resumed the attack. Lazaro saw him reaching for another stiletto, one with a metal blade, and attacked immediately. Moving in close he swept his blade up, knocking his opponent's blade back against his chest and securing an opening which allowed him to pivot on his left leg and swing in behind the man, trapping his blade with his own. With his free hand he reached in front of the man and, in a lightning move, grabbed his left hand, turned the stiletto, and drove it deep into the man's stomach.

In that moment he saw Zorzi drop his sword and clutch at his stomach. He heard the snap of the glass, then saw the other man turn, see that his partner had been dispatched, then thrust his sword into Zorzi for good measure. In that moment it was finished. Zorzi fell back against the wall and slid to the ground while his murderer extracted his blade and ran off into the night.

Lazaro hurried over to Zorzi, but, finding him dead, leapt to his feet and ran after the murderer. He turned one corner, then a second and found himself in a crowded street where black capes and white masks abounded. Though he scanned the streets as a wolf on the prowl he saw no one running, could not find that particular mask worn by the assassin.

He returned to Zorzi's body, removed the man's mask and closed his eyes. He had failed either to kill him or to save him. Behind him there was the scuffling of feet. Turning he saw that two masked men were checking the body of the assassin he had killed. Immediately behind Lazaro was a large dark figure, holding a blade tip to his neck. He looked up slowly. It was Beccaria. They stared at each other for a moment and Lazaro cursed himself for leaving his back unguarded.

Suddenly Beccaria's glance shifted and Lazaro heard the sound of someone running toward them from the direction the murderer had gone. Beccaria withdrew his sword, turned, and signaled to his men, who disappeared into the shadows, then pulled Lazaro to his feet and pushed him into a deep doorway opposite Zorzi's corpse.

The runner slowed as he approached the corner, hesitated, then turned into the alley and ran toward them. As he neared the body he slowed to a walk then stopped and knelt beside it, looking about nervously. Lazaro looked closely at him. He was about the same size as the man he had chased after but the clothes were different and he had no weapons. Then he noticed the face — it was Solomon, one of the Jewish proofreaders employed by Bomberg the printer. It was late and the ghetto would be closed. Solomon was in trouble.

In a moment Beccaria's men were on him; two more came out of the shadows. Solomon was wrestled to the ground, his hands and mouth bound, then he was dragged away. The other two men picked up Zorzi's body and carried it with them. Beccaria stepped out of the doorway and Lazaro followed. Beccaria looked at Lazaro for a moment, then put away his sword. Lazaro saw Beccaria's eyes move as two men approached from behind. The eyes returned to Lazaro and seemed to burn into him. Then something hit his head.

V

Lazaro tried to resist the pounding on the door, but it was incessant. "Go away," he shouted. The pounding stopped. The door burst open and banged into the stone wall. Four men wearing the insignia of the Secretariat stepped in. Lazaro sat up in bed, and immediately realized that it was not his bed but a wooden slab in a windowless room. Quickly his mind recalled the events in the *calle*, the death of Zorzi, the darkness which had flown over him with the assistance of a blow to the back of his head. And now he was in the prison cells of Venice. It was not a pleasant thought.

Abandon all hope ye who enter here.

His clothes, matted with blood, straw, and mud, were still on him. He looked, unnecessarily, for his sword, and saw in the corner a bucket. The two men closest to the door had their daggers drawn, the other two, standing nearer to him, seemed calm enough.

As he managed to stand, he saw there would be no opportunity of escape.

"I hope I've been invited to breakfast. My stomach is completely empty," he said as he straightened his clothes.

There were no smiles on the faces of his hosts. From the corner of his eye he saw one of the men lean over and pick up the bucket, looking inside. Suddenly its contents were hurled at him. Luckily it was only water. He stood silently as it drenched him, then smiled. "Thank you," he said as he ran his fingers through his hair, then dried his face with a corner of his shirt.

They marched out into a dark hallway where another guard waited with a lantern. Lazaro expected to climb stairs, but instead they descended. That meant he had been kept not in the *pozzi* but in the *piombi*, the cells in the roof of the Doge's palace, directly under the lead roof. He was glad it was not a hot day. He was also glad they were moving away from the prison area, for that meant they were moving away from the questioning chambers, the torture cells which were used so effectively to elicit explanations as to one's complicity in the crime accused.

The hallways were becoming lighter now, with the occasional window, and more ornate: carved wood, the odd painting, gilded ceiling and trim. The guards stopped at a beautifully carved door, opened it and thrust Lazaro inside. He stood between two guards as his eyes grew accustomed to the room. Though there were windows they were covered over with a heavy, rich cloth which blocked out all but a few rays of sunlight.

At least, he thought to himself, I have lived to see another day. He grinned cynically.

"You find your predicament humorous?" A finely balanced voice stabbed out at him from the darkness. His eyes made out the shape of a chair behind a large desk where sat a man in what appeared to be long black judicial robes, the official robes of the nobles of Venice. The man rose and walked to the front of the desk. "Wait outside," he said to the two guards, who immediately turned and left, closing the door behind them.

Lazaro could now make out the face of the man in front of him. His dark clothes and dark hair drew attention to his extraordinarily blank face. It was a face which seemed to betray nothing, as if painted by an unaccomplished artist who had not been able to inject any life into his creation. The man returned to his chair. Lazaro, by now accustomed to the darkness of the room, saw another man sitting in a farther, darker corner. It was Beccaria, dressed as he had been the night before, a white mask covering the top half of his face, sitting back in a large chair, dangling one leg nonchalantly over the arm of the chair while he fiddled with a dagger. Lazaro now recognized the man who sat behind the desk as one of the Grand Chancellor's Secretaries.

"You know who I am?" the Secretary asked.

"No, Domine," Lazaro said giving the Secretary as much station as he could.

"I am Tagliapietro, Secretary to the Council of Ten. You recognize Signor Beccaria," he said pointing to the corner.

Lazaro nodded.

"I will want your account of the events of last evening. But first I want to know a little more about you. Your name is Lazaro and you have occasional, albeit unofficial, employment in selling glass pieces?"

It was clear to Lazaro that these were not questions. "Yes, Domine. I have been befriended by Angelo, the mirrormaker."

"That old fool," the Secretary said with a smile. "But he does make beautiful mirrors."

"He does, Domine," Lazaro answered.

Tagliapietro looked up at him. "Drop the Domine. Of course you are aware that it is a capital offense to even think of assisting a glassmaker in flight. But you should also know that it is an offense for a foreigner to have any involvement in our glass. We have been aware of your association with Angelo but, out of deference to him" — Tagliapietro paused and Lazaro noticed an odd look cross his face like a shadow — "and out of a certain curiosity, we have allowed it to continue. I had wondered if you might be so foolish as to try and entice Angelo to leave Venice. Your failure and execution would have been a useful example to others. Apparently you are more intelligent than we had thought originally. But you haven't always been interested in glass and old men. I understand that you were a mercenary in the wars."

"Yes."

"And before that?" The voice arose from the dark corner, from Beccaria, and it sent a shiver down Lazaro's spine, not because of who he was but just from the sound of the voice itself.

"I have done many things. Before that, I studied in the north, most recently in Augsburg. Before that, I was a novice in a monastery in Ireland."

"But you didn't find your vocation," Tagliapietro added.

Lazaro smiled at the Secretary in answer.

"Your family?"

This question from Tagliapietro seemed more official than the others. Lazaro wondered for a moment how much information he should offer. He realized that they probably knew quite a bit about him already. Although the Secretariat did not concern itself with the background of Venice's mercenaries, he knew now that he had been watched more closely than he had expected. He hoped the Secretariat did not have eyes which could see into the soul. "My mother's father was Gabriel Ruzzini, Venetian, a trader in Cyprus."

Tagliapietro nodded, "I know the family. Your father?"

"As you may know Secretary, my father was a glass merchant from Constantinople, a Moor." Lazaro felt a pain inside of him which he had not felt for some time. He remembered his father, Ibrahim. He had never known his family name. They had lived in bright happiness: he, his mother, his young brother Nicolo, and his father, until the day the Venetians came to take his mother away from the "godless Turk" and back to his grandfather. There had been blood and screaming. His mother and he were the only survivors, carried back to a family of strangers. The memory sparked a pain which grew inside his head until he reached in and smothered it. "Both my parents are dead."

"So is your grandfather."

"I didn't know that, Secretary. I haven't seen him since I was seven."

Tagliapietro nodded. Lazaro noticed that Beccaria was leaning forward in his chair now, listening closely. He felt decidedly uncomfortable about this level of interest from the Master of the Assassins.

Tagliapietro rose from his chair and reached into the cabinet behind him, removing a decanter and two wine glasses. "You'll be thirsty," he said and poured a glass for Lazaro and took one himself. Beccaria continued to sit in the corner, watching like some bird of prey.

Lazaro drank the wine down and found the Secretary ready to fill the glass again. For a fleeting moment he thought of the reputation of the Secretariat for poisoning and noticed that Tagliapietro had not touched his glass. But, more likely than not, they wanted information from him. If they had wanted him dead they would simply have killed him, something they still might do. Besides, he thought as he tipped the glass back, he had already taken one drink.

The Secretary now took a drink from his glass and replaced it, nearly full, on the table in front of him. With the tip of his finger he took a drop of wine, then began pushing his finger around the lip of the glass so that it began to sing. However, he seemed not to notice the sound. "And now of course, we wish to know all that you know about the assassination of Signor Zorzi."

Now it came. Now he would be questioned and, if his answers were not accepted, he would be taken back to the cells and questioned in a less gentle fashion. And when they were satisfied with his "confession," he would be tried and condemned. Venice was famous for its justice.

In a moment, Lazaro decided on what he would say, and he unfolded the story like some well-woven cloth: he did not know that the man who had been killed was Signor Zorzi. He explained how he had been enjoying Carnevale, how he had been wandering through the city drinking and carousing to the point where his memory was very cloudy. He remembered a great deal of drinking with some young prostitutes, and that at one point he had stood in the Piazza, alone, trying to get his head clear. He tried to look into his glass often to give the Secretary an opportunity to betray himself with actions such as changes in facial expression, movements of the hands or fingers, knowing glances directed at Beccaria. Lazaro watched the reflecting surface of the wine and, adjusting his story slightly, followed such clues.

He continued with his recounting of a rakish night culminating with an encounter, in a *calle* he could not remember, with a fight just under way. He saw two men attacked by two others. He did not know why, but for some reason he went to the aid of one of the pairs, though he had no idea why the fight had begun or who was involved as all men were masked. He offered that perhaps it was because the ones whom he had aided seemed to be an old man accompanied by a younger, and he might have taken them for father and son attacked by two thieves.

The Secretary listened attentively to the entire story, and Beccaria remained silent and still. At the end, Tagliapietro paused for a moment, but in that moment Lazaro was sure, from the subtle changes to the man's face, that the story had been accepted.

"Perhaps God directed you to choose the proper side," Tagliapietro said finally, and filled both his now-empty glass and Lazaro's. "In any event, it is fortunate that you did what you did. Had you chosen the other side you would now likely be dead or facing death."

Beccaria moved in his chair but said nothing.

Tagliapietro noticed the wound on Lazaro's right arm. "I'll have someone look at that. Is it sore?"

Lazaro looked down and realized that though he had not felt it throughout the entire conversation, now that attention had been drawn to it, it was beginning to throb. "It didn't go deep."

"Still, I'll have my doctor look at it, the Jew Mantino."

Lazaro nodded his thanks but remained silent, ignoring the invitation to acknowledge the famous physician.

Tagliapietro stared into his glass for a moment then spoke. "We had uncovered a plan to assassinate Signor Zorzi when he came out in his gondola to visit his mistress, as he did most evenings. The Doge and the Grand Chancellor agreed that he might be safer at the palace and wanted him brought there by land. We had sent a messenger to accompany him back, but the assassins changed their plan. Somehow they had found out that he would be coming through the streets. We sent Beccaria and some of his men to help but they arrived almost too late."

"It was too late," Lazaro said and lifted the wineglass.

"Too late for Zorzi perhaps, and for our messenger, but we were able to arrest his murderer, thanks in part to you, though at the time your involvement was a bit unclear and so the precaution of your arrest. The murderer is now in the *pozzi*. Someone hired him and his accomplice to carry out the murder. You chased him off and I suspect he thought he could double back while you were looking for him and remove Zorzi's ring. He needed that in order to receive his pay. Beccaria knew this and that is why, when he arrived, he left the bodies as they were, as a trap."

"The Jew they arrested?" Lazaro asked.

"How did you know he was a Jew? He wasn't wearing the cap."

"I've seen him in the shop of Bomberg the printer."

"What business do you have with Bomberg?" Tagliapietro's voice indicated renewed interest.

"Books. There are certain books that I am interested in. From my days as a student. He prints some very interesting books, and from time to time I have gone there."

"Do you read Hebrew?" It was Beccaria's voice, but it seemed to Lazaro that it was not really of this world.

"No," he answered.

Tagliapietro softened. "I'm glad you traded the cloth for the sword. We can use more men like you. Yes, the boy was a Jew, from Venice. He was recruited by an agent from outside. We have reason to believe that this may have been motivated by developments in Rhodes. But then it may also have been business concerns. Most murders are," Tagliapietro said with a grin. "The Jew's father is well respected here — Mordechai, a scholar in the ghetto, and a member of their council. The matter calls for delicacy. Lent is fast approaching, and when our citizens are fasting they sometimes turn their pain and anger toward the unfaithful among us. That can be bad for business."

"What about the one I killed?"

"A Jew as well, though not from Venice." Tagliapietro gathered his robes and stood. "Come, I want you to see them."

Lazaro stood and followed him to the door. As it was opened he turned to see if Beccaria was coming, but the man had disappeared. "Don't concern yourself with his comings or goings. He has his own paths to follow," Tagliapietro said abruptly. "The wars are over and commerce is as always important, especially glass. But your arm and mind may be better suited to the heat of intrigue than that of the glass furnace." They walked through the door to where the guards waited, and Lazaro saw his weapons on a small table and hesitated. Tagliapietro smiled. "Take them. You look like a priest without a collection plate."

Lazaro returned the smile and buckled on his sword and dagger, then they were off, unaccompanied by the guards, a fact which surprised but pleased Lazaro. He followed Tagliapietro through a series of winding corridors, every now and then emerging into some magnificent salon, only to cross it and reenter a dark passageway. He knew clearly when they were near the *pozzi*, the lower dungeons which dripped with seepage; there was the smell of fear and pain in the air. And he could smell blood.

Tagliapietro stopped at a large wooden door and knocked softly. A dark-haired warder peeked through the barred square hole in the door, then opened it, nodding to Tagliapietro and closing it after they had entered. He handed a set of keys to Tagliapietro and a lamp to Lazaro but remained at the door while they continued on. Tagliapietro stopped at a small door which he unlocked and opened. Lazaro entered first with the lamp. On the table in the middle of the dark, damp room was the body of the assassin he had killed the night before, his mask by his side, the cape bloodied where the dagger had ripped into his stomach. The dagger lay on the table beside the mask. There was also a pile of gold coins and a note written in Hebrew.

"We don't know who he is, though I'm sure we'll find out. He's not one of the new Jews from Spain and he's not Levantine, so he must be an *ebrei italiano.* Men of principle often make enemies and Zorzi was a very principled man. Being a successful man of commerce only multiplied his enemies," Tagliapietro said with the air of someone professing a profound truth. "But we will investigate that. Perhaps this Solomon can provide us with some answers."

Lazaro picked up the mask and the hat. "After I became involved I was afraid from their dress that they might be Beccaria's men."

"That must have been the intent. If they had been more successful, blame would have been cast on Venice itself."

As they stood looking at the lifeless body on the table before them, Lazaro thought of his conversation with Fugger. Zorzi had been a thorn in his side and now he was gone, but not through Lazaro's actions. In fact, it was increasingly apparent that far from being an assassin Lazaro was being seen as a savior, more precisely a near-savior, of Zorzi. But from whom had he nearly saved him? Had the German hired these Jews to kill him? It wasn't Fugger's practice, especially when the situation was delicate, to have more than one assassin.

They moved now through the narrow passageways, dark except for the small lamp carried by Lazaro and the light which glowed at the bottom of ventilation shafts or from the torches in the walls at some of the cross passages. Lazaro had heard of these dungeons before, and, though he was sure he had been imprisoned in worse, he had no desire to test his hypothesis. They stopped at an imposing wooden door, locked with a thick metal crossbar.

Tagliapietro slid the wooden cover from the observation hole and peered inside, then shifted to the side so that Lazaro could see as well. On the wooden slab which served as a bed lay Solomon, chained by the arms and legs. There were bruises where his wrists had been chafed by the manacles but his heavy black hose had protected his ankles. He appeared to be asleep and calm. On the other side of the cell a lamp burned, not brightly, but enough for the warders to be able to check on him at irregular intervals. Lazaro also noticed that he had bruises on his face and a black eye. Lazaro looked away, and Tagliapietro shut the slot.

"The guards gave him a rough time as they were bringing him in. We haven't started any serious questioning yet. He is a Jew and he was out after curfew. That's a serious matter in itself. When we learned from an informer of the change in plans last night we were also told that Solomon was involved. I wish Beccaria had reached them in time. We could have arrested him for breaking curfew and banished him. It was probably the other who was the bad influence. Even that would have been hard on his father, but not as hard as this is going to be."

"Is there any doubt as to his guilt? Could he have been passing by?"

"Sadly, no. Leaving aside the informer, not far from where you lost him a man heard a dog barking and came outside to see a Jew running, leaving behind a cape and mask just like the other one was wearing. Our witness was brought in here and has identified Solomon. And while I am always a little suspicious of informers, this particular informer could not in any way benefit from this matter, and he gave us Solomon's name."

"It's unfortunate," Lazaro said. "Has his family been told?"

Tagliapietro turned. "Zorzi's or Solomon's?"

"Either."

"I've sent someone for Solomon's father. Due to his status, I thought he should be informed." They walked down the passageway. "Solomon will be questioned this evening. I may want to ask you some more questions as well," Tagliapietro said as they returned to the warder's station, "and the Zorzis are coming to see the Doge later. They have asked that you be present. They wish to thank you."

Lazaro thought of Marzia.

Tagliapietro turned and faced Lazaro, looking him up and down. "I'd advise you to have a bath and change your clothes. They won't be here until this evening, but I want you back here by five o'clock."

VI

Count Friedrich Erich Vom Scheidt stood by the doorway at the side of the Fondaco dei Tedeschi wearing a bright pink pig mask. "Lazarus," he called, as he noticed Lazaro walking along the *fondamenta*. He ran out into the passing pedestrians and knocked a couple over before he made his way to Lazaro. Reaching him, he clasped him and squeezed him closely to his chest, then pulled back, looking deeply into his eyes. "I have never enjoyed such a night as last night."

Lazaro pulled the mask down from his face, then noticed a couple of passing Venetians eye them with looks of disgust. He knew what they were thinking, but he didn't care at the moment. "More than I did," he said as he pulled Vom Scheidt against a wall and out of the way of the passersby. "Have you seen Béres?"

"He's around somewhere. Probably at Pander's. But where did you get to? I had to entertain the Circassian and the Moor myself.

The Moor kept asking for you. It's that deep tan of yours," he said, brushing Lazaro's cheek.

Lazaro thought it was better not to let the Count in on too many details. It wasn't that he didn't trust him, but until he knew more he was not going to involve anyone unnecessarily. "I went off for a little rendezvous of my own."

The Count stepped closer and took a whiff. "You smell like a bilge hole. I always thought you had better taste than that."

"Well, the night didn't turn out exactly as planned. I ended up taken by the Signori di Notte."

The Count laughed and for a moment the smile on his face was the same as the smile on the pig mask perched on the side of his head. "Too much fun, then?"

"I'm afraid so. Anyhow, I need a favor, if you're willing?"

"Well, it depends," he said with a grin.

They started walking over the Rialto Bridge. "I'm pretty sure the Lords of the Night are having me followed but it's hard to tell with this crowd and the masks. I need some time without them around" — he paused to see that no one was apparently following as they reached the center of the drawbridge span — "to conduct some business." The Count nodded. "I want you to switch clothes with me so that they'll follow you, then go to my lodgings, above an inn called the Dancing Mouse."

"I know the place."

"I thought you might."

"You have a room there?" Vom Scheidt asked incredulously. "Maybe you can get me in there. I'm above a cheese shop and it's fine for now, but I want to be out of there before the weather warms up too much."

"Why aren't you at Pander's like Béres?"

"Pander won't take my trade any longer. A small matter of a young girl who turned out to be his daughter." Vom Scheidt smiled and turned up his hands. "She moved like a married woman. How was I to know she wasn't? I don't mind husbands, and women like that usually have old doddering ones that don't bother their heads. But a father, that's another story. She wanted to see Il Doge," he said, pointing to his codpiece, "and her soft voice was so convincing that I had to give in."

"Some day you'll lose Il Doge."

"And what a crying and gnashing of teeth there will be that day," he added, his blue eyes sparkling under his dark hair. "So what, then?"

"Bathe, change clothes, and meet me back here. I'll change back with you and that's that. I want black clothes though. Respectful."

"You don't expect to change out here in the street, do you?"

"I had thought of an inn, perhaps, or some secluded alley."

"With the Secretariat's men on your tail and us candidates for being declared Barbarians — they'd have us burned for sodomy. My cheese shop is right off the Campo Rialto."

"Fine," Lazaro said, slapping him on the ass, "let's go."

Vom Scheidt made a great show of buying a distinctive mask for Lazaro, and a cheese, before they went up to his apartment, and as Lazaro watched Vom Scheidt depart and the Secretariat's agents follow, he saw that it had worked — the clothes might not have been enough but the mask and cheese gave them something to follow.

Though he had dressed in Vom Scheidt's clothes and donned the pig mask, he wanted to take no chances on being followed. When he was sure enough time had passed, Lazaro ducked out onto a balcony, scrambled across two more balconies, over a small roof, and down a flight of stairs into the next *calle*. From there he took a gondola out into the Grand Canal where it was lost in the crowded waterway. When he was let off at the *fondamenta*, he checked again to see if there was anyone following him, then headed for Pander's.

Béres was there and when he saw the clothes and the pig mask he must have thought it was Vom Scheidt, for he looked around nervously, and came immediately to the table. "Pander's away at the moment, but it's still not that healthy for you to be here."

"It's me," Lazaro said, then had to keep Béres from saying his name. "We have to talk but I don't want to be seen by anyone just yet."

"And so you masquerade as the Count. You haven't picked a very secure persona. You're liable to get your prick cut off."

"Zorzi's dead."

Béres looked into the pig's eyes. "I know. A fine job."

"But I didn't kill him."

"Yes. Don't worry. I'm not going to print a pamphlet."

"No, seriously. I didn't kill him. I tried to save his life."

"Well, don't ever try to save mine. I know Turks who could do a better job."

"Someone else attacked him before I could. Before I knew what I was doing I stepped in. But I wasn't able to help him. I killed one of the assassins and they took the other into custody."

"Who's they?"

"Beccaria."

Béres spit out his wine. "*Istenem*! What the hell have you done?"

"They have me figured for the savior and I'm to be introduced to the family and the Doge this evening."

"Well, who killed Zorzi?"

"They have a Jew in custody and the one I killed, he's a Jew too. Hired by someone. They didn't seem to have any ideas who."

"That bastard Beccaria always has ideas."

"There was another one. Tagliapietro. He questioned me and sent me home to change for this evening."

"Shit. That makes it worse. He must have had you followed."

"Not here. That's why I used Vom Scheidt. Did Fugger have another team?"

Béres was silent for a moment then said, "I doubt it. He wanted you. He wouldn't have gone to this much trouble and then found someone else. It would expose him too much." Béres said nothing for an uncomfortable length of time, then spoke. "This may turn out all right. They will be trying the Jew."

"They'll question him tonight."

Béres shrugged. "They'll have a confession tomorrow. Trial, execution, and then a grand funeral for Zorzi. It may be all right."

"What do you mean?"

"If the Jew is put to death quickly, there'll be no need to tell Fugger any of this. He'll figure you just used your head, kept your distance, and probably pulled off the cleanest contract he ever put out. If you're seen as a hero, he wouldn't be in trouble even if there was some linkage established between him and you. He'll be happy and he'll pay the full price." Béres held out his hands and smiled like some cardinal who had just solved the Church's problem with Brother Luther.

Lazaro shook his head. "Sometimes you are so . . ."

"Mercenary?" Béres offered.

Lazaro had to laugh, but Béres stopped him short.

"That's not the end of the problem, though. I wouldn't count on Tagliapietro being satisfied. He'll be watching you. But the extra security of having the Secretariat follow you might not be a bad thing at that."

Lazaro looked at Béres through the eyes in the pig mask. "How's that?"

Béres rubbed the pig's snout. "Because, *mon 'tit cochon*, if those two were carrying out a contract, the person who gave it out might not want the only witness left alive."

"So I'll stick with Tagliapietro," Lazaro said, then snorted like a pig.

"A sensible choice, unless of course the contract was his." Béres smiled. Lazaro didn't.

The sky was darkening when Vom Scheidt returned to his room. Lazaro had been waiting with relative patience since he had left Pander's, and he was starting to understand why Vom Scheidt was looking for somewhere else to stay. The smell of the cheese was beginning to nauseate him.

"You've got to get me into that building," Vom Scheidt said as he pulled a bottle of wine off the shelf and sat on the rough wooden chair beside the shuttered window. "That girl!"

"You didn't?" Lazaro said hopefully.

"No, no, I was incognito. But I wanted to. And she has friends."

"She's the innkeeper's daughter, but he's not as moralistic as Pander."

"That would be refreshing," Vom Scheidt said, pouring a glass of wine for each of them. "You got your business done?"

Lazaro nodded. "Were you followed back here?"

"Yes, the same two that followed me to your place. They aren't very good, or they want you to know they're following you. You must not have done anything that bad."

"Actually, I tried to save a man's life."

"Oh, that's bad." Vom Scheidt smiled. "A capital offense in Venice, isn't it?"

"Sometimes. Take your clothes — my clothes — off."

"You're so direct," Vom Scheidt said, putting his glass on the table. "And you do the same. I'd like to pay a visit to the innkeeper's daughter tonight as myself. I won't feel so restrained. And I imagine you will be off on some business?"

Lazaro nodded as he stripped.

VII

Though he was once more dressed in his own clothes, Lazaro felt naked in the crowd which surged in the *calle*. They were dressed in the gaiety of Carnevale, fanciful and fearful masks abounding, a multitude of colors, smells. He was dressed in somber black, his hair neat, his cape clean, though it dawned on him that he would not remain clean for long if he did not get off the streets. Stopping by a bridge he walked down to the *traghetto* below and stepped into a waiting gondola. The gondolier waited long enough to hear that he was headed for the Piazza and then poled off into the Canalazzo — the Grand Canal of Venice. Lazaro eased back into the cushioned seat and noticed that one of his followers had taken another gondola and was following at a discreet distance. The other man wove his way through the crowd along the *fondamenta*, keeping the gondola in sight. He felt secure. Vom Scheidt had been right. They were letting him know he was being followed and so they did not intend any harm, at least not for the moment.

Even though it was more sane in the Canalazzo, there was still too much traffic. As he looked about he wondered why he stayed in such a place. The city was overcrowded, the intrigue was omnipresent, like some oversweet dessert. And everywhere, it smelled. The city had been built on a swamp. True, the tide moved in and out to clean the canals and the lagoon on a regular basis, but still the refuse hung about. And not all of the human waste was simple excreta. It was not uncommon to see a body, or body parts — and sometimes bawdy parts — floating wistfully in some back *rio.* That was Venice. But then there was the glass. That was Venice too. Somehow in this city of darkness there was a light which glowed, sometimes difficult to see but oftentimes captured by the artists, especially the glassmakers, and, for him, by Angelo. Angelo would be wondering why he had not come. But Lazaro could not refuse a request from the Secretariat. The old man would understand.

The gondolier stopped exactly where the other gondolier had stopped the night before. Though he had spent so many nights in Venice, they had been eclipsed by this one night. Somehow he had been propelled into a different world. In one night he had moved from assassin to savior, soon to be presented to the Doge of Venice and to Marzia Zorzi. He had moved, surely he had, but he kept the truth to himself. Inside he knew that he had not changed, that he had been sent to kill Marzia's father, and that he would have, had fate not intervened.

Lazaro identified himself to the guard at the door to the palace and was immediately escorted into a waiting-room. He stood alone for some time until the guard returned and ushered him back out to the Molo. He pointed to the Ponte della Paglia, which crossed the Rio del Palazzo and led to the Riva degli Schiavoni. "Wait at the landing on the Slav side for the Doge's gondola."

Lazaro walked over to the bridge and crossed it to the Riva degli Schiavoni where he stood on the *fondamenta.* He had expected to see the boats of the firewood sellers who usually conducted their business here, but there were none. After waiting for a few moments he walked back to the bridge and down by its side to the landing. Peering down the canal he could see the Doge's barge but there was no way of knowing whether the Doge was in it or not. It sat at rest beside the *fondamenta* on that side of the palace, its two gondoliers at the ready. There was not much traffic in that section of the canal.

Suddenly he saw the gondoliers lean into their oars and the gondola swiftly moved toward him. As it neared the *traghetto* it slowed and came to a stop, swinging to one side to allow him to step on. The gondolier closest to him signaled for him to board and pointed to a small seat. Lazaro could not see inside the *felze,* but he assumed the Doge would be there. Before he had taken his seat the gondola was off. They headed out through the Bacino San Marco, rounded the tip of San Giorgio Maggiore, and then moved in between that and the Lazzaretto Vecchio, the hospital which had been established for plague victims in 1423, nearly a century before. The water was calm and the gondola moved effortlessly. The gondoliers were silent and Lazaro found himself enjoying the peacefulness of the lagoon. Here and there other gondolas were floating, no doubt carrying *nobili* who wished to watch the sunset over Venice.

Lazaro felt the gondola pitch slightly and heard the door to the *felze* open. Beccaria stepped out, masked, dressed in black, as he had been when Lazaro had seen him that morning in Tagliapietro's chamber. He pointed to the open door. "They want you inside." He stood waiting while Lazaro rose and walked to the open door. It was dark inside and as he entered Beccaria shut the door behind him. He heard Tagliapietro's voice. "Sit down, sit down. There is no ceremony here."

Lazaro looked to his side and saw that the seat was empty, so he sat, and then, his eyes adjusting to the dim light, saw that Tagliapietro and the Doge were sitting opposite him. The Doge smiled at him and then returned to the whispered conversation he was having with Tagliapietro. If he had strained his ears he might have been able to follow what they were saying, but he was drawn to the water appearing through the window of the *felze.* He enjoyed sitting low in a gondola, for it allowed him to be close to the water's surface. A water bird dipped to the mirror surface and took a silver fish up in its beak, effortlessly, leaving behind only a slight mist.

He was in the presence of power, the Secretary to the Council of Ten and Antonio Grimani, the Doge of Venice. Yet at that moment the mist on the water held for Lazaro a strange fascination. As he watched it he saw in it the face of a young girl and there beside her was her hand, delicate, beckoning to him. The mist seemed to glow translucent orange and then was gone.

Lazaro shifted his gaze across the Lagoon to Venice. He had never seen it this way before. When he had first entered Venice he was tired from the fighting and wanted only to rest in a city surrounded by the comings and goings which remind one of life. A contract from Fugger here and there and the possibility of delivering Angelo to a monied barbarian had kept him satisfied. But now he saw it, or perhaps more correctly, felt it, as it must have felt to the people who built it to protect them from the Hunnish horde which was devastating all that was civilized in northern Italy. These fishermen and merchants had fled to the islands across the shallow salt marshes and had built on piles what was to become the greatest sea power in the world — not so much a power military, though that she is, but a power commercial. From her warehouses she sought to rule the known world, and the unknown world. All commerce from east to west, from north to south, from sea to land, flowed through the dim accounting rooms of the merchant families. From the Arsenal, the shipbuilding yards, had come the ships which provided her with the power to enforce her commercial stranglehold. In the manner of an assembly line, ships were built and provisioned in one day. Her young men, trained in archery and the ways of the sea as well as commerce, manned these ships of power, not as galley slaves but as shareholders, respected by those shareholders who remained behind. And when force was of no assistance, there was always duplicity. In that she was rich. From her beginning she had encouraged the weaving of alliances to her benefit. The winged lion of Saint Mark would lie down with the lamb, if not for her benefit, then to tear her throat.

The spires of the churches were silhouetted against the evening sky and its hue and tone shifted with the sun. The lagoon was silver blue, the sky blue pink, the city black and gold. Everywhere about them the gondolas plied, bringing out to a perfect vantage point the *nobili* of Venice. It seemed the entire city was now engaged in this maritime constitutional, watching for the precise moment now arriving. The Secretary hushed and the Doge held his finger to his lips in anticipation. It seemed that even the lapping of the water and the creak of the gondolier's oar ceased. In that moment a celestial crescendo occurred. The bright wash of sunset poured into the lagoon and raced, golden, past the gondolas, chased by the shadows of the mountains and of Venice itself, shadows lengthening, grasping, scurrying after the gold of the sun, east to the riches on which Venice depended. Like a cormorant, the shadow spread its dark wings over the surface of the lagoon. In another moment it was upon them and silently past. Now all was soft blue to black below the sky golden with the setting sun. Lazaro looked to the faces of the Secretary and the Doge. They were transfixed. They were gazing upon God, not the bloody crucifix which the Church held up before men's eyes, but the glory of creation which could not be dissected into religious postulations. It was pure and inviolate. Then he saw Tagliapietro's face harden again. There was little which was inviolate in Venice.

"I believe that Lazaro would make a fine apprentice to the Secretariat," Tagliapietro said to the Doge. The Doge turned and faced Lazaro. Lazaro had wondered at the wisdom whereby, when all of Europe was ruled by young men, Venice had a Doge who was eighty-eight. But now he saw the power in Grimani's eyes, despite his aged exterior.

"Your mother's father was Enrico Ruzzini."

"Yes, Domine," Lazaro nodded. "But I understand he is dead."

"That chapter in your life is finished."

"It was finished long ago," Lazaro responded coldly.

Tagliapietro caught the Doge's glance and moved to soften things. "Lazaro served for some six years in our armies and gave good account of himself."

"But you are more than a soldier, lad. The Secretary tells me that you have had an education from the monks."

"And that my father was a Moor?" Lazaro knew this statement to be rude, but he felt little for diplomacy at that moment. The conversation had interrupted the beauty he had been witnessing.

The Doge waved his hand gracefully. "I don't need the Secretariat to tell me what my eyes can see. But you are here now and your future is before you, a future which, if directed skillfully, can erase the past. You do not wish to serve the Church?"

"No, Domine, I would serve Venice before the Church." Lazaro knew the Doge would question such a sycophantic response.

"A politic answer, young captain," the Doge said in a diplomatic fashion, though Lazaro saw his eyes harden slightly, "but you spent time in Germany as a wandering student. Who was your *bacchant*?"

Lazaro recalled the scholar he had been given over to by the monks when they had seen that he would not become a man of God. Paulus Ferrier had been educated in France but was a traveling scholar in Germany. As Ferrier's *bejaune* — the ignorant student — Lazaro had been saddled with the responsibility of begging in the streets and, at times, singing in taverns, to get money for them to live. He assumed that the Doge somehow had knowledge of these facts. As one skilled in law he would not ask questions for which he did not already have a fairly clear idea of the answer. Tagliapietro's men had quickly done their duty.

He explained his past, those parts of it which he was sure the Doge would know or which were of lesser consequence. He had wandered through a number of schools in Germany under the tutelage of Ferrier, and, as *bacchants* went, Ferrier was not bad. He beat him fairly often, but only when Lazaro disobeyed him or when he was too slow in his lessons. At least he did not do it for pleasure. Lazaro had heard the sad tales told by many of the *bejaunes*, and had seen the marks as well. Ferrier called his birch "The Motivator" and it had eventually motivated Lazaro to run away. He had confided in a merchant's wife who was allowing them to stay in her barn that he was running away and she had dutifully informed Ferrier that his charge was making a break.

Ferrier had allowed him to escape and had followed him secretly for eighteen days. Near Basle, Lazaro had been accosted and overpowered by thieves. When they found that he had no valuables or books, they were preparing to drown him, "baptise him" they had called it, when Ferrier came out of the trees. He had replaced his birch with a staff and with that and the advantage of surprise he had beaten the thieves away. Lazaro was more disposed to remain with his *bacchant* after that and was more attentive to his studies. However, Ferrier realized that his student was anxious to experience other things in life. During a sojourn in the Tyrol, he arranged for Lazaro to study with a cousin of Jakob Fugger's, an alchemist working with the Fugger mines in the town of Schwaz. It was there that Lazaro had met with a passing mercenary, and, interested in the profession of arms, Lazaro had left to join the forces of Venice.

Lazaro left from the tale the darker moments and the more personal ones. His thoughts of God, of his deceased parents, and the degradations he had suffered were no business of the Doge or Tagliapietro. Nor were his duties with the other Fugger. But they seemed more interested in his exploits during the wars. He recounted the massing of the mercenaries in the north, the arrangements with the Condottieri acting for Venice, the besieging of towns. The Doge seemed particularly interested in the second battle of Brescia.

"You served for some time with Nicolo Fontana and Gabriel Tadini, didn't you?"

Lazaro was aware of the revolution which Tadini and Fontana were causing in military science, though the thought was principally Tadini's. "I served with Tadini. Tartaglia, that was our name for Fontana, he was an apprentice to Tadini and learned his fortune from him."

Tagliapietro leaned into the conversation. "The nickname Tartaglia arose from his stutter, I believe, Domine. His head was split open by a French sword at the first battle of Brescia and, as Tartaglia tells it, his mother licked his wound for many days and nursed him back to health, but could do nothing for his stutter."

"He told the same story then, Domine," Lazaro continued, "though it took considerably longer. He is an accomplished engineer, but no match for Tadini."

"We felt the same way," the Doge said and adjusted himself in his seat, with a great rustling of silk. "That is why Tadini is in Crete, rebuilding the fortifications there. We must always be ready for the Turk. But tell me, is Tadini right and Aristotle wrong?"

Lazaro smiled. "I'm no scholar, Domine. I've left my books and thoughts behind. But Tadini knew how to make his cannon do his bidding. Aristotle's reasoning suggests that a cannonball should fly in a straight line and then, once its power is expended, fall directly to the earth. Tadini showed me once what would happen if he fired a cannon following that principle. The shot fell short and almost among our own troops."

The Doge smiled. "That explains why the Pope would have us adhere to Aristotle. These are fine tales. The birch of a scholar and the steel of a soldier prepare a young man well for higher service." He turned to the Secretary. "You are a good judge, Tagliapietro. I believe we have our man. The Secretariat needs eyes among the glassmakers. You have been associating with Angelo, the mirrormaker?"

The question was rhetorical, but Lazaro understood and nodded.

"Does the glass interest you, Lazaro, or mirrors?"

"Undeniably there is a certain beauty in glass, Domine, a beauty for which the world is willing to pay dearly. And the mystery of the mirror has value in many ways."

"Oh," the Doge said mockingly, and cupped his hands over his ears which were hidden beneath his *cornu*, "if I were a maid and you spoke of love . . ." His face shadowed. "But I am a merchant and commerce is the lust that pulses in Venice. The glass industry is one of our prized possessions and it is useful for apprentices to the Secretariat to know of it, and to learn how to serve. Too often soldiers and scholars serve secret masters. And, of course, priests." The Doge looked out of the small window of the *felze*. "Tagliapietro tells me that you have acted as Angelo's private agent in sales, and that you have recently attended at his furnaces." The Doge turned to face Lazaro. "And of course you know that it is unlawful for you to do either without leave from the Secretariat. The penalties can be severe, but Tagliapietro and my conversation with you have convinced me that another course of action is more profitable."

There was silence as the Doge looked again to the water, then Tagliapietro spoke. "Given your assistance in the Zorzi matter, we are willing to be convinced that your talents should be put to use in the service of the Secretariat and of Venice and so we suspend your punishment. I have sent word to Angelo that we will send you to him as a laborer and that you may act as his agent. In this way we have legitimized your contact with him. If things go well, it might even be possible to overlook your past and admit you as a citizen of Venice. Of course, the suspension of the offense can be withdrawn at any time, but I doubt that will be necessary."

The Doge's voice sounded. "This opportunity is a gift, young Ruzzini. If you aspire at all to greater things, this is the only path open to you. Tread carefully." He looked back at Lazaro and his face was again friendly, paternal. Tagliapietro nodded. Lazaro knew that the audience was over.

Tagliapietro cleared his throat. "You can wait outside, Lazaro. And ask Beccaria to come in."

Lazaro eased out of the cab and along the side of the gondola, noting that it listed little. The gondoliers, accomplished in their craft, would be leaning out farther on their platforms to compensate for the shift in load. Beccaria was standing, arms folded, watching over the waters — the Master of the Assassins. Beccaria looked him in the eye, and Lazaro felt something cold within. Lazaro signaled that he was wanted inside, whereupon Beccaria ducked into the opposite door of the *felze*.

Most of Venice would speak of Beccaria only in hushed tones, for he controlled an army of *bravi*; young, well-trained assassins, torpedoes who would do the bidding of the state, ferret out enemies, and dispose of them, quickly, silently. No one saw his face. Lazaro wondered if even Tagliapietro had had that honor. He wondered too if the mask hid some great scar. Then he realized that anyone might have seen Beccaria's face and not known it. And yet for Beccaria, masked or not, he must live within his disguise. Did this extend to family, friends, lovers? Lazaro had a thought of a man who by day had one identity and then, in his sleep and unknown to himself, stood and became another person, the wraith Beccaria. Perhaps there was no one who knew that the two people were one.

The gondoliers stood silently at their posts. Lazaro stared across the face of the Lagoon, hoping to find the mist again, but it was gone. All about him the gondolas of Venice began their slow return to the city. The setting sun made the sky brilliant red and gold and he took it as an omen foretelling the coming of a promising dawn. There was a rap on the wall of the cab and the gondoliers leaned into their oars, following the tide of black specks homeward bound. The Realtina sounded across the water and one by one the gondolas' torches were lit, as if calling to the stars which would soon appear in the night sky. Lazaro looked up into the sky and in the east he could make out the evening star, Venus and nearby Mars: pleasure and war — hallmarks of Venice.

Attendants tied the gondola to its berth while the gondoliers scrambled to assist the Doge up the steps. Beccaria followed them, then disappeared into the night. Lazaro hung back for a moment, seemingly forgotten. Then he saw Tagliapietro turn and wave to him as the Doge was met by his guard and made his way to the palace. Lazaro met Tagliapietro on the steps and they stood alone.

"You've been offered a good bargain today, Lazaro. Your activity with Angelo had placed you well within our jurisdiction," Tagliapietro said as they began walking across the Piazzetta. "Beccaria would have been entitled to arrest you at any time."

Lazaro smiled. "I'm beginning to feel that I'm under arrest now."

Tagliapietro stopped and turned to face him. "If you studied well you know the words of Thomas à Kempis — *de duobus malis, minus est semper eligendum.*"

"Of two evils, the lesser is always to be chosen," Lazaro replied suddenly, as if a schoolmaster had asked him.

"Difficult advice to follow sometimes." Tagliapietro paused and sniffed the night air. "I will call on you in the future and I want you to be ready to act for me if need be." He reached into his robe and drew out a small purse clinking with coins. "This is a reward from the Signoria for your attempt last night and for your presence at the trial tomorrow. But I want you to see Angelo early in the morning to arrange your duties with him."

Lazaro nodded and took the purse.

"The Zorzis will be meeting with the Doge now. Come with me." Tagliapietro turned and led Lazaro in through the hallways which were now becoming familiar to him. They entered a *salotto* in the Doge's quarters. The room was small, comfortable and warmed by a fire, but its normal opulence had been masked in black cloth which hung over the window as well as mirrors and paintings. The Doge was sitting on a small sofa and with him was a woman in black, the wife of Zorzi. Beside her on one side was the young man Lazaro had seen with Marzia only the day before in the Piazza. Between Signora Zorzi and the Doge sat Marzia. In the black of mourning she was still beautiful. Her golden hair was hidden in a black kerchief but her face was radiant. As they entered, all faces turned but Marzia's; hers turned a second later and it seemed to Lazaro that she recognized him. But only for a second.

Tagliapietro hurried across the room and the young man stood as he reached Signora Zorzi. She remained seated, her tear-stained face blank. Tagliapietro took her hand and said something to her which

Lazaro could not hear. He then turned to Marzia and the young man moved over to stand behind her. They looked again at Lazaro and Tagliapietro turned and motioned for him to approach. He walked into the circle and bowed his head.

"This is the young man I spoke of, Signor Lazaro Ruzzini," the Doge said to Marzia.

Lazaro was not quite sure what to do, so he bowed his head again. "I wish to offer my condolences."

Marzia reached out and took his hand. He looked up and stared into her eyes. "My mother is indisposed but I wish to thank you for everything which you did to try and save the life of my father. It was a noble act and for that my mother and I are in your debt. We would be honored to have you call on us following the funeral."

Lazaro nodded and was suddenly aware that all other eyes, save for Signora Zorzi's, were on him. Signora Zorzi's eyes had the blank stare of a woman who had lost touch with her mind. The man standing behind Marzia had a somewhat different expression, a dangerous one.

Tagliapietro seemed to notice the look and stepped in. "Allow me to introduce Signor Rodrigo Contarini, who is engaged to Signorina Zorzi."

Again Lazaro nodded politely but as he did so he caught a glance from Marzia and it made what should have been a somber moment somehow warming. He would think of it a great deal afterward, but at that moment it was as if she spoke to him through her eyes and her eyes betrayed that she was not fully in favor of the relationship which had just been announced.

Rodrigo Contarini cleared his throat. "You must come and dine with us. We are truly grateful for your efforts."

Lazaro summoned what courtesy he could. "I regret my failure but I accept your generous offer."

With that, Tagliapietro signaled to him that it was time to leave. Lazaro bowed again and left the room. Tagliapietro followed him out and pulled the doors closed behind them. They were alone in the hallway.

"The questioning of Solomon has gone rather well," he said with a smile. "It wasn't necessary to use very much force and he has signed a document which explains his complicity."

Tagliapietro shook his head and tried to seem saddened by what he was thinking. For an instant Lazaro saw through his skin, saw an evil mass of rotted flesh covered by a deceptive fabric stretched tight to resemble fine skin. Tagliapietro had enjoyed the questioning.

"He was not able to tell us who hired them, but he revealed that he and his comrade, his name was Eli, had been hired by a group of Jews who have interests in the island of Rhodes and who would prefer to conduct business under the policies of the Turk rather than under the Knights and so would benefit greatly from the defeat of the Knights. There has been much discussion recently as to whether or not Venice should support the Knights in their dispute with the Grand Turk Suleiman. Zorzi was among those who favor intervention to assist the Holy Order, and his influence was substantial. It is understandable that there would be Jews who would see Zorzi as an enemy. Apparently this Eli came into the city during Carnevale and had met Solomon at the home of Solomon's whore. The poor boy's confession is recorded but he has agreed to testify before the Consilio dei Dieci. And he will have to answer to two murders."

Lazaro looked at him questioningly.

"The whore. I sent men to question her, but she was found dead, her throat cut. Her neighbors said that she had last been seen with Solomon, early yesterday evening." Tagliapietro sighed and shook his head. "Solomon has confessed to that as well." He then became more formal. "I want you present at the trial tomorrow, in case I wish to call you for testimony. Four o'clock." The audience was ended and Tagliapietro turned and entered the *salotto*. Lazaro was alone in the hallway.

On the steps outside the Doge's Palace he tried to order in his mind the events which he had just witnessed. It seemed straightforward enough. He had tried to save the life of an important nobleman of Venice, and he had been rewarded. The family had thanked him and wished to show their gratitude by having him visit their *casa*. He was fortunate that they did not truly know why he had been so close to Zorzi at the time of his death.

But there was Marzia. He had seen her often during his time in Venice and had worshiped her in some distant way, as one might covet a magnificent house, or a fine horse, or gold. But she was unattainable, an image which he could hold in his mind, not a woman he could hold in his arms. And now he had met her, had seen the obvious difference in status, had been introduced to her future husband. Yet something in her eyes told him she was attracted to him. He decided it was his imagination, his fantasy.

He moved out into the Piazza and bought a flask of wine and an apple from a merchant. Pouring some wine down his throat to warm himself, he paid a few coins more and took a mask so that he would feel a part of the festival taking place in the streets.

From the Campanile the *cheba* — an iron cage — was suspended with a man imprisoned inside. From the crowd gathering beneath it to hurl insults and stones, he learned that it held a monk who had been giving singing lessons to young girls. Apparently he had tried to teach them skills for which their parents had not contracted. In the glare of the torches Lazaro could make out the man's sad face. He had seen imprisonments such as this before. They did not last long but they were for life. The imprisoned man would receive no food. His body would remain there after his soul had left it as a reminder to those who might transgress that they should not be caught. Venice did not take the position that a man should do no wrong, but that as a being of free will he must expect to be held accountable for his actions.

He finished the apple and fought an urge to toss the core up to the man in the cage. Instead he dropped it on the paving stones where it mixed with the rest of the refuse gathered there. Soon it would be mashed underfoot and would lie there, awaiting the street cleaners who moved about before dawn.

Somehow a breeze found him and he shivered, pulling his cloak tighter around him. He had an urge to be with friends in a warm tavern or with a woman in a quiet bed. He looked around, wondering if he was going to have an escort provided by the Secretariat. He realized that it might be difficult to tell, but he felt certain that the watchdogs had been called off. If they had suspected him he would not have experienced the audience he had had this evening. But it might still be too soon to look up Béres, and Vom Scheidt would certainly be out in the city somewhere.

Sleeping did not attract him for it promised troublesome dreams. But there was little point in pursuing much entertainment. Angelo would expect him at the furnace in the morning. He wondered how much, if any, of the events of the past two nights he would share with the old man. It would depend. There were times when the old man was so out of touch with the world about him that he appeared imbecilic, at other times his mind was sharp and clear as *cristallo.*

He wandered into Malatesta's glass market on the edge of the Piazzetta. He was well-known to Malatesta for the pieces of glass and the mirrors which he brought to the store. The shopkeeper made a good living from selling Angelo's work, even if Lazaro did make sure that Angelo wasn't cheated. He knew Malatesta would be up on the roof drinking with friends, and he nodded at the clerk who was watching the store and climbed the stairs. Malatesta saw him as he climbed out into the night air and came over to him with a flask of wine. The merchant's red nose was a good indicator of his mood, and tonight the nose was glowing bright. Somehow in his garbled fashion he explained that Lazaro was like a son to him and that he was welcome anytime. Lazaro nodded and grunted appropriately and Malatesta left him with the flask and went back to the boisterous guests.

Lazaro sat near the edge of the roof and looked over the Piazzetta and the Piazza. From here he could see everything that was going on, from much the same vantage point as the unfortunate monk. He glanced over at the two columns which stood in the Piazzetta. Solomon would have his trial tomorrow and he would be executed, most likely on a scaffold between the two columns.

Lazaro did not know Solomon well, and had met him only because he had worked at the printing press of Daniel Bomberg. Lazaro had first heard of the press from a surgeon he had worked with at the Fugger mines in Schwaz, a German named Von Hohenheim, though he went by the name Paracelsus. Paracelsus had introduced Lazaro to rare religious texts, many of which had been printed by Bomberg with the assistance of his master printer Hermann Liechtenstein and Fra Felice of Prato, a converted Jew. When Lazaro lingered in Venice he had found his way to Bomberg's establishment and was allowed free reading rights on the strength of his association with Paracelsus. And there Lazaro had met Solomon.

Bomberg was allowed four Jews as readers and Solomon had been one of them. In addition to the good money they made, the readers were allowed to travel through the streets of Venice without the yellow hats required of most other Jews. The readers took full advantage of the money and the special dispensation, but Solomon was probably the quietest of them all. It wasn't impossible that this affair had unfolded as Tagliapietro had explained, but there was something about it which did not fit, and Lazaro desperately wanted to sort it out. He wondered if it was Solomon's involvement which seemed farfetched. He supposed Solomon might have been involved in a plot such as Tagliapietro had described, but he doubted that he could have killed his mistress. Perhaps Béres was wrong — could Fugger have commissioned more than one team? It was not unheard of in order to secure success. But it was not Fugger's way. Lazaro knew that. Fugger chose people who would succeed at the tasks he set for them. That was why he had sought out Béres and Lazaro. But if there *had* been someone else, then Béres was right, and Lazaro would have to watch his back. He drank the last of the wine and decided he should head to his bed.

When the Marangona boomed out midnight he headed back to his room, though it took him longer than normal. Even with his newfound wealth there was not a gondola available, and the *calli* were crawling with Venetians in various stages of debauchery. The inn was filled with men and women who preferred to sit and be drunk than to stand and be drunk. For a moment he thought of joining in for a while, to drink away the dark thoughts hovering just beyond his understanding. But it took him only a few moments to choose against it. He felt that he could not even pretend to be a part of what was going on.

He climbed the stairs to his room, and as he passed the room beside his he chanced to look through the open door. By the moonlight coming through the window he could see Renata and Vom Scheidt, naked, cavorting on the bed. He stopped to watch, but they did not notice him. Suddenly he knew how the dead must feel, looking back at the living going about their lives. And he realized how self-centered it was of the living to think that the dead envied them.

VIII

The sky was beginning to lighten as Lazaro found his way through the winding *calli*, carrying a bundle of clean clothes, to the wharf in the Cannaregio. He found a gondolier sleeping beside his gondola, jingled some coins in the man's ear, and pointed to the pall which usually hung over Murano.

The air moved slightly with the dawn wind, and here and there in the Lagoon, birds swooped to the water's surface to compete with fish leaping for the insects abounding there. The fishermen were out as well in their small boats, gathering the last of the fish for the market which would open soon. The gondolier, though half asleep, was careful to avoid any of the *zeccho*, the marshy spots which appeared at low tide and which lay in wait to embarrass the novice.

Lazaro sat back in a contemplation which bordered on sleep as the island of Murano grew larger. During his many visits to Angelo's factory, the old man had often offered to let Lazaro take up lodgings in the factory, to save himself the trip, but Lazaro had declined. He had found Murano too singular in its devotion. In every *calle*, in every tavern, men were conspiratorial, discussing glass; not the export but the design. However, on this quiet morning, with his recent activity close in mind, he thought he might soon want to embrace Angelo's invitation. The conspiracy of glass would have been welcome in comparison to his life in Venice, and it might give him a better opportunity to complete his own conspiracy. In any event, Vom Scheidt would be happy with the vacancy at the Dancing Mouse.

As the gondolier rowed he talked of Murano, and it wasn't long before Lazaro realized that somehow he had managed to employ the same garrulous gondolier who had taken him, with Béres, to Mustapha's ship. However, the gondolier recognized Lazaro only as non-Venetian. In the mind of the gondolier all foreigners looked alike and craved nothing more than an explanation of something Venetian. Lazaro did not interrupt him, for the one-sided conversation guaranteed him time for thought.

The gondolier's patter started with the weather. "As hot as it may be in Venice today, wait for Murano. The furnaces there will call to mind Dante's Inferno, with seas of molten sand. . . ." The main furnaces of Venice had been moved to the island of Murano on November 8, 1291, by order of the Secretariat, which had responsibility for the glass industry. It was thought prudent, as it was necessary for the furnaces at the larger factories to be fired continuously, and there was always a risk that the fire might leap out of control. Better that a small island burn than the entire city. But this banishment did not mean that the glass industry was not valued. To the contrary, with the relocation of the factories and their masters to a smaller island, it was immediately possible to restrict the movement of knowledge and knowledgeable people. By controlling the secret of the manufacture of the best glass, and the crafting of fine objects and mirrors, Venice maintained control of a trade item which brought her considerable wealth.

This explained the laws which forbade the exportation of material central to the industry, and of industrial secrets as well. And members of the glassmakers' guild were included in that prohibition, on pain of death. This was not only the workings of a jealous Secretariat; the guilds, too, favored the job security guaranteed by such a decree. And being a glassmaker was not without its rewards. They received special privileges among the guilds, and in status-conscious Venice, where nobles were recorded in a golden book, where marriages were controlled, and where status was lost if one married beneath oneself, members of the guild and their children could marry into noble families and the offspring would retain the status of *Ene Aca*. So the guild members themselves, as much as the Secretariat, upheld the ban on a Doctor of Glass ever leaving Venice. But enforcement was normally left to the assassins under the direction of Beccaria.

Lazaro burrowed deep into his cape. Little of this had mattered to him when he had first arrived in Venice. He hadn't even intended to stay long; Tadini had asked him to come to Crete; Béres had offered him a place in his quiet village in Transylvania. But before long Lazaro had realized the value of the knowledge of glass, though his education in its mysteries began by chance.

About a year previously he had run into Angelo, quite literally, outside Bomberg's press. Angelo had come to Bomberg's wishing to examine a number of old manuscripts which Bomberg had purchased. He had brought mercuric oxide as an item of exchange. Mercuric oxide was always useful to Bomberg in the manufacture of red ink. After helping the old man to his feet and retrieving his bundle, Lazaro had bought him a drink in a nearby tavern. Though the old man had seemed a bit crazy, he had a certain light in his eyes which Lazaro could not ignore. Discovering that Lazaro had worked with mercury in Schwaz and knew something of glass, Angelo had leapt into conversation with him.

"Do you know what a mirror is?" the old man had asked.

"Something that reflects everything in front of it," Lazaro had replied.

The old man had laughed until tears filled his eyes, and people at nearby tables shied away. Then he had shaken his head and pulled Lazaro close to him. In a hushed tone he said, "A mirror is an instrument. You must begin with that understanding. And you must understand the instrumentality to enlarge your understanding. It is an instrument. But a marvelous one. Instruments possess potential but seldom act by themselves. Not that human direction is always needed. A knife can be used to cut by a man or a baboon. And a baboon can pluck a harp. But the mirror, it works on its own. And so there is the next important attribute to consider. It is a machine. But a very special machine for it produces something but it has no moving parts. The perfect mirror would never wear out. Next you must understand its capability for infinity. A shattered mirror produces many fragments but if you hold that fragment up to your face you do not see a fragment of your face but your entire face, smaller. Just as the smallest particle of the Host contains God, so too the smallest particle of the mirror holds all that the mirror in its entirety displays. And the entire mirror is itself only a fragment of the larger form which is the true mirror."

Lazaro had not been prepared for such a conversation, but he found it humorous and worth the wine. Still, though the old man was odd, he was not a fool. There was something in the old man's manner which fascinated him. He reminded him of the prophets, or at least of the representations of the prophets in paintings.

"So it isn't just a thing. But more than that it doesn't just reflect whatever is in front of it. Simple mirrors might appear to do that. But even simple mirrors perform a much more important function. They delineate the edge of existence. They are moveable windows to another world. And perhaps someday I will discover the true portal and pass through."

Lazaro was convinced by now that the old man had aspirated a bit too much mercury. He had received enough training to know that mercury was something to be treated with great respect. In Schwaz, part of his assignment had been to assist Paracelsus in preparing a treatise on diseases afflicting mercury miners. It was a miraculous substance which had the power to cure, especially with the *Morbus Gallicus.* And in an amalgam it could be used to coat glass and produce a mirror. But too much exposure to mercury unseated the mind. Watching this old man Lazaro began to believe that he might indeed fall through a mirror someday, with the help of mercury, and enter the other world which it represented to him. But if that happened his passage would be in one direction only. Still, Lazaro was enthralled by Angelo's stories, and when the old man invited him to visit his factory to witness the manufacture of mirrors and glass pearls, he agreed readily, though he vowed he would keep his distance from the mercury.

Slowly the idea came to Lazaro that this old man, or one of his acquaintances might be interested in a bit of lucrative travel. And then the knowledge of Beccaria and his assassins intruded. One night, soon after meeting Angelo, on his late return from Murano, Lazaro came upon a crowd of people crushing the head of a young man with a mallet. They explained that they were the young man's neighbors, that he had been observed dropping a message into the mouth of one of the carved lions set up as portals of truth to receive denunciations. The neighbors feared that he may have brought the assassins down on them, and they wanted their revenge first as, in that case, there would be no escape for them. Lazaro had not asked them what the accusation might have been. Strangers learned soon enough not to ask questions in Venice.

"*Signore*," a voice called, Lazaro opened his eyes. "*Signore*," the gondolier said, with a broad grin, "my wife says I have the gift of Morpheus. You agree?"

Lazaro stepped out of the gondola and onto the *riva* of the Rio dei Vetrai, noticing that the *calli* were filling with glassworkers heading to the various factories. Angelo's factory was a large squarish structure which abutted the Rio dei Vetrai and a small dead-end canal so that two of the walls could have large windows and yet prying eyes could not see in. Even so, precaution had been taken and the lower panes of glass were fogged sufficiently to protect the secrets within. The doorways which opened on the canals to allow the delivery of wood for the furnaces and to take away the shipments of glass were bolted shut. Above the factory area were Angelo's living quarters and his experimental laboratory where he kept his alchemical secrets. However, Lazaro had never been in those rooms. His experience had been restricted to the main-floor furnaces and to Angelo's private furnace where he performed many of his experiments and where lately, showing his contempt for rules and demonstrating an affection for Lazaro, he had exposed Lazaro to the rudiments of his manufacturing process. Lazaro had learned in Germany how to mix glass but he was continually impressed by Angelo's ability to produce *cristallo* or colored glass of high quality. But then, all of the master glassmakers of Murano had their closely guarded formulae which allowed them to produce glass coveted throughout the world. Lazaro was surprized that Angelo had allowed him to witness the mixing, though he was quite aware that Angelo kept some of the proportions and chemicals a secret.

Lazaro walked up the *calle* leading to the low doorway in the west wall which served as the entrance to the factory. Immediately inside was the porter's chamber. In earlier days this had been a stronghold guarded by a heavily armed servant to further protect the mysteries which lay within. Angelo had converted it to cramped living quarters for Domenico, a man of great size and strength, but having the mind of a child and the eyes and face of one who has been touched by God in a special way. Others referred to him as an idiot — but not within Angelo's hearing. Lazaro nodded at Domenico and he smiled back. Lazaro had seen how effective Domenico could be when a drunken foreigner had stumbled in and had not left when requested. Unfettered by anger, Domenico had simply picked the man up, carried him outside and broken his right arm, then left him there to contemplate his error.

Inside there was little activity. Though the factory often operated throughout the night, during Carnevale the workers were there only during the daytime. A young son of one of the glassmakers who assisted Domenico in keeping the fires going through the night was asleep on a cot in the corner. From somewhere on the other side of the furnaces he could hear the voice of Bartelemeo, the foreman, and an assistant, working in the area reserved for production of crown glass. As the day progressed and more ventilation was required, panels on the doors and in the arched ceiling would be swung open, but for now it was relatively cool. Relatively — as soon as he entered Lazaro removed his coat and placed it alongside his bundle on a shelf. He crossed the stone floor where all about were the remnants of designs traced out in chalk by the masters, and stood between the two large, beehive-shaped furnaces. Peering in through one of the glory holes which ringed the furnace he saw the clay crucibles which held the molten glass. Angelo would have mixed the proportions in his locked workroom and then had the young apprentices wheel the barrows out and load the crucibles to begin the transformation of the sand, soda, and lime into glass.

The doorway at the back of the factory which led to Angelo's private furnace was closed and so Lazaro continued around the furnace until he saw Bartelemeo, his face partly covered with a cloth veil to cut down on the heat from the larger glory hole used in the crown glass process. The foreman was busy and so just nodded to Lazaro and continued his work. Lazaro moved back to a cooler spot beside some of the spare crucibles and sat down on a barrel of quartz pebbles to watch the work as he waited for Angelo to appear.

Bartelemeo had already managed to get a sizeable gather on his *bocca*, the blow-pipe used by the glassmakers, and he carried it to the marvering table where he rolled the yellow glowing mass on the iron sheet, using a wet wooden forming block to give it the desired shape. Then his assistant began to blow into the pipe, and Bartelemeo moved the gather off the edge of the table and rolled the pipe back and forth. The glowing mass grew but also changed color to a bright orange. When it reddened, the assistant returned it to the glory hole to soften it for more blowing. The process was repeated until Bartelemeo was satisfied with the size of the globe. Taking a *punti*, a solid metal rod about four feet in length, he gathered a small bulb of molten glass and used it to attach the *punti* to the side of the globe opposite the blowpipe. The assistant then used a watering can to drip some cool water near where the glass was attached to the blow-pipe. With a careful tap the blow-pipe came free and the globe was now held by the *punti*. Quickly, the assistant worked with shears and a forming tool to widen the opening, and then Bartelemeo moved it back to the flash furnace for the final step. Resting the *punti* on a metal support he began to spin it quickly. The globe glowed yellow-white and began to open slowly, due to the centrifugal force. Lazaro leaned forward in anticipation, and suddenly the entire globe opened up with a pop into a flat disk of spinning glass. With the assistant's help the glass was pulled back through the opening where it would continue to spin until cool enough to rest on a bed of warm ash and then be cut into window panes. Lazaro had also seen them make window glass by blowing a cylinder and then slicing it open and spreading it into a sheet, but he enjoyed the theatricality of this process, and found the brilliant fire-polish of crown glass more attractive than broad glass.

He became aware that the factory was now abustle with glassmakers preparing for the day's work. As if in answer to the clatter in the factory, the door at the back opened and Angelo appeared. Lazaro stood and went over to him.

"I was visited by the bastards from the Secretariat yesterday," Angelo said in a tone of dismissal. "You are now an official apprentice to me. I have too much on my mind to discuss it now. We'll talk later." Lazaro knew of Angelo's moods. He was, as people would so correctly observe, mercurial. The old man moved over to the spot on the floor where he drew most of his final plans and squatted down on a small three-legged stool. He took a large piece of chalk in his hand and started sketching a rough figure. A light smock came down to his knees, and below that Lazaro could see his spindly legs, unstockinged, and his worn leather sandals. His feet were scarred from countless burns and, as he worked, it seemed to Lazaro that there was a particularly bad burn scar on each foot just where a nail would pierce the foot for crucifixion. Lazaro smiled to himself, thinking of the way in which the Church could still reach into his mind.

The old man had paused in his sketching, and Lazaro studied his face. Brown creased leather, it seemed at times a miraculous mask which could move so quickly from child-like joy to aged madness. Now it reflected only the master's concentration. Even the long white hair, at times so unruly, was pulled back and tied with a leather thong into a tail at the back. Angelo was prepared for serious work. As Lazaro watched he saw the idea unfold. The master intended to make a wide-mouthed bowl of clear glass supported by a ball of glass resting on a thick glass base. On each side of the base he had drawn a small animal shape.

Lazaro hunkered down beside him, sitting on his heels. "These aren't dragons," he said, pointing to the animals.

The old man looked at him for a moment as if he had forgotten who he was, and then nodded. "I know. All these bastards want to put dragons everywhere. It's the fashion. I think it looks like shit. No, these are salamanders. I saw one in the furnace this morning."

Lazaro had never seen a salamander, at least not the ones which could live in fire. "And you want the bowl to have rough edges?"

Angelo rubbed his hand over the edges of the bowl and drew again. "I want to leave it with some points rather than being a smooth circle," he said, leaning forward onto his knees and drawing more with his chalk. "The base is the flat world, the practical world, like when you're building a house. The globe is the Earth as a sphere. You must realize it's a sphere when you travel, especially when you are navigating on the ocean. But this," he said, pointing to the bowl, "this is the world in your mind." He sat back on the stool. "The salamanders will stabilize it. I may try to coat the inside of the globe like a mirror. I'm not sure yet." He slapped his knees then stood, picked up a *punti* with cloth wrapped around the handle and went back to the glory hole to check the metal.

Lazaro began arranging the tools which the old man would need to create this bowl. "I have business which I must attend to in Venice at four o'clock," he said with a question on his voice.

The old man didn't react.

"Will that affect the work today?"

The old man looked out, his face red from the heat. "Four o'clock. No, that won't affect this. We'll know long before that if it's working. I have mirrors to build after that. I won't need you then." The old man pulled out a small gather of metal and moved to his work bench. Marvering, then using his shears and wood-blocks, he quickly pulled and prodded the glass into the shape of a salamander. He looked up at Lazaro, who had been watching closely. "I want you to try your hand at this. I want you to have three ready for me when I need to attach them."

Lazaro nodded and took another *punti*. The old man watched silently as he took a gather and worked it in much the same way as the master had, though slower. The resulting figure was close to what Angelo had created. The old man smiled. "Not bad. It is a bit off balance but you have it. Try again." As Lazaro started on another the old man went to another glory hole where he had a second batch of metal working. "I don't know about the mirrored globe. It may not work, but I like the idea of a mirror to catch the action surrounding the bowl, to distort movement and size."

Lazaro agreed. "It allows the mirror to appear active."

The old man turned to watch him with the salamander. "Not all mirrors are passive. There was a mirror made once which had a great ability. It was produced by a master mirrormaker who understood his instrument. It appeared much the same as any other mirror but it was in great demand by the rich. You see, it was deceptive. Great instruments may be endowed with that capability. But its deception ran deep. In it, anything ugly appeared beautiful and anything beautiful appeared ugly. It was a novelty, but it had an even darker side. For in its power of deception it could eventually convince those with great ugliness in their souls that in fact they possessed there a great beauty understood only by the very wise. And those who depended on it greatly found that after a while they did not need the mirror any more, but that everything appeared exactly as the mirror had shown them. You see, the power of the mirror had entered their souls."

The old man turned back to the metal. "But the greatest mystery of all, and the most dangerous of all glasses was a glass manufactured for Emperor Tiberius, although the formula is lost." He paused again and looked at Lazaro. "The mixture is ready." He walked across to the tools assembled by Lazaro. "This glass was the most dangerous because it could not be broken."

Lazaro glanced at him incredulously.

"These are not children's tales," Angelo replied. "Bring me a bucket of water." The old man took a thin metal rod and pulled a small gather of white-hot glass from a crucible on the other side of his furnace and let a drop fall into the water. He waited a moment, then pulled it out and placed it on the marvering table. It lay there like a fragile teardrop. Taking a forming block he whacked it four times, but, to Lazaro's surprise, it did not break. "Now pick it up and try to snap off the tip of the drop." Lazaro followed the instruction, and the drop exploded in his hand, though the minute fragments had no sharp edges.

"You see," Angelo said. "Glass has so many properties which would defy what we know of it now. As Ecclesiastes says, 'The thing that has been is the thing that shall be; there is no new thing under the sun.' Someday I will find that formula."

Angelo's mind was now wrestling with the problem before him. He stood over the design he had traced out on the floor. Lazaro looked too and wondered if the old man had the strength to carry it out. Even with Lazaro and his other assistants, there were a number of stages in the creation of the piece which would call for the hand of the master. The old man saw the look in Lazaro's eyes and grinned. "We may die trying." He laughed and pointed to a particular *punti*. "Get me a gather on that one the size of a man's heart."

The assistants sat by the large open door, sweating, and drank wine with their bread and cheese. The piece was finished and was now in the annealing chamber above the larger of the beehive furnaces. It had taken a lot of energy on everyone's part, but most dramatically it had sapped Angelo. He sat, his hair untied now and falling about his shoulders, arranging and rearranging three small square mirrors.

Lazaro was tired. It had been a difficult job with many failures, but in the end the old man's vision had been realized. He had watched Angelo's face in the final moments of the formation of the bowl. Assistants had blown the glass, opened the lip, and waited as it had been trimmed by the master. As always, the glass had moved in and out of the furnace countless times. But then the moment had come. Everyone was ready. Some power flowed through the factory as Angelo moved to the hole and took the rod. At that moment his strength multiplied, and he worked the glass like a youth of twenty, but with the knowledge of the ages. Then it was finished. Malatesta would have another masterpiece for his shop.

Lazaro realized that it was getting late in the day and was time for him to change and head back to Venice and the trial. He looked over at Angelo and saw that the old man was gazing at him through one of the small mirrors.

Angelo swung around on his stool and walked over to him. "It's about time for you to go. I'll show you where you can change." Lazaro grabbed his bundle, and they walked out past the workmen and turned down the *calle* between the buildings which led to the *fondamenta*. Down the *fondamenta* they stopped at a door secured by a large rusty lock, at the back of the foundry. After that door had been opened and they had passed through, Angelo paused and locked it from the inside. This process was repeated with a second door down the hallway, and Lazaro found himself in a small room filled with the tools and materials of the chemist's trade. He had seen such laboratories at Schwaz, but this laboratory was different. Those had had countless flasks and beakers, storage bins and the like, all dusty with decay and secrecy, as if, true to the thoughts of many alchemists, life and gold would arise out of refuse. This place was clean and ordered.

Angelo crossed to a door at the rear of the room which led to a staircase inside the wall. Lazaro followed into the darkness, and they climbed to the second floor where Angelo unlocked another door which opened into his quarters.

As they passed through a black velvet curtain, Lazaro's eyes opened in wonder. There were no windows, and yet the large room was filled with light — natural light, not the glow of lamps, but wherever he looked for windows he saw only blue sky or a white light or trees and flowers. It was as if inside this building they had been transported to some hideaway in the mountains or by the sea or in the forest, depending on which direction he looked.

Angelo saw the wonder in Lazaro's eyes. "I deal in lies, whether it is the simple lie of constructing a piece of glass which gives the appearance of lightness but is, in fact, strong, or the more complex lie of a mirror which purports to most accurately reflect the reality which faces it. In the sense that it does this it tells the truth. In the sense that in doing so it gives such an image back to another mind which may then use it to lie and cheat, it is an accessory to a grand lie, and I, in my own way, am a contributing architect. If you don't mind being surrounded by lies, you can change here, and if it pleases you, you can stay here when you need."

Lazaro could not answer. He had already dropped his bundle and was wandering about the rooms with the slack-jawed wonder of a child. The windows were panes of glass which did not open but which had an image on them, an image of great accuracy of detail and filled with light from a source he could not see. Here and there in the ceiling there were windows placed so that he could see directly up into the blue sky. He looked into a mirror which reflected his face but showed it somehow differently, and when he reached toward it with his right hand the hand appeared on the left side of the mirror. He reached into a black box which held small perfect images only to find that the images were not where his hand had reached. He turned to Angelo. "This is amazing!"

"What the priests could do with such tricks, eh?" The old man picked up Lazaro's bundle and walked through a black velvet curtain into the next room. "What the priests *have* done with such tricks. Will this room do?"

Lazaro followed him into a small room with plaster walls and a small window leading to a tiny balcony and a ladder to the roof. From the window he could see across to Venice. After the wonder of the last room, this window seemed to be a deception as well.

The old man opened the window and grinned. "This one is real," he said, then sat on the bed. After a moment's silence, he looked up at Lazaro. "I don't really know how people feel about sons, but I've come to think of you as I believe someone might think of a son. I suppose it's better that the Secretariat has now acknowledged that you may work with me, but I care little for their rules. I enjoyed your company, and, frankly, I didn't show you much more than you already knew. My men trust me in that regard. Now you may see more, as much as you'd like. But this also means, at least in their minds, that you do so at their pleasure, with a threat hanging over your head that at any time they could withdraw their support and prosecute you. It means that they now have a right to forbid you to leave Venice on pain of death. It also means that they will watch you carefully, and will notice if your dreams of getting me to leave Venice become anything more than dreams."

Lazaro felt an odd embarrassment, as if he had been caught in some foolish prank by a father, but Angelo smiled and held up his hand. "Don't protest. I am flattered by your attention. But I trust you. Why else would I have allowed you in? So, just be careful. I enjoy your company. And if you ever decide you truly want to stay in Venice, and in glass, there are ways." Angelo got up quickly, as if to avoid the embarrassment of emotion, and left the room. From the hallway he called back, "Now change quickly. You don't want to be late for the performance."

IX

Lazaro arrived at the Piazzetta just before the Orologio struck four. Senators were gathered in the colonnade under the palace walls engaged in their favorite pastime — *broglio* — a lobbying session during which they would discuss various matters of business, political and mercantile, if such a separation was possible. He watched one shaking hands with a merchant, another dropping his *stola* from his shoulder to his arm as a sign of his desire to ask a favor. He grinned as he passed and entered the Ducal Palace. These politicians had learned their tricks from the courtesans.

A page took him to the antechamber of the Council of Ten. While he waited, the page entered the chamber and found Tagliapietro. The Secretary appeared in his long dark robe and ushered Lazaro into the room, seating him by a desk to the side. There were others about the room, scribes, witnesses, guards, the Grand Chancellor himself, and the rest of the members of the council, seated at the front of the room. The "Ten" was figurative, not literal. Lazaro noticed some of the young men who had arrested Solomon but Beccaria was nowhere to be seen. Lazaro was not surprised.

There was also a small dark area separated from the rest of the room by a wooden screen. Behind the screen Lazaro could make out a bearded old man wearing the yellow cap of the Jews. He presumed this must be Solomon's father, Mordechai. Tagliapietro had indicated that he was a man of some importance, and he must have been to be allowed to witness the trial.

As Lazaro sat waiting he saw, beside the old Jew, the face of an angel looking across the dusty space. All about him were representations of angels, beautiful angels with golden hair streaming about their faces. But this angel was different: her hair was the color of coal, her skin the finest alabaster, she was nineteen, twenty at most. As he watched her he felt that she was looking intently, longingly, into his eyes, searching for something. But then her eyes shifted as the unfortunate Solomon was brought forth. It was him she was interested in. Lazaro realized the obvious. A Venetian of such natural beauty would have spoiled it by bleaching her hair and painting her face. This was Solomon's sister.

Solomon was dressed in a clean robe and unshackled. Lazaro noticed that he favored one leg and that his right arm seemed to hang limply at his side. The sleeves of his robe were long enough to hide his hands but Lazaro knew they would show the marks of the interrogation. Solomon did not look up but took his seat silently to the left of the council.

Tagliapietro began his introduction of the matter, but Lazaro wasn't listening. He had switched his gaze to Solomon's father and sister. The old man was standing now, watching the proceedings and the young girl was supporting him. There was a great deal of pain in his face, the pain, Lazaro imagined, of a father who either did not believe his own flesh and blood would have done what was being read out, or of a father who feared that it was true.

Tagliapietro had finished the reading of the accusation and of the statements given by each of the witnesses. As he read them out, each witness was required to stand so that Solomon could see his accusers. Lazaro was the first called, and as he stood, he looked into

Solomon's eyes. There was little life there, just a distant hope that he would not take his family down with him. Solomon was already dead for all practical purposes, and there was nothing in the statement which was untrue. The statement did not accuse Solomon but simply was a transcription of what Lazaro had described seeing. Of course, the statement did not include the fact that Lazaro had intended to kill Zorzi himself.

More evidence followed, evidence which was circumstantial. At the end of the statements the Grand Chancellor bent forward and asked Solomon if there was anything in those statements which he wished to dispute. Solomon remained motionless. Tagliapietro then read out the statement which, he explained to the council, Solomon had dictated in the morning. The statement was an admission by Solomon that he had conspired with one Eli of Genoa, to kill Zorzi for payment which this Eli had arranged. Solomon stated that he had no knowledge of the person who had provided the funding. They had conspired at the home of the Christian whore known carnally by Solomon, and she had discovered their conspiracy and demanded payment for her silence. Instead, Solomon had cut her throat and then they had lain in wait for Zorzi. The rest of the statement dovetailed with the other statements read out by the Secretary and concluded with Solomon asking the council for pity. The Chancellor then asked Solomon if there was anything he wished to add. Solomon shook his head and a great sigh came up from behind the screen. Lazaro turned and saw Solomon's father tearing his hair and his sister holding the old man and trying to pull him away from the screen. A door opened behind them and two guards appeared and escorted them out. Little else happened.

The Chancellor asked the rest of the council if they had any questions and when they indicated that they did not, the Chancellor informed Solomon that they would retire and deliberate as to the penalty. Solomon was taken away, and the council retired.

Lazaro was surprised at how quickly it was finished. He had assumed that there would be a clear confession. There almost always was. But as he sat in the court listening and watching, he realized that his earlier suspicions had been borne out. Angelo had been right to refer to it as a performance. It had been successful in that it had publicly resolved the matter of Zorzi's death. But it didn't work for Lazaro. It wasn't clear to him exactly why, but he was certain that Solomon had not killed Zorzi. However, it was too late to do anything for Solomon. The confession had been given in open court and he was not about to set himself up as Solomon's savior. He wished the lad no harm but the matter was ended. All that was left was a sentence, and there was really no need to wait for an announcement. That, too, was part of the performance. It would be death, on account of Zorzi rather than the woman.

After the officials had left the room, Lazaro walked out through the cool hallways and onto the steps outside the palace where he stretched and stood looking out over the Piazza. It was pleasing after the chilled interior of the courtroom and the Piazza was alive with trade and festivities.

As he headed down into the market he was accosted by an old bearded man in a long coat. It took him a moment to recognize him as Solomon's father.

"Why have you done this to my son," he said as he pushed Lazaro and almost knocked him down the steps. Before Lazaro could answer or defend himself, Mordechai raised a cane and was about to strike him. People were gathering. Suddenly, the girl with the dark hair came forward and pulled the old man away.

"You must not listen to what my father is saying. That was my brother on trial. Solomon is no murderer." And with that she led the old man away into the crowd.

Lazaro was surprised by the attack. The old man should have known better. It was a serious offense for a Jew to attack a Christian, especially dangerous if the Christian had a sword. To disperse the crowd which had gathered, Lazaro straightened his clothes with studied nonchalance and smiled, pointing to his head as if to say that the old man was crazy. With some laughter and rude comments but nothing more, the crowd dispersed.

His mind still reeling from the foolish passion of Solomon's father, Lazaro noticed the time. It had been his intention to discuss with the innkeeper the possibility of having Vom Scheidt share his room with him. Vom Scheidt's plea to be saved from the horrors of cheese-inspired nightmares had been part of the motivation, but Lazaro had also thought he might spend some time in Murano with Angelo. It seemed to fit. He had hoped to catch the innkeeper and his wife alone without Renata, but unfortunately, by the time he was able to find Vom Scheidt and make his way to the Dancing Mouse, she was in the inn waiting on the customers. Her eyes lit up when he entered, but she turned a bright shade of red and he saw anger descend over her face when she saw that he was with the Count. Lazaro walked over to the innkeeper and asked to speak with him about his room. The innkeeper waved to his wife to join them and signaled for Renata to continue with her work, but the girl made a pointed effort to remain near enough to the table to hear all that was taking place.

Lazaro explained that he would have to spend a great deal of time in Murano at his work and that his friend the Count was looking for a better establishment to stay in during the rest of his visit to Venice. It made sense for the Count to take his place for the next while and, when necessary, they could share the room, though he agreed, without waiting for the innkeeper's wife to ask, that he would pay extra when they were both there. He assured the innkeeper that they needn't worry about the money, and as a sign of good faith he passed some coins across the table. They were so pleased that they called to their daughter to bring some wine. It was the wrong thing to do.

Renata had been hovering nearby, listening to every second word, and had missed enough to be sure that she was somehow being mocked, not by her parents, but by the two swaggering louts who had each managed to have their way with her. She forgot completely the interest she had shown in each of them separately and thought now only of conspiracies and barbarian debauchery and that her parents had somehow sold her. With a shout she flung a pitcher at the table and it broke, spraying the sour house wine over everyone. Her father cowered as was his practice and her mother was caught between the façade which she wished to present to the Count who would be staying with them and the harsh reality of her temper. In the end her temper won out and she and her daughter treated the entire inn to an entertaining shouting match, not to be rivaled anywhere in Venice. Lazaro knew that it would eventually settle itself, so he signaled to Vom Scheidt to go ahead to the room and arrange things and he would go out into the city for some fresh air.

The dream of finding some fresh air would not be realized in Venice that night. A warm wind had been blowing in through the day and the air had become warm and filled with the smells of the canals. At the best of times these sewers would be flushed by the tides and were bearable. At times like this even the rats gave up the ghost and floated dead amid the garbage and human waste.

Lazaro walked along the quietest streets he could find and eventually realized that he was standing at the entrance to the ghetto. His encounter with Solomon's father and sister repeated itself again and again in his mind. He remembered now that Solomon had once spoken of his father and sister and her name came to him: Margoleit. Lazaro had been asking Solomon questions about the Old Testament during one of his visits to Bomberg's. The printer had let Lazaro sit in the back to read the books which he could not afford to buy. He had been reading something recently translated by Fra Felice, a mystical Hebrew text, and he had been taken with the statements made. It had been a discussion of four types of light, a glowing light, a shining light, and a purple light, all which could be seen, and a light which could not be seen, which did not shine but which drew in all other light. And of Moses attaining a mirror that shines. He had asked Solomon about it but Solomon had just laughed and said he didn't understand it at all, that matters like that were only understood by his father and his sister.

Thoughts of Solomon were unpleasant and made Lazaro aware that he needed to be with people and to have wine. Glad that the Carnevale of Venice was not restricted to one night, he was back in more boisterous streets in a moment. For a little money he had all the wine he needed, and a skull mask which covered the upper portion of his face. He walked, enjoying the anonymity afforded by the crowd and the season, but wherever he walked, Solomon and his family walked with him. The wine would not wash them from his mind. What he had known of Solomon, the statements made at the trial, Solomon's face, the body of the other dead Jew, of Zorzi — all of it traveled along with him as he walked.

Lazaro knew that he wouldn't be able to outdistance the cacophony of thoughts — to free himself from them he would have to order them. He knew Solomon was innocent, but he needed to understand why he knew. He recalled the approach of the two assassins. In recalling the experience, he found that things became clear. The approach of the two had been very professional. They must have been following but he had not seen them. Perhaps they were not following. Perhaps they knew where he would be. Béres had had good information. It was not impossible that someone else also had the same information, or better.

Were Zorzi's assassins Jews? He tried to recall something about the man he had killed, but there was no image of him. He had been a dark blur of energy with a white mask. That Jew, Eli was his name, dead and naked on the slab in the prison cell could have been the man he killed. Lazaro recalled the fighting, the blade sliding into his opponent. The wounds were correct, the body size was correct. But he could just as easily have been an unfortunate Jew killed to make everything appear correct for a story meant to hide the truth.

But why was he so certain that Solomon had not been involved? The boy had some knowledge of the sword; all Jews in Christendom needed that. Zorzi was a good swordsman, but in a street fight luck sometimes provided a decisive advantage. Solomon had not appeared to be the sort of man to be involved in such things. In all the time Lazaro had seen him, Solomon had never given any indication of violence, or of passion for that matter. He had a Christian lover — that was known at the shop. But would he have killed her? She had uncovered the plot and was not going to keep silent, Tagliapietro had said.

There was something else about Zorzi's attacker which now leapt into Lazaro's mind. As he had been chasing him he had noticed a glint from the man's ankle — the glint of jewels sewn into a badge on the man's hose. Solomon's hose was plain black.

Lazaro thought of the badge on the hose as he wandered through the *calli* drinking, oblivious to what was going on about him. The young men and women of Venice belonged to clubs which were referred to as *della calze* after the badges which they wore sewn in their hose or, in the case of the women, sewn on their frocks. When he had first come to Venice, Lazaro had noticed them, but after a time he had grown as used to them as he had to the other things which had first appeared strange in Venice.

But Solomon's hose was plain black . . . the thought kept coming back into his mind. He recalled again and again the image of the assassin fleeing and always it was the same — the unmistakable flash of jewels sewn into his hose at the ankle. He could not remember what design it was but the sparkle was there. He wondered how long it would have taken Solomon to change his hose. It was one thing to throw off a cape and a mask, another to strip in the street while dogs barked — and when one was a Jew out after curfew . . . Tagliapietro had said that a dog was barking. And that a mask and cape had been found. Nothing more. Lazaro went back in his memory to the swordplay between Zorzi and his attacker. He had seen only glimpses of it; he was busy himself. Then he saw what had registered in his mind but what he had not recalled before. The swordplay was very good. Zorzi was good and would likely have had the better of his opponent, except for one thing. Lazaro had encountered it before and, in the heat of battle it could be decisive. Zorzi's opponent was left-handed. Solomon was not. That was the fact which had settled it for him.

Lazaro tipped the flask up, but it was empty. He realized that it was the third flask he had purchased as he had wandered through the streets. The thoughts in his mind had become an uncomfortable drone which even now threatened to leave him with a massive headache in the morning. Perhaps, he thought, I should have mixed some water with my wine. Reaching an abutment he stopped and looked down at the brackish water. A garbage barge appeared up the canal at nearly right angles to another canal. First the lantern appeared, dangling on a long pole, suspended over the water and casting strange tall shadows on the buildings. Then the barge moved slowly past, the two men on it using large nets to scoop from the surface of the water the more obvious refuse, the weeds, the stray cats, the bits of life which the people of this enlightened city had consigned to the sea. As they scooped they would fling the nets over their shoulders, emptying their catch into the barge where it would plop down on the black pile, glistening behind them.

Lazaro decided that he would meet them at the bridge in the next *calle* which passed over the canal they were in and toss the bottle into the back. They would go through their garbage and those items of value they would retrieve to be used again. As he walked he heard footsteps somewhere behind him. It was not his shadows from the Secretariat. In his wanderings this evening he had satisfied himself by patient observation that he was no longer being followed by them. But the footsteps were not random; when he paused to listen they stopped. When he started to walk again they shadowed his footfalls, as if trying to resemble echoes and thus avoid detection. He realized that there was not much light in the *calle*. He had not noticed it before. There were no torches, but the light of the moon had been enough to satisfy his need for illumination. Now that there was someone else, someone following him, he desired a little more light, but there was none. He pulled his mask down, freeing his peripheral vision. He had found that it was often only by not looking at something in the dark that he could see it. There was a scrape behind him in the *calle*. Without looking directly at the source of the sound he paused and let his eyes drift. There was a man there, dark against the wall. And he had a drawn sword. That was what had scraped against the stone wall.

A drawn sword, a dark *calle*, and I'm drunk, Lazaro thought. He had to control an urge to draw his sword and race down the *calle* to face his pursuer, if he was, in fact, being pursued. Instead, he leaned against the wall, his white mask dangling about his neck.

"Tell me, young sir, whom do you seek?" he yelled out. He waited but there was no answer. "Come, come," he said, turning and standing with his hands on his hips, "I am here for you, if you have not made a mistake." Again there was no answer. He looked away but could not tell from the corner of his eye if the man was still there. A cloud had passed in front of the moon and there was almost no light in the *calle*. He felt something move on the back of his neck, as if his hair was rising like the hackles of a wolf.

A fist crashed into his skull and he fell to the ground. He was aware that he was being dragged toward the bridge over the canal and then down under it. He felt water on the back of his head and then the water closed over his face. He tried not to struggle. Whoever it was wanted to drown him. His arms, limp beside him, suddenly steeled and swept up, crashing into the other man's head. He felt the grip relax and pulled himself out of the canal. The other man sat dazed beside him. Lazaro shook his head in an attempt to clear the water from his ears and then saw the man going for his sword. He kicked at him and caught him in the groin. The man doubled over and vomited on the paving stones between them. Lazaro cracked him on the side of his head with the back of his hand and watched as he rolled over on his side. Lazaro stumbled for a moment and wondered where his empty bottle was.

The man on the ground in front of him groaned and he turned to him. He took the man's weapons, tossing the sword into the canal but pushing the stiletto into his belt. Lazaro was interested in this street tough. He was not the normal vagabond lurking in these back *calli*. If he had been, he would have run Lazaro through and taken his purse. But he had tried to drown him. To Lazaro that suggested orders from someone, and Lazaro was interested in knowing who. The man tried to sit up but Lazaro slammed his fist into the side of his head and he passed out again.

It was then that Lazaro noticed the hose. On the man's ankle was the mark of his club. Lazaro took his stiletto and cut out both insignia. It was a jeweled pattern of a sword passing through a flaming heart. He had seen this pattern only a little while ago but he wasn't sure where. Since his recollection of the sparkle on Zorzi's assassin's ankle he had watched men's legs during his wanderings and had seen many different patterns — but this one, he wasn't sure. He stuffed the bits of cloth into his shirt. He next moved to his face, removing the white mask which hid the man's features. It was a youth of twenty at most, with blond hair and a scar across the left side of his otherwise unblemished face. His hands: the man wore a thick gold ring with a griffin on it. Lazaro turned his hands over. No heavy calluses, no signs of archery practice, but there was evidence that he played a stringed instrument. A rich man's son who fancied himself a troubadour perhaps.

He opened the man's eyes — brown — but there was no sign of consciousness. Lazaro decided that he would take the man to a more private location, revive him, and ask a few questions. He wanted to know who had ordered this. If it was the Secretariat it would be best for him to leave the city at once. But if it was not it might provide him with some information which could clear up the question of Zorzi's death and which might be of great value to the Secretariat, and to Marzia. In a way it might also ease his conscience. The glassmakers often said that conscience was like a shard of glass in your heart and when you did something wrong it moved and caused you pain. But if you did something wrong often enough the rough edges would be worn smooth and it would turn without causing pain. As Lazaro was lifting the thug onto his back he thought of that, for it had seemed to him that his shard of glass had been worn smooth long ago, and yet he was having strange feelings about this entire affair.

Rounding the corner of the *calle* carrying the man's body over his shoulders, he ran into two *bravi* of the Signori di Notte. They had been leaning against the wall of a building apparently watching the shadow of a woman undressing in a window on the second floor of the house opposite them. Luckily Lazaro had been hurrying, and the feet of his captive caught the first man square in the face, pushing him back against the stone wall and knocking him out. The second man leapt back and drew his sword but was obviously caught off guard. Lazaro was about to claim that he was carrying a drunken friend home when the guard started advancing on him menacingly. Not wishing any difficulty with the authorities, Lazaro tossed his bundle on the man, knocking him over. His sword flew from his hands and he scrambled to get away from Lazaro who had now drawn his sword. Instead of standing his ground, the man ran off down the *calle* and disappeared around another corner. Lazaro picked up his package again and started off but had turned only one corner when he heard footsteps running behind him. He knew it would be the *bravi* he had just left. Lazaro raced down another *calle* which led to a *rio* but realized before he was halfway there that he could not carry his package any longer. As he mounted the bridge he saw the garbage scow which he had noticed earlier passing underneath. He heaved his load over the side and the man crashed into the pile of refuse the bargemen had scooped in the evening's work. These two men immediately set up a great hue and cry. Lazaro ducked down another passageway just as the pursuing *bravi* came to the bridge. In the time that it took them to investigate the complaints of the bargemen, Lazaro was gone.

Lazaro did not return to the inn that night. Instead he wandered over to the shop of his friend Malatesta and asked if he could sleep on the roof. Malatesta was accustomed to Lazaro's anti-social habits and allowed the young glassmaker to do so, even gave him a blanket. But Lazaro did not sleep. He sat by the wall, wrapped in his blanket, watching the Piazzetta. At sunrise, as the Marangona pealed the *mezza terza*, they brought Solomon out and chained him to the column topped by the Lion of St. Mark. Beccaria stood there watching and, from a distance, Lazaro thought he could make out a curious smile beneath the white mask — the smile of someone who enjoyed his work. A functionary mumbled something which he read from a sheet of paper and a dark man stepped up behind Solomon and strangled him. Solomon began to shout something, but it sounded more like a statement than a prayer. And it was cut short by the garrotte.

They left his body hanging limp on the column for a quarter of an hour according to the Orologio, then, after Beccaria nudged it with the toe of his boot to check for any sign of life, it was cut down and loaded into a small barge. In the gathering dawn the barge was poled away toward the Lido, where the Jews were buried. As he watched the barge fade away into the sparkle of the rising sun on the water's surface, Lazaro looked again at the badges he had removed from his assailant. He knew now where else he had seen this pattern recently. It was the same pattern as that which appeared on the hose worn by Marzia's fiancé — Rodrigo Contarini.

X

Lazaro returned to the Dancing Mouse expecting to find Vom Scheidt taking advantage of his new lodgings. Instead, as he rounded the corner to the inn, he saw Vom Scheidt leaning in a doorway, with what appeared to be the intention of secretly keeping watch. Down the street Lazaro was able to see the furred shape of Béres sleeping in another doorway. Lazaro nudged Vom Scheidt's leg with his toe, and Vom Scheidt, recognizing him, gave a long low whistle to waken Béres. He hurriedly struggled to his feet, took Lazaro by the arm, and led him to Béres's doorway, where the Hungarian was busy stretching the sleep from his back. "Fugger's back, and he's asked to see you."

Lazaro wasn't surprised and fell in with Béres and Vom Scheidt heading for the Fondaco dei Tedeschi. When they crossed the Rialto bridge and entered the Fondaco, Béres and Vom Scheidt hung back and Lazaro proceeded alone to Fugger's suite. The guard at the door knocked twice, then, hearing a growl from inside, opened the door and let Lazaro enter. Inside, in the dim light, Lazaro could make out Fugger, sitting in his bed, swathed in bedclothes, going through a sheaf of papers.

"Lazaro, come in," Fugger said with a smile, then tilted his head to address his guard. "Shut the door and don't disturb us."

The door shut and the room returned to darkness save for the candle which burned on the table beside the bed. Fugger motioned for Lazaro to sit beside him on the bed. His eyes growing accustomed to the light, Lazaro climbed across the soft mattress and propped himself up with a pillow beside Fugger.

Fugger tossed his papers onto the table and turned to Lazaro. "There was a time when you would have found me warmed by a girl rather than a sheaf of favorable accounts, but I can only be what I am." He paused and listened to see that the hallway was quiet, then spoke in a lower voice. "Is what I hear about the Jews true?"

Lazaro shrugged his shoulders. "I don't know what you've heard."

Fugger said nothing and indicated for Lazaro to continue.

"Zorzi was attacked by two men before I could get to him. I killed one of them but the other got away."

"So it was the Jews," Fugger said, questioning.

"I don't know. The Secretariat appears to be convinced of that, but I think someone switched the bodies and framed the Jews."

"So it wasn't the Jews."

"I don't know."

Fugger was quiet for a moment, and stared into the darkest corner of the room. "You killed one of the assassins. Why?"

Lazaro responded with appropriate nonchalance. "I wanted to know who was moving in on my contract."

Fugger didn't look at him but Lazaro could see a hint of a grin on the banker's face. "And if they'd been my men?"

"You wouldn't have hired anyone else to do my job. And if you had, I'd have been justified."

Fugger laughed, then broke into a coughing fit. As it subsided he wiped his mouth with a lace handkerchief, then drew it across his balding head. "By God, you please me. If only you had a head for figures." He patted the papers he had placed on the table, then repositioned himself. "Zorzi is dead. That is as it should be. I've decided that the fact that you and Béres didn't actually do it won't interfere with your payment, but I may have you do a bit more work. Zorzi's death was necessary in order to secure a larger good for my house. If someone else has seen fit to have him killed in order to secure a larger good for their house . . . well . . . our larger goods may be in opposition. And you know how I feel about competition."

Lazaro nodded. "The story of the Jews doesn't satisfy you either."

Fugger shook his head. "I've heard the story from the Secretariat's official point of view. There are convincing elements, but the whole fails to satisfy me." He reached over to a dark bowl on the table where he had placed his papers and pulled out an orange. With a slight movement he offered one to Lazaro, but Lazaro declined. As Fugger began peeling the fruit, the room filled with the released scent. "And so it remains to be known — who went to this trouble? And why? What do you know?"

Lazaro renewed his caution. "The one Jew, Solomon, he worked for Daniel Bomberg. He couldn't have done it."

Fugger looked up. "Couldn't or wouldn't?"

"Couldn't. The man who killed Zorzi was left-handed. Solomon wasn't."

"So you are convinced there must have been a substitution. Does that mean the Secretariat is involved?"

Lazaro paused. He had no interest at this point in divulging his newfound suspicions about Contarini, or his feelings about Marzia. And whether Contarini was involved or not, the issue of the Secretariat remained. "At the moment I have no way of knowing. And even if the Secretariat, or some members of the Secretariat, were involved, they could have been involved in the murder itself, or in the cover-up after the fact."

Fugger coughed again, violently, and dropped his orange in his bed sheets. He reached to the table beside him and grabbed a bowl of tea. "An infusion of guaiac, Holy Wood from the New World," he said, by way of explanation. After taking a sip he replaced it on the table. "I have a monopoly in it. It's a better cure for the French pox than mercury." He grinned. "That's not my complaint, but if it's good for that it should at least help my cough. Anyhow, I need to know more. I want you to find out who killed Zorzi and why." He leaned toward

Lazaro and spoke in a lower voice. "I also need to know anything there is to know about the involvement of the Secretariat."

"I've met with the Doge and the Grand Chancellor's Secretary," Lazaro said. Immediately, he realized that he had told Fugger something he had not suspected, though Fugger tried to hide his surprise, and unease.

"What happened?"

Lazaro stretched out his legs and crossed them. "They saw me as a benefactor of the Zorzi family, and so they rewarded me. We met out in the lagoon and talked for a while the day before yesterday. They asked about my background but I only told them what they already knew."

Fugger was not comfortable with this new information. Lazaro could see this clearly now. "Be more specific."

"They asked me about my student days, my travels. They knew already that I had worked in Schwaz. But they were more interested in war stories. We talked about some of the campaigns . . ."

"Brescia," Fugger asked, "Tartaglia, Tadini?"

Lazaro was surprised that Fugger was able to guess the contents of the conversation. As he said yes, he saw the negative reaction begin in Fugger's eyes and spread to his entire body like some quick-moving plague. Fugger threw back the bed covers, got up, and began to pace the floor in his nightshirt. Lazaro noticed that in his haste and anger he had squeezed the orange which he had dropped into the bed, and a stain had appeared on his backside. "What did they want to know about Tartaglia and Tadini?"

Lazaro shrugged again. "Nothing really. They came up in the conversation. Tartaglia teaches military science here. Tadini is in Crete as Engineer General."

"Nothing ever just comes up," Fugger said with a bit too much anger. He controlled himself noticeably. "What did you tell them?"

"There was nothing to tell. I know Tartaglia and Tadini from the second battle of Brescia. We served together. They knew that much and once they grew tired of the tales of that battle they moved on to other subjects."

Fugger paced now, silently, for a few moments, then paused finally and turned to Lazaro who watched him from the bed. "I must leave today for Augsburg. I have matters there which require my direct attention. But there are things which I must ask you to do here. And I must give you some discretion to act. That discretion requires that I give you further information, and you know that my gift carries with it a very strict responsibility." Fugger paused again and Lazaro realized that the banker had found himself in a quandary. "I need you to seek out more information on the Zorzi matter and to report it to me as soon as possible. I will leave it to you to judge whether to use my couriers or to come to me yourself. My representatives here will know my whereabouts. I must know who killed Zorzi and why."

Fugger climbed back into the bed and sat uncomfortably close to Lazaro, so close that Lazaro could smell the rot of his teeth.

"I'm sure you're aware of the speculation about whether Suleiman will attack Rhodes in the coming year. I know that he will. The Knights of Rhodes have vaults upon vaults of plunder in their citadel. A large portion of that treasury is pledged to the Emperor Charles. A large portion is also pledged directly to me. However, I am more concerned about the portion pledged to Charles, for he has in turn pledged it to me as collateral for funds he has already received from me. Like his father Maximilian, Charles finds my finances useful — and given the military campaigns he is planning, essential.

"Suleiman was turned back in Hungary last year, but he dreams of triumph in Vienna. Before he returns he must replenish his treasury, and so he will attack Rhodes. If he succeeds and seizes the treasury, I will lose, and Charles will lose as well. But if the Knights move their valuables out, though I will not have lost from the Knights, Charles will receive from them sufficient resources to honor his pledges to me. Of course, I want to retrieve from the Knights that which is mine, but I want Charles to lose what is his." Fugger wiped his head again.

Lazaro could see in the dim light that his eyes had narrowed to slits. It was as if he was repeating a rosary. It was clear that in Fugger's mind, Lazaro was only barely present.

"You can see that the matter is a complicated issue of timing. But I'm not clear on Venice's position. De L'Isle Adam, the new Grand Master of the Knights, has asked for Tadini to help prepare for the attack. The Signoria appears to be of two minds, though I believe they are committed to instructing the Governor of Crete to refuse the request. Zorzi was adamantly opposed to this position, arguing that Venice should move to assist Rhodes and to strike at the Turk before he becomes too brave and threatens all of us. He was probably right, but I couldn't afford the possibility that he would convince the Signoria to give Tadini to the Knights. If Tadini were there now, there would be a very good chance he would have the ability to prepare the place to withstand a siege. And he would, as well, inspire confidence. I am willing to arrange for the confidence to be inspired, but not yet. In the end Rhodes must fall. You see now why I must know more."

Lazaro nodded. He knew there was more, much more, which Fugger was not telling him, but he was surprised and concerned that the German had taken him this far into confidence.

Fugger slipped out of the bed and onto the floor, then turned and leaned over to Lazaro. "And don't rule out the Jews yet. It may still be that they have a left hand in this, and have set up one of their own to be sacrificed. There are Jews who've been trying to rescue their comrades in captivity in Rhodes ever since the expulsion. Some of them are thinking this travail is a warning of their messiah. Others might be interested in taking a more active role. Suleiman is known to be very tolerant of Jews within his Realm of Peace. Given the troubles in Spain, I'm sure they would like to see the Moslems back there as well. They are more clever than you give them credit for."

Fugger turned and walked to the shuttered window, opening it to let in the light of day. "I will give you money for expenses but let us be clear about one thing: I trust you enough to let you refuse this request. But if you accept, I can't allow you to fail me." Fugger grinned broadly and exposed his brown teeth.

Lazaro nodded his agreement. He climbed out of the bed, and as he walked over to the window to shake hands with Fugger and close the deal, he couldn't help but notice that Fugger had managed somehow to squeeze the orange again and stain his clothes a second time.

When he shook Fugger's hand it was as if a current passed from Fugger to him. He could not decipher it at the time, but later he would think of it as if the contents of a book, normally imbibed slowly and sometimes painfully through the eyes, somehow had been poured directly into his mind.

"You've made a good choice, Lazaro, now sit."

He pushed Lazaro toward a chair and pulled another close to it. They sat face to face and close enough that Lazaro could again smell Fugger's teeth.

"I will have what is mine from Rhodes, and Charles will not — that is good financial planning. In the end he will be too indebted to me, and" — Fugger's tone changed to mock-humility — "it may be that he will be persuaded to cede to me the mercury mines of Almaden. You see, I could not have allowed Zorzi to give Tadini to the Knights and I cannot now allow the Jews to keep Tadini from them. He must come to the Knights by way of *my* beneficence, so that they will feel obligated to assist me. Though in the end he will probably come to them too late. And so you see, you have become so very valuable to me, because I believe you would be successful in negotiating with Tadini on my behalf." Fugger's eyes closed to a pig's slits and he turned away. "You will discover the intrigue of Zorzi, and the Secretariat, and the ghetto." He turned his slit eyes to Lazaro. "And it needn't be so unpleasant."

What Lazaro saw in Fugger's eyes was not attractive, but it was lucrative. He nodded in agreement.

XI

The early-morning meeting coupled with the late-night exploits had left Lazaro in a confused state. He wanted desperately to get some sleep, but he had a full day ahead of him. Tagliapietro had suggested that Lazaro attend Zorzi's funeral, and after his conversation with Fugger, it was necessary. Even without Tagliapietro's request, and now Fugger's orders, he would have wanted to attend, to see Marzia again. He had hoped, however, that he would have had time to go to Murano and explain the situation to Angelo, but he realized now there was no time for that.

Back outside the Fondaco, Lazaro saw that Vom Scheidt and Béres had disappeared. It wouldn't be possible to send either of them to Angelo with a message. He would have to speak with Angelo after, but Angelo would understand — this was Martedi Grasso.

At the appointed time he found himself at the Basilica of San Marco and paused in the Piazza to look up at its arches and mosaics.

This focal point of the Venetian state had been built with the plunder of the world, plundered from plunderers, and carrying with it a pedigree which pre-dated Venice. The old men said that even the marble on its outside walls, which had been plundered from Alexandria, had come originally from the marble facing of the pyramids of Egypt. The blending of a variety of architectural styles in the Basilica suited Venice, reflecting the changing moods and persuasions of those who were the power behind Venice. Lazaro found it to be, rather than a religious building, a political one.

People were milling about, but the funeral procession had not yet arrived at the Basilica. In some force of habit from long ago he checked his clothes and brushed some dust from his shoulder. He had changed hurriedly in his rooms, fearing that Renata would appear, and had donned the simple black which seemed appropriate for the occasion. He entered and didn't bother with any formalities, preferring to move quickly into the shadows along the wall. As he stood at the back of the church, he understood why he would never be taken for a Venetian. The Venetians arrived in finery disguised as black, and he had never seen so much golden hair. He felt vaguely out of place with his dark hair and simple clothing.

Abruptly, the Zorzi family entered, and he watched as they took their places, particularly mindful of the entrance of Marzia and her mother. The mother seemed out of touch with everything going on, as she had been at the Doge's Palace. Marzia was, as he had expected her to be, beautiful. She noticed Lazaro as they passed and he felt again that warm bond between them. Marzia was accompanied by Rodrigo, who seemed to have taken quickly to being head of the family and, busy in his role, did not notice the contact between Lazaro and Marzia. Lazaro noticed again the flaming sword and heart emblazoned on Rodrigo's hose.

The mass would be extravagant, and most of the nobility of Venice had gathered. Their names were not known to Lazaro, but he recognized many of their faces from the *broglio*. Of course the Doge, the Grand Chancellor, and Tagliapietro were there but he did not see Beccaria. He supposed it would not be seemly for a man employed to assassinate to come to the funeral of one killed by an assassin, but Lazaro also supposed most of the men here were murderers of one sort or another. How else to become giants of commerce? It was quite possible, even probable, that one of the great men here had arranged for the death of the man whose funeral they were now attending. But he knew he would find no clues here as to the murderer's identity. Church had a way of allowing truth to be hidden.

Once the mass was fully under way he slipped outside, having no stomach for the hollow rituals being performed. Zorzi's body was to be taken to the family crypt on the island of San Michele and it made good sense to follow the body to its final resting place, to see who else followed. However, as he stood in the crowded Piazza, listening to the cooing of pigeons, he was struck with a desire to go immediately to San Michele. It would be peaceful and there might be the possibility of rest, even sleep. Ignoring all else he went directly to a *rio* and signaled for a gondola. After giving directions to the gondolier, luckily not the garrulous one, he slumped back under the shade of the *felze* and, as they headed out into the Laguna Morte, drifted off to sleep. The rocking of the gondola and the soft sounds of the water coupled with his fatigue made it easy for him to sleep, and that sleep was dreamless.

Wakened by the gondolier's tapping, he felt greatly refreshed, though still a bit sleepy. Stumbling onto the *traghetto* and wandering into the island cemetery, he stood for a moment appreciating its quiet. Here and there men and women dressed in black wandered through the markers or stood or knelt by the crypt of a loved one, praying, crying softly or just looking. He passed the crypt which had been prepared for Zorzi and paused to listen to the two laborers who sat on a cart drinking wine and chattering. Though he attended within earshot for a quarter of an hour, they had no information of use to him, speaking instead of the quality of various nuns' breasts and facial hair. Bored, he wandered about this city of dead, reading some of the inscriptions.

Passing a particularly ornate obelisk he saw something which made him step back into hiding and peer out again carefully. A few rows over stood Beccaria, his hands clasped in front of him and his head bowed, in front of a small tomb, graced with fresh flowers. As he watched, Beccaria touched the tomb and then walked away, heading for a nearby *traghetto* where a gondola waited. When he was out of sight, Lazaro walked over to the marker and read the inscription. Beccaria's father. He hadn't thought of Beccaria as having a father. At least not a human father.

He looked around at the neighboring stones to see if perhaps there was a mother buried here, but he could find none. Glancing over at the wharf he saw that Beccaria had entered his gondola and was on his way back to Venice. Past the wharf, in the channel between San Michele and Venice, Lazaro could see the beginnings of the flotilla which would bring Zorzi to his final rest enter the Laguna Morte. It was time to wander back to watch the committal.

The city was no quieter as Lazaro returned to his room, nor was he wiser from watching Zorzi laid to rest. Tears were everywhere and a thousand suspicions, but nothing which pointed him in the right direction. He planned to call on Ca'Zorzi as he had been invited to do, to pay his respects, and see what more he might learn there.

But before that he had a few people to see, and he made his way to the Dancing Mouse in the hopes that Vom Scheidt might be there to help him. However, the German was nowhere to be seen. Instead there was a note written in a familiar hand. Fugger had taken Béres and Vom Scheidt back with him, it said in Fugger's code, and would await news from Lazaro. There was nothing more.

The door opened and Lazaro crumpled the note and stuffed it into his pocket. It was Renata, smiling. He got up and made ready to leave.

"So have you decided to stay here after all?" Renata asked, swinging her skirts slightly.

"I doubt I'll be here that often. I may be staying on Murano. But my friend has had to leave the city, and I have paid for the room until the end of the month."

"Bought and paid for so you might as well, is that what you think of me then?"

Lazaro could feel a storm gathering, so he started for the door.

"Where are you running off to now?" she said, in a pout that was not at all becoming or believable.

"I have to pay my respects at Ca'Zorzi."

"More likely to see the daughter. I know you always watch her," she said pointing to the window.

Lazaro opened the door, but she took hold of his wrist and stopped him. "I can give you more than she ever would or could."

He was moved by Renata's display, knowing that somewhere deep down she did mean it, after a fashion, but he just wasn't interested. He didn't want to insult her, and he struggled for the right words.

She pushed him back a step. "And don't stand there silent. I know what you're thinking. I'm not good enough for you. Maybe your barbarian friend told you something. Well, it doesn't matter. You can't just use me and walk away."

He tried again to find something to say, but in the end he just walked past her and went down the stairs. She yelled something about not hiding out in Murano either, but he couldn't make out all of what she said and he had no interest in asking her to repeat it.

His first stop was Bomberg's printing house. Lazaro needed to know more and he knew that Bomberg could be trusted and might have answers to the questions forming in his mind. He found him working in the shop, cleaning and inspecting his type. Lazaro signaled that he wanted to talk to him in private, and they headed for the small room in the back of his shop where he kept his account books. On the way Bomberg picked up a sheaf of paper.

"Of course Solomon didn't do it. He couldn't have," Bomberg said harshly as he pushed the paper into place in his storeroom, then carried on into the office. He pulled the door shut and leaned against a high table. "But there's no telling the Signori di Notte that. They sent men to question me but that's all I could tell them, and they didn't want to hear it. He worked his day here. He left. That's all that I had to say. They knew about Ottavia. They knew he had gone there that night. I knew it too, but I didn't say. I know he couldn't have killed her or Zorzi."

"Where did Ottavia live?" Lazaro asked.

"Two houses past where Federico lives, you know, my delivery boy. At a place with blue shutters."

Lazaro nodded. It was close to where Zorzi had been killed. "Did you know this other boy, the one they said was from Genoa?"

"That I can't say. I don't know Solomon's friends. There are always people coming and going from the ghetto. Maybe he did have a friend. What does it prove?"

Lazaro could see that Bomberg was angry and asked if he was angry at him.

"No. I don't blame you. You just said what you saw, and I can believe you. You had to do that." Bomberg paused. "But they executed the wrong man. And now they've taken away my readers. Fra Felice is furious and he will make representations to the Signoria. In the end I'll have to pay a few more ducats and then they'll give me my readers back. The ghetto is in the same boat. Their council pleaded for a pardon and offered a lot of money, but they couldn't get Solomon out. But the Signoria will threaten to pull their business licenses, and so in the end they'll have to pay the money, for nothing. And even that may not save them." Bomberg slammed the flat of his hand against a pile of paper. "I wish I could do business somewhere else, but . . ."

Lazaro knew how the sentence would finish. Venice was the best place to do business. That was why he put up with it. "After the trial I saw Solomon's father and his sister — I can't remember her name."

"Margoleit."

"Yes, Margoleit," Lazaro repeated. "How are they?"

"The father is out of his mind. Margoleit found him raving in the street this morning after they heard the news of the execution. They've drugged him for now, but it will be hard on him, on her too."

"Do you think I could see them?" Lazaro asked.

Bomberg shook his head and sighed. "Oh, I wouldn't suggest that, my friend, now or ever. Naturally they would display a certain animus toward anyone involved in the matter and you, unfortunately, are involved."

"Still, I'd like to try."

Bomberg shrugged, pulled a pile of woodcuts across the table, and began leafing through them. He paused at a woodcut made by Barbari. It was a beautiful view of Venice from the perspective of a bird and was very popular in the trade. Bomberg shook his head and continued until he found a print which showed the ghetto. He tapped the print with his finger. "This is the building they live in, on the third floor, I think, but take my advice and wait for a while. They aren't ready, even for kindness."

Watching Bomberg leaf through the prints, Lazaro had noticed one that he wanted a closer look at, and, as Bomberg finished, he pulled it out.

Bomberg glanced at it for a second. "Oh that. It's Rhodes. I guess you can see that. You're from that part of the world, aren't you?"

Lazaro nodded.

"Have it, if you like. Solomon was interested in Rhodes too. He used to complain about the conditions of the Jews there — at least he talked about it with the other readers." Bomberg rubbed his ink-stained hands together and looked at them. "I dream of clean hands." Without saying anything further, he stood and headed back into the work room.

Lazaro folded the print of Rhodes and stuffed it inside his shirt, but the parchment seemed oddly cold next to his heart.

He had no trouble finding the house near Federico's with the blue shutters. Ottavia had lived on the second floor. It was here that Solomon had spent a great deal of his free time, often staying past curfew and either staying over in Ottavia's rooms or sneaking back through the streets and finding a way past the guards around the ghetto. This and more Lazaro learned from Ottavia's friend and landlady, Francesca, as they sat in her rooms on the first floor of the house. Francesca had long red hair, the deep red of tiles, and she painted her face in heroic tones. She lived alone, widowed by the wars, and made a generous living investing in shares of the trading galleys. Even though the wars had taken her husband, they had been generous to her investments. Though she had no financial need, she rented out the upper floor of her house, to secure uncomplicated companionship. And for this reason she had become good friends with Ottavia.

"Ottavia was not a loose woman," Francesca assured him. "Her mother was dead, of the plague I think, and there might have been a young sister who died also, I'm not sure. Her father was killed in the wars and her brother, Constantino, became head of the family." Lazaro could see from Francesca's expression that she didn't take kindly to the brother. "He went on the galleys and did well at trade. But he was like all the rest: loud, possessive, too rough with the girl. He wanted her in a convent, but she refused. The Fathers suggested my house and so Constantino placed her with me. He even offered me money to look after her." There was a knock at the door to the *riva* and Francesca excused herself and went to it. The wood seller had arrived and passed a bundle of wood to her. She gave him some coins and shut the door, put the bundle of wood down beside it, and came back to the table, wiping her hands on her apron.

"You were saying that her brother left her here." Lazaro said to bring her back to her story.

"Yes. Yes, Constantino. When he was in town he was always bringing around potential suitors for her to meet. They were all friends, club members."

"What club was that?" Lazaro asked, knowing what the answer would be.

"I don't remember the name but their badge was a flaming heart with a sword through it. He didn't have to beat her. She just didn't like any of them, and she was strong enough herself to refuse. And then she met Solomon."

"I suppose her brother was not in favor of that match?" Lazaro added.

"Who would be? I told her myself that it would never work, but she loved him. He was a nice boy. You knew him?"

Lazaro nodded.

"She finally told him about a week ago, her brother. She shouldn't have. That night he beat her quite a bit and forbade her to see Solomon again."

Francesca was silent for a moment.

"What happened the night she died?" Lazaro asked.

"I don't know. I was out. Carnevale." Francesca wiped a single tear from her cheek. "I know they had planned to run away, Solomon and Ottavia. After her brother beat her she borrowed some old clothes of my husband's. She didn't tell me why, but I knew. Maybe she changed her mind. Maybe that was what she and Solomon fought about."

Lazaro could see from the woman's eyes that there was something else, but that she did not want to say it or even think it. "Is there anything left in her room?"

"No. Her brother came and took it all away. There is nothing left."

Tears were welling now in her eyes. He had gotten all the information from her that he could, and so he thanked her for her time and left.

Bomberg's advice was good, but Lazaro knew Fugger wanted fast answers and so he made for the ghetto next. At the gates he paused, watching the gondola which patrolled the canal around the ghetto turn from the Rio del Battello and enter the Rio di Ghetto Nuovo. It passed under the bridge and he and the guards watched it go by. The guards at the gates ignored him as he crossed the bridge and passed through the gates on the way to the Campo Ghetto Nuovo: it was common for Venetians and barbarians to meet with their Jewish business partners in the ghetto, or to go there for the superior medical advice offered by the doctors. Of course they would be more careful after nightfall.

When he arrived at the *campo* there were enough Venetians for him to feel comfortable, but still he felt out of place. And as he made his way to Solomon's house, he felt the mood shift. He had been in Jewish enclaves in the German towns and in the east as well, but the mood here was apprehensive. Small groups of Jews gathered at doorways talking, then became silent as he went by. No doubt they were wondering what the season might bring. The emotions of Carnevale often overflowed, resulting in an attack on the ghetto. The authorities would make a weak attempt to prevent it, but found it useful to allow the populace to vent their frustrations in this way. The bloodletting could have financial benefits as well, especially if bankers were killed and their records destroyed. And with the death of Zorzi, especially at this time of year, it was prudent for the Jews to be especially cautious. It became clear to Lazaro that he would have to wait a little longer or find his answers elsewhere. Attempting to speak with Solomon's family at a time like this would only make matters worse for Fugger's cause, and would do nothing for his conscience. Trying not to look too obvious, Lazaro retreated and started to thread his way back to the gate where he had entered.

Crossing the bridge and heading for the Fondamenta della Pescaria on the Canale di Cannaregio, he rounded a corner and ran headlong into Solomon's sister. It took a moment for her to recognize who he was, then she gathered herself and stepped out to pass. As she did he reached out to her and spoke her name. She pulled back, but still he held her, staring into her anger-filled eyes.

"What do you want with me? Haven't you done enough?" she said quietly.

He found it difficult to speak and just stood, dumb for a moment, staring at her face. "I want to talk to you, to help."

She seemed to take it indifferently. "You will do what you will, but leave us in peace." She pulled herself away from him and stepped past. Out of the corner of his eye, Lazaro saw the swift jab of her arm and he moved to the side to avoid the knife thrust. He grabbed her arm, and the knife clattered to the ground. There was no one in the narrow street, but he pulled her back into a deep doorway. "What are you doing?"

"If my enemy is preparing to attack, then I should attack first."

"I'm not your enemy."

She shook her head. "We are surrounded by enemies."

"I want to help," Lazaro said again, trying to quiet the situation.

"Will you raise Solomon from the dead?" She didn't wait for an answer but pulled her wrist out of his hands, picked up her bundle and her knife, and hurried off down the street.

Lazaro remained where he stood, watching her walk away, surprised by what had happened. There was reason for her to carry a weapon, but he hadn't expected murder. However, it made him realize that she lived in a world where it was better to have clear lines of demarcation and that regardless of what he felt, she saw him as being on the side of the enemy.

It was getting dark and near to the time when he would be expected to pay his respects at Ca'Zorzi. Whatever information he might have been able to discover from Solomon's sister would have to wait for a more opportune time.

The *casa* was alive with light, but all of the mirrors and paintings in the foyer were draped with black cloth. The doorman and the rest of the servants were dressed in black as well. Lazaro was greeted quietly and shown up a winding staircase to the *piano nobile*. He stepped to one side and stood for a moment by the rich tapestries hung on the wall, drinking in the gathering. On a dais at the far end of the room Signora Zorzi sat with Marzia by her side and Rodrigo standing behind. The rest of the room was crowded with the nobles of Venice, gathered to pay homage to one of their own, and to eat. Servants walked through the crowd with trays of food, stopping for a few moments at each gathering of people. He looked again toward the dais and saw that Marzia had noticed him. He saw Rodrigo look over at him a few seconds later — it was not a friendly glance. Lazaro felt Rodrigo's eyes on him as he moved through the crowd, but he kept his own eyes low, looking for badges displaying the heart and sword. He saw a few; any of these youths could have been Ottavia's brother, Constantino. He knew that somehow Rodrigo and his club members figured prominently in the deaths of Zorzi and Solomon, either as instigators or as men who followed the orders of another.

Too quickly he found himself at the dais and moved forward to pay his respects. He was acknowledged gracefully by Signora Zorzi and with a nod of the head by Rodrigo. Marzia, however, took his hand and held it as she spoke to him, thanking him for everything he had tried to do. He could see that Rodrigo was not pleased; he looked away, speaking to the man who stood beside him. Lazaro bowed, thanked Marzia, and walked away to a neutral area of the room. It was only then that he opened his hand and looked to see what was there. He had felt something as Marzia held his hand, but he had said nothing. Now it was there in the palm of his hand, wet from moisture, a small folded piece of paper. Looking to see that no one was watching him, he opened it. It said, simply, "Meet me in the garden when all are gone. I must speak with you." A hand clasped his shoulder, and he closed his fingers with lightning speed.

"I'm glad you came, Lazaro." Turning, Lazaro saw Tagliapietro and bowed his head slightly. The Secretary moved closer to him. "I also noticed that you didn't stay for the mass. It was wonderful, but they are a bore," he said in a conspiratorial whisper. "We will have to speak soon." He paused for effect, then waved his hand, assuming that such an invitation might strike fear in a normal man's heart. "Nothing of any great significance. There are some things I would like to discuss with you." With that he moved off in the direction of the Doge.

Lazaro looked about and realized he was out of place in such a gathering. He looked again to the dais, and Marzia caught his eye.

She looked to Rodrigo, busy speaking with another young man, then cocked her head ever so slightly. Lazaro responded with a nod, then edged his way to the door and left, walking through the garden and out into the *calle*. After turning two corners he paused to see that no one was following him, then doubled back and took up the same position he had held on the night he had lain in wait for Signor Zorzi.

He waited there in the darkness beside the wall for what seemed to be an eternity. In fact it seemed to him that this had all been a dream, that he had never received the note though he felt it in his pocket. The house took some time to quiet as people left and shutters were closed. It seemed so out of place, dark and quiet in the midst of a city of celebration. And then he heard his name softly whispered, and the long wait was over. Moving toward the gate, he saw her step from the shadows. The moonlight bathed her flowing soft green gown. She wore a small cap with lace streaming down her back, accenting her golden hair. She opened the gate quietly so that it would not alert the house guards, which the Doge had lent to her family for protection. He followed her in, waited as she closed the gate again, and then moved with her to a corner of the garden sheltered from the view of the house. A small raised area held a marble bench and a fountain.

They sat by each other and said nothing for a few moments. Finally Marzia began. "I don't know what possessed me to do what I have done. When I saw you at the Doge's Palace I felt I wanted to have a few moments alone to speak with you, and so I wrote that note. I wasn't sure that you would come tonight. But you have." She paused and seemed to blush, though Lazaro could not tell in the dark. "I want to thank you again for trying to save my father from those horrible Jews. He always said they shouldn't be allowed to live within the city, that they all should be sent back to Mestre. And now they've killed him."

He expected her to begin to cry, but she didn't. She just sat, dry-eyed, and looked at him. It had been a long time since such a beautiful woman had been so welcoming to him. Still, he wasn't completely sure of her intentions. "I lost my mother and my father when I was very young," he said, "but I remember that it was hard for me. It took me a long time to get rid of the anger."

She leaned against the back of the bench, her shoulder brushing his arm. "I don't think I ever will. It wells up, makes me want to see that boy executed again and again and again. And in the end I just want to put it all out of my mind."

"Perhaps if you think of more pleasant thoughts it will calm you."

"But I can't. I always see him."

They sat silently and the sounds of the garden filled their ears. Somewhere in the night two cats howled and hissed at each other, then were gone. A gondola passed and they heard gentle laughter echo along the *rio*.

She rose and walked to the edge of the garden and stood silent for some time looking through the wall to the *rio*. He did not interrupt her quiet moment, but sat by the fountain looking up at the sky. The soft gurgle of the water hid all other sounds from him, and for a while he was alone with the stars. The sky reminded him of another sky filled with the fluttering of an angel. He smelled Marzia as she passed and caught her arm, pulling her to the seat beside him. She had been talking and only when she sat beside him did he realize this. It was also apparent that she had been talking to him and, from the look in her eyes, expected a response. For a moment he paused and she seemed to get embarrassed.

"I suppose I shouldn't have said that," she remarked finally.

"Why do you think that?" The deception came to him naturally.

She pulled her hand away from his, though not in rejection. "You don't seem interested in my feelings and perhaps they aren't real."

"Sometimes," he said with the trick of the sleepy priest on confessional duty, "it is useful to repeat yourself. Sometimes it's easier to decide if you are telling the truth by doing that."

"All right," she decided. "I have been promised to Rodrigo, but I don't love him. Now with my father dead I feel I should continue with the arrangements, but I don't want to. And to complicate things, my father's death has allowed us to meet. I had seen you before we met at the Doge's Palace; in fact, I noticed you many times in the streets. But to be brought together by my father's death — I can't feel good about that, yet I do."

Lazaro depended on the darkness to shield the fact that he was both surprised and pleased. He found himself thinking again like a priest, though one who was now interested in the confession. "You have no feeling for Rodrigo?"

"I think I loved him once, but not any more." She looked away from him. "But it's not just that."

There was an uncomfortable pause, but it gave Lazaro time to feel his blood flow with increased power and temperature. He felt warmer, drawn to her. "There is something else?"

"It's bad enough not loving him," she said and her voice took on a trance-like quality, "but some thoughts are worse. Rodrigo was visiting the night my father was killed. A messenger came to the house to get my father, and Rodrigo seemed very interested in their conversation. Though I wanted him to stay, he left hurriedly, shortly after my father left. I feel horrible in saying this, but I can't help it, I feel that somehow he had something to do with my father's death." She paused. "To have lost a father is bad enough. To have lost him to the one he had chosen for me is a fate I would rather not face."

Lazaro felt twisted like a vine into this story. He was not sure, if the ax fell, that it would not cut his shoots as easily as the shoots of another. "Do you have any proof?"

"I know that he opposed my father in a business matter regarding the Pope and that as long as my father opposed it, Rodrigo and his family stood to lose a great deal of potential profit. I also can see that as my father's heir I would be a more valuable wife if the bequest materialized. I'm not altogether without mental faculties," she said with a glint in her eye. "But I can't see how he would have been involved with Jews. He hates them even more than did my father."

There was a parable which Lazaro could not quite call to mind but it was one which he was sure Fugger would heartily endorse; something about sowing good seed on fertile ground and reaping benefits, but it didn't quite fit. At this moment he saw Marzia more as a pump in need of priming. "I don't think it was the Jews who killed your father."

Marzia looked back at him, shocked. "But you were there. You killed one Jew and identified the other."

Lazaro recounted only as much as was necessary to show her that her suspicions might not be groundless. When he mentioned the club emblem she nodded, and when he told her of the attack on him the night before she stopped him.

"Your attacker last night had the insignia, yes. But was he wearing a ring with a swan on it? Did he have red hair and a scar on his left cheek?" She described further details. "Don't bother answering, for I feel in my heart the answer, and I don't wish to hear it. Zanipolo, a close friend of Rodrigo's, was hurt last night in a street fight. I have just described him to you." She wrung her hands and took a breath. "Rodrigo must have sent him to kill you. Even after he saw you at the Doge's Palace he seemed angry about you but he wouldn't talk about it. You are the witness the real murderer would fear."

"But if Rodrigo wanted your father killed, why didn't he just poison him, and poison me for that matter, if what you suspect is true?"

Marzia laughed, a sad laugh, and shook her head. She smoothed out her dress and looked at the Zorzi ring on her finger. "You all have the same view of Venice, don't you? We spend our days concocting poisons to be used in our nights of revelry. And I suppose the glassmakers have filled your head even more with their assertion that they can manufacture a wineglass of such perfection that it will crack if touched by poison." She paused. "I'm sorry. Yes, I suppose he might have resorted to poison, but to avoid discovery the poisoner must resort to a slow poison or must be sure beyond doubt that the chemist providing the poison is trustworthy, and dependable. The Secretariat controls the best poisoners. Besides, greed is like lust, and men seldom plan ahead when consumed by either."

Lazaro could attest to that. As he listened to her he felt the wine he had drunk earlier beginning to mix with his emotions, and it was not greed that was beginning to consume him. She turned her head and raised her eyes to meet his, and he saw that her cheeks were stained with the tracks of tears. He pulled her close to him, and she held him tightly. More questions might have been posed, such as how the Secretariat could not have known, though he could as easily furnish plausible answers; for example, Rodrigo could have had friends among the assassins and no doubt some of them were in the *calle* that night. He closed his eyes and his mind was filled with other images.

Some time later they found themselves in the far corner of the garden, lying on the grass, covered partially by their clothes, which they had pulled over themselves as the heat of passion died away. In moments of passion it was natural for people to cry out for what they wanted most, but he had never heard anything like this before. It made sense and yet it troubled him. He had said nothing, but afterward, passion spent but the wish remaining, she had repeated it. She wanted Rodrigo dead.

She rose up on her knees suddenly and leaned over him, retrieving her clothes. "I must go, my love, I have mourning to prepare for. And Rodrigo will be around. Can you meet me on Saturday night, late?"

Lazaro nodded, then watched as she stood and dressed in the moonlight; not the sagging hairy body of a Dürer or the lumpy body of a Raphael, but the angelic form of Botticelli's Venus. She bent over him once more to kiss him and was gone. He lay on his back, his hands under his head, staring at the sky. The moon was now shining through the boughs of the tree overhead and there was silence, save for the occasional bark of a dog, the hiss of a cat, and the gurgle which came from the canal. He knew he would leave soon, but for the moment he wanted to savor all that he had experienced that night. She was his. But was he hers? Could he shoulder the dark responsibility? He knew that she was right in her assumptions. And he knew he would kill Rodrigo.

The city was quiet, sleeping, as he made his way back to his lodgings. Here and there men and women had fallen asleep in doorways, lulled to sleep by the wine and the soft lapping of the water against the foundations of the buildings. The soft water sounds were punctuated every once in a while by the knock of the gondolas against their *palli*. Occasionally he saw a gondola pass by the mouth of the *calle* he was in, its light bobbing, and he could just see the faint outline of the gondolier bending to his oar. Not everyone was asleep.

"Taking in the night?" hissed a voice from the darkness.

Lazaro stepped back, his hand on his sword. With a laugh, the speaker emerged from the dark doorway which had sheltered him. It was Beccaria.

"Let go your sword," Beccaria said with a smile showing below his mask. "Come, walk with me."

Lazaro walked beside him silently, and presently they stopped in front of the Church of San Zanipolo. Beccaria sat on a bench at the side of the *campo* and said conversationally, "I like the night, don't you?"

Lazaro nodded, still wary, wondering what Beccaria could have in mind.

"I think it is because there are no people about."

Lazaro sat on the bench facing Beccaria. "Some people are afraid of the night because it's too quiet."

Looking at Lazaro, Beccaria said, "They are afraid of it because it gives them too long to think and they can't help but think of death. Death is quiet and dark to them."

"And to you?" Lazaro asked.

Beccaria smiled again, almost a warming smile. "Death is my trade." He sat back and turned his face to the sky. "Death just is. It's not like those liars say," he added, pointing to the church. "They call their place a house of God. It's a tomb. An empty tomb. It celebrates death, but they're too afraid of death to see that. They cover it with all sorts of rituals, with song and music, with incense to kill the stench. But it is just a large, ornate, empty place." He looked again at Lazaro. "You were a priest?"

Lazaro shook his head. "No. I was educated in the monasteries, but I had no vocation."

"So you were drawn to war."

"I couldn't give eternal life, so I brought death instead."

Beccaria laughed heartily. "You are well chosen, Lazarus."

Lazaro felt the hair on the back of his neck rise as Beccaria spoke his name. It was as if that voice called from beyond the grave. He looked into Beccaria's eyes, and, even though it was dark, seemed to see a light shining there. The eyes were at once welcoming and horrifying. He pushed the thoughts out of his mind. "Chosen for what?"

"We need men like you. At the Secretariat. Venice is always troubled. It's fitting that she is built on the waves. Her houses and her power are always endangered by the tides, by shifting loyalties. She needs men who can act in her favor, who can strike out with a sure hand at her enemies."

"Especially when he's tied to a column." Lazaro could almost feel Beccaria's eyes narrow. He felt the presence of a serpent preparing to strike.

"It's unwise to exhibit compassion for an enemy of the state, especially a Jew you helped convict," Beccaria warned in a cold voice.

"I told what I saw. Perhaps I didn't see everything."

"It's a bit late for doubts," Beccaria said, then stood and began to walk away, past Lazaro. Suddenly he wheeled about and, crouching behind Lazaro, put the tip of his stiletto to his neck. "Show a bit more wisdom in the future, Lazarus. And I would stay away from the family if I were you."

Lazaro hoped Beccaria was speaking only of the exchange he had had with Mordechai after the trial. "The father was distraught. He meant me no harm," he said without flinching.

"Don't be so trusting of fathers. Abraham would have slain Isaac. Even God let his son die." Beccaria relaxed the pressure on the stiletto. "The Old Man of the Mountains had the best assassins because they believed they were already dead. I could have killed you the night we arrested Solomon, but I have let you live. I think you will see the merit in the opportunity being offered to you."

"I'm not sure I could live my life in a mask."

Beccaria stood, sheathed his stiletto, and started walking away. "Oh, you'll find a way, Lazarus, believe me. We're cut from the same cloth, you and I. And in the end, you'll see that." The darkness along the side of the church seemed to swallow him, and he was gone.

Lazaro continued to sit on the bench, wondering if Beccaria or one of his hirelings was watching from somewhere in the darkness. He also wondered whether Beccaria had known he was at Ca'Zorzi or whether he had just been waiting for him to come home. In any event, it had not been a chance meeting. Cut from the same cloth, he had said. Perhaps he was right, Lazaro thought, though he wanted to believe otherwise. One thing had become clear — but for the possibility that Lazaro might be of use to the Secretariat, Beccaria would gladly have cut his throat. And Beccaria was watching him closely, almost jealously. It was a time to be very careful.

Lazaro noticed that first light was breaking and made his way to the Dancing Mouse. The tavern was still, littered with bodies thrown off by their inhabitants in the last rites of Carnevale: here nakedness, there sickness. He climbed the stairs as quietly as possible, stole into his room, and began changing his clothes. As he was doing this he was drawn to the window and glanced out, knowing he would not see Marzia but wanting, for some strange reason, to look at her *altana*. Saturday could not come soon enough.

Looking down to the *calle* which ran beside the *rio* he saw a water merchant carrying two jugs on a yoke and crying out, "*Acqua fresca, acqua fresca*," but even the water merchant was tired and quiet. Slowly he eased out of his room and down the stairs, not wanting to awaken Renata. With care he again stepped over the bodies strewn about and was out in the *calle*. As he made his way toward Canareggio where he would be able to find a boat to take him to Murano, he was struck by the fact that the city was still relatively quiet. It seemed no one was stirring, as if everyone had finally exhausted himself and was resting behind his shutters with a mixture of satisfaction, shame, and fear. Most, he reasoned, would either still be asleep or would be readying themselves to attend mass where they would receive their ashes — gray powder which cured them of their madness.

The light of this Wednesday was always a difficult light to face.

XII

It was this sort of morning which made Lazaro recall, with a certain lack of veracity, the life of a mercenary. On mornings such as this, that life beckoned with the promise of sleep when sleep was due. It was a life which contained terrible moments of fear, pain, and deprivation, but when concluded, there was luxury, licentiousness, and rest. While he had passed a night with some degree of licentiousness, still he was too tired to be about Murano this early, with the laborers coming to the furnace. It was like the life of a priest responding, without clear thought or desire, to the prescribed diurnal duties.

Again, Angelo's door remained closed while the glassmakers began their tasks. Many of the men were busy with the manufacture of crown glass and broad glass, while others worked on a variety of objects, from goblets and vases to tiny glass balls which would later be transformed by Angelo's mercury amalgam into fake pearls. Lazaro busied himself gathering up the cullet, the pieces of waste glass that were strewn about the factory. This would be added to new batches of glass to aid in the fusing of the ingredients. Very little was wasted. Before long, Bartelemeo called him over to help with some cane production. Canes, long rods of glass, clear or colored, which might contain intricate patterns running their length, were widely used for decoration in the production of many pieces. Angelo had most of his canes produced by a master cane-maker. However, as a glass factory was also a school for apprentices, all facets of the trade, even the building of crucibles and furnaces, would at times be carried out.

Bartelemeo had shown the apprentice, Pasquale, how to marver a gather of white glass into a fat rod and then force it into a long star-shaped mould. This star-shaped rod was then rolled into a bed of clear glass so that Pasquale now had a rod of clear glass about six inches long, with a star in the center. Lazaro brought blue rods over to the table and Bartelemeo showed Pasquale how to arrange them in a bundle around the star rod and secure them with two pieces of wire. The bundle was returned to the glory hole and heated until it glowed orange then, with the wires removed, rolled on the marvering table to fuse the rods. After further heating, a *punti* was attached to one end of the rod bundle. Now Lazaro anchored the other end while Pasquale, under Bartelemeo's supervision, pulled the fat bundle of rods out thinner and thinner, occasionally cutting the rod and bringing more apprentices into the pulling operation, until in all there were ten four-foot canes one-quarter inch in diameter. Of course much more elaborate embedded patterns were possible, but Bartelemeo wished the apprentices to understand the general principles first. And he wanted the star-shaped design for a bowl he was making. He planned to cut the canes into thin slices — *marina* — and then roll a *cristallo* globe in them as he was blowing, to fuse the stars in the sides of the vase and give a simple but attractive mosaic effect.

As the cane production was coming to an end, Angelo emerged from his private workroom and called Lazaro in. He touched Lazaro lightly on the shoulder and said, in a conspiratorial whisper, "I have something important to show you. It has been annealing and should be ready." He signaled for Lazaro to close the doors so that the other workers would not be able to see them. When Lazaro did, he realized that the windows had been draped in cloth and the room was quite dim. Angelo opened the door to the annealing furnace and a blast of heat warmed the room. Inside was a sheet of clear glass, thick but not overly so.

Angelo brought it out and supported it between two blocks of wood. "I've been working with the formula for the glass which cannot be broken, and I think I have something." Angelo turned and went to the furnace where he picked up a long metal rod with a bulb of iron at the end. He handed the long hammer to Lazaro. "Try to smash it."

Lazaro shook his head. "I don't want to break it. It's a nice sheet of glass."

"You haven't listened," the old man said, shaking his head. "It is unbreakable."

Lazaro shrugged his shoulders and took the metal rod. He gently tapped the glass sheet.

"Harder," the old man said, crowding in behind him, "hit it as hard as you can."

Lazaro pulled back and swung the rod into the air then brought it down on the sheet. It turned white and hung there for a moment, long enough to surprise Lazaro. Then it shattered into a million pieces. The two of them stood silent for a few moments, then Angelo chuckled.

"I'm sorry," Lazaro offered.

The old man was laughing louder now. "No, no," he said shaking his head and wiping tears of laughter from his eyes. "I thought I had it, and it almost worked. I saw it in your face. You were so surprised. You really don't believe me, do you?"

Lazaro was laughing by now as well. "No, I don't. I believe that you believe in it, but I don't believe it will come to be."

Angelo sat on a stool and motioned for Lazaro to sit beside him. "Oh, ye of little faith." He dried his eyes. "I'll do it before I die. You'll see."

"If you are successful, you will die. The Secretariat would never allow such a thing to happen. The value of glass, and so many other materials, would diminish to nothing."

Angelo nodded. "Not just the Secretariat. The glass guild would do me in first probably. They would stand the most to lose. So much for science." They sat quiet as the humor of the moment dissipated.

The old man pushed the pieces of the broken glass into a pile with his feet, then, without looking up, added, "Although I suppose you could always find me another city."

Lazaro waited through an uncomfortable silence, broken finally, and knowingly, by Angelo.

"I had expected you to return sooner. How did things go?"

Lazaro raced through the story of the death of Solomon and of his belief in the boy's innocence, enough that Angelo was not insulted but not so much that he would be placed in any jeopardy by the knowledge.

Something seemed to take the old man's attention and though Lazaro looked in the same direction he could see nothing. Then Angelo's eyes focused again. "You're in a nest of vipers." He paused, then clapped his hands and stood. "So, now I want you to help me with the mixtures," he said with a grin, "and remember you're sworn to secrecy."

Lazaro arranged the barrows which Angelo would use to mix the various types of glass. Sand from the Venetian islands formed the largest proportion of the mixture, although Angelo also used ground quartz pebbles and sand from Syria. Over two-thirds of the mixture was sand and the rest was made up of lime and potash. There were other additives, of course, many which Lazaro did not recognize. For the *cristallo*, to remove the green which would normally be present in the glass due to the iron in the sand, Angelo added pyrolusite, or glassmaker's soap. The manganese contained in this substance would wash away the color and leave a brilliant clear glass. Angelo also prepared mixtures to bring color to the glass. He had heated copper and sulfur to produce a black mass which when roasted produced a red *ferretto*. Replacing the sulfur with copperas produced a green pigment. For a yellowish brown he had subjected iron and sulfur to a similar process in order to produce *crocus martis*. Of course, there was *zaffre* from Damascus for a deep blue, and other chemicals which produced almost any color imaginable. The quality of the colors varied depending on the knowledge and skill of the alchemist. Angelo's colors were of the highest quality, as were his mirrors, though he didn't show Lazaro his formula for the special amalgam of tin and mercury with which the mirror was made. However, Lazaro had no desire to be involved in this production. As he had learned in Schwaz, even during the preparatory phase the mercury could well enter the body and begin its journey of destruction.

As the week wore on, Lazaro found himself dreaming of Saturday, when he would again be with Marzia. It was not all self-interest, he told himself. No doubt she would have more information regarding Rodrigo and, after skillful questioning, she would give it to him. All of this, he told himself, would aid Fugger. Fugger himself had said that the investigation need not be unpleasant.

Making up for the time lost to Carnevale, everyone worked long and hard hours, under the watchful eyes of Bartelemeo and Angelo. Most of the work was mundane; broad glass and crown glass were in demand for windows. And Angelo also needed the broad glass for mirror surfaces. A few of the workers were busy with small goblets and two were kept busy blowing penis-sized glass tubes for the specialty shops. By Saturday Lazaro was ready for some time off. He stayed behind when the other workers left, as was normal, cleaned up the blow-pipes and *punti* rods and gathered the cullet which was strewn about. He then went up to his room above the factory, and as he walked down the hallway, noticed Angelo, lit by a candle and warmed by a small brazier, poring over his books and accompanied by a bottle of wine. "I'm going into Venice and I may be gone for a couple of days," said Lazaro.

"Is it me or my trade?" asked Angelo, then added with a mischievous grin, "the young courtesan asked with a painted smile."

"I have some things to attend to," Lazaro stumbled.

Angelo cuffed him lovingly on the side of the head. "Did you say the same thing when you left the monastery?" Angelo leaned forward in the darkened room and the light from the brazier caught his face in warm red. "You will be back when you are back."

Lazaro felt caught somehow, like a child, and tried to move the conversation along. "How has my work been? Would the guild have me?"

Angelo smiled and shook his head. "The guild. If you want to be had by the guild I'm sure they would accommodate you. You have enough talent to be a good worker. But it isn't for you. You'll never be a glassmaker."

Lazaro smiled and pulled a low stool over beside Angelo. "Probably not."

Angelo took a glass and filled it with wine, then handed it to Lazaro. "Stay with me for as long as you are able. Or as long as you need to," he added, and Lazaro knew he referred to the Secretariat. "I'll still teach you as much as you are interested in learning. But if this isn't your life, there's no need for you to try and make it so. It only results in a struggle." The old man scratched his head, and his hair quickly became unruly. "There are other things which interest you more, and it's important that you follow them. I could never be anything but a mirrormaker. It's everything for me." Angelo leaned back and put his hands on his knees. "You must seek your muse. I've found mine — the mercury." Angelo noticed the surprised look on Lazaro's face. "You think of it more as a madness, a debilitating thing, don't you? Well, maybe it is. When the mercury overtakes me, I am gone for a while, given to strange habits and sounds. Nonsense outside. Inside it is wonderment, and in the throes of that madness which comes often unannounced I see and hear and sometimes feel the most fantastic things. And when I return, well, I twist the glass to make it resemble where I've been."

"It's the vapor from the mercury, when you paint the mirrors or the inside of the pearls . . ." Lazaro began.

Angelo put his hand on Lazaro's shoulder. "I know that mercury loosens reality's hold on me, but is that such a terrible thing?"

"It'll kill you."

"And otherwise I would have lived forever?" Angelo asked. "Don't twist my meaning. I don't say that you should go out and diminish yourself and enslave yourself. But some things happen which are meant to happen, or at least which open new doors, allow you to see things differently. And the opportunity should be embraced. I have my muse; you have yet to find yours, and it isn't at this glory hole. You have too much of the warrior in you. But there will be something which will transport you, transform you. You'll toil with the truth and the lie, but not in glass." Angelo slapped his legs with his hands and stood. "I just want you to know that I understand."

Lazaro changed quickly and headed out into the cool night, ready to meet again with Marzia. As he walked past a tavern near the factory he heard a woman's voice call his name and stopped. Peering in the door he saw Renata. She was dressed in a loose skirt and blouse, her blonde hair falling on her shoulders and ringlets drooping in front of her eyes. Her lips were parted in a friendly smile, and she was pulling herself away from two men who were too obviously dressed in the uniform of the Secretariat to be anything other than Beccaria's men. She quickly got up from the table and came out into the street.

"Are you surprised to see me?" she asked coyly.

Lazaro nodded.

"My mother has an interest in this place," she said, pointing to the tavern, "and she agreed that I should come here to oversee it. I'm living upstairs," she added. "Why don't you come in?"

"I have some things to do," Lazaro said with a smile. "Really."

Renata's lip curled slightly. "Business again." She pushed him gently. "Part of the reason I wanted to come here was so I could keep my eye on you." She pulled him closer to her body, brushing her breasts against his arm. "There's no need for you to be a stranger."

The young assassins called out Renata's name, and she leaned back in the door and told them, in shrewish tones, to be quiet.

Lazaro disentangled himself. "I really do have to be somewhere."

Renata let him go but remained smiling. "Well, at least you know that I'm here. Drop in and visit."

"Sure," Lazaro said, without meaning it, and started off down the *calle*. He turned once as he reached the corner expecting her to be hanging in the doorway waiting to give him one last wave but she was already back inside. She, at least, had found her muse.

Back in Venice he headed toward the Dancing Mouse, thinking he might spend some time there drinking until it seemed late enough to pay his visit to Ca'Zorzi. When the *calli* had quietened sufficiently, he made his way to the *casa* and found a shadowed vantage point. He watched the house for some time, until he began to fear that Marzia had forgotten or had decided not to meet him. Finally, when he had decided that it might be best for him to leave, he saw Marzia's face in an upstairs window. She noticed him and signaled to him that she wanted him to wait away from the house. He walked down to the next corner and waited for what seemed to be a long time but finally he heard the sounds of a woman walking and turned to see her approaching. She hugged him and pulled him into an alley which turned in behind another building. There, shielded from any passersby, they kissed and held each other for a long time without speaking. Finally she pulled herself from his arms. "My mother isn't well. I had trouble getting away, but I felt I had to meet you, as I had promised. I don't think I can meet you again. What happened before was wrong."

Lazaro shook his head and pulled her back. "You don't believe that."

The moonlight spilled onto the narrow *calle* and Marzia's blue eyes shone. "I don't know what possessed me. My father's murder, maybe it made me crazy." She turned her face to the paving stones. "I am promised. I must marry Rodrigo."

"Even though you know he had something to do with your father's death?"

She turned from him and took a step away. "There isn't anything I can do. He was here earlier, but he left. He said something about a meeting in the Campo Rialto." Stepping closer to Lazaro she pushed her blonde hair away from her face and furrowed her brow. "I don't know what is right."

Lazaro held her face so that they looked into each other's eyes. "If you don't want to marry him, you shouldn't. What do you want?"

She pulled away from him and leaned back against the wall, her arms folded across her chest. "What I want doesn't matter. My father gave his word. I can't dishonor my family." She took Lazaro's face in her hands and looked deeply into his eyes. "I have no choice. As long as Rodrigo lives I will be his." She turned and ran down the alley. Lazaro didn't bother to follow her. It was clear to him what she was asking him to do. It was nothing he hadn't done before.

He wandered through the *calli*, much quieter now that Lent had arrived, and before long he was at the Campo Rialto. He had not been sure what to expect but when he arrived there were about twenty young men milling about, all of them wearing white masks. Had it been a normal club gathering there would have been boisterous singing and drinking, but too many of them murmured and glanced at each other in a conspiratorial fashion. One of them came up to Lazaro and handed him a mask. "Best to wear this," he said and then was back in the crowd.

Lazaro realized what was afoot. As a mercenary, he had seen it in towns they had taken. If there was a Jewish section, the attackers would go there first. It was partly because the Jews kept a store of valuable commodities pawned to them by the Christian population of the town. But the attackers had to be quick because it would not be long before the people of the town, realizing that law and order were temporarily disbanded, would prey on their Jewish neighbors. So there was always a mad race to see who would loot and rape in the Jewish section first. Here there was no war, but it was Lent, with Good Friday at its end, and two Jews had been found guilty of murdering a respectable *Ene Aca* of Venice. In that instant, Lazaro was torn between his duty to Fugger and what felt like guilt. If the *bravi* succeeded in what was no doubt their quest, there would be little information he might be able to discover from Margoleit or her father. And if the *bravi* were truly about to do what he suspected, to what extent was he culpable? He had not accused Solomon, but his testimony had been used to ensure that two Jews would be blamed for this murder. And now there would be theft, murder, and rape as a result of his testimony.

It was no longer clear in his mind why he had come to the Campo Rialto. He could think only of the ghetto. He moved slowly out of the square, then raced quickly through the winding *calli*, across more bridges, and through more *sottoporteghi* than he had thought existed in Venice until he reached the street leading to the ghetto.

Lazaro stopped at the gate and saw that the guards who should have been there were not. Missing, too, was the patrolling gondola. He wasn't sure how much time he had but he knew it would not be long. Things were too quiet. He raced along the route which had first been traced out for him by Bomberg to the home of Margoleit and her father. In the distance he could now hear sounds of shouting. The *bravi* were on their way. And this house would be a prime target for them, perhaps even one they had been directed to, the house of the murderer of a Christian *zentilhomine*. And a house which held a beautiful sister of the murderer. Lazaro battered on the door. He saw a light shining through the cracks of the shutters on an upstairs window. There was some noise from within and then the shutters opened. It was Margoleit.

He removed his mask. "Quickly, there is no time to explain. You must leave now."

She hesitated for a moment, and in that moment the vanguard arrived. Two *bravi,* masked, with swords and firebrands, rounded the corner and ran up to the house. They had received clear directions. For a moment they didn't notice Lazaro, and both looked up at Margoleit. One of them moved forward, then the other one pulled his arm, and they looked in Lazaro's direction. He saw then that they recognized him. The first man dropped his torch on the ground and drew a stiletto. In the flickering light Lazaro saw that they both wore the emblem of the flaming heart and sword on their ankles, and that the man who had dropped his torch carried his sword in his left hand.

As they stepped back and crouched, Lazaro, readying for their attack, drew his sword and shouted to Margoleit, "This is only the first of a mob. Get your father and get out." The two *bravi* circled for a moment, then attacked him from either side. The man to his right, still holding his torch, seemed to be less accomplished than his partner and Lazaro decided to use this. He attacked the better man first, pushing him back and managing to trip him. Instead of continuing with his advantage he turned on the other who had raced to defend his partner. Whether it was the mask, the torch, or stupidity, it mattered little, for the young man impaled himself on Lazaro's sword. There was a flash of surprise on the man's eyes and he dropped his sword and his torch, then grasped Lazaro's blade with his bare hands, endeavoring to pull it out. Lazaro withdrew it and the man rolled onto the paving stones, and pulled himself into a ball, clutching his stomach.

The second man was up again and circling. Lazaro had been right; this man was experienced. He could be one of Beccaria's men. The thought shone clear as *cristallo* in Lazaro's mind. Neither of them could be allowed to escape. He engaged the man and they slashed at each other furiously. He knew that he was fighting much too hard and that he could not do it for much longer. The other man could afford to expend more energy as he expected his accomplices to arrive before he was exhausted. For him it was worth the risk. Lazaro was at a distinct disadvantage. He had no help on its way and he was aware that the lives of Margoleit and her father now depended on him. Though he wished he couldn't, he could see them, huddled in the doorway of their house, their way blocked by the fighting men.

His adversary swung his stiletto so close to Lazaro's face that it touched the mask which hung about his neck, then lunged at him. This man was most definitely skilled at street-fighting. They circled each other and Lazaro saw in the eyes something familiar. He had seen this man before, though where he was not sure. Now the man changed his approach and slowed. He was waiting, hoping either to tire Lazaro or that his comrades would arrive. Then he spoke. "Bitch" was all he said, but it rang clear in Lazaro's mind. Though he could easily have taken it to be an epithet hurled at Margoleit, something told him it had been directed at Marzia. In that moment he recognized his opponent. It was Rodrigo. Rodrigo sensed he had been recognized and renewed his attack. They stood face to face, swords crossed, and stared into each other's eyes. Lazaro gathered his strength and pushed the crossed swords away. Rodrigo was caught off guard and banged hard against the wall. Lazaro gave him no time to recover but leapt at him with sword extended and dagger held back as a side block.

The mask was Rodrigo's undoing. He parried the sword and misjudged the stiletto. Too late he sensed his error. Lazaro's blade moved between Rodrigo's ribs and he stiffened. His face was close to Lazaro's when he spoke his last. "She'll bring you death," he said, then his eyes took on the empty stare of the dead. Lazaro pulled out his blade, and Rodrigo slid to a sitting position.

Suddenly, the other man ran at him from behind. Lazaro swung his sword around, deflecting the blow aimed at him, then felt his feet kicked out from under him. He fell and saw his opponent looming over him, still clutching his stomach, crimson now with his own blood. Lazaro pushed back quickly with his heels and the man leapt toward him. He rolled his body as far out of the way as possible so that only his hand remained in line with the man's falling body, his hand holding erect his stiletto. The man's body fell with the full force of his weight firmly on the stiletto and Lazaro quickly rolled back and threw his legs over the man's back. He released his grip on the stiletto, sat astride the man's back and, grabbing the hair on the back of his head, slammed his face into the paving stones. There was no more movement. He checked his neck, but there was no pulse.

He stood slowly, making sure he had not been cut. One glance to Rodrigo assured him there would be no more danger from that quarter. Lazaro quickly went to the doorway where Margoleit and her father stood. Mordechai was disoriented and Margoleit was angry. "You can't leave those bodies there."

"What are you talking about?"

"Two dead Christians outside our house . . . we'll be burned at the stake."

"Where can you hide?"

"It depends on who we're hiding from."

"I'm not really sure. The men who are responsible for your brother's death, I think."

"Are we to hide from you, then?"

"There's no time for this. You can hear them." The noise of the *bravi* was now echoing through the *campo*. They had reached the gate to the ghetto. Watchful Jews had barricaded it, but Lazaro knew the size of the mob. They would get through. He thought of Francesca. "I have a place, but how do we get out of here?"

For a moment it seemed Margoleit was not interested in his assistance, but a loud crash at the gate brought her to her decision. "I know a way." Lazaro took her hand but she pulled away. "What about the bodies?"

"What do you want me to do, carry them with us?" Lazaro asked in anger.

She stared at him long enough for him to realize that she meant for him to do just that. He grabbed the closest body and slung it over his shoulder, then followed her as she dragged her father back into the building and through a curving hallway. She stopped at a doorway which had been boarded up but which showed signs of having been used often. He realized now how Solomon had been able to slip in and out of the ghetto after curfew. He dropped the body and pulled two of the boards off. The *rio* was dark, though filled with echoes from the bridges leading into the ghetto. He turned to her. "How do we get across?"

"You just get the other body," she said, pushing him back, "and remember to bring the weapons."

As Lazaro raced back through the hallway he heard a loud splash. When he returned moments later with the body and the weapons, Mordechai was standing, Margoleit's crumpled dress beside him on the floor, staring out into the dark water. As Lazaro watched, Margoleit swam up to the *riva*. She pulled her dark hair out of her face, took the rope which she held in her teeth, and handed it to him. Lazaro could now see that a gondola was drifting toward them. She pulled herself, naked, out of the water and grabbed her dress. "Drag the gondola in, and hurry. I'm going back to lock the door." She saw that Lazaro was looking at her in a quizzical fashion. "There is no use making it easier for them."

He loaded the bodies in, and when she returned he made her lie down in the bottom of the gondola with her father then poled out into the canal. He tried to stay to the dark sides of the Rio San Girolamo. As they drifted out into the canal, Lazaro could tell from the sound of the fighting that the *bravi* had broken through the gates and were in the ghetto. It also looked as if a fire had broken out in Margoleit's house. That didn't surprise him in the least. The fighting had spread out to the streets and bridges leading to the ghetto as young Jews tried to repel their attackers. Most, however, would huddle behind their strong doors, ready if need be to defend their families from actual harm. In the morning, the council would go to the Doge's Palace, there would be discussions, apologies, and perhaps a payment for damages. If they were very lucky, the payment would not be followed by a special tax which would recover the damage payment.

Lazaro's original plan had been to go quickly to Francesca's house. He had no doubt she would help the family of Solomon. But as he poled along he decided it would be better not to go there directly in case some *bravi* had had instructions to visit that house as well. And so they drifted, up one *rio,* down the next, pausing from time to time in convenient shadows, avoiding detection. Margoleit's father did not look well. He looked gray and strained, and she stroked his head until he drifted off to sleep. Then she just sat, looking out over the water, and from time to time staring at Lazaro. At one point when he pulled into a small *rio* to avoid a barge that was passing in one of the larger canals, she spoke to him as they waited in the shadows.

"I remember that my brother mentioned your name. Did you know him well?"

"Not really," Lazaro said in the darkness. "I saw him when I went to Bomberg's."

"Are you a scholar?"

Lazaro smiled. "I suppose I once thought of myself as a scholar. At least I thought that is what I would become. But there are easier ways to live." He realized as he said it that she might take it the wrong way, and he could tell from her silence that she had. "I'm sorry about what happened to him. I told them only what you heard me say, what I saw." He heard her sigh.

"He was foolish. Father always said so. And too strong-willed to stay in Venice. I knew he was going to leave with that woman of his, Ottavia. Father didn't know. It would have worried him sick. But maybe he should have known. Maybe he would have stopped Solomon." She said nothing for a few moments. Lazaro strained but he could not make her out, sitting in the dark well of the gondola.

"I know he didn't kill Zorzi." The words should not have been spoken, but in the darkness he felt he had to say them to her.

"Then why didn't you tell them?"

"I didn't know for sure until after he had been executed. And now I'm not sure I should tell them."

"They won't believe you. Do you know who did it?"

Lazaro had already said too much, but he continued. "I think it was one of these two. At least they had something to do with it."

Again there was no sound for a few moments.

"Can we go now?" Margoleit said softly.

Lazaro listened and hearing nothing poled the gondola out into the rio. In a short while they were at the riva of Francesca's house. Lazaro tied the gondola to a palle, climbed out onto the step, then knocked on the door. It took three knocks before a light appeared. Francesca opened the door slightly and peered out. Lazaro started to whisper something to her, but she recognized him and quickly unlatched the door and opened it. "What do you want?" she asked.

Lazaro turned so that she could see Margoleit and her father, awake now and shivering in Margoleit's arms. "It's Solomon's family. I didn't know where else I could bring them."

Francesca opened the door wider still. "Bring them in, quickly."

Lazaro helped Margoleit move her father onto the *riva* and into the house where Francesca settled them in the next room, then returned with him to the *riva*. Taking a few coins from his pouch, Lazaro pushed them into her hand. "In case there are expenses."

"They'll be safe here," Francesca said with a nod.

"I'll be back before dawn," Lazaro whispered as she started to shut the door.

He poled the gondola from *rio* to *rio* until he was in the Grand Canal, which was largely deserted. Here and there the gondola of some lady of the evening or some drunken nobleman wandered about in the water. Lazaro avoided any contact with these and finally reached the Molo. Off from the Piazza in the Bacino San Marco the barges of the courtesans glowed with light and the sound of revelry. Quietly he poled the gondola in to shore and tied it to a mooring pole. Making sure no one was about he took the bodies of the *bravi* and carried them, one by one, to each of the columns in the Piazzetta. He tied a body upright to each column, choosing the column where Solomon had been executed for the *bravo* he did not know, though he suspected him to be Constantino. As he tied Rodrigo to the other column, he thought of Marzia.

He paused for a moment to be sure that no one had seen him, then returned to his gondola and poled off into the dark night.

XIII

The city had begun to stir as Lazaro slowly returned through the *rii* toward Francesca's. "She will bring you death," Rodrigo had said. Sour grapes? Rodrigo had engaged in a gambit and he had lost. Still, there was more to be determined, Lazaro thought as he poled along, before he could report to Fugger. He would have to speak more with Marzia, though it would not be for a while. When the bodies were discovered, a messenger would be sent to her house, to acquaint her with Rodrigo's death. She would have to mourn — it would be expected. And then . . .

However, for the moment, it was Solomon's father and sister who occupied his concern. Tying the gondola to the *palli*, Lazaro stepped out on the *riva* and tapped on Francesca's door. She was faster to answer this time and roughly pulled Lazaro inside, barring the door behind him. She quickly pulled a bit of cloth over her face and spoke to him in hushed tones. “I shouldn’t have let you leave them here. They are sick, very sick, both of them.” She pointed up to the second floor and pushed Lazaro toward the stairway.

Lazaro dropped his bag and quickly went up the stairs and into a dark bedroom. There was enough light coming in through the cracks in the shutters for him to see Margoleit kneeling beside the bed where her father lay, fully dressed, his eyes shut. For a moment he expected her to look up but he realized quickly that she was unconscious.

Crossing the floor, Lazaro knelt beside her. He checked her pulse, and it was strong but fast, her skin was clammy and he could see reddish blotches around her neck. Reaching gently under her he lifted her and placed her on a smaller bed on the other side of the room. In the little time he had known her he had found great beauty in her face. It was as the finest alabaster, almost translucent, allowing the soft light of her soul to shine through. But now the light was very dim indeed.

Lazaro returned to Mordechai. His pulse was weak and irregular. Lazaro could see in the old man’s fingertips the gray of death beginning its travel through the body. He had seen it before among the seriously wounded, those who were not dispatched by the battlefield scavengers or saved by the surgeons. They would lie for a while with their friends, if they had any, or in a ditch if they did not. And the gray of death would spread, first along their fingers and toes and then through their arms and legs until finally it seemed to reach into their hearts.

When battles were over he had been quick to volunteer to bury the dead, for in that way he avoided seeing the pain of those who were in the process of dying. So, too, in his work he had always tried to make death quick when it had to come. But in this death, for which he somehow felt responsible, he had not delivered a quick blow. It was as if he were the glass stiletto of one of Beccaria’s men and had been plunged through Solomon and into the old man’s heart. And now the shard of glass called to it the gray death creeping along the old man’s limbs.

Francesca was waiting for him when he came down the stairs, still holding the piece of cloth over her face. “Is it the plague?” she said in a hoarse whisper.

Lazaro walked over to a chair and sat. “No,” he said, shaking his head. He was silent for a moment and he could feel Francesca hovering near him, afraid to ask any more questions. “It’s not the plague. But Margoleit is very sick." He looked up at Francesca and saw the concern in her eyes. "I don't know what it is, but I know it's not the plague. Her father though, he will die soon, before this day is half gone. His heart."

Francesca sat down at the table with a great sigh and started fiddling with the cloth that only moments before had been her only protection from the grim reaper. "I'm not surprised. To lose a son that way, and then to be chased out by a mob. But he can't die here," she said suddenly.

Lazaro shrugged. "I doubt it's his choice, but there's little we can do, unless you want to turn them out?" Lazaro looked at Francesca and she shook her head.

"Her fever is bad," Lazaro said, rising from the chair and looking around the kitchen. He found some herbs and gave them to Francesca. "Make an infusion of this but let it steep until it's black. I'll need some fresh water as well, and a piece of cloth."

Francesca tossed him the piece she had in her hands, then grabbed a pot and filled it from a water jug which sat on a low table along the wall. "Go ahead," she said and began stirring the brazier. "I'll bring the tea up as soon as it's ready."

Back in the sick room, Margoleit looked no worse. Lazaro put a light blanket over her, then attended to her father. As he looked at the old man's face, his eyes deep in their sockets, his neck sinewy with age, he thought of his own father. He had been cut down in his prime, the pain had been brief. Still, in a selfish way, Lazaro silently wished that he could have had a moment with his father, a moment to make whatever peace could be made at such a time.

Gently, Lazaro smoothed out Mordechai's beard and placed his hands on his chest, the right over the left. There was a flutter in the old man's eyes, and they opened, just a bit. The whites were yellowed with age and much of the life had drained from his eyes, but still there was life there. He looked at Lazaro but it was not Lazaro he saw.

"Solomon," he whispered.

"Yes, Papa," Lazaro said, at peace with the lie.

The old man's eyes shut and the corners of his mouth attempted to smile. He moved his right hand and Lazaro took it in his. The moment was brief. The old man's grip loosened, and his breath grew shallow, so shallow that it barely moved the fluff of down which Lazaro held to his lips with his left hand, then that too stopped. It was a minute before Lazaro let go of his hand.

There had been no pain — the pain had come earlier, when he had learned of his son's death. From that point it had been a slow descent and now, for him, it was over. Though he had long been away from the church, Lazaro's mind turned to the Bible, and he remembered the story of Moses being taken to God. The recollection was like a silent prayer and he hoped Mordechai's spirit would not be offended.

Now his attention shifted to Margoleit. Though he had tried to appear confident when he answered Francesca's questioning, he was not at all sure that what was wrong with Margoleit would not attack them as well. He believed it to be nothing more than a severe chill coupled with exhaustion, but he had seen before strange diseases arise from simple symptoms.

As he dampened the cloth and wiped it across her brow he was aware that she reminded him of someone, but he could not remember who. He stared at her face, at the dark hair, the strong eyebrows and full lips, the rounded forehead, but he could not manage to rein in his memory. Two days before he had had all but no knowledge of her existence. But now it seemed to him that he must preserve her life above all else.

Francesca arrived with the infusion and he forced some of it past Margoleit's lips, then returned to bathing her face, neck, chest, arms, and ankles. Throughout the remainder of the night and the early morning he repeated his actions time and time again, pausing only when he needed more water and Francesca had dozed off. Finally, as it neared midday he saw the fever break and Margoleit's breathing, and her heartbeat, approached normalcy. Though she did not regain consciousness, the worst had passed. He had no doubt that she would be ill for a few days, but that she would live.

After he had explained to Francesca that Mordechai was dead but that Margoleit would live, and when she was calm enough to go out of doors, he sent her to the ghetto. By now there would be no danger and the guards at the gate and in the *rio* would not be back until sunset. Francesca assured Lazaro she would have no trouble finding Solomon's friends, some of whom were known to her.

While he waited for her return, Lazaro opened the shutters and let the light of day enter the room. It changed the entire character of the place. In the dark there had been something which separated the living from the dead and softened the entire situation. Now, in daylight, there was simply the corpse of an old man and the strained face of a woman whose brief respite from pain would soon end with a return to even greater sorrow.

The sound of Francesca's return startled him and he quietly stepped outside onto the balcony overlooking the small *rio* outside Francesca's house, closing the shutters behind him. Francesca had suggested that it might be better if she told Solomon's friends only that Margoleit and her father had been brought to her house by a stranger, and that she had cared for them through the night.

From the balcony Lazaro listened to the men as they entered the room. Some quickly bundled Margoleit off, and he heard them downstairs telling Francesca that she would be all right. The rest seemed to stand by the bed for a few moments, and Lazaro thought he heard them mumbling some sort of prayer, then they took the body and followed their comrades down the stairs and out into the narrow street. Lazaro made out the sound of a cart, and then he heard Francesca calling out that they were gone.

"Can I make you something to eat?" she asked him as he got to the kitchen.

"No," he said, shaking his head and picking up the jacket he had left on the floor. "It's kind of you, but I have business to attend to." Under his jacket he saw the mask he had been given the night before. He picked it up and tossed it on the brazier, watching for a moment as it smoked then burst into flames.

Francesca open the door to the *riva* and a fresh breeze blew through the house. "They'll let me know how she is. Come by later."

Lazaro nodded and stepped out onto the *riva*, untied the gondola he had used the night before and stepped in. He waved to Francesca, then poled out into the canal as she shut the door. At the first opportunity, he turned into a small *rio* and stopped the gondola by a footbridge, tied it up, and wandered off in search of a gondola to take him to Murano.

XIV

Lazaro knew that Marzia would be expected to be in mourning for a week, and he had no desire to be linked to the murder of Rodrigo. He expected as well that there would be no point in trying to question Margoleit any further, until the pain of her father's death had dulled somewhat. He toyed with the notion of contacting Francesca to see how Margoleit was, but decided against it because he didn't want to have Margoleit involved any more than she already was, and he wasn't sure how closely he would be watched. With no way in which he might serve Fugger, he served instead the master who was closer at hand, at least physically. As there was no need for him to go to Venice, Lazaro spent his days in the factory and his nights in the room which Angelo had prepared for him, much to the chagrin of Renata. She made a point of inviting him often to her rooms, but he continued to refuse, as graciously as possible.

It wasn't until late on the evening of the eighteenth of March that Lazaro returned to Venice. It had been ten days since Rodrigo's death and he expected he would be able to see Marzia in relative safety. Of course there would be questions, for Fugger's benefit, but he looked forward to more than that. The heat of the furnaces had sapped him of strength, and as he didn't want to be tired when he visited Marzia, he decided to stop first at the Dancing Mouse to rest for a few hours. The inn was quiet and there were few customers about. Even Renata's father seemed to be asleep at the fire in the main room, so he went to his room without anyone noticing he had arrived.

It was after midnight when he roused himself, eased open the door to his room, and stole down the stairs and out the door, waiting at the first corner in the *calle* to make sure that no one had been waiting for him outside. A light rain began to fall and he pulled his hood over his head and set out, pausing a few times again to ensure that he was not being followed, and finally reached the wall of the garden of Ca'Zorzi. He tossed a couple of stones inside the grounds to see if there were any dogs or guards about, then hoisted himself over the wall and dropped behind the bushes on the other side.

After pausing for a moment to be sure there was no one in the courtyard, Lazaro ran across the soggy ground to the house and stood beneath Marzia's window. There were no vines or drainpipes on the wall, so he found a few small stones and tossed them at the window. It was only a moment until the window opened and Marzia leaned out. Lazaro stepped back and pulled his hood from his head so that she could see him. She smiled and signaled for him to wait by the door which led from the garden into the house.

He moved over to the doors and waited. Through the window he saw her come down the stairs wearing a soft white gown. She threw a hooded cloak over her shoulders and came to the door.

"You shouldn't have come at this hour," she said as she closed the door and stood in the rain beside him.

"I know," Lazaro said with a sheepish grin, "but I missed you."

She held out her hands and he took them. She kissed him gently on the cheek, then pulled him with her as she walked toward the gate. "We cannot stand here and talk and I can't invite you in." Reaching the gate she produced a large key which opened the lock. She pushed Lazaro outside, then followed. They scurried down a *calle* and across a small bridge, then she unlocked the door to an old warehouse and pulled him inside.

She drew him to her and kissed him, then pushed him away. "We can't be seen together in public, at least not in any way which might be misunderstood."

Lazaro wiped the rain from his face and pushed his hair back off his forehead. "I hadn't planned to kill him so soon. It was unexpected."

Marzia's blue eyes flashed green in what faint light there was. "It was better this way."

Lazaro nodded, though as he watched her remove her wet robe he remembered Rodrigo's death and what he had said. Suddenly he felt something gnawing at his roots. "Rodrigo spoke to me before he died," he said. He watched carefully, and his heart sank. Though she hid it well, he could see the truth. He wasn't sure exactly how it all fit together, but he knew in that moment that she had used him. She had used Rodrigo before him, and her love for him had nothing to do with wanting Rodrigo out of the picture, of that Lazaro was sure.

"What did he say?"

There again, hidden deep within the voice, the clear bell of betrayal. Had he held before her a mirror of truth, he imagined, what ugliness would he see? Or would he simply see a merchant, a Venetian? It came to him in a flash, yet slowly, as in a dream. He saw it approach, more and more ugly as it neared. Somewhere in his baser nature he wished he had not asked any questions until after they had made love. But now what he saw in his mind was so clear, it took little effort to speak it. "You knew Rodrigo had killed your father before I brought it up."

"What do you mean," she said, tilting her head, smiling.

"You knew he had killed your father. It wasn't his idea."

"I don't understand."

Lazaro was angry, most of all with himself. "Take off the mask, it doesn't become you.

"Lazaro . . ."

"Rodrigo spoke to me."

"You can't believe him. He was crazed."

Now it all seemed so obvious. Lazaro didn't want to look at her, but he did. "He was in your thrall."

A change came over Marzia's face, like the change in still water when a storm crosses. The beauty remained, but it was frozen in place. "He loved me."

"And for that he would die."

Marzia was silent and, as Lazaro watched, a tear welled in her eye but only for a instant. Then it seemed that she drew it back inside. "There was good reason for my father to die. Very good reason. More than you'll ever know."

"And when Rodrigo had served his purpose he was of no further value."

"He wanted his reward," she said venomously. "He would have forced me to marry. He wanted to own me."

Lazaro thought for a moment that he heard a crack of lightning, but there was nothing save the drumming of the rain on the roof tiles. He looked into her cold blue eyes. There was no warmth, love or pain, just truth. "And now, what of me? I'm the next station in your passion?"

The fountains opened now, at least enough to send two rivulets down through the powder on her face to drip from her chin. "Not you. It's different."

Lazaro laughed and leaned back against the wall. "I've heard that story too many times." He found it easier to laugh. It was his armor.

She pushed herself away from the wall and leaned hard against him. Her robe slid from her shoulders and underneath it her white gown was thin silk. His arms wrapped around her almost in a reflex action and he found himself being kissed by her. The heat of her body warmed him through his wet clothes and he felt her arms reach behind him and pull his jacket up over his head, his shirt with it. She was saying things that he could not make out, but the intention was clear. Though the words seemed to speak of love and trust, the movement was one of growing passion. He felt his body responding, overpowering his cautious mind. The heat grew as they pulled off their clothes and sank onto her robe, spread over a pile of straw in the corner.

He was underneath her, but she pulled and tugged at him until he was on top of her. There was barely enough light for him to see clearly, but he watched in gathering excitement as she stretched her arms back and her hair fell over her shoulders and across her breasts.

The invitation was more than he could resist and he leaned forward.
Suddenly two pairs of hands shot out and grabbed each of his arms. He turned and saw the mask of the assassins, then saw Beccaria step out of the shadows. Two more assassins stood by Marzia, pulled her to her feet, and threw a cloak over her nakedness. It was then that Lazaro saw the dagger in her hand. She looked into his eyes, then turned her head and pulled the cloak around her.

"Tagliapietro wants to see both of you," Beccaria said with a smirk.

Lazaro felt anger sweep over him and struggled with the men holding him. A hood was thrown over his head and he continued his struggle until someone hit him on the back of the head.

The *pozzi* were wet cells built in the lower levels of the Doge's Palace, far from the fine rooms so that the sound of inquisition and the smell of death would not offend the *Ene Aca*, and far from the cells where Lazaro had been held before. When Lazaro awoke to the dripping of water he knew that he was in serious trouble. His head throbbed like a deep wound and his stomach was painfully empty. There was no window so he couldn't really tell how long he had been there but he felt the night had probably passed. Under the door and around the peep hole there was a bit of light, but except for that everything else was dark. And wet. Even the straw he was lying on was damp. He swept it off the sleeping platform and then, like a blind man, felt about the cell until he found some which was a little drier and set about rearranging things so that he could wait in comfort. But he tried not to think of what was awaiting him.

It was not really a surprise that he had ended up here. Killing Rodrigo had made such detention a distinct possibility. And then to have Marzia try to kill him. In the wet darkness it came clearly to him what had been going on, that he had been used as a fool.

"A fool," he said out loud and startled himself. Suddenly he felt sick and felt around for a pail. He found one, but the feeling passed. He wrapped his arms across his chest and rolled over on his side. Prisoners seldom returned from the *pozzi*.

The door clanged shut and woke him from a dreamless sleep. He could smell food in the cell. Carefully, he sat up and felt around near the door until his hands found a piece of bread and a warm bowl. He tasted it and found it to be some sort of fish soup. They planned to keep him alive, he thought as he wolfed down the bread and drank from the bowl. It wasn't necessarily a good sign, but at least there was a chance.

Nothing more than the arrival of food disturbed the dark quiet of his cell for the next four days and in that time he had an opportunity to review everything which had happened to him since the eve of the new year. It had been barely three weeks but it had spun his world upside down.

On what seemed to him to be Monday, the door opened and two guards entered. They said nothing but indicated that he should follow them. The time has come, he thought to himself as they headed through the long corridors under the Ducal Palace. However, instead of heading for the inquisition chambers, they traveled down corridors which began to bear resemblance to those he had walked down when he had first been a guest of Tagliapietro.

Roughly, the guards opened the door to a small chamber and shoved him inside, then bolted the door behind him. As his eyes adjusted he saw that there were a desk and two chairs in the middle of the room, but no other furniture. Stumbling back to the door, he tested it, just in case, but it was securely bolted on the outside. He brushed his hand against the rich tapestry which hung on the walls and walked the perimeter of the room, checking behind the drapes, but there was only stone, no windows or secret doors. Here and there, where there were no drapes, hung dark, disturbing paintings, representations of hell and damnation. Lazaro felt the throbbing in his head and all interest in art ceased as he returned to one of the chairs where he gladly sat, waiting.

Finally hearing the sound of footsteps in the hallway, he stood and walked halfway to the door. Tagliapietro entered, followed by Beccaria. Tagliapietro nodded to Lazaro and motioned for him to sit at one of the chairs while he took the other one. Beccaria stepped away from them and busied himself looking closely at the paintings.

Tagliapietro looked over at Beccaria for a moment, then cleared his throat and leaned toward Lazaro. "My apologies for not being able to see you until now, but it was necessary. It came to my attention that you were in the city and were visiting Signorina Zorzi. I had hoped to have this conversation with you at some more opportune time, but" — an insincere smile spread across his face — "I believe it was in your best interests that we invited you when we did."

Lazaro remained silent. He had no idea what direction the conversation would take and he was not about to provide Tagliapietro with signposts.

Tagliapietro glanced again at Beccaria but he was engrossed in a particular representation of hell as a demon's banquet where the evil ones feasted on the bodies of men and women, bodies in the full bloom of sexual development and, from what Lazaro could make out, of sexual arousal as well.

Tagliapietro caught Lazaro's eyes and began speaking. "It is difficult to find an appropriate place at which to begin this tale." He paused again and put his fingers to his lips, as if praying. "Your relationship with Signorina Zorzi is at an end."

"I don't have any desire to be with her."

Tagliapietro grinned. "Don't speak so surely of your desires. They have a way of tripping up a man when he isn't watchful. And what about your desire for revenge?"

Lazaro felt himself flush, though he couldn't tell if it was embarrassment or anger.

Tagliapietro noticed and held up his hand. "I can understand how it would be ordinary for a man who has been employed by a woman, paid in false love, and almost dispensed with permanently, to wish some revenge. But you are no ordinary man."

"I feel quite ordinary at the moment."

"To the contrary," Tagliapietro said, sitting back, "you are far from ordinary. An ordinary man would have been allowed to die in Marzia's arms. But I am convinced that you are more valuable alive than offered up as a sacrifice to that questionable goddess."

Lazaro looked around again, expecting Beccaria to be joining in the conversation, but he was still looking at the painting. There was something ominous in the assertion that Lazaro was thought valuable, because it carried with it an additional, if silent, phrase . . . "for the time being."

"He's not listening," Tagliapietro said, putting his hand on Lazaro's shoulder. "There is no room in our plans for revenge. Our justice must serve the state. And to the state, each person has a different value. We had known of her intrigues with her father, or I should say of her father's intrigues with her. That kind of '*droit du seigneur*' is always troublesome." Tagliapietro stared off in the darkness for a moment. "I wonder if part of her reaction was jealousy of her father's involvement with his mistress." He raised his hand in a gesture of dismissal. "It doesn't matter. While a father has rights over his children it should not extend to such unnatural acts. Men or women who engage in such actions are burned at the stake. I am sure Marzia thought of it, in part, as a less painful and less embarrassing execution when she arranged for the assassination of her father by Rodrigo Contarini. However, the more important result was that she would secure her family's resources, albeit through a violent takeover. Her father had been planning some business investments which in all likelihood would have failed. Marzia is better at business than her father ever was. And when the Turks entered the picture, hoping to bestill Zorzi's political influence, she had the strength of mind to negotiate. If she had not, someone else would have taken the contract and she would have been out in the cold. In this way she had secured for her company an important concession with the Turk, through a trader named Mustapha."

Lazaro did not react to the name, and Tagliapietro continued. "Rodrigo was only too happy to assist his true love, and Constantino's troublesome sister just made the entire thing a bit more convincing."

Lazaro looked up at Tagliapietro and Tagliapietro laughed. "Oh, don't misunderstand me. We can't permit patricide, at least not in this case. Given his intimate activity with his own daughter, there is some justification to the act. As well, Zorzi was not a favorite of the Secretariat. Even with his power and persuasion, he was losing ground. Not that we side with the Turk, but his attempt to involve Venice in the mess which is coalescing at Rhodes does not find favor within the Secretariat. Had we known of Marzia's plans before the event it is likely that we would have stopped her. But we were too late, even with your interference. I suppose in the end it has turned for the best."

"And Solomon?" Lazaro asked.

Tagliapietro sighed sadly but unconvincingly. "We arrested him in good faith. Unfortunately some of the *bravi* who work for the Lords of the Night were members of Contarini's club. They were able to substitute Solomon's friend for their own fallen comrade. It was unfortunate but, after all, the law would have put Solomon to death in any event. He had planned to run away with Constantino's sister, with the help of this Eli of Genoa. And this Eli had, with Solomon's assistance, been speaking with the Jews of the ghetto to find ways to assist in the overthrow of the Knights of Rhodes. For this, he would have died.

"Constantino in his anger had provided his friends with an appropriate body and another charge against Solomon. And it did fit neatly. The Jews furnished a plot which has convinced those who might have decided otherwise that we should not involve ourselves in Rhodes. For Zorzi, how do the Turks say it? 'God appeared unto him unexpectedly.' If his death came a little sooner than it might have, well" — Tagliapietro raised his hands and shrugged his shoulders like a merchant — "we all die." Tagliapietro stood and walked around the desk.

Lazaro stared at Tagliapietro.

Tagliapietro anticipated his thoughts. "You find it hard to believe?" he asked. "The truth is always so simple, Lazaro. It revealed itself to you, and finally you embraced it. We often prefer an elaborate lie." Tagliapietro walked back behind his desk and sat down. "But to your good fortune, Beccaria likes things to be a little more complicated. I would have believed that you were deeply involved in this from early on in the tale. But Beccaria was curious."

Lazaro saw Tagliapietro look in Beccaria's direction, but he was still examining the paintings.

"There was something which did not appear neat to him, and so he investigated. I think what first convinced me of your innocence were his reports of your belief that Solomon was innocent."

Tagliapietro held up his hand in anticipation of some comment from Lazaro, and though Lazaro had had no intention of speaking he made the beginning of a movement to speak so as to satisfy Tagliapietro and encourage him to continue.

"You weren't that easy to follow or to read, but we found enough information to convince us that we should investigate further. The wounding of Zanipolo, for example. He had been one of our *bravi* but we had not placed him on your trail. Why had he been following you? By the time we had enough information, Marzia had already arranged for Rodrigo to kill Solomon's sister and father, in case you had told them anything when you had spoken with them. They were then to kill you. It was at that point that the tables turned. Still, things moved a little more quickly than we had anticipated and so you have Beccaria to thank for your life."

Lazaro heard Beccaria clear his throat and when he turned, the Master of the Assassins was leaning against the wall, listening and smiling. Lazaro couldn't decide whether the smile was friendly or threatening.

"There is danger in emotion or devotion," Tagliapietro continued after a brief pause. "It displays your vulnerability. In the heat of the moment we often do things we regret later. Think of you and poor Rodrigo. I realize that Marzia encouraged you, but you could have chosen a better time and place. Defending an enemy of the state, the family of Solomon. Who would believe anything you might say with that known? Your life would be worth nothing if the news of Rodrigo's murder is allowed to circulate. There are enough Barbarians who would gladly kill you to rid themselves of their banishment. Then, of course, there's Rodrigo's family. Not only *Case Grandi* but *Apostoli*, his is one of the oldest families in Venice, quite large, and male."

"What do you want?" Lazaro asked. "Why tell me this?"

"The truth makes us strong, Lazaro," Tagliapietro said as he leaned forward across the desk. "The truth makes us free. Free to act in our best interests and strong enough to succeed. You have skills which are valuable to us. You have a future here."

The Secretary paused and the silence hummed in Lazaro's ears.

"I want you to do only what you have already done. From time to time there will be an assignment, nothing too difficult. You will do it quickly, quietly, professionally."

"And if I refuse?"

"I haven't taken away your free will. But choices have a cost." Tagliapietro laughed. "Why would you? I didn't get you into this mess, you did it to yourself. You wove webs around yourself and now I have simply brought this to your attention. I am a friend to you. Beccaria convinced me that you had the touch. In fact, at one point we were contemplating doing away with Rodrigo, and he suggested you for the job."

"Marzia just beat you to it," Lazaro said with a grin.

Tagliapietro laughed. "She beat us all. We would have paid you well to kill Rodrigo. What did you get from her?"

Lazaro said nothing.

Tagliapietro smiled and clapped his hand on Lazaro's shoulder. "The fire of youth's passions should have burned out of you by now. It's a liability in your line of work."

Lazaro remained silent. He realized now she had not cast that spell over him — he had done it to himself. But she had seen it and had used it. She had used him, defeated him. And to rub salt into the wound, her success was not dependent on his defeat in particular. It could have been just about anyone. There was an urge deep within him to seek her out, to . . . But she had simply taken advantage of a business opportunity. And now, foremost on his mind, was a way to make sure he did nothing to upset his chances to continue with Fugger's interests, and to do that he had to remain alive. Above all, he had no interest in becoming part of the nether world of Beccaria and his assassins. "What will happen to Marzia?"

Tagliapietro smiled. "Part of the reason we held you for this length of time was to allow us the opportunity to rid ourselves of the *bravi* who were disloyal and to arrange for Marzia to leave Venice." Tagliapietro shrugged. "She must be punished, but we have taken into account the mitigating circumstances. Her mother is unlikely to recover her senses and so we have made Marzia her nurse, to care for her in a convent in Rome. As there are no other members of the immediate family, the Secretariat has taken over the Zorzi property and will administer it in trust. However," Tagliapietro said with a smile which was unsettling, "I believe her stay in that city will be eternal."

Lazaro thought it best to remain silent, but he saw the method in the Secretariat's actions. With one fell swoop they had taken over a major financial concern and dispensed a form of justice which allowed them to maintain the fiction of the assassination of Zorzi by Jews.

"I understand that you have a place to stay in Murano, with the mirrormaker Angelo," Tagliapietro said.

Lazaro nodded.

"Good. We've gathered some clothes for you from that inn you stayed in. Perhaps it would be best if you stayed in Murano for the next week. Understand me, your room is still there for you. You have paid for it. Just a week to let things quiet down. Not that I expect any real trouble, but we'll be watching over you."

The door opened and a guard stood there with Lazaro's weapons and a bundle of clothes. Beccaria remained leaning against the wall, but Tagliapietro walked him to the door. "We have a gondola waiting for you." Lazaro followed the guard down the hallways and out to the *riva*. He climbed into the gondola and lay back in the *felze*, taking its black into his mind.

The factory was now more useful to him than ever. Angelo had him working long hours building mirrors and when he wasn't needed at that task, he volunteered to fire the glass. Standing in front of the flame of the glory holes helped to sear his mind and he threw himself into work, trying to ignore the memories of Marzia which flared from time to time. It wasn't easy, for when he rested from his work he could feel the ache for her. And to make it more difficult, Renata intruded as well, though this was in the flesh rather than as a thought.

On the third evening Bartelemeo asked Lazaro to watch the factory between shifts as Domenico was going to accompany the other workmen to the tavern for something to eat and drink. Lazaro had no interest in the camaraderie of the tavern and was glad to remain behind. He began to gather the *punti* and blow-pipes left behind by the glassblowers, knocking piece after piece of glass to the floor where it shattered into a million small pieces like sugar powder. There was the sound of someone behind him and he turned, expecting Bartelemeo returning with some final instruction. It was Renata. Her dress was cleaner than he had seen it before, but was still far from godliness. Undone buttons revealed an admittedly enticing cleavage and the press of her bosom on the worn fabric of her bodice tugged at the remaining buttons and allowed a glimpse of the round underside of her firm, high breasts. She noticed his eyes exploring her, smiled and tried unsuccessfully to look demure. "You're working hard."

"So are you."

"I'm not working now," she said and walked, swaying her hips, to the finished glass pieces piled on a rough table to the side of the room. "Why don't you take a break?"

He glanced over at her and realized his mistake too late. She had picked up a rod of glass with a partially melted end which had formed a ridge. As his eyes caught hers she slid it into her mouth then smiled, showing the white teeth of which she was so proud. He was not close enough to see but knew that the glass would be smeared with the rouge on her lips. She raised her hand and pulled back the tangled, bleached-blonde hair which had fallen over her eyes, then pulled the rod out of her mouth with a smacking sound which, to an innocent, would resemble only the sound of a child disengaging from a stick of candy or a bare foot being pulled forcefully from muck. "No one is here. Why not?"

Lazaro paused for a moment, troubled by this parody of Marzia, aching for her. It was as if Renata were a demon sent to tempt and torture him. He turned his back and said nothing, returning to his work.

She picked up a tiny glass ball and threw it against the wall. He ignored her. She picked up a larger one and threw it. Again no response. Still another and another and another. Lazaro threw down his tools and rushed toward her, grabbing her wrists with his hands and pushing her against the wall. She banged her head against the wall and for a moment went limp. He thought she might be unconscious, but a smile crept over her face. He looked down to see that her bodice had popped open, and her breasts were exposed and pressed firmly against his chest. She began to writhe against his body as he pinned her to the wall. He felt himself go erect and she slid her right hand out from under his and into his pants.

He drew back and the rejection altered her mood dramatically.

"If I was that Zorzi bitch you'd curl up with me, wouldn't you?" She didn't wait for an answer but began straightening her clothes. "But now she's gone to the convent and you're still pining for her. Well, don't expect me to be there when you change your mind."

"Renata," he started.

Her eyes sparked and she picked up another glass ball and hurled it at him. "Don't give me any excuses. I should have let you starve in the prison." She saw the question which spread over his face. "You don't know, do you? Do you think it was that bitch who brought you the food? Not likely. And it wasn't just the bringing. I had to lie on my back for the jailer just to get it to you." She turned and started out the door then stopped. "That part at least wasn't a waste." Then she was gone, down the *calle* toward her inn.

He hadn't thought of her. In fact he had just assumed that it had been Tagliapietro who had arranged for the food but he realized now that he had been wrong. Part of him wanted to go after her, to thank her. But he knew that would be folly. It was better to leave it all as it was. That she had the information she did would have been troubling to him had it not been for the fact that some of the *bravi* employed by the Secretariat frequented both the Dancing Mouse and the tavern she worked at now. Clearly she had made valuable friendships among the assassins.

In the days which followed he saw her often, wandering about near the factories, speaking with the craftsmen, wandering off to the inn at the end of the day with the most attractive of them. And if she happened to see him glance her way, immediately she would be more friendly with her client. He wished he had been able to find the right words to thank her for what she had done for him but he knew it was better to let it be.

A part of him wanted to get a message to Fugger immediately in those first few days, in the hopes that he could get on with whatever Fugger's interests demanded and be done with Venice. Yet it was necessary to keep a low profile with the Secretariat watching him. Though the days were long, the nights were more unpleasant. His time with Angelo was a pleasant diversion. When they shared a meal or when he helped the old man try to find the formula for unbreakable glass, they would speak of the trade and its history. But in the dark quiet of his room, Marzia would return to him. In his dreams he saw her beauty and that beauty, inflated by desire, was bright enough to make it difficult for him to realize the less attractive aspects of her being. When he tried very hard he was able to see her as she really was, but he then found himself wishing he could find some way to even the score between them, permanently.

During those sleepless periods, in the little light there was, he would look over at his image in the large mirror which leaned against the wall. Though he normally avoided mirrors, especially while he worked in the factory, at night he would allow himself a longer gaze. Try as he might he could not find a way to see the image as himself. At the best of times the eyes in the mirror seemed alien, not correct for his face. At the worst, it was as if what he saw before him was a beast of the forest with its hair pulled off, in imitation of a man. But the thought he wished most to avoid was that the mirror simply spoke the truth, that he had, by his own actions, driven himself further from all that was good within him.

One image he could conjure in his mind brought him a more peaceful feeling. Toward the middle of the week he began to think more and more of Margoleit. She would come into his mind cool and clear, and he found himself wondering if she was now over her illness, if she was safe. It pleased him that she looked so little like Marzia and he imagined her to be everything Marzia was not — honest, dependable, tender. There was relief, but it would not last long and, like some avenging angel, Marzia would return.

On the eve of the first of April he found the thoughts that invaded his dark room too troublesome, and so he roused himself from near sleep and wandered along the *riva*, looking across the lagoon to the lights of the barges around Venice. He found a cool breeze and sat where he could watch the moon rise and cast its light down the center of the canal. For a while he looked over the surface, thinking of nothing in particular.

A hand tapped his shoulder. It was Angelo. "You shouldn't sit like that," he said as he tugged at Lazaro's shoulder. "You might fall in, and that water stinks like a pisspot."

Lazaro looked down at his reflection in the water. He no longer looked like some depilated beast, only like a foolish man. And the morrow was the day on which everyone celebrated the fool within them. He smiled, then stood, and he and the old man went to a tavern for a drink. Tomorrow it would be time to go to the Fondaco.

XV

After that first drink, the night stretched out, and Lazaro and Angelo talked, and drank, as they never had before. Once when Lazaro was young he had almost drowned and afterward, when he was revived, he had felt clean and new, a feeling similar to the way he felt after a battle. He felt that way as he talked with Angelo. He had sunk to the bottom, but he had come back up to the air. When dawn did arrive it seemed the cobwebs of the past weeks were cleared from his mind. The old man simply nodded when Lazaro mentioned that he would not be at the furnaces but instead had business in Venice.

As he sat in the gondola approaching the Molo, Lazaro watched the business taking place there and in the Grand Canal as if from a great distance. Not that it was foreign — it seemed to him that he had been there his whole life — but more as if everything that was

Venice was now so far away from his heart that it had diminished in importance and, oddly, in size. He thought of the bird's-eye view which Bomberg had printed from the woodcut by Barbari. Though he was deep within the sights and sounds of the Grand Canal, the entire city was spread before him. He could see the Dancing Mouse and the streets surrounding it. Not far away was Ca'Zorzi. He felt nothing and wondered why. And farther on, the ghetto. That too left him with a strange feeling, but not an empty feeling. He pulled away from that and, like an eagle searching for his daily meat, set his eyes on the Fondaco dei Tedeschi, where the gondola now stopped.

The Fondaco was crowded with German and Venetian merchants, but they paid him no attention as he made his way across the courtyard and back into the recesses of the building, to Fugger's area. The guards who lounged there, pretending not to be guards, allowed him to pass. He identified himself to the clerk who had been there when Béres had brought him to Fugger only a month before, a man named Gottfried, and passed to him a coded message he had written out in the early hours of the morning, when his sobriety had found him again. The message was clear and to the point. The assassination had been a family matter, and the Secretariat had now solidified its position of non-intervention in the affairs of Rhodes. Though Lazaro was reluctant, in the end he had decided to include some information about Marzia and his relationship with her. Still, his vanity had counseled him to present himself, not so much as the fool, but as a dutiful agent of the merchant banker, willing to subject himself to all manner of danger in the body and the heart to secure the valued information. Given the sort of knowledge Fugger probably already possessed, it didn't matter too much either way. But he knew Fugger would allow him at least this measure of face-saving.

Gottfried made no effort to ascertain the contents of the message but simply placed a drop of red wax on it and pushed it back across the table to Lazaro. Lazaro pressed into it the ring he wore on his right hand, a circled cross — he seldom even noticed this ring, given to him long ago by his mother and enlarged many times since — and shoved it back across.

The agent looked at the seal in the wax and, as if this was the sign he had been told to wait for, he signaled for Lazaro to come with him into a small room. "Fugger sent a message that when you came here I was to make clear to you that if you wished to come to him in Augsburg we would make all necessary arrangements. Do you have any plans to travel?"

Lazaro shook his head. "Just see that he gets that message as soon as possible."

"We have a courier leaving today. It'll be in his hands in five days."

As Lazaro walked back along the riva toward the Rialto Bridge, he thought of what the agent had said — Fugger would make sure that he reached Augsburg. Given his recent arrest coupled with the prohibition against travel by anyone associated with the glass industry, it was reassuring to know that the merchant prince had left him with that option. However, he knew that if Fugger had wanted him to come he would have said so. The message was clear — unless it was impossible, he was to wait in Venice.

As he walked, he caught sight of a girl turning the corner in front of him. Before he could think he was off after her. It was Margoleit, or at least it looked like her. Lazaro followed her as she turned corner after corner, kept from reaching her by the crush of people shopping in the markets of the area. He broke through a particularly thick pack of people and burst into a small *campo*, sending the pigeons off in a short noisy flight. They circled and settled almost immediately about his feet as he stood in the center of the *campo* looking down the mouths of the six *calli* which converged there. She was nowhere to be seen. The twists and turns had proved too much for him, and he had lost her, if in fact it had been her. He made his way back to the Rialto Bridge, and as he crossed it he wondered what he would have said to her if he had caught up with her. He knew he wanted to see her soon.

At the Campo Rialto he stopped and bought a piece of cheese from a vendor and sat under the arches. All around him under the arches Venetians haggled with each other in loud attempts to secure private loans. And farther along the wall some street children were engaged in an even noisier pastime. A group of them had surrounded an unfortunate beggar and were hounding him. As Lazaro watched he recognized the beggar whom they were attacking. It was the ragged, hairy man he had seen in the Piazza San Marco when he had gone there with Béres. He swallowed the cheese and went over to the crowd of children, kicking a couple in the ass and pushing the rest away. They were reluctant to leave such easy and enjoyable prey, but they soon tired of Lazaro and ran off toward the bridge to find someone else to abuse.

The ragged man, whose hair reminded Lazaro of a wolf, lay on the ground huffing and growling. Lazaro held out his hand to help him up and the man took it with a hand bandaged tightly with blue cloth. The thought raced through Lazaro's mind that this bandage might hide some repulsive disease, but he reasoned that if it was deadly it was probably too late to protect himself. The man was now sitting on his haunches in front of Lazaro, his begging bowl placed in front of him, his arms resting between his knees. He looked up at Lazaro with eyes of deep blue shining through the mane which fell about his face. A chill passed over Lazaro, as if a cloud had suddenly cooled the sun. He felt unnerved and absent-mindedly fished in his pocket for a coin to drop in the wolfman's bowl. There was a nod and grunt and that was the end of the matter. Lazaro walked back to where he had been sitting only moments before, but he had lost any desire to remain in the *campo*. He felt restless, but it was still a bit early to leave for Murano, too early even for a drink. Impulsively, he decided that he would visit Bomberg.

The printer was busy cleaning his presses after the day's run when Lazaro arrived. When Bomberg saw Lazaro he seemed nervous and signaled to him to follow into the back room where the readers worked. The only one there was Jacob ben Hayyim, a reader Lazaro had been introduced to before, and who had been working with Solomon on what Bomberg had described as a rabbinical Bible. Bomberg asked Jacob to leave them alone, and when the reader had gone he shut the door.

Lazaro smiled. "What's this all about?" He noticed that Bomberg didn't return his smile.

"They're still watching this place," he said, without having to say who *they* were. "I don't want any more trouble."

Lazaro felt somehow responsible and stumbled toward an apology but Bomberg interrupted him. "No, I don't mean it that way. I'm glad you came by. I was looking for you, but I just want to be careful."

"At least they've given you your readers. Did they force you to pay much?"

"Not really. It was reasonable," Bomberg answered absent-mindedly, listening for a moment to the muted sound of Jacob reading aloud in the next room. Then he seemed to relax. "You remember Solomon's sister, Margoleit?"

Lazaro nodded.

"Well, she wants to thank you for what you did for her. She was very sick for a few days, but somehow your ministrations helped get her over whatever it was. At least she believes that. Except for her faith I would have counseled her to thank St. Roch instead of you. Anyway, she sent a message asking me to contact you but there's been no way of reaching you without alerting the Secretariat."

"Why are they watching you so closely?"

Bomberg grinned cynically. "Apart from my association with a recently deceased enemy of the state and of the faith, they see printing as a dangerous science. But it isn't just me. I'm told they're watching you very carefully as well."

"Because of Zorzi?"

"That, maybe more. I really don't know. But I don't want to get Margoleit in any deeper than she is. Can you make it to Francesca's house this evening without being seen?"

"Isn't that a bit risky?"

"No more so than anywhere else." Bomberg scratched his chest the way he always did when he was thinking. "Probably less so. I don't think the Secretariat knew you took Margoleit and her father there. If they had there would have been trouble. What do you think?"

"That depends. I take it you want me to meet Margoleit there."

"I don't want you to do anything," Bomberg said indignantly. "I told Margoleit I would try and arrange it. You're here. I'm trying to arrange a meeting."

Lazaro held up his hand. "All right. I didn't mean anything by it. It probably is as safe as anywhere else. I can be there at nine."

"Fine," Bomberg nodded. "I'll send a note with Jacob. He's honest enough not to read it. But be careful."

Lazaro moved to the door. "I will," he said as he opened it and headed out toward the street.

Bomberg reached for his arm and stopped him. "Why did you come here?"

Lazaro smiled and shrugged. "No reason, really. I was just passing by and wanted to say hello." Bomberg smiled and they parted company.

Back in the street Lazaro wondered about Margoleit wanting to see him, and about why he had come to see Bomberg. He had pretended in his mind that it had been to visit, pure and simple. But he admitted to himself now that it had been to find out about Margoleit.

The sun had set and the *calli* were dark when he ventured out of the Dancing Mouse. Renata's mother had been nowhere to be seen and her father seemed more than friendly to Lazaro, though he left him to drink in the corner by himself, pausing at the table occasionally with a flask of wine which was better than that normally served to the drinking public. Lazaro had reciprocated with a larger payment than would have normally been tossed on the table. A cool wind was blowing in from the north, chilling the night. Lazaro pulled his cape about his neck and looped the hood over his head. It was time for him to start for Francesca's house, and, after the customary checking at a couple of corners to see that he was not being followed, he began to walk in the direction of her neighborhood.

However, his decision had been taken too soon. It became apparent to him, after about five minutes of walking, that he was being followed, and it was as apparent that it was the Secretariat. Changing his course gradually, he made instead for the Zorzi home. Pausing outside the gates he looked into the deserted house. There was a lamp in the first floor, a guard left by the Secretariat, but all else was in darkness. And from the one lamp he could see that the house had been emptied. The Secretariat had allowed Marzia to take her family's furniture with her to Rome. Lazaro looked up to the *altana* and wondered if the nuns would allow her to bleach her hair on the rooftop of the convent.

He heard the sound of feet scuffing the paving stones to either side of him, but did not reach for his sword. Their capes and masks identified them as Beccaria's men and so he stood his ground but left his hands to dangle at his side. He could hear steps behind him and turned slowly to see Beccaria, at least two sword lengths away from him.

"A minute of your time, Mirrormaker, if you please," Beccaria said tauntingly, and beckoned with his gloved hand. Lazaro walked slowly over to him, sensing that the other two men were very attentive, watching for the slightest movement. Beccaria was on guard. It was enough to make Lazaro cocky. Beccaria walked with Lazaro to a nearby doorway and leaned against one side of it. Lazaro took the other post. "Taking the evening air?" he asked, and saw a grin spread over the lower half of Beccaria's face.

"I take what pleases me," Beccaria answered.

"You take the leads I give you," Lazaro said, then looked back at the two *bravi*. "Bodyguards?" When he looked back at Beccaria the smile was gone.

"Don't push it, Mirrormaker. You were at the German's Fondaco today. There are some who suggest you might be considering a trip abroad."

Lazaro burped and chuckled at the unexpected sound. He pulled his hand across his face in feigned boredom. "Choice is something I value highly. I would recall if somehow I had lost it."

There was a grinding of teeth, or so it seemed, before Beccaria spoke. "The Secretariat will say when you may leave Venice and they will not give you permission until I am ready to release you. You're mine."

"I think you have me confused with someone else, someone who would listen to you."

Beccaria pulled out a metal stiletto, stepped across the doorway and held it tight against Lazaro's throat. "You should be more respectful in the manner of your speech. I can take your life or I can give you employment. Frankly you are alive now only because you are more valuable to me alive than dead."

Lazaro smiled. "You shouldn't give away your secrets. When you do that you lose power." He put his hand under Beccaria's and began to push the blade into his throat. He saw Beccaria's eyes widen as the blade pushed through the skin on his throat and a drop of blood ran down the blade. The wine in his system dulled the pain which he knew was there. He felt Beccaria's arm stiffen and try to pull the blade out, but Lazaro kept the pressure up. He could feel the point of the razor-sharp blade push against the bottom of his tongue. Still he would not release Beccaria's hand.

And then, as quickly as he had started it, he finished it. He allowed Beccaria to remove the blade. Beccaria stepped back and stood silent, the bloodied blade in his hand.

Lazaro smiled at Beccaria, then walked away into the night. He was cautious, more cautious, it seemed, than he had ever been before. Four times he doubled back on his trail to watch for Beccaria's men, or the man himself, but each time there was no one there. With the nose of a wolf they would have had no difficulty in following him — the handkerchief which he held to his throat was quite bloody by now, and he knew that he should soon find his way to Francesca's and treat the wound which he had inflicted on himself. But he took Bomberg's warning seriously — the pain in his neck reminded him that he should. Beccaria would not take kindly to him meeting with Margoleit. And he might take it out on her.

Finally he felt secure, and so, knowing that he was about an hour late, he made his way to Francesca's. He knew that Margoleit would still be there: the gates to the ghetto would now be closed; she would stay at Francesca's for the night. He slipped around to the back of the house and made his way along the narrow *riva* to the door he had carried Mordechai through on Martedi Grasso. With one last pause to listen for any sounds from inside the house which might indicate danger, he knocked. He waited. There was no reply. He knocked a second time. There was a rustle within. He waited. The door opened as far as the safety chain would allow it and the light of a lantern illumined his face. Francesca's face was pressed up to the door opening.

"Just a minute," she said, then closed the door again.

He heard more scuffling and then the door opened again. There was no light in the room as he stepped in. The hair on the back of his neck wavered, ready to stand on end should danger present itself. It did not.

When the door was closed he heard Francesca beside him say, "All right." Across the room the lantern was turned up and above it the light slowly revealed the face of Margoleit.

He was reminded of that first day he had seen her, in the court when Solomon's fate had been decided: alabaster skin framed in dark tresses which fell to her shoulder, a small cap on her head, lips red not from rouge but from life, and eyes which drew him in. He watched as her eyes fell on the bloody handkerchief which he held to his throat, heard her tell Francesca to get some water, saw her cross the floor to him and touch his hands gently, exploring the wound. He felt no pain.

"How did this happen?" she asked, as she bathed the wound in water and wiped it gently with a piece of soft cloth.

He hesitated and looked around, but couldn't see Francesca anywhere.

Margoleit pulled his face back. "How?"

Lazaro looked into Margoleit's eyes and had trouble focusing. He wasn't sure if it was the wine or her proximity. He shrugged and smiled. "I was making a point."

She shook her head. "The point almost made you" was all she said as she poured alcohol on the wound. Lazaro winced and said "Ouch" in such a surprised but earnest fashion that Margoleit began to laugh, dropping the cloth and falling back on a small sofa behind her. Lazaro turned to face her. "It hurts."

Margoleit had trouble stopping her laughter. "Such a brave man," she said between chuckles as she wiped her eyes. She leaned forward and took the cloth from him then tied a fresh one over the wound. "There."

Francesca left them alone for the evening and, after the mutual thanks and condolences were passed, they spent a pleasant night discussing one thousand and one topics all equally capable of being considered meaningful and meaningless, all the while keeping the small fire burning and watching each other closely. During the conversation, he felt the effects of the wine and the exchange with Beccaria diminish to the point of unimportance. Though he had no desire to do so, he found himself comparing Marzia with Margoleit. With Marzia, he had been drawn by the lust which surfaced quickly between them, and he had felt satisfied with it, like some sweet dessert which put an end to hunger, for the moment. But this was so different from anything he had experienced before that he was comforted. He felt drawn to Margoleit now in a way he had never felt before: it was most pleasant to listen and watch her as she spoke. Too often he had not taken the time to listen to a woman speak. Too often when there had been speaking it had been of no consequence. And far too often there had been no intention of speaking.

Yet this conversation drew him in. Solomon had often said that it was his sister and not him who his father considered to be the scholar of the family. And as he talked with her, Lazaro saw what Solomon had meant.

Still, a part of him sat apart, watching, cautious, not believing that he had truly found a pearl in the foul oyster which Venice could often be.

First light was nearly upon them before they realized how late it was. They had been able to avoid the discomfort which sometimes accompanied the road to intimacy and found it almost embarrassingly easy to agree that they would meet again in a week's time.

The door shut and he stood for a moment amid the swirls of fog rising from the *rio.* He could hear only the sounds of water lapping against the stones and the gondolas. Somewhere far off in the fog a dog barked, hesitated, then barked again. He wondered if the fog would trip him up and land him in the *rio* but the sounds were his guide. And from somewhere suddenly there was the sound of a woman humming. Lazaro paused for a moment, wondering whether she was at hand or had been transported so near by the fog, then ducked to stay within the fog's cloak and hurried off to find a gondola to Murano. As he waited at the end of the Fondamenta dei Mendicanti for a gondola, he saw the ragged man, the wolfman, sitting with his back to a building staring out into the fog which drifted in from the Laguna Morte. He wondered if this had been the dog he had heard barking.

The night shift was finishing its work when he arrived at the factory, and the next shift was gathering, trading stories and admiring some of the better pieces which had been crafted in the night. Lazaro nodded to the workmen then slipped up the back stairs. Angelo was sitting in the middle of his study, surrounded by books and paper. At first he seemed asleep, but then it became clear that he was deep in thought.

Lazaro noticed a bowl of fruit by the brazier, picked out a pomegranate, and began to eat. The sound of his eating broke Angelo's trance. "You're back early," he said, shutting the book resting on his lap.

"There were a few things I had to attend to and it took longer than I thought."

"Thought." The old man smiled. "I think your brains have slipped below your belt."

Lazaro sat down beside the old man and shook his head. "No, nothing like that. Business."

"The German, then."

Lazaro nodded as he worked the pomegranate seeds around his mouth. "And you" — he tilted his head at the books opened and strewn about the room — "the glass which can't be broken?"

"The secret which can't be broken." Angelo stood and opened the window to look out over the water. "I know it's there. But no recent alchemical work can come close to it. There is some special blend of metals which allows their properties to meld in just the right way." He turned back to Lazaro. "It's there, all right. And if I could live forever, I'd eventually find it. The number of combinations is much closer to infinity than my lifespan."

"And staying here doesn't make it much better. If there were a place for you, where you would be given everything you need without care of expense, would you go there to work?"

"Would that be in Heaven or Germany?" Angelo looked out again over the water. "I don't know if I could. For either place. Not because of the Secretariat. You'd find a way for that, I'm sure. But this is where I work. I know my furnaces well. I know how the air affects my chemicals. And the sand is wonderful. But even if all that could be taken care of in some other place, and forgetting for a moment the weather, I don't know if my eyes could adjust to some other place. It's the water and, of course, the light. For most people one place can be just about like any other. It's harder for a Venetian."

Lazaro pulled off his boots and stretched out on the cot which Angelo kept in the study, and before he was aware of what was happening he was moving quickly toward sleep, guided by a comfort he had not felt in some time.

XVI

The next week passed quickly due to the pace of work being carried out at Angelo's factory. Angelo had decreed that there was no value in Lazaro spending any more time in front of the furnaces and instead had him delivering goods to Malatesta's shop in the Piazza and negotiating for the best price. This allowed Lazaro good reason to wander through the Mercerie and the Rialto Market, watching the Fondaco for signs of Fugger. It also allowed him to watch for Margoleit, in the hope that he might see her sooner than in a week's time.

The trips also provided Lazaro with diversion. Beccaria had pulled back somewhat and had assigned less experienced *bravi* to the task of following him. Entertainment consisted of losing the *bravi* in a crowd, then turning the tables and following them as they searched high and low for some sign of their assignment. However, by the end of the week he had tired of everything, even Malatesta's wine and conversation.

As he stood in a shop on the Mercerie on Tuesday evening and saw Margoleit walk past on her way to Francesca's, he felt something within him that he had feared; he wanted desperately to be with her. He spent an hour moving from shop to shop, trying to find some small gift for her, in the end deciding on nothing, and then another hour walking through the city to make sure he wouldn't be followed to Francesca's house, and all the while he could think of nothing but Margoleit.

After Francesca had left them alone and they sat in the dark room, lit only by the red glow of the brazier, watching the lights along the *rio* disappear one by one as a heavy fog rolled into the city, Lazaro could tell that Margoleit was feeling the same. Although their conversations ranged from an exchange Margoleit had had with a cloth merchant to the flavor of the cheese Francesca had left for them, it was clear there were more private things which they wished to talk about but could find no way to begin.

"Will we meet again?" he finally asked, feeling immediately as if a fever had gripped him.

Margoleit hesitated and blushed. "I don't know. Do you want to?"

"I enjoy being with you."

"And I enjoy being with you. But . . ."

"But I am a Christian."

Margoleit laughed. "Well, to hear your exploits, your membership is technical at best."

"Technical," Lazaro said, smiling. "And are you as technical a Jew?"

Her face went blank, not from surprise but from deep thought. "That is less possible, but right now I'm not sure of anything. Except that I want to see you again."

Lazaro leaned closer to her and she tilted her head back. There was a subtle fragrance which filled his head with images of a fresh stream and flowers. It began as a touching of lips. Tender at first, it became more pronounced and then rapidly escalated into a kiss far sweeter than anything he had imagined, though it reminded him he had been imagining this. And that memory in turn made him want to kiss her even more. He felt her hands pull at his tunic and he moved his right hand to her side and cupped it over her breast, firm and warm through her clothing.

Suddenly she pushed him away.

Lazaro sat up. "I'm sorry. I thought . . ." There was an uncomfortable silence. Margoleit sat straight-backed. Lazaro thought of touching her shoulder, but he held back. "Let's go out for a walk," he said finally.

Margoleit didn't look at him. "Where could we go?"

"There's a place," Lazaro said and she looked at him. "It's not far from here. We can wear masks."

"But Carnevale is over," she said, though it seemed like a question.

"Carnevale is never over at this place."

It seemed to take a long time, because they went not by gondola but on foot through narrow, twisting *calli* and the fog altered all dimensions. But before too long they arrived at Maddelena's. She was an aged courtesan, and though her beauty had fled, and she had trouble walking due to her age, her house was one of the warmest houses among the less monied of Venice. Lazaro and Margoleit had donned masks which they had found at Francesca's, he the sun and she the moon. These were popular masks among those who were enjoying themselves at Maddelena's, and no one noticed that two more had arrived. There was much wine and music, Maddelena said to them as they entered. Her hair was a brighter red than Lazaro remembered, but the blue mud caked about her eyes was still the same. They paid a fair price and she kissed Lazaro on the masked cheek and then threw open the curtains and led them into the main room, setting them free to wander through the old rambling *casa*, enjoying themselves. The masks and those masked about them allowed Lazaro and Margoleit to enter a different universe, one in which they did not have to concern themselves with the differences which had separated them. Instead they danced, flirted, wandered about the rooms and engaged in ridiculous conversations with people they did not know, all the while watching each other.

There was something about Margoleit as she wandered through the smoky room, her long dark hair hanging on both sides of her moon face, which drew Lazaro in. It was more than her beauty, more than her graceful manner. It was as if through the mask he could see her smile.

Three hours later they took a gondola back to Francesca's, and, as she had not yet returned, they let themselves in and stumbled up the stairs into the room which appeared to be set aside for them. Lazaro opened the shutters and let the fog roll into the room. The brazier was still burning and it set the mist aglow with a ruddy hue. He and Margoleit stood in the center of the room in the swirls, and though they left their masks on, they removed their clothing and made love.

Lazaro awoke with a start. His mask was on his chest and Margoleit sat on the edge of the bed, her dark hair tapering down the center of her bare back. On the table beside the desk lay her discarded mask. Without a sound he pulled himself closer to her, then held out his hand and stroked her shoulder. The touch startled her and she tried to stand, but he pulled her back to sit on the bed.

"Have you been awake long?" he asked.

"I have to go," she said in a distant voice.

Though the wine still had a hold on him, it was clear that something was wrong. "I'm sorry if . . ." he began.

Her eyes flashed with the light from the brazier. "Don't apologize. Don't say anything." She paused and all he could hear was their breathing and the sound of the water lapping against the sides of the *rio*. "It's just that this shouldn't have happened." She stood and gathered her clothes from the floor.

Lazaro tried to speak, but she shook her head and reached out to put her hand over his mouth, then sat beside him. "I wanted it too. Very much." She was silent for a moment, then leaned over, kissed him, and fell back on the bed with him.

It was noon before they took leave of each other, promising again to meet in a week.

The weather grew warmer and with the heat came a thick moist carpet of air which hung over the islands, making even breathing a chore. Each day Lazaro was in Venice conducting business on Angelo's behalf and watching for a sign of Fugger. The sign came without premonition on the day before he was to meet with Margoleit. In the early hours of Monday morning he and an assistant had arrived at the Molo and while the assistant was unloading their wares, Lazaro strolled over to the column topped by the winged Lion of San Marco. He leaned there in the warm morning sun watching the business activities in the Piazza. Over by the steps of the Ducal Palace he noticed the wolfman and was ready to wave hello when a beggar in black bumped into him, nearly causing him to fall. As the beggar stepped back and tried to offer apologies, Lazaro made a sign with his hand to dismiss him, but the beggar leaned closer. "Fugger wants you," he mumbled, then lurched away into the crowd.

Lazaro wasn't sure at first what he had heard. But when he let it sound again in his head it was clear — "Fugger wants you." The old banker had strange ways of passing messages, but as Lazaro walked over to Malatesta's shop he realized that this was probably the safest way. The beggar must have been one of Fugger's men, but as a beggar would have gone unnoticed in the morning market crowds. When he had finished his business with Malatesta, Lazaro sent his assistant back to Angelo with the details of the arrangements he had negotiated and went on through the Mercerie, as he did most days. With careful nonchalance, he made his way across to the Campo Rialto, engaged in some business there as well, then on his way back, stopped at the Fondaco and identified himself to Fugger's clerk, who acted as if he had expected him. The banker was definitely back in town.

As Lazaro waited in the dark room at the Fondaco, he thought of Fugger's office and counting houses in Augsburg. Fugger *was* Augsburg, from his control over commerce to his Fuggerei, retirement houses built for the use of his retired workers. But it was Fugger's office which stuck in Lazaro's memory. The room spoke of power, from the gold-leafed carvings to the massive table topped with marble and supported by four black lions resting on the skin of what must have been a giant of a lion. By contrast, this office was poor, but therein lay the deception.

The wait grew long and Lazaro bored. As he sat he noticed a small curtained archway leading out of the office, something he hadn't noticed on his earlier visits. Pushing the curtain aside, he came upon a small room lined with shelves of books. There were as many different titles as there had been at Bomberg's but the selection was quite different: more accounts of travels, more histories, and fewer volumes which covered religious subjects. And there was another thing. It was clear to Lazaro that this was a collection, an investment. Fugger, he was sure, would have read these volumes from time to time. In fact there was some evidence that they had been fingered in a way which suggested actual reading rather than proprietary fondling. But in the end they were possessions to be collected, an investment which was sure to appreciate in value.

The footsteps coming down the hall had barely registered in Lazaro's mind, but when the doors opened and Fugger entered he stepped out through the curtains quickly.

"Looking for something to read?" Fugger asked with a smile. He dismissed his bodyguard, locked the door, and walked past Lazaro to take his seat behind the desk. "Lazaro" — he waved with his hand like an old friend, as he slid his carved chair up to the desk — "come closer."

Lazaro pulled the heavy chair closer to the desk, then sank back into its soft velvet upholstery and looked at Fugger's desk. It was covered with reports written in a variety of styles and bearing differing evidence of great distance and importance. Some of the papers had drawings of strange plants, others had painstakingly drawn maps.

"I like to keep track of my holdings," Fugger said as he noticed Lazaro's glance. "The world is a changing place and information is the keystone of my empire. Take a look at this." He pulled out a sheaf of paper with many drawings on it, some of plants, some of animals, and others of people. "The new world which the Spanish and the Portuguese are conquering is filled with wonders — animal, vegetable, and mineral — and ours for the taking, especially the mineral. And if the Church wants them, there are millions of souls, though it seems easier to dispatch them to the afterlife than to convert them." He chuckled and Lazaro saw that he pointed to columns of figures indicating deaths. He looked up and noticed Lazaro's surprise. "Oh, don't credit the Castillians with that much ferocity. Most of these deaths are from simple diseases which apparently were unknown before our arrival. The natives often die before the Castillians even reach their villages — condemned to everlasting damnation when they're so close to salvation at the hands of the holy fathers." Fugger shook his head and laughed again. "I wish I could see that world but I shall never go there. That is where a young man would go to make his fortune. But my businesses and my emperor need me here." Fugger smiled again and Lazaro saw those teeth which always bothered him. He wondered for a moment why a man as rich as Fugger could not do something to make his teeth at least appear more attractive and healthy. But then, he thought, a man as rich as Fugger didn't really need to care.

Fugger closed his books and pushed them to the side. "When I heard this business with Marzia and that you had been taken by the Secretariat again, I was quite worried. You understand I could do nothing. The Secretariat would have been too suspicious."

Lazaro nodded.

"But it's been long enough and the matter with Marzia is closed, I take it? So you're ready for a trip?"

Again Lazaro nodded. "A change of scenery would be nice."

"Good, good. Crete first and then, God willing, Rhodes." Fugger held up his hand in the pretense of holding back comment. "And I'm pretty sure God is willing. I know it isn't the best time for idle travels in those parts, but it will be profitable."

"For me or you?"

Fugger narrowed his eyes. "That's a stupid question. For me, of course, but then, have I ever been unkind to you?"

Lazaro only grinned. "I take it now is the time for you to deliver Tadini to the Grand Master in Rhodes. Are Béres and Vom Scheidt to be involved?"

"Most certainly, but you meet up with them later," Fugger said, smiling broadly and moving his papers about until he found the one he was looking for. Like the rest, it was a table of numbers. He paused over it for a moment, then sat back in his chair and opened his coat. "I need Béres and that German of his. You deliver Tadini, they will assist. They will remove my resources from Rhodes, you will assist."

"Will the Grand Master be happy to see that you are deserting him in his hour of need?"

"That is where your assistance is most necessary. There are things he needs more than jewels in his treasury. Suleiman is already massing his troops and he will be moving against Rhodes in the near future. The Grand Master knows Tadini is worth everything I will take out. As you confirmed, the Governor of Crete has been ordered by the Signoria to keep him on the island and improve the fortifications there. They don't want to risk the wrath of Suleiman. They know if the Turk attacked their holdings they could expect no assistance from the rest of Europe."

"But you could just snatch him," Lazaro said, wondering if Fugger already had tried and failed and so needed him.

"Maybe I could, but I need him to be a willing partner in the great battle facing the Knights. I know Tadini values his friendship with you. Comrades-in-arms have ways of convincing people to embark on quests, no matter how foolhardy. And there will be honors for him, admittance to the Order, and money as well, as much as is necessary."

Lazaro nodded. "He's the best, especially with sieges — he proved that at Brescia. But I doubt it will save Rhodes."

"I know it won't," Fugger agreed. "I think De L'Isle Adam knows it too. He won't admit it, he can't. The Knights can't just give up. And who knows, maybe God will decide to be on their side. But unless he has someone of Tadini's stature, he'll have one hell of a time keeping his mercenaries and the Rhodians. He's paying for hope. And the deal is good. I provide Tadini, further provisions during the siege, and as many troops as can be mustered."

"And in return you take out your goods."

"Some as payment, some as collateral against the day when the Knights may have to relocate."

"And Charles?"

"You do have a good memory. Charles will find his portion taken by the Turks. Should they be successful," Fugger was quick to add. "And by the first of next year he will owe me over four hundred thousand florins."

"But isn't Charles bringing in enough gold and silver from New Spain?"

Fugger's eyes narrowed to slits. "Questions, when answered, can become chains." Then he smiled. "But perhaps you should know the stakes. He's bringing in lots of gold and silver, but that will just push prices up. He will need even more gold and silver, and the financial expertise which my agents can offer. Within a year I will be able to press him for the quicksilver mines of Almaden."

"Why not take the gold mines?"

"Don't you remember anything my cousin Sigismund taught you?"

Lazaro remembered working with Fugger's cousin in Schwaz. There had been a great concern with the sickness experienced by the mercury miners in the Tyrol and Sigismund had hired Lazaro, on Jakob's recommendation, to work as an assistant to the company doctor, Paracelsus. Good workers were valuable, but mercury was more valuable. "Charles will need the mercury for refining the gold and silver."

Fugger smiled. "Exactly. Oh, I'll take gold and silver, but I want all the quicksilver as well."

"All?"

Fugger's eyes again narrowed to slits, and he bowed his head in mock humility.

"Quite complicated," Lazaro said with a smile.

"And fragile as fine glass. I didn't want Tadini going until it could be to my benefit. If Zorzi had convinced the Signoria to assist Rhodes, that would have been my downfall. Had Tadini not been ordered to stay away, I would have had no bargaining power."

"Nor would I," Lazaro mumbled.

Fugger grinned broadly and held out his hands across the desk toward Lazaro like a loving uncle. "Have I ever been unkind to you? There will be a great deal of money for you, but it will mean remaining in Rhodes during the siege, at least until I get my resources out."

Lazaro was silent longer than he had wanted to be. For many reasons it was the right time to leave Venice. Remaining here meant death. But then leaving meant the loss of Margoleit, and Angelo, unless they were willing to leave. "I have a price which involves more than money."

Fugger clutched his heart in mock concern. "I'm not sure I want to hear of things unnatural. I am an old man and set in my ways."

Lazaro leaned forward. "You remember my interest in glass? Well, there is an old mirrormaker, a master, Angelo . . ."

Fugger shrugged his shoulders and pouted. "I don't really need a mirrormaker, and with the profits from this job, you won't really need the extra money. But, if you want . . ."

"No. He's not well — mercury — like your miners." Fugger nodded knowingly as Lazaro continued. "I want you to give him a place in your Fuggerei, but with a factory."

"If he will leave, and if you can get him out alive" — and it was clear that Fugger felt the odds would be in his own favor — "I will provide him with a place in the house and with a pension. And what about the Jew?"

It didn't really surprise Lazaro. He should have anticipated that Fugger's spies would have been watching him. But he realized as well the danger which this implied. Not just that the Secretariat's spies might be as knowledgeable as Fugger's, but that Fugger now had something which he could use to control Lazaro. And given the stakes, Fugger would not let anything stand in his way. For the moment there was nothing he could do but continue. "You haven't lost your touch," he said with a smile. "If she is willing to come along, I would hope for your help in finding a safe place for us."

"I'll do what I can. I can make arrangements for her to stay in Crete while you are in Rhodes. But I will only guarantee her protection while you remain in my service. And when our business is done, I'm sure we can make suitable arrangements." Fugger stared into Lazaro's eyes for a moment, then nodded and held out his hand.

Lazaro stood and shook. "Then it's a deal."

Fugger explained that he would need Lazaro with him the rest of the day and most of the next, in order to review the accounts with which Lazaro would be dealing. Calling in his bookkeeper, Fugger began immediately, reviewing with Lazaro lists upon lists of transactions which, as Fugger's bookkeeper continued to explain, related to Fugger's holdings currently in the hands of the Knights. Lazaro had been enthralled by the mysteries which he had experienced during his study of alchemy but he had never expected bookkeeping to hold such a power. It did. The finances of the Fugger empire were tied to transactions in a number of commodities but, more important, to risk. Fugger's capital had been invested in a variety of projects, some of which showed profit immediately, others which seemed to fail as quickly, and many which demonstrated a gradual but steady profit.

Fugger made it clear that he viewed Lazaro as an investment. "If you survive Rhodes, the training I am giving you will make you very valuable indeed, at least to me. And if you do not succeed, well, the magic of double-entry bookkeeping is that a venture is no longer a singular enterprise. These sheets of figures allow us to look at the larger picture. If there is a God," Fugger said, baring his brown teeth and doffing his furred skullcap in mock humility, "his account books would not be unlike these."

However, in order to allow Lazaro to understand fully, they examined related documents as well, especially reports from company agents stationed in various trade centers. The reports dealt not only with Fugger's business concerns but with the climate, political and otherwise, possible new resources or products to export or import, trends which might be important. Of the highest concern were two items: the trade routes being built up by the Atlantic nations and the effect of Suleiman on trade in the Mediterranean and overland to the east.

The schooling ended at sunset on Tuesday. As Fugger intended to leave Venice the next day to return to Augsburg, they reviewed the arrangements for Lazaro's trip to Crete and Rhodes. Fugger sorted through his maps until he found one of the Dalmatian coast. "I'll get word to Béres and he'll meet you in western Hungary, along the trade route to Belgrade and the lower Danube," he said, pointing with his stubby finger to an area marked with mountains. "The Secretariat has too much control over the shipping from Venice so you'll have to take your ship on the other side of the Gulf. But you'll have to travel with caution. I do not want them to notice you are gone until your trail is cold, but once you get to the other side of the Gulf you run the risk of meeting with Turkish skirmishers and that wouldn't be pleasant."

Lazaro nodded. "I won't need the map. I've been along that route before."

"Good," Fugger said, rolling the map and pushing it into a satchel. "The less for the Secretariat to discover the better."

"When do I go?" Lazaro asked.

"After Easter certainly, but before Pentecost. There are still some things I have to arrange. Yes, unless you hear from me, you should leave in six weeks. The travel arrangements are up to you, though if you need anything you can contact my agent here. I'll get word to Béres," Fugger said, looking at a calendar, "and have him there from about the thirtieth of May until the end of the first week in June. But until you leave I want you to be a model Venetian and do nothing to interest the Secretariat. This deal has been a long time in the making and I want as few variables as possible."

After appropriate circumnavigations of the center of the city, and stops in a few taverns just for safe measure, Lazaro made his way to

Francesca's. Under cover of darkness he approached the door by the *rio*, waiting and listening for a moment, then knocked and was admitted. Francesca was busying herself to leave and pointed to the stairs leading to the second floor. "Margoleit is up there," she said with a smile, then exited the way Lazaro had entered, though with less stealth.

Opening the door to the room where they had slept before, he saw her sitting by the window, looking out over the dark rooftops of the city. There was a moment when her eyes were clouded, or so it seemed to him, like the moment just before a new log, superheated on the coals, bursts into flame, and then the hesitation passed and her face opened in a smile. She ran to meet him in the center of the room and they embraced, kissing long. The weight of the week's absence was upon both of them and the gentle caresses only fueled the fire. It was not long before their emotions, encouraged by the wine from the table by the window, took over.

Lazaro awoke from a deep, comfortable sleep to hear Margoleit crying softly in the dark beside him. He reached out and felt for her head, then put his arm around her and stroked her wet cheeks. "Was it a dream?"

She was silent for a few moments, then he felt her nod. "A dream and more. I've had it many times since I met you. I am usually wandering in a city, though once or twice I have been in the country, calling to the ravens instead of the pigeons on the battlements, looking for my lover, calling his name, but always there is no answer. Last night I dreamed I was wandering through these streets and I wanted to call out my lover's name but I couldn't. My mouth was full of sand. I reached down to the water to wash the sand from my mouth, but the *rio* was filled with blood."

Deep within him, Lazaro felt the urge to tell her of his feelings, but the urge was so far away, like a voice in a deep cave. "I don't understand," he said, though it was close to a lie.

"When are you your true self — when you are with me or when you do your work?"

Lazaro knew that she didn't mean his work in glass.

Margoleit turned away from him, lying on her side, and he turned as well, so that they curved together, his left arm under her neck, his right hand holding her hands in front of her.

"This Thursday is the beginning of Pesach. Do you know what that means?" Her voice sounded clear as a small bell.

"Passover. This year it coincides with the anniversary of the Last Supper," Lazaro answered.

Margoleit was silent.

"The day before Good Friday," he added.

"I know that," Margoleit snapped. "But what does it mean?"

Lazaro said nothing.

"It's so different now without my family, without my father to repeat the words. Sabbath is lonely enough. And they'll put extra guards on the gates to try and keep people who worship one of us as a God from attacking us. If I could live without any thought of the past or the future, and if you could be who you are when you are with me, what you and I have would be fine," she said, her voice ringing in the black.

"What do you want to do?"

"What I want and what I must do are two different things. There is too much difference between us."

"We could leave Venice."

"Leave. And go where?"

"Germany. Hungary maybe. There are lots of places. I'm in a position to arrange it now."

"Now you're being naïve. You can't change who you are and I can't change who I am. I'm not in the market for a lover. And between you and me there could be nothing more."

Again there was a long silence.

"We could find a place."

"There is no place." The statement was final.

Lazaro lay in the dark, unable to respond. The moment stretched out, and it was then too late to say anything. Bells chimed out night hours, but they didn't break the silence which had enveloped him. He lay without moving, hoping she would say something else so that he might then speak, but she said nothing. As if he had been buried alive, Lazaro felt the darkness press down upon him, heard the hum of the black silence.

Margoleit moved in the bed beside him and then got up. He listened to her movements, then felt her sit on the edge of the bed, pausing. Her voice rang out clear. "I'm leaving now."

"Where are you going?"

"We can't do this. I'm leaving." With that she turned, pulling her shawl up over her head and before Lazaro realized what she was doing, she had run down the stairs, opened the door and gone out. He pulled on his clothes, grabbed his sword and cape, and went after her, but she had already disappeared. All he saw was what seemed to be a trail left in the fog but that too disappeared quickly. He heard her footsteps receding into the night and tried to follow but soon the city as he knew it was gone and in its place was grayness and, here and there, massive stone structures surrounded by the sounds of water close by and of people far off. He kept moving through the *calli* cautiously, every once in a while hearing footsteps and following them, but not seeing anyone. He was alone. And in that loneliness he heard deep in his mind, deep in that cave he had felt earlier, a voice which said, "The wolf is about." It wasn't clear to him if he had heard that voice or the other sound first but the other sound lasted longer. It was the howl of a lone wolf. Lazaro knew it was not possible but then he heard the howl again.

He made his way toward the ghetto, watching for signs of Margoleit, but seeing neither her nor anyone else. The fog gradually turned into a warm mist and the mist to rain. At the bridge over the Rio di Ghetto Nuovo he waited, wet, in a doorway, to see if she would pass that way. He kept watch as well on the *riva* they had used when they fled the ghetto when it was attacked by Rodrigo and his club. In the remaining hours of the night the guards patrolled in their gondola but Margoleit did not appear.

As he watched he thought of what he would say to her if she passed, but each time he tried out some logical argument, it fell sadly short of the mark. And each time he thought of something he might do, he realized there was little he could do which would change her mind. That, she could only do by herself, and he felt little hope she would do so. He had never before experienced such difficulty. In the past when he had been presented with a situation which required action, he had taken action. But here, there was no action which recommended itself. Margoleit had made it clear that she had reached a decision. To take any action in opposition to what she had said she must do would have meant that he didn't respect her decision. And yet to do nothing — that was not his way.

Marzia had been different. There, there had been passion, excitement, but over all had been a sense that they were involved in a business transaction. The feelings he had experienced when he found out what she was up to had much more to do with having been beaten at his own game than with love. Lazaro sank down on his haunches and the rain blew past in sheets, soaking him through. He didn't want to confront the reality which faced him — that he was in love with Margoleit, and that he was thus more vulnerable than he would ever choose to be. He had allowed this to happen. He wanted to turn his back on the rain and lean his head into the corner.

Margoleit had asked him if he could always be the person he was when he was with her. In truth, he wished he could be, but he doubted it. Perhaps when he had been a student, he might have been able to do just that. But he had moved so far away from that life. He had done what he had to do to survive, and he had come to enjoy it, but it had left its mark on him. And she had seen the mark.

As he watched he listened too, for the wolf, but heard no more.

With the approaching dawn he rallied himself from the damp doorway and headed back toward the Piazza to gather Angelo's funds from Malatesta. It was clear as he walked along the *riva* that the warm mist and rain had been the harbinger of the *acqua alta*. He could hear the booming of the sea on the Lido, beyond the Basin, and he could see the water in the *rii* ruffle uncomfortably and take on a curious pea-green color. As he neared Malatesta's the smaller *rii* were already beginning to overflow their banks and when he reached the glass shop he could see that the Piazza was in danger of flooding. Under the covered area on Malatesta's roof he drank a glass of wine and watched as a thin film of water began to spread from the edges of the Piazza, eventually covering the entire area. Already people had begun the task of laying out wooden walkways which would allow pedestrians to keep out of the water. But to the storekeepers this was of little value. *Acqua alta* meant that very few

Venetians would visit their shops. Malatesta just shook his head. "No business today. Let's go inside and drink some more. You don't have anywhere to go, do you?"

Lazaro shook his head and followed Malatesta inside. He wished Fugger had ordered him to leave sooner. To be in Venice and not to be with Margoleit was something he did not think he could bear.

XVII

On his return to Murano he found that Angelo had come down with a cold. With the weather turning damp and cool, Lazaro tried to convince the old man to get some rest, but his efforts were in vain. Within three days the cold had moved deeper into Angelo's chest until he was unable to go to the furnace or even to sit up and pore through his books. Lazaro decided not to make any trips to Malatesta's and sent an assistant instead. Though part of the reason was so that he might remain close to the old man, part of it was due to Margoleit. If he had gone to Venice he might have seen her, and if he had not seen her he might have gone looking for her. It was better for him to stay clear of that temptation. And he nourished some hope that Margoleit would, in the time before he left Venice, discover that she could be with him, perhaps leave with him. A thousand times he dreamed this dream in front of the glory holes. And just as many times, in the dark quiet of night, he knew it could never be.

His feelings for Margoleit didn't extinguish his thoughts of Marzia, though they refocused them. He couldn't deny the sensual pleasure he had felt with Marzia. He felt embarrassment that he had been duped by her, and he thought to himself that if he were to meet her again, he would deal with her in a businesslike fashion — though at times he felt that might mean he would kill her. But the painful irony for him was that while Margoleit had been driven away by the mark of the beast which she had seen on him, he knew that it was that mark which had attracted Marzia.

While Margoleit and Marzia plagued him in spirit, Renata plagued him in body. She made herself quite apparent but was unable to secure from Lazaro the response which she desired. Twice she walked off with junior workmen when they should have remained at the furnaces. From the look on her face it was clear that she expected him to do something — to be jealous even if he had to rely on the pretense of concern for the work of the factory — and was disappointed when he did nothing. Twice, as well, Lazaro saw *bravi* who worked for Beccaria stroll through Murano and end up visiting with Renata at her establishment. Their presence reminded Lazaro of Fugger's warning to do nothing which might attract interest from the Secretariat.

Good Friday and Easter came and went, and Passover as well, Lazaro realized. So many times before he had been less than aware of the havoc which some communities wreaked against the Jews on Good Friday, but this time he listened intently for news. There was none. Probably in part due to the attack on the ghetto a little more than a month before, there was no outburst of anger against the Jews. They celebrated their festivities in peace, and the Christians celebrated theirs.

For three weeks more, the wet weather remained, and though Angelo's chest began to clear in mid-May when the weather improved, his strength was slow to return. At the beginning of the next week Angelo seemed stronger and was able to toss off the lingering effects of the cold. It would soon be time for Lazaro to leave, and at midweek he traveled to Venice to drop in at the Fondaco, just to make sure that Fugger had sent no messages indicating a change of plan. As an excuse he took a shipment of glass to Malatesta, then strolled along the Mercerie as he had done so many times before. Gottfried was there as always and informed him that there were no messages from Fugger. However, on his way to and from the Fondaco, Margoleit was more in his mind than Fugger's dreams of a mercury monopoly. As he walked along, Lazaro thought many times that he had seen her, but it was not she. Though he was tempted to look for her near the ghetto, he forced himself to stay away. In another moment of weakness he found himself stopping by Francesca's house. It took him close to a quarter of an hour to resolve not to knock on her door and see if she had heard anything of Margoleit. Instead, he made his way back to Murano.

While the weather had warmed considerably, the rain returned that evening and continued through Friday. Lazaro busied himself preparing mirrors under Angelo's intermittent instruction. He worked in the old man's laboratory, learning how to prepare the reflective amalgam, and how to coat the various shapes of glass which had been prepared below under Bartelemeo's direction. Though he knew the danger of the mercury and had avoided it in the past, he now found something compelling about this quicksilver, this silver which was alive. While waiting for the chemical processes to complete, he used his finger to chase small reflective balls across the table top, squeeze them into a million drops and then reform them effortlessly into a seamless bead.

Marzia. She held for him the same fascination and danger as the mercury. A fatal combination of beauty and poison, she gave the appearance of life, but underneath she was cold metal. And did she not reflect all which was about her? Whatever soul she had had not been enough to protect her from the lessons which Venice had to offer. But as Lazaro looked into the mercury which was Marzia he saw himself reflected. In what way had she been that different from him? In her situation might he not have done the same thing? He didn't like what was being reflected and pushed the mercury back into its container.

As he labored, Lazaro also planned his departure from Venice. Originally he had determined to leave without any assistance from Fugger's agent, and even though he had had the opportunity the day before, he had asked for nothing. However, as he reviewed his options and set the following Thursday as his day for departure, it occurred to him that rather than try to arrange for a horse and provisions, he would simply get Gottfried to have things ready for him in Fusina. It would be simple enough to get a gondola to take him to the Terraferma.

The work with the mirrors had tired him and so, after checking in to see that Angelo was now back to studying his texts, Lazaro fell into bed early and was deep asleep the moment his head hit the pillow. As he slept he dreamed of the patter of rain, the dripping of water into a pail, the far-off sound of woodsmen chopping in tandem at a huge tree, the smashing of a mallet against a man's head.

He awoke with a start. Someone was tapping lightly at his window. As he rose from the bed it stopped. Cautiously approaching the window, he peered outside. Though he could see nothing, he was sure there was someone out on the small balcony. He reached to the bedpost where he always hung his sword. With one movement he kicked the door open and leapt naked onto the balcony. In the darkness to the side he heard a whimper of surprise and watched as a bedraggled woman stepped out of the shadow. In that uncomfortable moment he recognized that she was Margoleit, and that he stood before her in the rain without any clothes on.

For a few heartbeats they said nothing. He relaxed his sword arm and then saw that she was smiling at him.

"I suppose I should be frightened at the sight of your sword," she said, masking a giggle.

Lazaro noticed that he had an erection and quickly re-entered his room and pulled a sheet over himself. "What are you doing here?"

Margoleit hesitated at the door, her smile gone, and Lazaro realized that he must have sounded uninviting. "Please. Come in." He waited as she entered and pulled the door shut behind her. "I've missed you."

Margoleit pushed the wet black hair back from her face. "I didn't know if I should come," she said, then paused and sat on the edge of the bed. Lazaro sat beside her.

She pulled off her wet shawl and tossed it over a chair beside the bed. "I'm out of my mind for being here, that's what. I know I shouldn't be here but I wanted to see you. I came out here but I wasn't brave enough to go to the glass factory with everyone around. I saw you come here, but I thought you might come back out. It's

Sabbath and I know I should have left, but I couldn't. And I didn't want to face another Sabbath alone. I guess I waited too long — it was too late to go back — and so I waited until there was no one around and then I climbed up here. The truth is I wanted to see you." She looked up at him with large dark eyes.

"I wanted to see you too, but I thought it was best not to," Lazaro said, relaxing a bit.

"It was," she said, but didn't give Lazaro time to say anything more. "I've decided to leave Venice. There's nothing left for me here and I know that worse is coming. Every day I see the men who work for the Secretariat." She caught the look in his eye. "They haven't troubled me; they just watch, because of Solomon. But I don't want any more of it."

Lazaro put his arms around her, and they stood close in the dark for a long time, saying nothing. He listened to her breathe and felt her pulse push at his chest. Her hair felt rough but pleasing against his face, and it smelled of a small flower whose name he could not remember. When it seemed as if they had been standing there for hours he said quietly, "You can stay the night here if you wish."

Margoleit pulled her head around and faced him, her hair caught in the stubble of his beard. She said nothing but stood clear of him and slipped off her robe and undergarments. They lay down on the bed and made love as if for the first time.

He awoke clearheaded from a deep sleep. He knew that he had been dreaming but of what he had no idea. It seemed that before he even opened his eyes he knew why he was awake. He felt Margoleit by his side, deep in sleep. The window was open and Beccaria stood at the foot of his bed.

"You're a light sleeper, Lazarus," Beccaria said in a whisper, "much more easy to awaken than your namesake. I only had to think your name, and you opened your eyes."

"Don't wake her," Lazaro said as he pulled himself slowly from her embrace and slipped a robe on. He pulled the door to the balcony shut then signaled for Beccaria to follow him to the next room. As he bent over the brazier to light a taper he said, "What are you doing here?" He lit the candle, then, hearing no response, glared at Beccaria. "I asked you a question."

Beccaria stared out through the mask, so close that Lazaro, even in the dim candlelight, could see the color move in his irises. "Perhaps you have forgotten your manners. For that I will forgive you. But I will not forgive you if you forget your duty." Beccaria spit the words out and pushed Lazaro back from him so that Lazaro landed sitting on a dusty chair in the corner. Beccaria made a flourish with his cape and turned to face Lazaro. It was then Lazaro saw that he had drawn his stiletto. "I have a job for you. A certain Sanguinetti, a master glassmaker known to you, is planning to leave the guild, and Venice."

Lazaro knew the man to whom Beccaria referred. He was truly a master glassmaker, and his *cristallo* pieces were unequaled. "It will be a pity to lose his talents," Lazaro said with little respect.

Beccaria stared coldly out through the eyeholes in his mask. "Yes, a great loss. But better the world loses him than Venice loses him and France gains him. You will kill him before he leaves."

"I will not." Lazaro's answer was clear and rang out even before he had completed thinking it.

Beccaria smiled. "Oh, you will reconsider, and in the end you will agree with my reasoning, and you will accept the task which is placed before you. Of that I can assure you." Beccaria approached him and put his blade away. "And don't think of turning on me. That won't stop what has already been set in motion. You're mine. At any moment you could have been killed, except that alive you have a value. But if you turn against me you have no value to me. And I will gladly take care of you.

"How many times have you walked past a spider, let it live, and not even been conscious that you had the choice to make or that you made it. But if the spider was crawling across your arm or had just bitten you, you would make the choice and likely without much hesitation. Most men are like that for me. As long as they mind their own business they are safe. If they do not bother me I will not bother to kill them. However, you . . ." Beccaria walked to the window and opened it. The wind blew in and filled his cloak. "You bother me." He smiled again as he turned. "But I see a use in you. I see a skill which I should not waste." Beccaria paused. "You will kill for me." Beccaria picked up a fine goblet from the table.

He held it to his eyes, then felt the weight of it. "This is fine work," he said. "Yours?"

Lazaro was silent.

"I thought not," Beccaria said. "Has anyone ever told you the story of the visit of Emperor Frederick III? The Doge presented him with a fine goblet, one much more ornate than this. A real work of art. The emperor praised the workmanship, but as he examined it he let it slip from his fingers and crash to the floor, on purpose. 'This is a thing of great value,' he remarked, 'but you see,' he said, pointing at the pieces, 'as a vessel it has great value but in pieces it is worthless. Now gold vessels, even in pieces they are worth something.'"

Beccaria paused and Lazaro expected him to drop the glass but he placed it on the table instead.

He turned to Lazaro again. "He didn't understand at all. The value of our glass is that it is beautiful and fragile. People want it, want to possess it. And it does break, so much more easily than a metal vessel, which a common craftsman could repair. Our glass shatters and can never be repaired. It must be replaced, and it can only be replaced by us. And so it has so much more commercial value. Don't you agree?"

Lazaro yawned rudely. He noticed that Beccaria stifled a show of anger.

"People are like that. Marzia, for example, she is like a vessel of gold — beautiful, valuable — but if you drop her, she won't break. She sits in Rome knowing that we have beaten her and waits to do something of value for us. In time, probably once her mother dies, we will find someone who needs a wife, a wife we can control. She is beautiful and valuable, but no one could say that woman is fragile. No. But then your Jewess in there, what's her name — Margoleit?" He picked up the glass again. "She reminds me of this. She has such a great beauty, and much of that beauty lies in her fragility. You glassmakers say that the finest glass will shatter if poison is poured into it. She would surely shatter if some of my *bravi* poured their poison into her." He dropped the glass and it shattered around his feet. He looked down at the pieces then slowly looked up, smiled at Lazaro, and pulled a parchment from his cloak. "My apologies." He placed the parchment on the table and then stepped through the door and onto the balcony. "Post that notice on the door to Sanguinetti's factory once you have completed the job.

It is a warrant for his death." He stepped out onto the balcony, then turned. "And by the way, I'd stay away from the Fondaco dei Tedeschi if I were you. Fugger's not powerful enough to protect you from me. I won't allow you to leave Venice." He turned and was gone.

Lazaro listened for a few moments, but he could hear nothing. The wind rose again and spit rain into the room, some of it striking the brazier and hissing. He shut the door to the balcony and went back into his room where Margoleit lay sleeping. For a moment he sat on a low stool against the wall, then he quickly dressed and went out.

Margoleit was wakened by the door being slammed in the wind. She looked up and saw Lazaro standing by the window, dripping wet. "Where have you been?" she said, sitting up and pulling the sheets around her.

Lazaro pushed his hair from his face. "I've been making arrangements. Did you mean what you said about leaving Venice?"

Margoleit reached for the cup on the table beside the bed and took a sip of the wine. "Of course."

"Tonight?" he said with a grin.

"What's gotten into you?"

"If you're ready to go tonight, now, I have a way."

"You're going to come with me?" Margoleit asked.

"I'm ready to leave. There's nothing here for me but trouble."

"There's trouble if you leave. You know what they do with runaways from the glass industry."

Lazaro shook his head. "By the time they know I'm gone, we'll be far enough away."

"They say you can never get far enough away."

Lazaro felt a touch of impatience. "This time it's possible. I can't explain to you now, but you must trust me. Will you leave with me tonight?"

She seemed not to hesitate. "Yes."

He left her to get dressed and bundle those things which she had with her. Down the corridors he went and ended up in the old man's room. It frightened him to go in there when the old man was asleep. He was always afraid that he would find him dead. But, as always, the eyes opened. When he told him of his plan, the old man just shut his eyes.

"Are you running from what you have done tonight or because you will have to do it again if you stay?"

"What do you mean?"

"It's clear on your face. You've killed someone. I see it. You are flushed with the excitement of having taken another man's life."

"Angelo . . ."

Angelo opened his eyes. "Don't insult me with lies." He shrugged and fumbled in the pile of cloth beside his bed. "I don't mind who you kill. But be clear on what you are doing." He pulled out a small mirror. "Here. Look," he said and handed it to him.

Lazaro humored him and took the mirror in his hand. It was a finely made piece, decorated metalwork with a round, convex surface. He glanced into the mirror and saw that there was a fleck of blood on his cheek. As he quickly wiped it off with the back of his hand, he wondered if Margoleit had noticed. Then he saw what the old man meant. What he had always disliked about his reflection seemed to leap out of the mirror at him. He tried to hand it back quickly, but Angelo pushed it back toward him.

"Keep it. Let this be your conscience. The next time you are going to kill a man in cold blood, look at your face. You'll see the wolf that lurks in there."

Lazaro took the small mirror and held it for a moment. He avoided looking into it again, but stuffed it in his pocket. He hugged the old man and left without saying anything else.

He and Margoleit hurried through the dark, wet *calli* to a boat that was waiting not far from Sanguinetti's factory. Lazaro left her by the corner of a building as he went forward and woke the gondolier. There was a brief conversation and an exchange of coin and then Lazaro signaled and Margoleit came from the shadows and climbed into the gondola. It immediately moved out into the misty lagoon and was lost in the darkness.

All that anyone talked about the next day was that Sanguinetti had been found draped over his sack as he was packing it to leave Murano. While everyone agreed that it was necessary to protect the industry, as they spoke in hushed tones they were surprised that retribution had been so swift. And so precise. But when they saw the death warrant signed by Tagliapietro and the Master of the Assassins, they understood.

Part Two

XVIII

The horses were there as Sanguinetti had said they would be, rest his soul. With a small additional payment to the man who had tended the horses, and the fact that the man understood them to be heading for Trento as Sanguinetti had intended, Lazaro reasoned that they could be sure of a day's advance. If they were lucky, that would be enough. They loaded their small packages and before long they had left the sight of Venice and headed down the road to Trento until they had traveled far enough to break across country and make for the road which led north and east, toward the Friuli.

As he rode, Lazaro tried to push any guilt from his mind. That fat glassmaker would have been dead in any event, but his death gave them time to get away. He knew that the rationalization was shallow, but it covered the grave. In time, of course, the soil would sink and the grave would show. And there were so many other graves to keep it company. The old man had seen it right away. And Margoleit? Had she seen it? He looked over at her, riding beside him, alive and free from Venice. He was with her, but to achieve it he had once again been the kind of man she would not want him to be.

By now Beccaria would know that he was gone and that Margoleit had come with him. The Secretariat would not be too rough on the old man. He could depend on Tagliapietro's business sense for that; Angelo was too valuable a commodity to trifle with. There was more danger to Francesca, but she knew nothing. He hoped that Tagliapietro and Beccaria would realize the futility of trying to get answers from either of them and would simply begin the hunt. Or, better still, acknowledge that the hunt was not worth the expense and simply ignore his absence. But even as he thought of Beccaria, Lazaro knew again the chill he felt when he looked into that man's eyes. There was something there which promised that he, at least, would never erase Lazaro's face from his memory.

It had been a while since he had been out of Venice and it seemed strange to him. There were no streets with buildings crowding over them, no narrow canals snaking here and there through the labyrinth. Nor were they on the flat water, shifting blue and ripped with the wind but devoid of elevation. They had left behind the blue, green, and gray of the Lagoon and the colors and smells of Venice.

Margoleit had ridden poorly at first, but Lazaro could see a great improvement. There must have been something in what she had done when she first mounted. He had seen from her eyes that she was not happy — she had never ridden before — but he knew that she saw the necessity of this form of travel. With her eyes closed, she had spoken softly to herself, as if repeating an incantation. He had leaned toward her and she opened her eyes but ignored him, leaning instead closer to the horse's ear. "Man and beast you save, oh Lord" was all she said, but by nightfall she was adept, at least, at staying on.

They had not gone as far as he had hoped but through heavy riding and good fortune they had crossed the Piave and were nearing the Livenza when night fell. Finding a grove of trees on a hilltop which afforded them a good view of the surrounding countryside, they stopped for the night. As they spread their blankets she felt the pains of the first day's riding. Her breasts had been hurting most of the day from the constant jiggling. She had stopped once to bind them, but the day of riding had shaken them free and now they pained her greatly. And her buttocks hurt even more. There was still plenty of the bread and cheese which Lazaro had found in the pack and so they settled down to a late meal then rolled up in the blankets to keep warm. The pain and fatigue of the day's ride excluded passion. Instead they lay there watching falling stars and the moon cross the sky, until the quiet of the night began to lift from them the weight of what lay behind.

At first they spoke only of what might lie ahead. Lazaro chose his words carefully. There was only so much of their journey which he wished to discuss with her, partly for her own safety and partly because he was afraid it might somehow change things. He told her she would have to wait in Crete alone while he traveled on to Rhodes, but was purposefully vague about the length of time. She had not pursued it, but Lazaro knew she was aware of what was left unspoken.

"Will they find us?" Margoleit asked in a tired but peaceful voice.

Lazaro tried to be honest. "They're good, but if they think we've headed for Trento we should have enough time to get to Béres. From there we're safe."

"But they could find us in Crete."

"I suppose they could find us anywhere, but it may not be that important to them," he lied. "And once I'm finished with Fugger's work we can head for Augsburg. From there, with Fugger's assistance, there are a lot of places where we could go. France, even New Spain."

"What would we do?"

"Could you imagine me as a merchant?" Lazaro asked, then laughed as he thought of it.

Margoleit turned her head and smiled. "You're too thin."

"And I'm getting too old to be a soldier."

In the moonlight Lazaro saw a change come over her face, and he thought she would ask how he had made the arrangements for them to leave, but she said nothing. Then, after a long pause, she asked, "What was it like to be a soldier?"

The question was close enough to the mark, but still Lazaro was relieved. "Truthfully?" he asked, taking a bite of an apple. "I found it pleasant. The fighting wasn't, but it was over so fast. And then, well, we had good times — it was the only way to purge the sights and sounds, even the smells, from your mind. And it was a living. If you could convince a Condottiere you had experience, he would offer a contract which allowed you a share of the spoils. Otherwise, you were just a freelance.

"There was one battle, I can't remember the name of the town, but I can still see it, on a hill top north of Trento. It was hot, but it smelled as if there would be a thunderstorm by nightfall. We were to take the town that night and I was assigned to a captain who held a frontal position, not the safest place. By the way the Condottiere had arranged his men, it was clear he expected to lose a great many of them as he hurled them against the defenders of the town. Most of the troops around me were inexperienced. They had fought in the battles which children and schoolboys have and some had even killed. But fighting the Landsknechts when they're defending a town is a different story."

"I don't understand," she said.

"Attacking, you're swept along by the rush of your comrades and the frenzy of the battle run carries you through a lot. Defending means standing your ground, when an army is rushing at you with sword and fire and noise. It can sap you of your strength and whatever else can be called bravery." Lazaro paused. "Sometimes bravery is just not soiling yourself out of fear.

"The fighting was thick and warm, and there are just bits I can remember, like a mosaic. Things started slowing down just before dawn. I remember standing alone, and the noise seemed much farther away. Suddenly a tall blond youth with ill-fitting clothes and a strange wool cap on his head ran full tilt into my sword then staggered back, dropped his sword, and fell.

"I looked at him for a moment, then found a tree stump and sat down. It was barely first light and the dawn wind blew through the bodies, stirring the mist into horrible shapes. The noise had moved into the city and around me there was only the faint sound of the wind and the moans of the dying on the field. Then the women began to come up the hill — the camp followers — slowly at first, then more and more, their skirts hitched up to avoid the mud. And the scavengers too. Not the crows — I didn't mind them feeding — the human scavengers. You see, the Condottiere would sell the right to loot the bodies and bury them, those not claimed by comrades or by the women. The women, however, were no match for the scavengers and often were far too late. By the time they arrived, a hand had been hacked off because the rings had been too tight to remove, an ear had been lopped off to be relieved later of its jewel. The women would still find the body, what was left of it. The burying would take place later, after the booty had been collected.

"There were also friars giving last rites to those who needed it, but they too watched for rings. Here and there a man seemingly dead would begin to move, his life depending on who saw him first: if a woman, a friar, or a comrade, it might last awhile longer; if a scavenger, no.

"And somewhere down below in the tents and in the places where there was still some grass there were surgeons working to save men who had received smaller wounds. An arrow in the arm, a sword wound to the head, some puncture which was relatively clean, these wounds could be treated in relative safety. There were amputations of limbs, extractions of eyes, and all to the screams of the patient. Still, it was marvelous what these surgeons could do with a drill, a saw, an ax, and a red-hot poker."

Margoleit pulled the blanket tighter around her and moved closer to Lazaro, but he didn't notice.

"As I was sitting there, I saw a headless torso that looked familiar but I couldn't place it. Then one of the camp followers came up and fell on it, sobbing. When I saw her I recognized him. They had been quite open about their lovemaking in camp, and I had seen them earlier that day making love. It had been fierce. She had plowed the earth with her feet then thrust them into the sky. They had rocked back and forth and held each other close, striving to unite.

"She cried for a while, resting on the chest, then stood, sobbing, and began searching around the body in ever-widening circles, looking for her lover's head. Finally she stumbled on it and stepped back. She picked the head up carefully and carried it back to the body. She knelt and aligned it carefully with the rest of him and draped her scarf over the space which had been the neck. Gently she bent over, closed his eyes, kissed his lips, then stretched out beside him.

"I couldn't watch. It was somehow more personal than when they had thrown off their clothes in passion. There was complete fidelity. She would never desert him. I looked away and saw a man approaching, leading a horse, picking through the bodies. As he found something of value he would pause, retrieve it, and toss it into a basket fixed to the saddle. He was headed for the couple. As I walked up to him he started to say something, but I didn't wait. I just put my sword into him, then walked away, leaving him writhing on the ground beside his horse and basket of jewels."

Margoleit was silent and Lazaro realized he had been speaking for too long. Then like a firefly her voice appeared in the dark. "There's a passage in the Zohar, 'God created man, male and female. And the Holy One does not place his abode where man and woman are not found together.'"

She reached out and took his hand, then they lay still, watching the stars again. When they fell asleep it was without pain or fear.

With the next day's sun they were up and on their way, hoping to cover even more ground than they had the day before, putting a greater distance between themselves and the tentacles of the Secretariat. Lazaro knew that by now they would be on their trail. He prayed that the headstart they may have had would be enough. By nightfall they had crossed the Tagliamento and were just north of Marano.

"There's a miller I used to know who lives near here," Lazaro said as he pulled up by a tree for a brief rest and to get his bearings. "I think we'll be able to stay with him for the night. It isn't far."

It was dark when they crested the hill and saw in the valley below the outline of a mill by the stream. They rode down and, as they got closer, saw how this structure had been ravaged by battle and time. The bricks were twisted out of place in many spots from cannon fire and the wind had wreaked havoc with the tiles on the roof. Lazaro wondered what had become of the miller. His name was Roberto, a large man, heavyset and strong, with a hearty laugh and a very crooked face. Roberto's son, also named Roberto, had been wounded in a battle, he couldn't remember now what the battle was for, and he had brought him home to his father. The boy had died before they arrived, but Lazaro brought the body home anyway. Roberto had been stricken with grief but was grateful to Lazaro for what he had done. It looked now as if war had touched Roberto even more directly. At least there was enough of the mill left to provide shelter.

There was no one about and little evidence of any recent use, except for some hay, still fairly fresh, which lay on the floor of the room where Roberto had stored his grain. It must have been left by some farmer who had used the building for a temporary barn, perhaps to hide his animals from roving bands of mercenaries. They stabled their horses in the next room, then, as Margoleit set about making a bed in the hay with their blankets, Lazaro gathered some wood, most of it damp, and started a small fire. While they lay beside the fire watching it there was a movement within the flames which startled Margoleit. She reached for a branch to jab at the fire but Lazaro stopped her.

"It's only a salamander."

"In the fire?"

"They say they can live in flames, though I imagine it was just sleeping inside one of those wet logs and was finally rousted out by fear of being roasted."

Margoleit smiled. "It can live in flames, then."

Lazaro nodded and chewed on a piece of cheese. "So they say. Angelo believes that. He says he's seen them in the glass furnace, in the coals."

Margoleit took the cheese and finished it. "You said he sees a lot of things." She lay back on the blanket.

"And they're supposed to be extremely poisonous. I read that just one salamander once passed through a river upstream from where the army of Alexander the Great was camped. In the morning four thousand men and horses lay dead."

"A Venetian creature," Margoleit said and stood, then walked over to the ruined wheel room where the water from the chute cascaded over the broken wheel, spraying the paving stones beside it. Without a word she pulled off her clothes and stood naked in the water, cleansing herself of the day's travel.

The full moon had risen and Lazaro felt its pull as he stared at it through the ruined roof. The moon also shone in the wheel room. He turned on his side and watched as Margoleit rubbed her white skin, washing the caked dust from her feet and her arms. Her breasts reacted to the cold water and her nipples tightened. She turned from him and let the water run over her dark hair. It swayed like seaweed down the center of her back. She grasped her hair with both hands and threw her head back, letting the water splash on her face. A spray resulted that, when illuminated by the moon, created a rainbow halo about her.

He took off his clothes and moved beside her into the force of the water. The chill startled him but his presence was not a surprise to her. When she felt his body she turned and embraced him. They stood together in the water, letting it wash away the stress of the long ride, massaging each other's back.

Later they lay on the blanket with another over them and watched as the moon passed through the trees which showed through the broken ceiling. Save for the splashing water which did not seem like noise, it was quiet, still. He wanted to speak but he was afraid to, as if his intrusion would break whatever spell there was. He could feel her warmth beside him, the soft hair on her legs as she curled them around his, her moist warm locks against his shoulder.

Morning came gently. The sun warmed them as they slept and when they awoke it was as if they had been transported to another world. The darkness of the night before had hidden from them the colors surrounding the mill, the spring flowers, the budding leaves, and, of course, the birds. They were in full voice, darting here and there, filling the air with their songs and colors. Above them, through the hole which had been the upper wall and roof, vines had sent out shoots. The sky was a full blue and cloudless. In the gentle breeze the upper branches of the trees swayed gracefully. They lay together, enjoying the warmth of the sun, the hiss of the water, and the birds. Margoleit slid her hand down Lazaro's thigh and caressed him. He turned to her and they joined with a slow rhythm dictated by the water and the sway of the limbs of the trees.

In the midst of their lovemaking they did not hear the birds grow quiet or the horses grow restless. They did not see the shadows dart past the openings in the walls or the glint of sun on steel. They did not feel the eyes upon them, hungry eyes peering through white masks. Uncovered, they made love passionately, as if it would be their last time together. When they were finished Margoleit collapsed on top of Lazaro, then slowly slid over and rested again beside him.

"What a pretty picture."

The voice stung Lazaro's ears and he sat up, then scrambled to his feet feeling for his sword.

"The Turk and the Jew bedded down like dogs in heat. The beast with two backs."

Margoleit was on her feet as well and had grabbed a dagger. They stood back to back, not sure where the voice was coming from. Their clothes were in the next room, by the broken water wheel, and they dared not go in.

"Who?" Margoleit whispered.

"Beccaria," Lazaro answered back. He wasn't sure if it actually was Beccaria but if not, it was his men. There was a sound to his right and he spun around, instinctively pushing Margoleit behind him. A man stood in the rubble of a tumble-down doorway, blocking the sun. Lazaro could see only his silhouette, the Venetian hat, the short black cape, and the light of the sun illuminating the mask from the sides so that the light seemed to spill out of the eye-holes. He knew that it was not Beccaria. But before that man moved, another rushed Lazaro from behind, expecting to make it past Margoleit. He must not have seen her dagger, or if he had, had assumed she would not know how to use it. He crumpled to the ground, holding his belly and writhing, and rolled to the wall where he stayed. Margoleit stepped over and took his sword from where he had dropped it. They stood again back to back and naked, like Adam and Eve facing the minions of a wrathful God rather than give up their Garden of Eden.

Again the voice. "The bitch has claws. We might have pleasured her, but now I don't know that we will do her that favor."

The man in the doorway attacked and Lazaro sprang to action. The man was good, and not nearly as rash as his comrade had been. He matched Lazaro stroke for stroke and in the time it took for the fight to end, Margoleit was able to retrieve her clothes and bring Lazaro's to him. When the second assassin lay beside the doorway where they had first seen him, Lazaro dressed while Margoleit kept watch. He was sure that he had heard Beccaria, but now he seemed to have disappeared. Lazaro checked the roofline but could see no one on high and there seemed to be no movement about the windows. Cautiously they checked the horses but they were undisturbed. Lazaro signaled for Margoleit to untether the horses while he got their belongings. There was still no sign of Beccaria. They mounted inside the mill and Lazaro rode out first, circled in front of the door, and when he saw that the area was clear, he signaled for Margoleit to follow. They rode quickly away from the mill and didn't stop until they had crested a hill to the north. From that vantage point Lazaro checked for Beccaria but he was nowhere to be seen, as if he had vanished like a spirit into the air.

They rode through the entire day, checking many times to see if they were being followed, and changing their direction as often as they could. But there was no sign that anyone was following them. Lazaro wondered if this had been part of the cat-and-mouse game which he expected from someone like Beccaria. They stopped for the night on a hill overlooking a small town. As they watered the horses and rolled out their bundles, Lazaro noticed that Margoleit was particularly silent. They lay for a while under the stars, not lighting a fire just in case. Finally he could wait no longer.

"What is it?" he asked. There was a long silence, too long, but somehow he felt he could say nothing more until she spoke. The silence rolled on and he watched the stars. The moon was not yet out and he could see so many that the sky seemed white with their light.

"Will it always be like this?" she asked finally and with finality.

A lie would not have been accepted. "Beccaria will be determined, but if he's alone he's likely to wait for more men or go back and try to find me later." He could see that she too was staring at the stars.

"Just you?"

He moved closer to her and felt comforting warmth. "They were lucky to find us. Beccaria must have seen our tracks when we turned east off the road to Trento, so he expects we're headed to Hungary — to Béres. And given the Akinji there's no reason to expect he'll follow us there."

"Akinji?"

"Turkish irregular cavalry. They're outriders, skirmishers. We'll be entering the Dar-ul Harb. When Suleiman targets an area for invasion he decrees it to be Dar-ul Harb — Lands of War — and his Akinji are sent in to soften any resistance. And sometimes that's enough to let him add it to his realm with a minimal amount of full-scale fighting."

"But they're there for us as well."

Lazaro knew well what she meant. He didn't relish the thought of running across them. Compared to the Akinji, the assassins would be welcome sport. But there was no way to avoid it. "Béres has grown up with them. We won't have any trouble getting through, and we'll be with him before we get deep into the area where the Akinji will be."

"Perhaps Beccaria knows our route."

"He can't. Fugger has been able to become who he is by being in control of information."

Margoleit said nothing for a moment. "And how did you become who you are?"

Before Lazaro could answer she turned her head to face him. "The night we left you came in from the rain and said you had made arrangements, but how did you do it all in that night? What happened?"

Lazaro felt his heart beating faster. He had hoped that somehow it would never come up, but he had known it had to. "I fulfilled a contract."

"You killed a man," she corrected. "A glassmaker?"

"Yes. He had made arrangements to leave Venice. He would have been killed anyway. The Secretariat knew where he would be heading."

"And so we got his gondola. His horses. His food." Margoleit turned back to face the sky. "You did this for Beccaria?"

"It was the only way I knew to get us both out of Venice quickly. Beccaria knew you were there with me. You would not have been safe." Lazaro listened to Margoleit breathing. He glanced over and saw that tears had welled up in her eyes.

"That night when you asked me to leave I saw the light of passion in your eyes as I had never seen it before. I thought it was me but now I'm not so sure." Again she turned her head to face him and he saw her cheek glisten. "What do you feel when you kill?"

Lazaro looked into her eyes. "I don't know. When I fight, it's different. When I killed Sanguinetti, it was business. I put my feelings deep inside."

"Are they so deep you might lose them?"

He moved so close to her that he could no longer see her clearly and they held each other tight.

"I will never lose my feelings for you. And we never need to see Venice again." Lazaro felt Margoleit's arms tighten around him. They lay together in each other's arms until sleep took them.

Sometime in the night Lazaro awoke to hear the baying of a wolf in the distance and then fell asleep again.

XIX

For the next five days there was no indication that they were being followed, but still they took care to avoid the cities and towns, sleeping in the most secluded places they could find, watchful always for any sign of pursuit. On the few occasions he entered small towns to bargain for food and to hear the news, Lazaro left Margoleit secreted somewhere out of the way and rode in from the opposite direction in which they traveled. The people talked of only one thing — the Turks.

By the sixth night they were deep in the mountains and stopped in a secluded place which offered a pool of clear cold water. During their travels they had discussed many times the route which would take them to Crete, that she would wait for him there while he made a delivery to Rhodes, and that once Lazaro's business with Fugger was completed they would head for Augsburg and be in greater safety. However, he had avoided discussion of the fact that she might have to wait in Crete for some time before they could leave for Augsburg. He thought it better not to discuss it, partly because it seemed reasonable to save her from the worry, at least for a while, and partly because he harbored some hope that he might be able to conclude his business in Rhodes before Suleiman tightened the noose.

Much of their time had also been spent in talking about themselves. Lazaro had been fascinated by Margoleit's childhood memories of life with her father and brother in Mestre and Venice, of her pain at finding out that her mother died giving birth to her, of her schooling by her father, of the abuse which she and her family had suffered at the hands of the Christians. The abuse of Jews was not a surprise to Lazaro, but a personal view of that abuse was. Previously it had been no more to him than something which happened to an unfortunate group of people. To some extent he could understand, having been a stranger in his grandfather's house, a child of a Christian mother and a Moslem father, born out of wedlock.

"My father was a trader from Constantinople, dealing mainly in glass," Lazaro explained that night as they stretched out on their sleeping robes. "He did business with my grandfather, a Venetian merchant stationed in Crete. He met my mother and they fell in love. A Moor and a Venetian could never be allowed to marry and so they ran off to Rhodes, thinking they might be safe there. I don't know why. Perhaps he had friends, I have no idea. And if my grandfather had not sent men after my mother, I might be now with the Akinji we're trying to avoid."

"You don't remember much about them?"

"Sometimes too much," Lazaro answered.

"What's your first memory?" Margoleit asked, rolling up onto her elbows and looking down at him.

"It's hard to know what was first. I remember being in a courtyard with my father, and I wanted to be inside with my mother. But my father kept telling me stories of famous generals and of the Yenicheri, the 'new recruits,' the foreign-born converts who are the backbone of the Sultan's army. Then I heard my mother screaming. Before I could run, my father grabbed me and said it was all right. But I didn't believe him. I guess my mind was filled with horrible images — like Kaziklu Bey catching my mother."

"What's that?"

"Who. He was an infidel, a king who battled the Turks, impaling whole cities of them just for his pleasure. Stories were told about him to scare children into obedience. Then an old woman appeared, one of the old women of the neighborhood, grinning toothlessly, and held the door open for us. We went in and there was blood — I remember that clearly — and then I saw my mother, dripping with sweat and red from blood, her eyes closed, smiling. Cradled between her breasts was my new brother, Nicolo."

Lazaro smiled. "I suppose it's natural not to be too happy when someone comes along and takes the attention away from you. I don't think I treated him very well at all. I remember once — I don't know what I had been doing to Nicolo, but my father was angry with me. Maybe I was pulling his hair. Anyhow, my father punished me in a more lasting fashion. He told me Kaziklu Bey would carry me off and chain me to a wall where he would drink my blood each day for all eternity if I ever hurt my brother again. And he said the same thing would happen to my mother, unless I watched over both of them. From that day Nicolo was safe. Until the men came."

"What happened then?"

"My grandfather had hired them to bring his daughter, his property, back to him. It took them a while to find us but when they did they went about their task with precision. They killed my father and my brother. I was taken back to Crete with my mother but she died soon after, I suppose of a broken heart," he said, feeling the lie turn in him like a shard of glass. "I was left with my grandfather, unwelcome, sure that he was Kaziklu Bey. I remember losing my voice for the longest time, unable even to cry, feeling like a caged animal. Finally I was sent away, and I've been wandering ever since."

"Was she beautiful, your mother?"

"She was like an angel," Lazaro answered. It struck him at that moment that it was his mother that Margoleit had reminded him of that evening he had rescued her from the ghetto and bathed her to cool her fever. He hadn't realized.

Margoleit rolled over and lay back beside him, looking up into the stars. "My father told me that my mother had been a treasure chest filled with jewels, and that when God took her away he left me, a pearl, so that's what he named me."

The next day threatened rain from its beginning, and about an hour after their midday rest it started. As the cold and damp pressed through their cloaks, Lazaro began to feel as if there were eyes watching them. There was no one in sight, but the feeling grew stronger as the day wore on. They moved up from the valley they had been riding in and into the trees on the hills which flanked each side.

It was well past midafternoon when Lazaro heard the soft whinny of a horse. He whirled his horse about, and there behind Margoleit stood a troop of Hungarian horsemen with Béres at their head. Almost before Margoleit could turn to face them, Béres gave a signal and his troop melted away into the trees. Béres rode forward to greet them.

"It's good to see you, both of you," he said, smiling at Margoleit, "especially with all the Turks around here."

"We haven't seen any, but we've been careful," Lazaro said as he leaned forward, stretching his back.

Béres laughed and slid from his horse. "You've been loud. The trinkets you wear with your tack announce your coming from far off."

Lazaro dismounted and took Béres's hand before introducing him to Margoleit.

"I didn't expect you for another week," Béres said. "We just got here yesterday. Did Fugger send you out early or did I get the dates wrong?"

Lazaro shook his head. "We had to leave a little earlier than expected. But it's all worked out fine."

"Just as well you're early. Fugger wants us in Valona by the tenth of June and it's a long ride through the mountains."

"Just what we need," Lazaro said, looking at Margoleit. "Is Vom Scheidt with you?"

Béres nodded. "He's right behind you."

Before Lazaro could turn he heard Vom Scheidt's laugh. He wouldn't have recognized the Count. Where in Venice he had presented himself in the height of whichever fashion might attract a woman, here he was fitted for battle with the Akinji. He was in fur and felt with a huge felt cloak draped over his horse. A dull brown cloth was tied over his hair and his face and hands were darkened with soot.

Vom Scheidt slid out of his saddle and took Lazaro's hand. "I've been riding point ahead of you for the last two hours." His gaze shifted to Béres. "There's nothing up ahead." He stepped past Lazaro to Margoleit. "I wish the circumstances of our meeting were better."

Margoleit pushed her wet hair from her face and smiled. "I would have wished for better circumstances as well, but these are probably the best circumstances I could expect at the moment."

Béres took strips of cloth from his saddlebags and pushed in between Margoleit and Vom Scheidt, handing strips to her and to Lazaro. "You can talk later. For now, tie up your buckles. There's a place not far from here where we can rest for the night. According to Vom Scheidt we can have a hot meal." The Count smiled and nodded and helped them tie up anything that might make a noise.

Béres's men had gone on ahead and when they reached the camp, the men had already prepared a small fire in a shallow cave and staked out some shelters circling it to benefit from the heat. After the afternoon of drizzle it was pleasant beneath the tall pines with a surprisingly dry bed of needles underfoot. A meal was cooking, and, though he knew it would be some kind of greasy stew, Lazaro welcomed it. He noticed as well, while he unrolled his bedroll, that the men were cleaning their weapons.

"We had some fighting just after dawn," Béres said, noticing Lazaro's gaze. Farther north and west of here, between us and home."

"Are things all right at Krakoi Boros?" Lazaro asked, remembering the town Béres held.

"My son is there and he has enough men, but I'm sending these out now. They've already eaten and they can be over the next pass before they rest for the night. We can travel faster alone."

Vom Scheidt joined them holding three bowls of stew, obviously hot, and quickly gave one to Lazaro and one to Margoleit then sat down beside them. Béres stood and headed over to the fire where he talked with his men as they readied for their journey.

"It isn't good, then?" Lazaro asked as he filled his mouth with the greasy stew.

Vom Scheidt shook his head. "He wants them back there as soon as possible. But Transylvania will hold until next year at least. By then, if Suleiman gets through Rhodes, he'll sweep in with everything he's got and nothing will stop him. That's why Béres needs the money."

Margoleit swallowed a piece of stew meat she had been struggling to chew. "To get out?" she asked.

"No, to get in. If it's inevitable that these raiding lands will become vassal states, Suleiman will become quite the peaceful and understanding ruler, but it will take a bit of money to keep on top of things during the transition. Fugger is paying dearly for Béres, but he's worth it."

Lazaro glanced over at the Magyars who said goodbye to Béres in that language he had never been able to understand. "They look seasoned."

Vom Scheidt smiled and his teeth shone out of his mud-stained face. "They're berserkers."

"You mean crazy?"

"I mean berserkers." He put his bowl down and wiped his mouth. "They're mushroom eaters — *bolond gomba* — the mad mushroom. They drink *soma*."

Lazaro put his bowl down and looked into it. Margoleit paused in her chewing, waiting to find out where the conversation was going.

"No" — Vom Scheidt smiled — "it's just stew. Bad stew." He took another spoonful and hit Lazaro with his elbow as he filled his mouth, encouraging him to do likewise, then smiled at Margoleit as he chewed. "*Bolond gomba* is a mushroom, small and white with a red cap. It grows around the roots of birch trees. Properly prepared and consumed it allows your mind to, well, it's difficult to explain, but the world changes for you and fear vanishes."

Margoleit paused in her eating. "I remember a phrase from the Zohar, 'Out of the scorching noon of Isaac, out of the dregs of wine, a fungus emerged, a cluster, male and female together, red as a rose, expanding in many directions.'"

Vom Scheidt nodded. "I'm not sure exactly what that means, but sometimes that's what the mushroom is like."

The conversation was cut short by the departure of the horsemen and Béres's return to their circle. "Fugger has made arrangements for us to be met in Valona by a Knight of Rhodes named Antonio Bosio. I will remain there while you three make for Crete." He turned to Lazaro. "That's where you will find Tadini and convince him to accompany you to Rhodes. I take it Margoleit will remain in Crete until you've finished your business with the Knights?"

Lazaro nodded and looked at Margoleit. It was clear that she was beginning to realize that her stay alone in Crete might be longer than Lazaro had implied.

"Bosio will provide the transportation," Béres continued. "While you are in Rhodes, I'll arrange for a series of ships to bring in the supplies and reinforcements Fugger has promised the Knights. Those ships should turn around and carry out Fugger's cargo."

"I didn't know you had a fleet," Lazaro said, baiting Béres.

Béres grunted dismissively. "I've got my ways. It's getting late and I want an early start," Béres added and began to spread out his sleeping robe. The others followed his lead.

"And when exactly do the ships carry you out?" Margoleit whispered to Lazaro when they had bedded down for the night.

"It's difficult to say, really. I have to take Tadini in and arrange for Fugger's property to be taken out. The Turks haven't laid siege yet . . ."

"And when they do?"

"I hope to be out of there before that. But if they do, it will just mean a delay. You'll be protected in Crete. Fugger has guaranteed it."

"I'm not sure that comforts me sufficiently," Margoleit said, yawning and rolling up closer to Lazaro.

"We don't have that much choice at the moment."

"Still not comforting," she said sleepily and pulled his arm around her. The wind blew the mist in around their bedrolls and fanned the small fire.

Lazaro opened his eyes and saw the dark trees silhouetted against the stars of the night sky. The rain clouds had moved on, but there was still a chill in the air. He had been dreaming of Marzia. "Will I ever be free of that witch?" he thought as he got up to relieve himself. Margoleit stirred briefly, but Béres and Vom Scheidt looked to be deep in sleep. He reached for his sword and walked off, away from the fire and into the dark night. He wondered if there were wolves about; they had heard them earlier in the day, before he had run into Béres, but since then the forest had been silent.

He stopped by a small evergreen a respectable distance from the camp, leaned his sword against the tree and unbuttoned his pants. The air was filled with the sound of the wind in the high pines and the occasional grinding of two tree trunks against one another. He finished and stood, watching the heavens. The moon was just about ready to rise. The stars were bright and so numerous that the sky, though a deep blue-black, seemed, in some impossible way, white.

And Marzia. Why could he not rid himself of her memory? When he found himself thinking of her it was as if he was being unfaithful to Margoleit. Perhaps she sensed something, for often, when he was thinking of Marzia, Margoleit would ask him if something was wrong. He found it easier to lie and suggest that he was thinking about Fugger's business. Then it would pass and he would wonder how he could think of that woman the way he did. It was clear to him that he had never loved her, had never felt for her the way he did for Margoleit. And yet, when he least expected it, she would return again, like a plague. Perhaps only time would wash her from his mind.

Lazaro turned to head back to the campfire. The soft pine needles carpeting the forest floor muffled the sound of his feet. His movements were so quiet that he was able to approach an animal pausing by a tree, just beyond the circle of light. He watched it as it looked over at the mounds of sleeping men. Then his pulse quickened. It was a wolf, silently watching his sleeping comrades. He moved toward it quietly, his sword raised above his head. His heart leapt. It wasn't a wolf, but a man with a wolf-skin and head on his back, for as he looked to the wolf's paws he saw that they dangled lifeless beside the arms of a man on all fours, clothed in the soft garments of the Turk. And beneath the wolf's head was the darkened face of a Turkish scout. He stepped closer and swung his sword down with a clean and sure stroke. As the blade descended, the wolfman turned his eyes up and saw the face of Lazaro, saw the blade catch the light of the coals as it flashed. Lazaro saw his lips move to a smile, and, as the blade found its mark, he was sure the lips had been about to say "There is but one God, and that is Allah."

The Turk's head dropped beside his body and blood spurted out as the torso collapsed. Lazaro knew now why the wolf's howls had stopped. There were greater wolves roaming this mountain — the Akinji. He hurried over to Béres and roused him from his sleep. The old Magyar was quick to his feet. He told Lazaro and Vom Scheidt to ready their horses, then disappeared into the darkness of the forest. Vom Scheidt buried the glowing coals while Lazaro moved to Margoleit and awakened her, warning her to be quiet. She read the danger in his eyes and asked no questions but moved over to her horse, ready.

For what seemed a long time there was no sound except for the wind high in the trees, and then Béres returned. "It must have been a scout. But I think there's a camp nearby, in the opposite direction to the way my men went, thank God. I can smell the smoke." They mounted their horses, then followed Béres off into the dark forest, climbing the mountain on which they rested. Béres stayed out in front, his horse surefooted, his great bulk impressively silhouetted against the night sky.

"He's worried now," Vom Scheidt whispered as the horses took them through the trees.

Lazaro turned to Vom Scheidt. "What do you mean 'now'?"

Vom Scheidt leaned in his saddle and spoke in hushed tones. "There have been too many Turks and they've been too well prepared. Béres is afraid they've been sent to hunt him, and that they've found his trail."

"Why would Suleiman hunt Béres?"

It was dark but Lazaro could see in Vom Scheidt's face that he too was worried. He even imagined that a wind from nowhere rose and stirred the trees. "Béres has a special place as a warrior. You must have heard the stories from your father. Béres killed Vlad Tepes."

Lazaro shook his head in ignorance.

Vom Scheidt leaned precariously far out of his saddle and whispered into Lazaro's ear, hoping that such spirits as might inhabit these mountains would not hear and would not be raised by the name which he spoke. "It was Béres who killed Kaziklu Bey."

In an instant the terror of childhood fears returned to Lazaro and he felt transported, though he was not sure to where. There was darkness all around him and he awoke in a sweat to be held by his mother. She was soothing him from the dream which had driven him to screams. And in his babbling he was repeating the name which he had just heard on Vom Scheidt's lips. Lazaro had asked his father to tell him a scary story and his father had obliged. The story had been of the Impaler, the king who killed so many Turks by impaling them on stakes, thousands of stakes. It was said that he reveled in the pain that he caused, that he drank of the blood of Turks to replenish himself after battle, that he was not human at all but a demon who feasted on men's souls. And even though his earthly form had been destroyed by a great Magyar warrior, he still could be seen, in the dark of night, prowling through the narrow streets in disguise, looking for children who had been disobedient. The dream had terrified him, for Kaziklu Bey was feasting on his brother.

Lazaro looked back for Margoleit and stopped his horse, allowing her to move up between him and Vom Scheidt. He crested the next rise just behind Margoleit and saw that Béres and Vom Scheidt had dismounted, tied their horses to a tree and were crawling toward the next rise on their bellies. Over that hill Lazaro could see the glow of fire and could hear sounds which were not peaceful. He slid silently from his mount and signaled for Margoleit to stay with the horses while he dropped to the ground, joining Béres and Vom Scheidt as they peered through the grass at the top of the knoll.

In the valley below they could see fires burning brightly throughout a Turkish camp. Like obscene decorations, five men, likely taken from some mountain village, had been impaled on stakes driven up through their rectums. They writhed in an agonized dance of death. One in the process of being impaled, was held bound and bent over by two Turks beside the hole which would receive the stake as two others positioned the stake and another pounded the end with a heavy mallet. Elsewhere there was the scuffle of repeated rape. It was as if the bowels of the earth had opened and the steaming putrescence of Hell itself had spilled forth.

"*Aut deus aut lupus*," Béres said.

Vom Scheidt turned to him.

"*Homo homini aut deus aut lupus* — as Erasmus says, man is to man either a god or a wolf." Béres moved back from the crest and mounted his horse. "We'll go around. I want to be far away from here by morning."

Nothing else was said but Lazaro knew what was in his mind. He wanted to be finished with this job and back in Krakoi Boros before the Turks got there.

When they rejoined Margoleit she asked nothing. As they moved silently away from the hilltop he wondered if she had been able to see what he had seen. Even if she had not seen it, he was sure she had felt it.

They traveled through the night, saying nothing until they were off that mountain. Continuing south, they rode hard and long at first, then as they felt the distance grow between them and the Akinji, they assumed the speed of merchants, fat merchants, it seemed to Lazaro.

Béres had stops along the way where the people knew him and trusted him. Lazaro was a little surprised but he realized that while he had known Béres as a mercenary, he was also a merchant and as a merchant, he knew the value of honesty among the people through whose land he traveled. It was for this reason that Fugger had chosen him.

Margoleit had taken to the saddle and both Béres and Vom Scheidt were taken with her. Lazaro felt the comfort of a return to the camaraderie he had known when he had traveled before with Béres and Vom Scheidt. And there was the added bonus of time spent with Margoleit. When they had begun their journey from Venice he had felt the full weight of caring for someone. He had never felt so responsible for someone else's safety. This was not business. Her ability to take care of herself had shone at the mill, but as they journeyed he came to realize that it was more than bare ferocity and will to survive; she had a capacity, a depth, which meant that she depended on no one unnecessarily. There were, at times, feelings of something which resembled embarrassment when he became aware of the fact that his comrade was also his lover.

However, against the light of his time with Margoleit, there was a small darkness, a question which sat like some little gremlin on his shoulder until finally, in the calm of an early-evening campfire, high in the mountains by a cold, clear lake, he roused enough courage to inquire. Margoleit was down by the edge of the lake trying to catch fish for their evening meal when Lazaro turned to Béres and asked his question.

Béres smiled when asked about Kaziklu Bey.

Vom Scheidt smiled too and put another piece of wood on the fire. "I think I'll go down and help Margoleit find some fish. I'm too hungry to be lazy any longer."

"It was a long time ago," Béres began, "before you were born. But then I guess you know that. As a young man I sometimes rode with Vlad Tepes, the Dragon, they called him — Dracul. My father had known his people, and I was sent to learn the trade of arms from them. They were kings in their own lands, south of the Danube. And strange, all of them, but Vlad was stranger. He had little fear and seemed not to understand pain. I learned later that he understood it only too well. And the handmaid of pain — fear — he understood that too. They were free there until the Turks came. And then it was Hunyadi who helped to set us all free. Hunyadi's son, Mattyas, he had no time for Vlad and when Mattyas was made king he imprisoned Vlad."

"Why?" Lazaro asked, pulling back from the light of the campfire.

Béres shoved the ground with his booted foot, pulled up a piece of dry grass and tossed it into the fire. "Vlad had bad habits. If it had just been with the Turks it might have been all right. The impalings were cruel, but in the eyes of some they served a purpose. But when there were no Turks, he would turn on his own people. And on the Hungarians who lived among them."

"And drink their blood?"

Béres looked into Lazaro's eyes but just carried on with his story. "Mattyas held Vlad captive in Buda and at Solomon's Tower for twelve years. But then it became necessary to rouse the people of Wallachia against the Turk. Basarab Laiota ruled Transylvania under the Turks but he and the boyars who kept power were not of the Roman faith. Mattyas, a descendant of St. Stephen, wanted someone there of the proper faith, at least on the surface, and someone who could rally the people and terrify the Turks. Vlad was a perfect choice. He had been away long enough that his people had forgotten his excesses but not so long that the Turks had. But Vlad needed a wife. And Mattyas had a sister." Béres sighed and moved into the heart of the story.

"Mattyas promised her she would not have to suffer long. And I was that promise. In that campaign Vlad taught me how to fight as I had never fought before. We rode through the camps of the Turks and nothing could stand before us. We were armored by *bolond gomba* and were berserkers. We were the storm wind.

"And then word came from Mattyas. The message was for me to come home. And so I prepared. There was a battle approaching, near Bucharest I think it was, and I spoke with Vlad, arranging to leave after it was finished.

"He had a habit of slipping into disguise and wandering off to the flanks, when the terrain allowed, so that he could watch battles from a different vantage. The terrain allowed. That morning he chose to dress as a Turk.

"His men found him later, after they had won the day, though his head was not with him. For that I earned the gratitude of my king, though he stayed far away from me. A man who can kill one king can always kill another."

A wind blew up and fanned the flames of the campfire, pushing embers dancing into the air. Lazaro was startled by a cheer from Margoleit and Vom Scheidt at the lake's edge. They had finally caught their first fish. Margoleit stood proudly, holding the fish high then tossed it to Vom Scheidt who nearly fell into the lake.

"We'll eat soon," Béres said, then stretched back and looked up at the sky. "She's young, Lazaro," he said, after a short pause.

"What do you mean? She's older than her years."

"I mean young. Not yet old. Born long after the rest of us, with a life that will go on long after we're gone."

Lazaro grinned. "She's a lot younger than you."

"And you," Béres retorted.

Lazaro sat up and poked the fire with a stick. "She's twenty. I'm thirty-five. That's fine. I doubt I'll ever get old enough for our ages to make a difference."

"Probably not," Béres said, still looking at the sky. "This is the first time she's been away from her people."

"I guess that's right," Lazaro said, uncomfortable with the direction he sensed the conversation to be taking.

"I'm sure you're not looking for advice, but I'll give you some anyway. Guard your heart until she has learned whether she can be outside the law."

"You mean be with me as an outlaw?"

"No, I mean outside the law. Her law."

Another cheer arose from the lake side, and Margoleit and Vom Scheidt started back toward the campfire.

"Looks like our meal has finally arrived," Béres said, sitting up and pushing a log with his feet so that it rolled onto the fire.

Lazaro stood to greet Margoleit and help with cleaning the fish. As they prepared them for the fire, Lazaro, for the first time since they had left Venice, thought about the difference between what he had left behind and what she had left behind.

By the end of the week they had come through the mountains without incident, thanks mainly to Béres, and they saw the Adriatic stretch out before them. As they picked their way down a trail which joined with the coast road, the marshes by the sea erupted into a silvery cloud, turning on the wing, spiraling away from them and out over the shallow sea. There were more birds here than Lazaro had ever seen before, and the spectacle repeated itself again and again as they traveled along the coast to Valona. The weather was now very warm and the cool breeze from the ocean made it most pleasant. When there was no whitewashed town perched on the cliffs over the sea, they made their beds under the stars and watched the moon over the Adriatic. On those nights Lazaro found himself thinking of Venice, off to the west across the water. Uninvited and unwanted, Marzia's face would appear, sometimes to entice him like some daughter of Lilith, as often to mock him for his foolishness. But when he found himself in the midst of those thoughts, he had only to look beside him, to the face ringed in dark hair, angelic, and Venice would recede from his mind.

XX

Though their trip had taken on a leisurely air, they arrived in Valona on the tenth of June, as Fugger had requested. Valona was a Venetian port and that gave Lazaro good reason to be cautious. Still, it seemed that if Beccaria had any men there, they too were lulled into restfulness. The sun and the sea combined with the white buildings and green hills to create a most peaceful atmosphere. It took them the better part of the day to find Antonio Bosio at the docks, and when they did, Lazaro's first impression of Bosio's galley was surprise, for it appeared to be in a state of disrepair. Even the sails were a filthy brown rather than the bleached white of most. However, Bosio assured them that once they were on the sea, they would realize that the ship's appearance was quite deceptive.

Bosio was a short, fat, balding man who, although he was a Knight of Rhodes and a defender of the Catholic faith, was nevertheless a pirate. After some brief introductions and even briefer farewells, Béres went his way to begin making the arrangements which would fulfill his part of the bargain with Fugger, and left Lazaro, Margoleit, and Vom Scheidt with Bosio. Bosio had received his instructions from the Grand Master De L'Isle Adam and knew the outline of the operation to bring Tadini to Rhodes, though, as Lazaro expected, he had no idea of the traffic of goods which would flow out of Rhodes should their endeavor be successful. He made it quite clear that he was not pleased with having to carry a woman and would only discuss the details of their voyage when Margoleit had been stowed below deck. Without pretensions of friendship, Bosio explained that he expected Lazaro to produce Tadini quickly once they put ashore on Crete. Recent developments in Rhodes made it necessary that they complete the operation with no more than ten days spent in Crete. In the interests of security, he asked Lazaro and Vom Scheidt to travel as natives of a nearby village, under the names Conversalo and Scaramosa, and for Margoleit to be the sister of Conversalo. As he explained it, there was no point in his crew knowing more than they had to, and so he had told them that they had been hired by two men who wished to leave Valona before they were located by creditors. With what seemed to be misplaced reluctance, he noted that the presence of Margoleit would require more lying than he had anticipated.

It was in part due to men such as Bosio that Suleiman had turned his attention to Rhodes. There was no doubt that he needed to replenish his treasury, but if he should be successful in capturing the Rhodian treasure he would retrieve much of what had been his to begin with. For years the Knights of Rhodes had used the island as a base from which to attack Turkish shipping. True they also protected pilgrims, operated hospitals, and were an outpost for the Christian west, which, like Hungary, would slow down the juggernaut of the Turkish horde. But they were also pirates, Christian pirates who believed in divine inspiration when plundering the Turks.

By the next morning's tide, Bosio's men had readied the vessel and they set sail down the coast. Bosio wished to raise no suspicions, either en route or on their arrival in Crete, and so they traveled as a normal trading vessel, slowly, putting in at a number of ports along the way to pick up various goods which he knew would be easily traded in Candia — within a week, as he constantly reminded Lazaro.

During the trip Lazaro had more opportunity to get to know Bosio and though he was a relatively distasteful man, particularly with respect to his attitudes about cleanliness and education, he was an excellent sailor. The storms they passed through would have sunk lesser captains, but for Bosio they were nothing. For Vom Scheidt and Margoleit they were much more; though they were not impressed with the food on board, they had not expected to cast it over the side so often. Lazaro felt a bit of seasickness as well but he was able to keep his food in his stomach. He was, however, pleased that Vom Scheidt and Margoleit were able to develop such a close friendship.

But it seemed that Margoleit took longer to recover from the effects of the constant motion; even when they were ashore in ports, her sickness continued.

"I was afraid to tell you until I was sure," she started one evening as they lay in the hot darkness of their room in a small tavern in Sapienza. "I'm pregnant."

The idea had crossed Lazaro's mind but he had tried to keep it at bay. This was not the time for such matters. There was too much to do, too much danger. And he could not avoid his time in Rhodes. "When?" he said, stroking her hair.

"I don't know when," she said and pushed his arm away from her, then smoothed out her long hair. "Part of why I was so intent on leaving Venice in the first place was that I thought maybe I was. It must have been in April." She smiled at him. "I guess we should have been more careful."

Lazaro looked down at her belly, browned, shining in the moonlight. It seemed a little tighter, just a bit more rounded. "But when will it be born?"

Margoleit smiled. "The middle to end of January, I think."

"And we don't even know where we'll be in January."

"It'll work out," Margoleit said and slid closer to him.

"But I have to leave you in Crete."

"I know."

"Don't mention a word of this to Vom Scheidt, or anyone else, for that matter. It's better if no one knows."

"Thanks," Margoleit said, hitting him on the arm playfully.

"You know what I mean."

"I guess so. But don't you think anyone will notice?"

"Not unless they see you naked," Lazaro answered, running his hand over her belly. Margoleit smiled.

They didn't sleep the rest of the night but just lay together, holding each other, waiting for the dawn and the call to board Bosio's galley.

They arrived at Candia in the afternoon of the nineteenth of June. With a last warning from Bosio as to their timetable, Scaramosa and Conversalo, accompanied by Conversalo's sister, thanked their benefactor and wandered off into the port area to find simple lodgings. The market area was abuzz with business activity. It seemed the gathering storm to the east was not having a negative effect on business at all. The Signoria knew only too well that to make a profit it should not take sides, and so it had been adamant about Tadini remaining in Crete.

However, there was more on Lazaro's mind than finding Tadini as he headed into town from the port, leaving Margoleit in a tavern with Vom Scheidt watching over her. His first task was to arrange secure lodgings for her. That would require contacting Fugger's agent in Crete but Lazaro wanted more protection than that which could be afforded by Fugger.

In the white canyons of the poor area of Candia he found who he had been looking for. After his mother's death there had been one woman who cared for him, even though she had been dismissed from the service of his grandfather. Lucrezia had been his mother's nursemaid and had been held responsible for her escape to Rhodes with the Moor. When she had heard of their return she had tried to see them, to no avail. And when she had heard he was alone, she had found a way to contact him. The kitchen servants, who had been given the responsibility of finding some useful work for Lazaro to do about the house, had brought him to her. At first she had terrified him. Though she could only have been forty or forty-five at the time, she was even then an old woman. Now as he knocked on the door of the house where she had lived, he hoped that the old woman was still alive.

The door opened. It was Lucrezia, and although she seemed somehow different, she appeared no older. Her back was bent, her black hair white, but her eyes shone with the love he had felt briefly so many years ago. It took no longer than the time it takes to splash cool water on a face for her to recognize the man before her as the boy Lazaro.

He knew that while she still lived she would not refuse him and she did not. The arrangement was clear; he would bring to her a woman he loved, who was with child and in need of protection. There would be a man who would provide money, though Lucrezia was not to trust him too much. Lucrezia herself proposed the method by which she would explain Margoleit's presence — a daughter of a distant friend who was hiding from a bad marriage arrangement. She promised this would provide Margoleit with the protection of every woman in Crete. With apologies for having come back after all these years of silence and promising to return the next day with Margoleit, Lazaro left to contact Fugger's agent.

Gaspar Lomann seemed too young to be Fugger's agent, but the beardless German produced credentials at Lazaro's request and didn't seem to mind the questioning of his authority. He passed an unopened packet to Lazaro and retired to his accounts, giving Lazaro the opportunity to read in seclusion.

"God smiles on you and on my fortunes." Fugger's hand was unmistakable. "As you are reading this, my faith in you has been well-placed. Lomann will take care of your Jew while you are in Rhodes, but remember that you must satisfy our contract before you and yours will be afforded the full extent of my protection." Lazaro saw the threat, plain and simple, in the banker's letter. Given the child which Margoleit now carried, the threat was even more serious. But thoughts of Beccaria made him remember Thomas à Kempis — *de duobus malis, minus est semper eligendum.* He had to pick the lesser of the two evils. The letter continued, giving Lazaro information about the whereabouts of Tadini and the habits of the Governor of Crete. With little choice but to trust Fugger, he left Lomann with directions regarding Lucrezia and set out on his last errand of the day.

The heat had been building throughout the day, and had peaked at some less-than-bearable temperature hours ago. However, the sea now worked its magic and the cool winds of evening blew in over Candia. Lazaro climbed a steep street leading up to a hill overlooking the bay, then found his way to the large whitewashed villa surrounded by trees and a high wall, which had been his mother's home at one time. As he stood by the gatepost a flood of emotion swept past him and, as if a mouse in the shadow of a hawk, he shivered. The weight of the memories of this place had always followed him, dragging behind him in the dust. On too many occasions had it felt as if those memories were tethered to his heart. Though he had no desire to enter, there was something in the house that he had to get, something that he had often seen in his dreams. He knew that it would still be within that house, knew exactly where it would be. But he would have to wait until nightfall to get it.

As he waited, the sight of the house brought to his mind memories long buried of his mother. They had returned from Rhodes in the company of the men who had attacked and killed his father and brother. The assassins had hurried them from the boat to the house, along the same route taken by Lazaro earlier. He had never before seen Crete and the sights, sounds and smells were new and frightening to him. The house had seemed oppressive from the first moment they entered. He had hugged his mother's skirts as she stood, like a captive, head bowed and silent, in her father's foyer. When Ruzzini had entered it had been a great shock for Lazaro. In Rhodes he had heard Italian being spoken and had seen Italians, but he didn't understand the language and given their recent incursion into his child's world, he feared them greatly. He understood that this man had been the instigator of that attack and he wanted to run out and kill him. But he also understood this man to be the father of his mother and so he waited to see what she would do. Ruzzini dismissed the guards and stood facing his daughter, silently. Then his anger broke loose and he yelled, shook his fist, and paced back and forth. He looked at Lazaro, scowled and shouted words at him as well. Lazaro had never before seen eyes so blue as this man's, and this, combined with everything else, terrified him. He was sure he was looking into the soul of a demon, a murderer who had ordered his family killed. But his mother said nothing. She remained silent, staring at the old man. He grew more and more angry, then finally, in a fit, lashed out at her, striking her on the side of the face. She fell to the floor and Lazaro rushed over to her. Lazaro remembered with amazement that he saw no pain in her eyes. It seemed she had not felt the blow. But, if she had not, he had. As she regained her feet Lazaro attacked the old man.

His memory failed him; he remembered only that he had awakened that night in a dark room, alone with his mother. She was standing by the open window. He was sure she was speaking softly with someone, but when he reached the window there was no one there. She had not noticed him but continued talking softly in Turkish — it was to his father. Lazaro had looked out and seen the Mediterranean lying peacefully before them, moonlight shimmering on its surface. He had returned to his bed. Sometime later his mother had turned to him and he saw that there were tears in her eyes. She sat beside him and spoke to him in Turkish, telling him stories of his father Ibrahim and his little brother, Nicolo. She talked and sang softly to him far into the night. Then she dried her eyes and looked at him. "Forgive me for my weakness," she said. He looked into her eyes and saw that she was not herself. Somehow, during the storytelling and the singing, she had left. He watched as she stood and pulled a chair over to the window. She stood on the chair, took her belt, and tied it around her neck, then looped it over the beam, securing it. She turned to him once more and again began speaking softly. In an instant she was dangling freely from the rope, the chair overturned.

She hung there, twisting gently in the wind, her netted headdress billowing about her in the soft sea breeze. Lazaro watched her for a while, thinking of the stories of the beautiful angels, the houris, who inhabited paradise. She seemed to be looking at him and he waited for her to say something to him. Then, realizing that she was dead, he turned and faced the wall. He spent the night sobbing gently and when all his tears were gone and he could cry no more, he sat, mute. When the suicide was discovered he was brought before his grandfather, but he would not speak.

His mother was buried outside the church and black cloths were placed over all the mirrors in the house. He had wondered about these black cloths on all the walls throughout the house, and in the night he rose to find out what was under them. He crept down to one and climbed onto a stool. Holding a candle he removed the cloth. There he saw his face and the eyes of his murdering grandfather in his own face. It terrified him and he let out one last scream, then spoke no more.

His grandfather, filled with remorse, hated him even more but could not bring himself to kill the boy, and so Lazaro was put to work in the kitchens. It was there he had become acquainted with Lucrezia. Any kindness shown to him during that time came from her. Eventually, his grandfather, consumed with anger and guilt, could not bear to have Lazaro around as a living reminder, and gave him to some Irish monks passing through after a pilgrimage to the Holy Land. Thus had Lazaro begun the long journey which now brought him back to Crete.

It was night now and time for him to do what he had planned. As a kitchen servant, he had learned well the many paths about the gardens and had used them often to sneak out and wander about the town. Quietly he moved to a part of the wall which had been repaired while he was still a child. The stonemason who had done the work had not been interested in fitting the stones back together exactly as they had been, and the result was a series of outcroppings which the young Lazaro had used to pass over the wall from either side, almost like a stile. As he stood by the spot now, the wall seemed so small in comparison to the one he had carried in his memory. He was quickly over it and down the other side. Moving through the squat olive trees toward the back of the house, he had to freeze in the shadows twice as people moved past the windows: Ruzzinis, his mother's cousins who had taken over the house to carry on the trading tradition. He finally reached the back wall of the villa and found the vines still there, strong as ever. But this night he would not climb the ones he had usually climbed to his garret in the attic. He moved along the wall to the vines he knew would lead him to the room which had been the refuge of his grandfather. Large wooden shutters were closed over the window to that room, though they were open at every other window on this side of the building. He took that to be a good sign that the room was not used.

The vines felt cool and comforting to him and for a moment he buried his face in them, drinking in the memories which he had left behind. They were not pleasant memories, but they linked to things which he knew would be more pleasant if he could only remember them. There was little in his memory of the time spent as a family with his father, mother, and brother. But this house and the memories of it were the only link to that lost time. The vines creaked with his weight, though he shifted it very gradually and carefully in order to minimize the sounds. From inside he could hear laughter and music. A feast was in progress, not a boisterous bacchanal, but a lively enough feast that the few sounds made by him would not be noticed.

Reaching his grandfather's window Lazaro found the shutter was not latched from the inside and swung open with ease. He pulled himself onto the ledge and pushed on the windows. These were latched, but he quietly slid his stiletto between the wooden sashes and the latch lifted. Slowly he let his feet down onto the floor, testing each step before shifting his weight. The moon lent its light to the room and as his eyes sharpened he saw that the room had not changed from the one time he had seen it so long ago.

He had been brought here the night after his mother's burial, when he was found collapsed under a mirror. His grandfather had been standing in a robe staring at a picture on the wall. Words which he did not then understand were spoken harshly, and he had been taken away. But in that brief visit he had seen what his grandfather had been staring at. He looked for it now and found it under a piece of tattered black cloth — a small painting of his mother.

Margoleit was awake when Lazaro returned, but with Vom Scheidt asleep in the next bed, they stepped out through the window and onto the roof to be alone and get the benefit of the cool breeze.

"I was a bit worried when you didn't come back."

"It took longer than I thought, but I've made arrangements for you to stay with an old friend of my mother's — Lucrezia. She can be trusted. It'll be best if you go there tomorrow. What I have to do in the next few days, it's better you don't know."

"Will you be gone long?"

"Two months, maybe three. It's hard to say. Will you be all right here?"

"I don't have much choice," she said, then realized that that was the wrong thing to say. "I'll be fine. This woman, you trust her and so I trust her. And Fugger needs you. Things will work out, and before you know it, you'll have completed your bargain with Fugger and we can be on our way."

"I'll take you there tomorrow, but after that I'll stay away. I don't want you mixed up in any of this." Margoleit nodded. Lazaro reached into his pocket and pulled out the small piece of canvas. "There's something I want you to keep for me while I'm gone." He handed the miniature of his mother to Margoleit.

She opened it and he could tell that she recognized immediately who it was. He also saw that she was more than a bit surprised at the resemblance between herself and the woman in the painting.

"I'll keep it safe for you," she said, and they sat down on the roof to watch the sky.

Vom Scheidt was still asleep when they left and walked through the streets to Lucrezia's house. To Lazaro's satisfaction there were few Candiots about. Their goodbyes were brief: to have taken any longer would have betrayed the fear they both harbored.

When Lazaro returned, Vom Scheidt was just awakening, stretching his arms and sniffing the air. "Where's Margoleit?" he asked Lazaro.

"I've taken her to a safe place." Lazaro's tone made it clear he wanted no more discussion of Margoleit.

"Right," Vom Scheidt said, swinging his legs over the edge of the bed. He smelled the water in the pitcher before pouring some into a shallow earthenware bowl and rinsing his face. Lazaro went over to share the water. Vom Scheidt had moved to the small window and was looking out over the water. "Will it be difficult to get in touch with Tadini?"

Lazaro pulled his wet fingers through his hair. "No. This is Friday. Gabriel Tadini is a man of habit, and each Friday he selects his own fish in the fish market."

Vom Scheidt smiled. "And if your attention to his habits is more enduring than his own?"

Lazaro shrugged. "Fugger has provided me with his address."

They didn't need the address. As they stood in the fish market, Lazaro saw a tall man with graying hair and an aquiline nose making his way through the crowd, followed by a servant with a basket. Unmistakably, it was Tadini.

Lazaro watched for a while and saw, as he had expected to see, three guards following Tadini. The Governor, the Duke of Trevisiano, would take necessary precautions, especially if ordered by the Signoria to keep Tadini in Crete. The bodyguards appeared to be seasoned men, though they were not in the least apprehensive, and seemed as interested in the young women of the market as in keeping a watchful eye on their charge. Lazaro sent Vom Scheidt off to find two attractive and available girls, and before long they were in motion. As Tadini sifted through the fish market, the two girls found their way to the bodyguards and kept them busy long enough for Lazaro to pull Tadini back in between two stalls just as Tadini sent his servant off to another area of the market.

"Lazaro," Tadini said with surprise as he straightened his robe. "You find a strange way to greet an old comrade-at-arms. I didn't know you were in Crete."

"I'm not," Lazaro said with a crooked grin and stepped past Tadini to catch Vom Scheidt's eye. Vom Scheidt nodded that no one had noticed Tadini's disappearance. "I apologize for the rough greeting, but the Signoria has some young men following you and I would rather they did not know we had talked."

"The Knights have sent you, then."

"Someone trying to help the Knights asked me to speak with you. They are interested in having you come to Rhodes."

"I'm sure they are," Tadini said, stroking his beard. "Suleiman will move on the island this summer. But the Governor has placed me under military orders not to leave. I have to get Crete ready, in case Suleiman decides to move on us, though we all know that's highly unlikely. So even if the price were right, no shipping would accept me."

"I can arrange for you to be kidnapped" — Lazaro stepped back to check with Vom Scheidt again and received a nod — "kidnapped right in front of the men who are guarding you. If you are taken against your will, there is nothing anyone can say. And the Knights sorely need someone of your talents."

"The Signoria doesn't seem to understand that if they want to stop the Turk they should do it in Rhodes."

"They should have sent more help to Hungary. I came from there," Lazaro said, sensing that Tadini was in favor of the venture.

"Was it bad?"

"Bad enough. It will be better this summer. But if Suleiman has a success at Rhodes he will return there, and if he can break through he can move right up the Danube to Europe."

"Getting rid of Rhodes would give him freer rein in the Mediterranean as well," Tadini added.

"You will come, then?"

Tadini sniffed the air. "I'm getting a little too old to be running off on wild-goose chases. Even with me, I don't know if there's enough time left."

Lazaro remembered Fugger's hope that there would not be. "Maybe not, but it's quite a challenge, and the Knights are very rich."

"I am growing tired of this place," Tadini said sweeping his arm around. "The fish are good but the way they prepare it here, it just isn't to my liking. But who do I know in Rhodes?"

"We'll be there," Lazaro said and Vom Scheidt nodded.

"It will be costly," Tadini said.

Lazaro smiled. "I'll guarantee you will be satisfied with the fee. And you'll be made a Knight."

Tadini's eyebrows raised. He paused, and nodded his head from side to side as if arguing with himself. Finally it ended. "If you're going, I'll go with you. How will it be done?"

"It's better that I don't tell you anything. It will be more convincing to the Signoria's men. But it will happen soon."

Tadini nodded and leaned toward Lazaro. "It is good to see you again." With that he shuffled back out into the market.

The next week was taken up with preparations. Bosio and Vom Scheidt kept themselves busy provisioning the ship while Lazaro watched Tadini, following him throughout the city as he went about his tasks. The only difficulty he encountered was in forcing himself to stay away from Lucrezia's house.

It didn't take long to spot the other guards who had been sent by the Signoria. There were five in all, three for the day and two for the night. All were young, rough, but obviously well trained for their task. It was understandable that Tadini had not spotted them. The three who followed him by day would take turns, one following while the other two hung back, so that it would be difficult for anyone to notice them. The two night watchers followed the same plan, though Tadini's habit was to remain at home most evenings. This meant they had to do little more than take turns watching from their rooms, which allowed them a view of the main entrance to his house. It seemed they did not expect trouble. Lazaro was now convinced that his plan would work.

On Tuesday Lazaro and Vom Scheidt rode east of Candia to a remote section of the Bay of Mirabella which Lazaro had known as a young boy. Nothing had changed, and it was sufficiently deserted to be used as the place to rendezvous with Bosio. They then turned their attention to the streets around Tadini's house, watching the route Tadini took as he returned for the evening and the actions of his watchers as they delivered their charge to his house, then waited to be relieved by the two men who kept guard at night. By Thursday evening Lazaro was satisfied with the plan, and he asked Bosio to cruise the coast past the Bay of Mirabella, then to work his way back so that he would be there on Saturday, waiting.

The heat was building on Saturday evening and there seemed to be no respite in sight. The sky was still clear and there was little movement of air through the streets of Candia. Lazaro, hidden in the mouth of a narrow alley, watched for Tadini to return home. Across the street he had positioned Vom Scheidt in clear view. He was to wait until Tadini had passed, then knock him unconscious, as gently as possible. Lazaro had worried about this part of the plan, but he knew it had to look real. As Tadini did not know Vom Scheidt well, it was easier to have him strike the blow. They had also positioned three horses in a nearby alley. Lazaro would be there to surprise the bodyguards as they rushed Vom Scheidt. After that it would be a simple task of riding east to the rendezvous with Bosio. Once on the sea, either by wind or oars, they would put a safe distance between them and Crete.

They didn't have to wait long. Lazaro saw Tadini as he turned the corner. He pulled his head back in so that he would not be seen. Unfortunately, Tadini was not alone, as he had been on previous nights. A man walked at his side, talking, and Lazaro assumed he was one of the governor's men, by his dress and by his weapons. From his vantage point he could see that Vom Scheidt had noticed the complication and was preparing for it. The men walked past Vom Scheidt and he made his move, first striking Tadini on the back of the head with the pommel of his sword. Lazaro winced, then readied himself. Part of him wanted to rush out immediately but he knew he had to wait until the bodyguards rounded the corner.

What happened next was unfortunate. The man who had been walking with Tadini turned to face Vom Scheidt, drew his blade, then, with only a moment's hesitation, ran away. Vom Scheidt, crouching at the ready, straightened himself and turned to Lazaro, smiled, and replaced his sword. Lazaro was not as pleased. He had not counted on cowardice. That man was by now halfway to the governor's palace and would be returning with more men. Suddenly the bodyguards turned the corner. They had abandoned their normal formation and all three rounded the corner together. Vom Scheidt was busy pulling Tadini over the back of one of the horses. While two of the *bravi* stood their ground, one advanced with his sword drawn. Lazaro stepped out of the shadows and stood between the bodyguard and Vom Scheidt. No words were spoken but Lazaro could see in this man's eyes that he would not turn tail and run. Instead he waited, standing back two paces from Lazaro, then circled him, sizing him up. As Lazaro drew his stiletto he saw a second bodyguard approach Vom Scheidt. The third left and he too was probably headed for the governor's palace, unless there was help closer. Lazaro caught Vom Scheidt's eye and they nodded to each other. This matter had to be finished quickly. Vom Scheidt was the first to strike and as the sound of steel on steel hit home, Lazaro slashed at his opponent. The man was good on his feet and moved back and to the side as he returned a thrust. Sweat dripped from Lazaro's brow as they exchanged blow after blow, and he became concerned that this matter would take too long to conclude. Both of the *bravi* knew that all they had to do was keep Lazaro and Vom Scheidt busy until others arrived. There was no need for them to endanger themselves, and so they parried where they could and assumed a defensive posture. Lazaro watched and each time he saw an opening he pressed it, yet he was gaining no ground. He heard from behind him a gasp and the sound of a body fall, but he couldn't spare the time to turn to see who had been successful. And then the look on his adversary's face told the tale. A knife whistled past him and stuck in the man's stomach. He dropped his sword and stiletto and tried to pull the blade out but it had sunk deep and sapped all of his strength. He fell to his knees, then his face smashed into the paving stones. Lazaro wiped the sweat from his brow and turned to see Vom Scheidt.

"Sorry," Vom Scheidt said as he stepped past Lazaro to retrieve his knife, "but I don't think it would be a good idea to stay any longer."

"Don't let it bother you," Lazaro answered, sheathing his blades, "I couldn't get to him." He looked over at the unconscious body of

Tadini, sprawled over the back of a horse. "We've got to get him out of here. He's going to have a bellyache to match his headache."

They made it out of the city without incident, but as they topped a rise about two miles out and looked back they could see the dust of horses following them. They stopped and revived Tadini with water and got him back on his horse. He accepted Vom Scheidt's apology for the blow, and assured them that he could ride, but Lazaro noticed that he was still a bit groggy. This, he knew, would slow them down enough to make it dangerous. However, there was nothing they could do but ride. It was when they topped the ridge by the shore that Lazaro saw what would be their real problem. As Vom Scheidt and Tadini rode on, Lazaro stopped and watched the shipping from Candia. Among the boats he could make out at least four sleek galleys propelled by oars and sails. Two were headed east and the other two west. These were the customs boats. The governor had been quick to respond, and these galleys, used to hunt smugglers, would be hard to outrun.

When they reached the bay, Bosio was already waiting for them at the shore with a small boat. His ship was anchored in the bay, ready to sail. Three young men were put ashore, as Lazaro had requested, to ride off with the horses to lead the pursuers away. He told Bosio of the customs ships and Bosio sprang into action. Even before they had reached the ship he had been shouting commands and already the anchor was up and men were scurrying here and there in the rigging and on the deck. The sails were taken down and the masts dismantled. Once everyone was aboard he let down another boat and had everyone at the oars both in the galley and in the boats which were now being used to tow the ship. Lazaro could see as he pulled at the oar that they were headed for a cliff face on the east side of the bay. He smiled. Bosio had scouted the area well. He knew from his youth that there was a cave there, and at low tide Bosio could have slipped the galley in. But now that the tide was high it would afford little protection, and even though Bosio had unstepped the masts, he wondered how he intended to hide from the watchful eye of a galley captain.

The answer was quick in coming. As the galley pulled up to the cliff face Bosio had men in the water with ropes and tackle. They found a few spots to attach ropes to and they used winches to pull the galley up close to the rocks and secure her under the overhang afforded by the cliff. Bosio had his men drape the dirty brown sails over the boat from stem to stern. On more than one occasion during the trip, Lazaro had wondered why the Knights of Rhodes could not afford a more well-equipped and modern galley. However, he saw now the value of the ship's appearance. Once the sails had been lowered to water level they formed a curtain which all but blended with the color of the rocks. From the sea it would be next to impossible to make out as it lay tight to the cliff. The test came immediately. Bosio had been correct to move with great haste because no sooner had the sail touched water than two customs boats came into view. One stayed out while the other swung in to take a closer look at the bay. Bosio signaled to his men and they remained silent. There was no sound save the groan of the ropes which held them tight to the rocks.

Within an hour the customs galleys had moved on along the coast, but Bosio held fast to the cliff face. He had survived as long as he had by taking chances only when absolutely necessary. There was no need to run now, and they might find more galleys waiting for them as soon as they cleared the headland. Instead, he waited until nightfall, and then, before the moon rose, he untied his ship and sailed off into the night, for Rhodes.

As Lazaro looked back at the dark coastline, he said a short prayer for a quick end to the task before him and a safe reunion with Margoleit and the child she was carrying.

XXI

When Bosio anchored his ship in the galley port at Rhodes it felt to Lazaro as if he had been poured into a deep crucible with slippery, glassy walls and a fire beneath it being fanned hotter and hotter.

The city was a nest of activity, an anthill of whitewashed buildings and gray stone walls amid the blue of the Mediterranean. It was clear that De L'Isle Adam had been busy. His spies had given him early warning of Suleiman's intention and De L'Isle Adam had used the time wisely, gathering in all crops, refortifying some of the battlements that had fallen into disrepair, especially the Tower of St. Nicholas which could guard both the galley port and the commercial port. There had been green on the island, but around the city of Rhodes it had been either harvested or burned back. Lessons learned in the siege of 1480 were being applied in the hope that perhaps Suleiman would not have been as successful at learning from the mistakes of his father.

The Grand Master had also sent out envoys to gather troops and provisions from all quarters. Still, the Knights numbered only about five hundred, including their servants-at-arms. De L'Isle Adam had managed to recruit another thousand mercenaries and perhaps five hundred of the Rhodians were capable of serving as militiamen. Another two thousand Rhodians had come inside to serve as sappers and pioneers under the direction of Tadini.

And then there were the Jewish slaves kept by the Knights. Lazaro had wondered how true the stories which Solomon had told could have been. But now, inside the city, it was only too clear that the tales had been true. The Jews were not mistreated in any material way but it was clear that they were kept as captives. Under Suleiman, Jews were allowed to live peacefully, to carry on business, and practice their religion. These freedoms were denied them by the Knights. For that reason, a significant number had remained outside the walls, in hiding, to take their chances with the Turks.

While Tadini was only one man, his arrival was a crowning achievement for the Knights. With Tadini in Rhodes, the final preparations could begin in earnest. The first of August was set for Tadini's formal investiture as a Knight of the Langue of Italy, bypassing the normal period of service in apprenticeship. As a Knight he would cease to be a citizen of Venice, for whatever worth that might have in diplomatic circles. However, he was treated immediately as a Knight and given command of all preparations of fortifications, positioning of artillery, and deployment of sappers for countermining. Quarters suitable to his station were made available to him, and he was provided with a valet who also was rumored to be a good cook. When he invited Lazaro and Vom Scheidt to join him, they accepted without hesitation.

Lazaro had a small room to himself, a luxury in a city crowded with men and provisions. There was a little table in the corner of the room, and he cleared it to use as a writing desk. He set out paper, pen, and ink that he had carefully packed. It was his hope that he would not be here long, but he knew it would ease his mind if he could write to Margoleit, even if she might not receive the letters. He also unpacked his battle dress; black leather shirt and pantaloons, generously studded with metal. Though at first he thought it might be premature, as he watched from his small window the preparations within the wall and beyond for the imminent siege, he realized it would be best to be prepared, and so, rather than hanging them up, he donned the leathers. In his pack he also found the small mirror which Angelo had given him on the night of his departure from Venice. As he stuffed it into the pouch tied around his waist, he heard footsteps stop at his door.

"Ominous," Vom Scheidt said, leaning in the doorway.

Lazaro turned and smiled. "When in Rhodes . . ."

"Tadini sent me. His manservant has found a chicken and prepared it for us. It is likely to be the last fresh meat you will have for some time so I have been sent to bring you. It may also be the last time Tadini eats with us. No doubt he'll be supping with the Knights from here on in." Vom Scheidt walked over to the window. "This is more than I have." He leaned out, watched for a moment. "I'd rather be on the outside trying to get in."

Lazaro finished tying his boots and walked over to the door. "Wouldn't we all."

Vom Scheidt took a last look at the setting sun, and then the two of them walked off to join Tadini for the evening meal.

Late that night word came to Lazaro's quarters that the Grand Master would see him in private. The guards remained outside the heavy wooden doors as Lazaro entered. Dressed in the long black robes of the Order, the Grand Master shut the door himself and indicated that Lazaro was to follow him to a desk and two chairs positioned so that they allowed a view of the city's walls. There was wine on the table and the Grand Master poured two glasses.

De L'Isle Adam had a hard face, not scarred as that of a footsoldier, but scarred inside from the decisions he had made during his military career. In the black robe he resembled more a chancellor of the Signoria than a great general.

"Fugger has placed a great deal of trust in you, and it seems justified. I had all but given up hope that Tadini would get here."

Lazaro nodded and took the glass of wine. "He was eager to be of assistance."

De L'Isle Adam smiled cynically. "I'm sure he was." He paused and looked out over the walls where even in the dark of night there was furious activity. "There's never enough time. Or money." He emptied his glass of wine and filled it again. "You will not have use of any of my ships. Fugger has arranged with this Hungarian of his, Béres, to send in a number of ships with provisions and mercenaries. As they arrive, you will supervise the flow of material." He handed Lazaro a sheet of paper, drawn up like a ledger, indicating how much gold and other precious commodities could be transported, and when. "I want to make it clear that you will do nothing to make this transfer of securities apparent. My men must know none of this. You will work directly with me and you will be under my military discipline. I will expect you to fight as the need arises, and I assure you it will arise."

As Lazaro scanned the list, checking it against the information he had memorized from Fugger's accounts in Venice, he became fully aware of the wealth of the Knights, and of the brilliance of Fugger's plan. By giving the Knights Tadini at this late juncture, he ensured that they would remain on this rock and that, inevitably, the Turk would have all the riches which the Emperor Charles was hoping to retrieve in order to continue his activities in Europe. Charles, in turn, would have to become even more indebted to Fugger, and Fugger's wealth and influence would increase dramatically. But the hardest part remained — making sure that De L'Isle Adam kept his part of the bargain, and that the plunder that belonged to Fugger moved safely through the Turkish blockade which would soon begin to strangle Rhodes.

When the audience was over, Lazaro was escorted back to his room where he found Vom Scheidt asleep and Tadini standing out on the balcony, hands on his hips, watching the night workers about the city.

"This will probably not work," he said to Lazaro without looking at him, "but it is quite a challenge."

"If any one can do it, it's you," Lazaro responded.

Tadini turned to him with a grin and nodded his head in agreement. "Me. Or God."

On the next day, the feast of Corpus Domini, the first Turkish ships reached Kalitheas Bay. There were not many but they sailed past the city with the bands of the Yenicheri — the Janissaries, the Europeans called them — playing martial Turkish music. Tadini signaled to his gunners in the Tower of St. Nicholas and they opened fire. The ships were not hit, but it didn't matter. Tadini wished only to remind them of the fort which had held off the most fierce of attacks in the siege of 1480, when Suleiman's father had failed in his bid to take Rhodes. Lazaro wondered which way the omen should be read. This was the first time he had entered a fray expecting his side to lose, betting on it. He hoped he would not be there when it happened.

Though the ships were only a vanguard, and there was no sign of Suleiman, the invasion had begun. The defenders of Rhodes watched as flotillas continued to arrive during the following two weeks, and yet their reconnaissance reports indicated that no men were disembarking. Lazaro was busy for most of that period helping Tadini and readying those goods which De L'Isle Adam had agreed could be sent out with the first ship. He had seen riches before which equaled those hoarded by the Order, but only in dreams or in paintings. Centuries of plundering the East (and by the presence of some articles, the West as well) had led to an accumulation of wealth which could only be appreciated by the truly wealthy, such as Fugger. As he worked in the treasure rooms Lazaro polished a precious thought. With the delay of the Turkish disembarkation, it was his hope that Fugger's ships might arrive quickly and that before the true siege began it might be possible to complete his task and return to Margoleit.

On the tenth of July a vessel flying the colors of Florence made its way into the port, successfully running the Turkish blockade which had by now established its presence. Its captain, Bertoluzzi, had been sent by Béres and brought with him a good store of food and wine, five mercenaries, and a pouch which bore the Fugger coat of arms. When Lazaro arrived at the door to the Grand Master's chambers it was open, guarded by one Knight in battle dress. Within he could see Bertoluzzi surrounded by De L'Isle Adam and three other Knights all dressed in the black robe normally worn by the Knights when out of battledress. Tadini was similarly attired but was standing by the window, looking out over the harbor as a great boom was being hauled across from St. Angelo to Fort St. Nicholas.

Tadini noticed Lazaro and signaled for him to enter. As he passed the Knights arguing in the center of the room he recognized the other three as Commissioners of Gunpowder: de Pommerois, Buck, and another man he had seen about but whose name he did not know.

Tadini whispered the identity for the third Commissioner to Lazaro. "That's D'Amaral. He contested with De L'Isle Adam for the position of Grand Master but lost in the final vote. He didn't take it too well, but De L'Isle Adam has been playing up to him. D'Amaral holds sway over many of the Knights." Tadini had obviously been enjoying the argument which occupied the Grand Master and his three Commissioners and smiled as he explained it to Lazaro.

"Bertoluzzi wants to lead a night attack on the Turkish ships — send in fire boats and boats loaded with gunpowder to destroy the fleet while the troops are still on board."

"It sounds reasonable," Lazaro answered quietly.

"But he wants to do it with your ship."

Lazaro strained to follow the discussion more closely.

De Pommerois and Buck were quite in favor of the bold plan. D'Amaral, on the contrary, argued that the store of gunpowder would need to be preserved and that the number of ships required should not be risked in what he saw as a foolhardy venture. As Lazaro listened he saw the good strategy behind Bertoluzzi's plan and, though he would rather have not risked the first of his ships, he was surprised and, to some extent, disappointed when De L'Isle Adam took D'Amaral's advice and rejected the plan.

The Grand Master thanked the Commissioners, then indicated that he wished to be alone with Tadini, Lazaro, and the bold Captain. When the Commissioners had gone and the guard had closed the door, De L'Isle Adam came over to them at the window. Tadini walked over to the other side of the room where Bertoluzzi stood at a table which had a pitcher of wine and some glasses. He poured glasses for himself and Bertoluzzi, and they spoke quietly.

The Grand Master stood beside Lazaro and they both looked out over the Post of France. "This man has presented credentials from Fugger. You can send your German friend with the first shipment, but remember, I want no one to know of this." He looked over at Tadini and spoke loudly enough for him to hear. "Experience is sometimes an expensive commodity."

Tadini smiled. "But often worth the price."

The Grand Master returned the smile but paused and looked out over the battlements. The smile left him and he mumbled, "I hope so," then turned and left the room.

Lazaro joined Bertoluzzi and Tadini in a glass of wine and Bertoluzzi reached into the Fugger pouch and handed Lazaro a packet addressed to him. Inside was a message from Béres, in Fugger's code, directing him to send Vom Scheidt back with Bertoluzzi to Valona. Béres would meet him there to take over the shipment and, by that time, would have another ship provisioned and ready to sail for Rhodes, and Vom Scheidt would return on it.

After everyone had retired for the night, Lazaro returned to his quarters and, in what was becoming a habit, he pulled his chair over to the small window and looked out over the city's walls. The night was calm, uneventful, and Lazaro wondered if the fighting would ever really begin. Below him the laborers continued their preparations under the watchful eyes of the Knights, but above him the stars hung peacefully in the clear sky, and out on the Mediterranean the moon rose, sparkling.

In some ways he hoped for some action, just to occupy his time. Accompanying Tadini about the walls or taking care of Fugger's business interests left too much time for speculation — speculation about their child Margoleit was carrying, about their future, even about his feelings for Margoleit. Lazaro found himself questioning whether he had been truthful to Margoleit and to himself. There was no doubt that he felt keenly the pain of separation, but deep within himself, though he tried to ignore it, he wondered to what extent his feelings for Margoleit might have been in proportion to the wound Marzia had left in him. And in the shadows, Marzia still appeared to taunt him, to twist the knife.

Finding it impossible to sleep, he sat up into the late hours at the small desk in the corner, as he had on other nights, writing a letter to Margoleit, looking forward to being with her soon. By the time he had written all that he could, it was quite late and he, quite tired. His last thoughts before sleep took him were of her and the chance that he would soon be able to leave.

Bertoluzzi sailed on the evening of the fourteenth, carrying Vom Scheidt and the goods which were to be delivered to Béres. Vom Scheidt also carried a packet of letters which he would try to forward to Margoleit in Candia.

The next morning Tadini received word in his chambers that the Turks were landing. Lazaro accompanied him up onto the battlements of the Post of England, where they watched the first Turkish batteries being set up. Other batteries followed throughout the day until the city was ringed with cannons and soldiers of the Sultan. As he watched from Tadini's observation post, Lazaro began to understand how defenders of the cities he had attacked in the past must have felt. For those in Rhodes there was no retreat, they would have to stand their ground. Arrayed in a huge crescent beyond the city walls were soldiers from all the lands of the Sultan: Persians, Circassians, Anatolians, Wallachians, Arabs, Egyptians, the Turks themselves. But most noticeable were the troops of Janissaries, the Sultan's personal army. Young boys were given up by Christian families as part of a levy — the *devshurmeh* — exacted by the Sultan. These children were put through extensive training in religion, literature, music, horticulture, and, obviously, warfare. What made them nearly invincible, however, was the military indoctrination, the lifelong camaraderie of the barracks (for they were not allowed to marry), and the high status they enjoyed. Their distinctive headdress, a large white ostrich plume, made them recognizable by sight, but they were also recognizable by ear. The Janissaries made use of martial music in preparation for and during their attacks. Even though they were not attacking at the moment, the sound of their music struck a chord in Lazaro. It reminded him of things for which he had no real memory, and that troubled him. For an instant he wondered if he would have been with the host outside the walls of Rhodes if his grandfather had not sent mercenaries to gather his mother from this very city.

There was little time for such thoughts in the days that followed. Sortie after sortie was sent out to harass the Turks. From the battlements Tadini orchestrated a rain of fire and shot, using much more gunpowder than the Commissioners would have liked. And under the walls Tadini waged war as well, though there the fruit would be slower to come. Sappers from the Turkish side had set to work almost immediately on taking up their positions, digging tunnels and trenches toward the foundations of key positions at the battlements. Theirs was the traditional and most successful of siege maneuvers. A series of tunnels would be dug to the foundations of a tower, a cavern would be hollowed out and filled with gunpowder or firewood and the tower would then either be shaken by the blast or overheated by fire until it crumbled. However, total success called for expert miners and an unimaginative and inexperienced enemy. The Turks had the first but not the second.

Tadini had constructed a number of sensing devices, tambourine-shaped objects with bells attached, which, when placed on the outer walls, could detect the vibration of miners, and he was training a cohort of listeners. Armed with that information he would be able to direct his sappers to countermine, constructing ventilation shafts which would completely dissipate an explosion. He also had his men constructing larger tunnels which would snake out to the Turkish tunnel so that they could be filled with armed men waiting for the Turks to break through. Still, all of this would take time and for the moment he had to turn his attention to the artillery. With the agreement of De L'Isle Adam, he asked Lazaro to assist him in the planning of his tunnelwork and, when the need arose, to supervise the construction of the larger tunnels and the deployment of soldiers beneath the earth.

By the last week of July the Knights had been so successful in their tactics aboveground that there was rumor of mutiny in the Turkish camps. Spies reported men refusing to fight, sappers refusing to dig. Lazaro's hopes of a quick resolution rose again. However, on Monday the twenty-eighth Suleiman arrived and made a great show with his Janissaries and their band. He visited the entire siege line, personally overseeing a number of impalings of some of his less-successful commanders in the hopes of encouraging his troops, then headed for Megasandra where his headquarters had been set up. All hopes of the siege being lifted were dashed. Immediately the defenders of the city noticed changes in the array of siege weapons; siege lines were reformed to be more effective, guns were repositioned to increase their accuracy. But the most telling aspect of Suleiman taking charge was that there was a drastic increase in the activity of the sappers. In addition to tunneling, to the great consternation of Tadini, they built a huge earthen artillery mound which, when completed, would allow Suleiman's gunners to fire directly into the city.

Despite artillery tactics which rained death on the mound builders, and mounted forays to attack them, the mound grew until not only the battlements but the inhabitants of Rhodes began to feel the true weight of Suleiman's attack. And though there were cannonballs of immense size, some more than eight feet in circumference, it was Suleiman's exploding artillery shells and his *carcasse* which caused the most damage. The exploding artillery shells were something new, and Tadini was suitably impressed by the military science of the Turks. The *carcasse*, on the other hand, was more common and quite effective. Small balls of metal, covered with razor-sharp points, wrapped in cloth then dipped in a mixture of excrement, rotting flesh, and, whenever possible, extract from the swellings of plague victims, would be hurled into the city. It took only a small cut to infect a man and any military commander knew that an injured man could be more costly than a dead one.

Belowground it had been quieter, but just as busy. The sappers had been working in shifts, constructing a series of tunnels leading here and there about the base of the fortifications, seeking the tunnels of the Turks. More men had been trained in the use of Tadini's listening device and it was clear that once the mound was of a suitable size, the Turkish sappers had turned their attentions back to mining the city walls. Tadini personally directed the construction of the ventilation shafts which would displace much of the anticipated blast. In other areas, large open trenches were dug deep to act as a barrier to approaching tunnels. Lazaro directed his sappers to dig deeper in search of the larger tunnels which the Turks would use to allow their soldiers to enter the city. Lazaro's tunnels were just as large, so that he might bring men-at-arms to the subterranean battlefield. On a number of occasions those on the surface might be experiencing a lull in the battle while below, in the tunnels, blood flowed in pitched battles fought in near darkness with no room to move. Often the tunnels were packed with men waiting their turn to advance farther along in the darkness where the fighting was taking place. Here, a Roland was all that was needed.

The morning of the twenty-second of August dawned cool. Lazaro had awakened just before first light and pulled on a robe to keep him warm as he stood on the observation deck. At some point in the night the pleasant dreams of Margoleit had stopped abruptly and Marzia had returned to torment him. Then these visions ceased as well, and in their place came the dreams he had hoped were gone forever.

He had dreamed again of his mother. The dreams had stopped after he had returned to the house in Crete, as if by visiting that room the ghosts had been swept from his mind. But in the deep of his dreams last night she had returned. Perhaps it had been the bellicose music of the Janissaries, who seemed to play all night. He had come close to the surface of consciousness a number of times, and though he had never really awakened, he had been aware of the music. It seemed to writhe in the black night. His mother had been there in his dream, floating in the gentle breeze, but it had not been Crete. Rather, it had been here in Rhodes. He had run out of the room and as he ran down the twisting streets he had grown into a man. As he turned a corner he ran into a Janissary. When he stepped back to look at the Janissary there was something familiar in his face. Lazaro had reached for his sword but found it missing. He looked up at the Janissary again and saw that his sword was sticking through the young soldier. It was then that he realized why the face was familiar — the Janissary was his brother, Nicolo. The drums of the Janissaries began to beat faster and faster.

He had awakened with a pounding headache, drenched in sweat. There seemed to be no air in his room and he had gone out to the balcony for some fresh air. In the early morning sunlight, the scene spread before him was like a representation of Hell. Fires, smoke, trenches, living men crawling over dead, and everywhere mud. And below that hell lay another — his tunnels.

After a quick breakfast he was back underground, his dreams far behind him, checking the work which had been done by the night shift. At first the tunnel seemed cool but as he approached the work area, the cool dampness gave way to the fetid air of the workers' sweat. Here and there dead rodents added their shovel-split innards to the slime, and more than once men slipped and fell from this rather than any seepage. He was glad that they were sensitive enough to remain silent when they fell. There was no way of knowing how close an enemy tunnel might be. Any moment the walls could split open and murderous barbarians could roll out, blades in hand, and kill a work party. It was somehow more troublesome to the nerves than walking in the streets where an errant cannonball might drop from the sky. Even duty by the walls was more relaxing. There there was air, light, room for movement. Here there was only the constant reminder of the grave.

Lazaro moved now, following a red rope that led out to the tunnel Tadini had asked him to check on. The digging had proceeded well, and Tadini was sure that the tunnel was now far enough out that it should be mined and left to await an advance by the Turks. As Lazaro turned the last curve he saw one of the sappers bending close to the wall. He had his ear against a listening stick stuck into the earth. As he saw Lazaro he motioned quickly for him to come, silently, and listen.

Lazaro put his ear to the stick. He could hear the voices of the Turks through the soil which separated their tunnel from his; perhaps thirty feet, perhaps no more than two or three. It was hard to say underground. The quality of the soil, the presence of water or of stone, all could deceive. There was now a gathering of sappers about him. Without moving he signaled to them to hurry back to the supply tunnel and bring gunpowder, all they could carry. He replaced his ear to the stick and strained, trying to make out the words but failing. He glanced back over his shoulder and saw his sappers heading back for the gunpowder, moving past the shafts of light which came down the vents. These created rings or bands of light in the otherwise dark and murky tomb. His candle flickered and went out, and for a moment he was afraid. In that darkness he saw the deception of the mind as all manner of fear swept over him and created strange shapes. Then his eyes grew accustomed to the light level and he again could see the rings of light, though his sappers were now out of sight.

The voices of the Turks had stopped. He tried the listening stick. Nothing. He moved along to the absolute end of the tunnel and listened, holding his breath, straining his ears.

A sound began and moved toward him with fearsome speed. The walls of the tunnel shook and he glanced back again to see the rings of light but they were gone. He cradled his head in his hands and everything went black.

XXII

There was a bright light, like a gather of molten glass fresh from the glory hole, and Lazaro moved from the darkness toward it. As he got closer, what had been white was now pale in comparison to that brighter light which seemed to come from the center. He was closer now, so close that the light was blinding, but still it grew brighter. He saw someone there, a woman, he thought, in a long flowing white dress. There was a soft breeze and the smell of a flower. He could not remember what the flower was called. Suddenly he spun wildly back into the darkness and felt his mouth fill with sand.

"Lazaro!"

He did not recognize the voice. He barely recognized the name as his own. He could see nothing.

"Lazaro!"

Louder now. He could feel hands on his body. He knew that he had little clothing on and he was cold. There was a hand touching a cool wet cloth to his forehead. He did not want to open his eyes and find himself naked in front of strangers. And he could sense that there were others about.

"Lazaro! Open your eyes!"

He did not want to open his eyes. This voice had no authority over him. He would not rise up and come forth.

Cold water splashed his face and he gasped. A hand slapped his cheek and that voice called to him again. He opened his eyes.

Tadini was kneeling above him and Vom Scheidt was crouching behind Tadini. At first he didn't really recognize them. He knew their names, but he had no clear idea of who they were. Finally it dawned on him that Vom Scheidt should not be there, and he said as much.

Tadini and Vom Scheidt smiled, and Tadini straightened and sat on a chair near the bed. Vom Scheidt knelt down and rested against the side of the bed, sitting on a pillow that lay on the stone floor. "I wish I weren't here. You missed the best of it, I think."

Lazaro looked over at Tadini. "What happened?"

"Your friend's right, I hope. The Turks set off their mines. It took us the better part of a day to get to you. That was five days ago. They must have had five-sixths of the *enceinte* mined. Our shafts vented most of the blasts, but we've taken some serious damage at the Post of Auvergne and we lost a lot of the old wall. Poor masonry to begin with. Vom Scheidt arrived three days ago with Emeric Depreaux, but we've probably lost a third of the men he brought in."

"Béres is in good spirits in Valona," Vom Scheidt added. "Too good for what you have to put up with here. Fugger arranged for twenty mercenaries and provisions and we carried in four Knights who had been unable to arrange transport. It put a smile on the Grand Master's face, and I think he's ready to send me out again."

Lazaro nodded and sat up, though the pounding in his head made him wish he had not. He noticed that he was clothed from the waist down but that his stomach and chest were heavily bruised. The way his face felt, he expected that it would look the same.

Vom Scheidt moved over to a chair so that Lazaro could swing his legs over the edge of the bed. "Depreaux won't go back out, though. He said it's honor, I think it's fear. The shipping lanes are pretty bad. Turks everywhere. But Bosio has volunteered to head out to Naples then to Rome for more men, so I think you could arrange for him to drop me in Valona."

Lazaro nodded and made an effort to stand.

"Don't try it right now," Tadini advised. "You'll need to build up your strength. You used most of it just staying alive. The sappers who found you were ready to leave you there rather than drag you out for burial. But your mirror was beside you on the ground and one of them checked you for breath. That convinced them to bring you out." Tadini stood and reached over to Lazaro, handing him the small mirror which Angelo had given him.

Lazaro said a silent thank-you to the old man and looked at the mirror. The face in the mirror was not quite his own. It was thinner, stubbled, a very different color. His own blue eyes still shone out, so he knew that he was alive, though not if he was still human. Something in his face reminded him distantly of a wolf, and, feeling the old discomfort, he put the mirror down quickly.

Vom Scheidt laughed. "You're not much uglier than you were before. Don't let your vanity fool you."

Lazaro managed a smile and turned to his friend. "When does Bosio leave?"

"Tomorrow," Tadini answered. "So you'll have to make arrangements tonight."

Lazaro heard the hesitation in his voice. "What else?"

"Things aren't going to get any easier here." Tadini was uncomfortable with his suggestion. "It might be advisable for you to ship out with Bosio. Suleiman will not be happy with the ships that have been coming in and out. He'll tighten the blockade."

Lazaro shook his head and again felt the pain. "I can't leave until I've completed the deal for Fugger." He looked to Vom Scheidt and then to Tadini. "I gave him my word. If I don't keep it I could lose everything."

Tadini raised his hands. "As you wish, but you could lose everything by staying. I like your company, don't get me wrong. But we're in trouble here, serious trouble."

There was not much time for discussing the state of the city's defenses or for visiting with Vom Scheidt if he was to sail with Bosio. De L'Isle Adam expected Lazaro, though it was clear that he had begun to feel sour about his arrangements with Fugger, and reluctantly gave Lazaro the approvals he required to send a shipment with Bosio.

As Vom Scheidt prepared for departure Lazaro brought him a small package, a bundle of letters. "I want you to try to get these delivered to Margoleit in Candia. Fugger can arrange it through his agent there, a man named Lomann."

Vom Scheidt hefted the bundle. "You've been busy."

"I write quite often. And after this last accident, I just need to get these to her."

"Are you sure you don't want to come out with us? That explosion wasn't an accident, you know."

"I can't leave yet," Lazaro answered. A night had not passed when he had not thought about leaving and getting Margoleit out of Candia, but he felt he had little choice. "With the next shipment I'll have done all Fugger has asked of me. Otherwise I can't depend on him for Margoleit's protection. Between Beccaria and Fugger there'd be no place to go."

Vom Scheidt shook his head. "It's your choice."

"And tell Béres that De L'Isle Adam is getting a bit reluctant. He sees his fortunes here dwindling in too many ways. I don't want to be held up with the next shipment. Encourage him to bring in something a little extra." They embraced, then Vom Scheidt headed out to the galley port and Bosio set off into the dark night on schedule.

With Vom Scheidt and Fugger's cargo safely on the way to Béres, Lazaro toured the city with Tadini and saw more clearly what he had meant when he said things had taken a turn for the worse. There was not a portion of the walls which had not received some damage and in many areas it was substantial. Repairs had been effected and the stonemasons were continuing to work at a feverish pitch, but it was clear to Lazaro that the tide was turning.

They walked through the merchant's quarter and into the Jewish quarter below the Post of Provence. The Turks had been lobbing mortars into this sector and there was much more rubble here than in the western part of the city. The quarter left Lazaro with an odd feeling. It was not just memories of Margoleit. He had seen her face so many times in his dreams and in the faces of some of the inhabitants of the city, that now when he saw women who looked like her, he didn't give it a second thought. It was farther back in his memory than that. This was the quarter where his parents had lived when they had run from Crete. This was the quarter where he had last seen his father and brother alive.

"I don't want to see this city fall," Tadini said as they climbed the battlements at the Post of Provence and looked out over the countryside. There were fires and tents everywhere, most just beyond the range of the guns. Tadini saw Lazaro smile.

"I don't mean it just like that. I would rather live than die, that's understandable. But this place has always held for me a strong attraction. This is the outpost of the West and if we ever lose it we can lose everything. I've worked for Venice most of my life and I've been treated well by her, but staying out of this was a mistake. It's not possible to win every battle, but we shouldn't give up Rhodes too easily. Suleiman will roll over Europe if he breaks us here."

Tadini's eyes swept the city, or what was left of it. "When I was young I heard stories from my father about the Colossus of Rhodes, and tales of the Knights as well. I even wanted to come here when the siege was on in 1480."

"For me, this place could burn."

Tadini turned to Lazaro. "Had enough, have you?"

Lazaro looked down into the Jewish quarter. "My father and brother were killed right down there. By Venetians," he added. "My mother had run away with a Turk. Her father wanted her back. I was unlucky enough not to be killed here and so I saw her die later."

Tadini was silent for a few moments. "You never told me that."

Lazaro turned and walked along the battlement. "I didn't mean to tell you of it now. It's past. I hope the men who did it are now dead. I don't even know who they were. Just men hired by my grandfather. Men like me."

Tadini walked quickly to catch up with Lazaro. "Leave the past, then. Chances are it will die here with us." He slapped Lazaro on the shoulder in friendship. "I need to check the sharpshooters by the Post of Aragon. Do you feel strong enough to come with me?"

Lazaro nodded and they started off down into the rubble of the city, heading for St. Mary's gate.

The following month saw the city rebuilt, as much as it could be, given the lack of materials and men. Tadini had planned a massive counter-mining operation and, with Lazaro's assistance, it was successfully exploded on the evening of the fourth of October. The blasts rocked the city, but without damage. From the mouth of the main tunnel came the cries of dying and wounded men, but the secondary explosions took care of those. Lazaro lit one last charge to seal the shafts, then returned to Tadini's quarters to report. When he arrived he was surprised to hear the sound of Vom Scheidt's voice. And doubly surprised when he heard Béres answer. He didn't bother knocking, but entered to find his two friends sharing a bottle of Tokay with Tadini.

Béres was in the middle of one of his jokes, and though he waved Lazaro in, he continued, but switched to Hungarian. "*Hol al a kurva macska had baszom meg!*"

Béres and Vom Scheidt rocked with laughter. Tadini turned to Lazaro. "It was something about a mouse that got chased into a bottle of Tokay by a cat."

Lazaro shook his head. "He always does that to me. When he gets to the punch line he starts speaking Hungarian, and I don't know what the hell he's saying."

Vom Scheidt wiped his eyes. "It's the mouse," he said stifling his laughter. "The mouse staggers out, beats his chest, and says, 'Where's that cat? I want to fuck it.'" He curled up again in laughter.

Tadini shook his head. "It loses something in the translation."

Tadini had found a glass for Lazaro and complimented him on his work in the tunnel that evening, and Béres, after he regained his composure, explained that he and Vom Scheidt had come in with a Knight by the name of Jean de Bressolx, who had brought his galley into port that evening. On board were fifteen mercenaries, two expert sappers, and a young man whose uncle had been a Knight.

They and the provisions carried had been Fugger's latest offering to the Order. As for Béres and Vom Scheidt, they didn't expect to stay very long, just until they could come out with Fugger's next shipment. As Béres explained it, "With Suleiman putting all of his troops to work here, things have become considerably more quiet in Hungary. I decided to come here for a visit and so I sent for one of my sons to oversee the work in Valona."

Lazaro knew Béres was lying and he expected Tadini knew it as well. But Tadini didn't pursue it and, after another bottle of Tokay, wandered off to his private chambers to pass out. Vom Scheidt had drifted off to sleep as well in the chair in which he had been sitting. Lazaro left him where he sat when Béres signaled for them to go out onto the balcony to talk. The air was cold, and they huddled over the brazier, their cloaks wrapped tightly around them.

"Fugger doesn't think the Order can hold out much longer," Béres said as he rubbed his hands over the brazier.

Lazaro smiled. "Everyone in the city seems to be thinking that, except maybe De L'Isle Adam and Tadini."

"What about D'Amaral?"

It was clear that D'Amaral's name had not been raised by chance. "My guess is that he thinks we can hold out. He's trying to conserve our stores."

"I'm sure he is," Béres snorted. "Fugger wants his things out of here faster and so he sent me in to arrange for it."

"I doubt the Grand Master would go for that. If anything he'll delay. If he can break the siege before all the goods are out he'll renegotiate with Fugger. And if he can't win he may need to buy his way out. That's strong incentive."

Béres looked up. "Fugger does not want this plan to fall through. His mind is made up. Once his funds have been extracted from here the Knights can lose, but not a moment before that."

"I'll see what I can do," Lazaro joked.

Béres let his cape drop from his shoulders as if the cold weather had disappeared. "Fugger has everything riding on this. If he is successful, the Emperor Charles will recover none of the funds which are held here for him by the Knights. Without that money behind him, Charles will be so deeply in Fugger's debt that the mercury mines and a large portion of the gold and silver from New Spain will be Fugger's for the asking. He'll sit on his ass in Augsburg and control a financial empire larger than Rome at its height. And without an army."

Lazaro sat back. "He has us, though."

"He has us by the balls."

"I don't think De L'Isle Adam cares much about our balls. He'll need more incentive than that if Fugger is going to speed things up."

"Well, Fugger sent me with a new incentive. The way things stand at the moment, the Order doesn't have a hope in hell. Even if things change it's unlikely the outcome will be altered, just delayed. But in this game, delay is everything. The new ticket is D'Amaral. He had been in the running to be Grand Master but De L'Isle Adam's supporters outvoted his. D'Amaral had originally counseled that the Order should evacuate Rhodes, and Fugger had word that he was also against Tadini being recruited. That's why De L'Isle Adam had to go outside the Order to get him here."

"And the Grand Master must know all of this and more. His men are everywhere."

"But they are getting fewer in number. My guess is that if a vote were to be held today, given the way this siege has gone and the number of men killed, D'Amaral might stand a chance of being elected."

"There's no election unless a Grand Master retires or dies, and De L'Isle Adam is not planning to do either."

"D'Amaral has plans."

The meaning was clear to Lazaro. Intrigue was nothing new to power politics and in tense military situations, coups should always be suspected.

Béres pulled a flask of Tokay from his cloak and took a swig then handed it to Lazaro. "Fugger has some pretty convincing evidence that D'Amaral is not only plotting against the Grand Master but has been dealing with the Turks. His valet, Blasco Diaz, has been sending messages to Ayas Pasha for some time now; information on tunneling, stores, morale. And there has been dealing too. Talk of possible terms should the Grand Master meet his maker — the surrender of Rhodes."

"You've got hard evidence with you? Not just contrived forgeries?"

"I think I have enough to convince the Grand Master. Half of it is in his hands at the moment. And don't worry, your name isn't on the list."

"How many?"

"Five Knights are named but you know how these things can grow once people are put to the question. A bit of a stretch and all sorts of information can start spilling out. I imagine they'll take Diaz first. And once they start to feed on themselves, it won't take long for all of this to be over."

Béres was right about De L'Isle Adam being interested, and he had no problem arranging for an early-morning audience. While Béres spoke with the Grand Master in seclusion, Vom Scheidt filled Lazaro in on what had been happening outside Rhodes. Though the battle raged here with the Turk and his designs on Europe were clear, things were relatively quiet, surprisingly quiet elsewhere. News from Venice revealed nothing. And there was no news from Crete. Vom Scheidt had arranged for a Fugger courier to take the letters to Candia and had hoped to hear something before their departure. But there had been nothing. He was quick to add that that was not a bad sign. Shipping had been disrupted greatly by the Turks.

Their conversation was disrupted by Béres storming out of the Grand Master's quarters and signaling for Lazaro and Vom Scheidt to follow him.

"The man's a fool" was all he was able to say before he lapsed into Hungarian. Only after a few glasses of Tokay was he able to explain that De L'Isle Adam wanted to wait a bit longer before allowing another shipment of Fugger's merchandise. "He agreed that the information is worth it but said he had to wait, maybe a month, to see how things turn out. *Istenem!* I can tell him how things are going to turn out. He'll be riding a pole before another month has passed. I should've held it back. I could have negotiated a better deal with D'Amaral."

"Softly," Lazaro said as he filled his glass. "If the Grand Master hears that he'll have you negotiating with D'Amaral, and sharing the rack with him as well."

Béres stooped and looked at Lazaro for a second, then burst into a laugh.

With no hope of taking goods out immediately, Lazaro busied himself to try to mask his concern about Margoleit. Tadini had asked him to be responsible for tunneling in two sectors and as well, to spend time deploying sharpshooters with muskets on the south-facing roofs to harass the Turkish gunners as they adjusted aim. As the work in the tunnels was well ordered, Lazaro found himself spending more time on the rooftops. In every location on the church roofs and on the battlements overlooking those areas of greatest Turkish activity, Lazaro had his sharpshooters construct small protected enclosures, often using bags filled with soil from the excavations, to protect them from the Turkish musketmen. He had found the bags to be much better than stone — they reduced the chance of ricochet and provided a more comfortable resting place during the long hours of waiting for a good target to present itself. Janissaries, richly clothed Turks, and gunners were the preferred targets and Lazaro was usually quite harsh with any of the sharpshooters who wasted shot on an Azab.

The morning of October eleventh was decidedly colder than the last week had been and as he climbed out onto the roofs Lazaro wished, almost, that he was in the warmer tunnels. However, dawn seemed to be one of the better times for hitting targets, partly because the night gunners were exhausted by that time and tended to become sloppy. After making his rounds he settled into his hiding place above the Post of Aragon. Glancing to the streets below, he saw Tadini making his way out to the walls. It was his habit to carry out an early inspection each morning in order to determine by light of day which areas merited attention from the stonemasons engaged in repair work. Materials and men were scarce and so he had to be quite judicious in his decision making.

His perch put him in mind of Marzia on her *altana*. He shivered, but it was clear to him that it was the temperature, and not the thought. In that moment, seated on the rooftop, a musket by his side, he realized that Marzia had all but disappeared from his mind. And it was just as clear to him that at whatever cost, he must get back to Margoleit and their child. He was filled with the conviction that his feelings for her were and always had been genuine. This crucible that was Rhodes had cleansed him to the point where he could now see clearly what was in his heart. He almost felt thankful.

Turning his attention back to the task at hand, Lazaro surveyed the pitted band of earth surrounding the city. It had been ripped by explosions, churned by thousands of marching feet and watered with blood and sleet until it had become a land which no man could want. Directly in front of and below him was a collapsed tunnel, cutting diagonally between the walls and a gunnery position, just beyond his range. He noticed a tree branch, twisted and gnarled, sticking out of the mud halfway between the Azabs and the walls of the city, a mute reminder to the carnage. It had likely been a beautiful tree, standing in that very spot only a few months before. Then it dawned on him that he could not remember a tree having been there, or a remnant of a tree. He looked more closely at the tree branch and it seemed to sway in the breeze, an odd thing, he thought, for a branch stuck in the mud. Suddenly a flame shot out of the end of the branch.

Lazaro heard a cry erupt below him, and looked down to see Tadini fall to the ground, surrounded by his engineers and stonemasons, his face red with blood. He looked again at the branch — it was clear now. A Turkish sharpshooter had tied a branch to his musket and had crawled out in the dark and buried himself in front of the wall which had been damaged by cannon fire, waiting for Tadini. The Turks knew his habits and they wanted nothing more than to kill one of the men most responsible for their delay in capturing Rhodes. Lazaro aimed and fired into the small hump behind the branch but there was only the sound of a ricochet. The Turk had been smart enough to put a piece of metal over his back. Seeing that Tadini was being carried away to the hospital, Lazaro crossed the roof to his nearest man, a young Genoese named Christoforo. The instructions were clear. Christoforo was to go to the next two sharpshooters and have them cover the sniper while he went to the nearest cannon and had the gunner blast the area. Tadini's killer would not escape.

Lazaro hurried off the roof and down to the hospital area. He spotted Tadini on a table surrounded by Knights, but before he could get closer one of the surgeons of the Order grabbed him. "There's nothing you can do here. He's had half his face blown out and he's lost one eye. We'll send someone if he regains consciousness."

Rather than return to his rooms or to the roof, Lazaro decided to wait and slumped down in the open space outside of the surgery where the minor wounds were treated. As he sat there, some voice other than his own said it might have been avoided if he had spotted the Turk, if he hadn't been thinking of Margoleit. Lazaro pushed that thought from his mind. Near midday he was joined by Béres, who had just heard the news and shortly after that they were summoned into the surgery area by the Grand Master.

De L'Isle Adam was deep in thought when Lazaro entered the room with Béres; however, he did not wait long before looking up. "Please," he said, indicating some chairs. "He's survived the operation but he's still not out of trouble. We may not be able to keep him alive, and even if we do, he won't be able to move for some time, a couple of months if we have that long. This may postpone Fugger's shipments even longer."

"I don't see how," Béres was quick to answer. "Tadini was delivered to you in good condition. It's not our fault if you didn't take care of him. And the information about D'Amaral you agreed was value beyond what Fugger promised you. A deal is a deal."

"These are dangerous times," the Grand Master said, as if repeating an old proverb. "I need everything I can hold on to."

Lazaro leaned into the conversation. "Tadini will continue to work for you and I'll guarantee him. You discuss it with him yourself. He can work through me. I'll stay until he's well enough to get back on his feet."

"And if he dies?"

"I'm betting my presence here that he won't."

The Grand Master thought about it for a minute, then gathered his robes and without further discussion left in the direction of Tadini's room.

Béres slapped Lazaro with his cap. "What in hell are you doing? He would have given us the goods. At least enough to send you out," he said, pointing with his thumb in the direction of the departed Grand Master. "This place is sinking into Hades and it'll take everyone with it. This isn't some little backwater town that we're charging into with a bellyful of wine and the promise of booty. This is already over. And you know what those Turks will do?"

"There's no point in talking about it," Lazaro said. "I promised Fugger I'd bring this deal through. If I don't, I can't collect. He's watching over Margoleit in Candia, and afterward we'll need his protection."

"Oh shit," Béres responded and stood. "We've done enough for Fugger. He can straighten out the rest. If the Master reneges, it isn't our loss. And I'm sure Fugger has factored that possibility in to his equations anyway. You and Margoleit can always come to Boros Krakoi. The fools in white masks would never get to you there."

"And Suleiman?"

"Just a passing storm. And at least you'd know who your enemy is."

The Grand Master appeared at the door before Lazaro could answer. "Tadini can't speak too clearly but he seems in agreement with your proposal, Lazaro, though he wants to see you first. On his recommendation I will accept. I'll arrange for transport, but it will have to wait until after I have dealt with D'Amaral. I guarantee that you'll have shipment within a month."

Béres shook his head and looked away, but Lazaro agreed and went in to see Tadini.

Tadini hung on the edge of life, one minute waxing, the next waning, for three days. On the evening of the third he had a particularly bad bout with fever but it broke in the middle of the night. Lazaro had not strayed from his bed, mostly out of friendship, but also because he did not want to risk an attempt on Tadini's life. Given the information of spies within, and in high places, his fear was well grounded.

And so when Tadini's withered hand grasped him by the shoulder as he dozed by the bed, he was not surprised. Tadini had done that often through the ordeal, when the pain returned. But this time there was no pain in his eye. Rather there was a firm resolve.

"This can wait no longer. If it is the end of me I must tell you."

Lazaro took a wet cloth and wiped his forehead. "I think it's better that you sleep."

Tadini pulled the cloth from his hand and flung it across the room, then fell back on the bed. "That evening, when we walked by the Jewish quarter — you said you had lived here."

"Yes," Lazaro answered, "with my parents, until I was taken away to Crete."

"And your father and brother murdered."

Again Lazaro answered, "Yes."

"When I was younger, when I was first employed by Venice, I was assigned to the Master of the Assassins."

Lazaro sat back. "I didn't know that you worked with the Assassins." He felt the hairs on the back of his head rise up.

"It was a long time ago. I wanted a position and I had not yet proved myself. They knew my skill was in mathematics, but even a clerk must make his bones. Improves loyalty. Someone had ordered an assassination, but the target was in hiding. We received word that we could find him in Rhodes so we came here, in three groups. The ship I was on was blown off course by one night. By the time I got here they had already completed their task, here, in Rhodes, in the Jewish quarter.

"The bodies were buried and one group was headed back to Venice while the other had taken the women and a child back to Crete. One of those family quarrels. She'd run off with a Turk. Anyhow, she was returned to her father and I avoided spilling any blood that time around."

Lazaro felt as if he was encased in glass. He had listened to Tadini's story and it sounded as if it was recounting events from another lifetime. But they were events from his. Anger burned in him, not newly lit but newly fanned. He didn't feel it toward Tadini, though it might have been justified, save for the coincidence of a breeze. "Who killed my father and brother?"

"I wasn't there. I don't know. But I was told later that a young man named Beccaria had taken charge of the attack, and that as a result of his success, on his return to Venice he was appointed Master of the Assassins."

Beccaria. The fire burned so high in Lazaro that it caused pain. Beccaria had known all along. He had asked enough questions, questions which had seemed normal, though Lazaro now saw that they were part of Beccaria's need to confirm in his mind who it was he was dealing with. But Beccaria was far away. Tadini was here, at his mercy. Lazaro felt his dagger under his hand, and for a moment there was a taste of revenge in his mouth. Then it passed.

"I had to tell you," Tadini said. "I couldn't go to my grave with that. It was something from so long ago, I had forgotten. And I didn't know until we spoke that night that it was your family."

"It wasn't by your hand," Lazaro said after a moment of reflection. "But when I am quit of this place I will make my peace." He stretched over and picked up the cloth which Tadini had flung and dipped it in water. He vowed, as he wiped Tadini's brow, that once he had taken Margoleit to a safe place, he would settle things with Beccaria.

With his time now consumed by being Tadini's eyes and mouth, Lazaro asked Vom Scheidt to take over the sharpshooters. Béres was kept busy by a different task. Somehow the Turks had found out that the executioner of Kaziklu Bey was now in Rhodes and they would sometimes gather outside the wall calling to him, challenging him to come out and fight. The Janissaries especially would stand on the embankments, risking sharpshooters and small cannon, to play their music and pay peculiar homage to Béres. One evening the taunting got to him. With the agreement of De L'Isle Adam, Béres gathered a small force of mercenaries who were willing to give themselves to the *bolond gomba*. They gathered in Lazaro's quarters and prepared themselves, passing the cup from mouth to mouth, sitting in the dark and waiting, as Béres explained, for the glow. As Lazaro watched he saw a change come over them which he could not fathom. Somehow the men transformed, not on the outside but inside, so that it showed only in their eyes.

When they were ready, Lazaro led them down into a tunnel which took them out past where the Turks had gathered to taunt the great warrior. After positioning them underground, Lazaro hurried back to the nearest gate and had the keepers readied for what was to come. He himself climbed onto the battlements above the gate for a better vantage point.

For the Turks it was a nightmare come true. Behind them the ground erupted in fury and Béres leapt up with his soldiers, soil clinging to them, and they rushed forward, toward the gate. The Janissaries, caught off guard, tried to flee from the berserkers but were caught by the maze of trenches which had been constructed there. In the fray, Lazaro saw the dark fury of the berserkers mingle in a strange frenzied dance with the tall, feather-topped Janissaries. Most were killed before they could even put up resistance, and Béres and his men reached the gate without injury. From that night on, at irregular intervals, Béres and his small band would gather to wreak havoc among the Turks nearest the walls.

Though he was invited by Béres to join them, Lazaro had little time. Instead he crawled back and forth through the tunnels which ringed the city, listening, building vents, and at times setting off countermines. When he was not in the tunnels he was with Tadini, watching over him like a hawk, making sure that he would regain his health, and making sure that there would be no more attempts on his life. The old Brescian was strong but the wounding had taken a lot out of him, figuratively and literally. The musketball had entered his right eye and had taken out much of that side of his face as it traveled to his right ear and tore that off on its exit. Only the expert surgeons and the herbs for which the Order's hospitals were famous allowed him to fight off the infection and heal. Still he wore a leather mask on the right side of his face to protect others from the hideousness as much as to protect himself.

But if his flesh was weak, his spirit was willing. During his waking hours, when the painkillers which were administered to him did not cloud his mind, he was busy with Lazaro, directing the defense of what was left of Rhodes. And of his exploits in years gone by he made no mention. Lazaro had made it clear that no further comment was necessary.

While Tadini and Lazaro were concerned with the walls and the tunnels, De L'Isle Adam watched the inhabitants and the members of the Order, holding in reserve the information Béres had brought to him, until the last week of October. On the twenty-seventh a Candiot woman, Rachael, reported that she had witnessed D'Amaral's valet Diaz, a Jewish convert, preparing to shoot a bolt with a note attached into the Turkish lines. Within a few hours of arrest and questioning under the watchful eye of the Grand Master and his Inquisitor, Diaz confessed and implicated D'Amaral and three others, as well as a few townspeople. Fugger's information was used by De L'Isle Adam with precision, and D'Amaral, the most senior Knight of the Order, fell from grace, taking others with him. Two days after Diaz had been executed, on the eighth of November, D'Amaral was carried to his gallows in a chair, unable to walk due to the Grand Master's questioning. Afterward his body was quartered and piked along the battlements in a gruesome reminder to those within the city and without that the Order would not easily abandon Rhodes.

For Lazaro, it was also a gruesome reminder of Fugger's abilities. He had divided this house against itself.

XXIII

In need of supplies and of reinforcements, and to honor his commitment to Fugger, the Grand Master arranged for another venture through the Turkish blockade: on the fourteenth of November, Nicholas Fairfax would sail for Valona with Vom Scheidt and the major portion of what remained of Fugger's cargo. After delivering it to Béres's son, Fairfax and Vom Scheidt would then sail to Candia for whatever provisions and men could be secured there. De L'Isle Adam gave his word that on their return the remainder of Fugger's payment would be released to Lazaro.

Lazaro took Vom Scheidt aside and gave him an added task. Explaining to him where to find Lucrezia's house, he asked him to visit Margoleit, see that everything was good with her, and give her the message that Lazaro would be out with the final shipment within the month. Vom Scheidt encouraged Lazaro to take his place but given his arrangement with De L'Isle Adam it was impossible. It was clear to Lazaro that the end was close in many ways and it would have been folly to confound it at this point. He pressed into Vom Scheidt's hands a letter he had written to Margoleit explaining as best he could what the next month would hold and his hope that he would be with her soon, no matter what the outcome.

The days which followed Vom Scheidt's departure were dark, dreary, and fraught with senseless battle. For the Turks, no advances were made; for the Knights, no advantages were achieved. Only death tallied a win. And for Lazaro, the pain of separation had somehow come to a point with the knowledge that Vom Scheidt, not he, would soon see Margoleit. That point pressed deep into his chest, but the distraction of near-death at every turn kept him from wallowing in his sorrow.

In the dark, pouring rain on St. Andrew's Eve, the Turks attacked with great force, preceding their general assault with a devastating artillery barrage. The barrage hit as Lazaro was resting in his quarters after a day in the tunnels. Béres had been there as well, having called together his berserkers to prepare for another foray. When Lazaro crawled out of the rubble he could barely recognize the room. The outer wall and door had fallen in, probably due to a direct hit from an exploding cannonball, and there was a gaping hole in the roof. Most of the berserkers were sitting, dazed, and shaking dust out of their hair, some getting wet as rain dripped in through the hole, but Béres was nowhere in sight. Again and again Lazaro and the berserkers dug through the stones and broken furniture until at last they uncovered Béres, saved from being flattened by a ruggedly built refectory table.

Trumpets were sounding throughout the city and men everywhere were being called to the walls.

"They seem to have gotten the jump on us," Béres said as he regained his wind. He called to one of his men, another Magyar named Locsi, to find the *bolond gomba*, and it wasn't long before Locsi called from the next room that he had found it. Smiling, he returned holding the large bowl in both hands to the circle of berserkers now gathering in the center of the room. "Why don't you join us this time?" Béres said, looking at Lazaro. "It may be the last chance you have to take the flesh of God."

Lazaro looked out through what was left of the balcony and saw the Turks streaming through a gap in the wall. It seemed the time for a new communion. "It may be the last chance I have to do anything."

Béres threw his arm around Lazaro and pulled him into the circle. "We will all be changed in the twinkling of an eye."

The men quickly gathered broken pieces of furniture and piled it in the center of the room, then poured oil over it and tipped the contents of a brazier on top. The fire leapt to life, billowing up to the hole which had opened in the ceiling. Most of the men stood around the fire feeling its warmth but saying nothing, while Locsi and another were moving around the circle, handing out drinking horns filled with the milky substance which had been in the bowl — *soma*. Lazaro took the horn offered to him and tasted the drink, sweet with honey, potent with the mushroom.

He hesitated, not wanting to slip into what he now saw happening, but it was too late. Even now he felt the warmth of *soma* growing in his being. Energy began to flow along his limbs. He glanced down at his fingertips and saw tiny sparks rolling off the nails. At his feet was his sword, placed there by the *soma*-bearers. He and the other men reached down as one and picked up their swords. They stepped back and waited. It seemed that a wind rose in the room and the blasts of the Turkish cannon became louder, though less frightening.

A murmur, low and guttural, began, rising in the dry throats of all. Lazaro could not make out the words, but he joined in the sound of the chant. It was wrong to say he joined for he was no longer a separate person. He was out of his time and unsure of anything. All he knew was the *soma* glowing within him and the others, the heat and light of the fire, the sound of the chant, the wind and rain, the slight movement by the circle as they began to move toward the center, and the feel of the blade in his hand. The blade. He glanced down at it and saw that the sparks which had been dropping from his fingertips were now shooting from his hands and into the blade, infusing it with a strange crackling glow, like the fire only cold, darker, blue.

Then a sound which Lazaro could not even begin to understand rose from the deepest part of these men's souls, from a part buried but not forgotten, fed from the memory of their forebears. The roar rose too in Lazaro's throat, for he now was one of them. Their blades touched to the fire at the center of the circle and the flame which had been rolling off the tips of their individual blades now fused with the fire into a clear blue-white light.

Deep within him an eye watched what was happening but could not control or even influence it. A larger, darker force entered and assumed his being. They had become one mass of arms, spiked at the end with a glowing cold blue-white talon or claw. Then the mass broke into smaller groups and then into men — though not men any more.

Lazaro found himself moving through the streets of Rhodes at breakneck speed. All about him in the black and rain were others, racing to find the Turks. He was no longer a man. The *soma* had flowed into his soul and dredged from its depths the wolf on the hunt. His legs were strong of sinew and his paws, surefooted, found their way over tumbled rocks and fallen bodies. And he was not alone. The shapes about him, those darker than the surrounding darkness, all had the same purpose. He could sense about him Béres's berserkers, though they now seemed wolves, were-creatures, and birds of prey.

As they moved through the streets they were stopped a number of times as the ground beneath them erupted and Egyptians, Anatolians, all manner of Turkish soldiers issued forth from tunnels which the sappers had dug into the heart of the city. The attack had been sudden enough that it would be some time before order could be brought to the defense, though the buglers were trying to do just that. For the time being, though, it was to be hand-to-hand fighting, singly or in small groups.

They made their way through the twisting street — somewhere deep in his mind Lazaro wondered if this was the Jewish quarter — where the majority of houses had been reduced to rubble. Though there were a large number of Turks in the city, the narrow streets made it possible to survive even when the odds were against them. By the time they had made it to the Post of Aragon the walls were being defended as best they could, but the Turks kept coming, wave after wave. The trenches which the Turks had dug there hampered them as much as they hampered the defenders of Rhodes. The feet of perhaps ten thousand Turks churned the ground into sucking clay through the night and though it was bitterly cold and they were slashed with sleet, the soil was kept warm and would not harden.

Lazaro rounded one of innumerable corners and saw before him a Janissary who had just dispatched a Knight. With a howl that was neither wolf nor man, Lazaro was on him, even as the scimitar was raised over the Turk's head. The blade fell on Lazaro's shoulder and cut through the fur and flesh, exposing a bone. Lazaro felt no pain and his fire burned bright within him. His jaws closed about the Turk's throat as the talons of a falcon on a sparrow, and closed tighter and tighter. The Turk dropped his scimitar and clawed at Lazaro, trying to break the hold on his throat but to no avail. He fell to the ground under the weight of the man-wolf and Lazaro felt his adversary's skin open. The flesh of the throat was ripe and sweet in his jaws. He tasted blood and drew from the Turk his life force. Lazaro threw back his head and cried to the moon hidden beneath the storm clouds which whipped freezing rain down on Rhodes. This was the last he remembered as the *soma* took over, and the watching eye deep within him was put out.

Lazaro opened his eyes. The night was gone. He saw above him only clear blue sky. But he could smell the smoke and blood of battle done and for a moment he had no interest in turning his head to either side or rising. He was alive and he was again human. Beneath him he could feel the rock of Rhodes. Rolling to his side, he sat up and saw that he was by the Post of Aragon. All about him men were busy building fires for the Turk bodies and digging graves for their comrades. Lazaro rose and walked through the remains of the city. Here and there were dead Turks, and dead Knights, and withered, blackened things the loyalty of which he was unsure. The memory of the night's battle flooded back over him and he slouched against a still-standing wall.

Béres came up behind him and put his hand on Lazaro's shoulder. "Don't fight the *soma* now, it's leaving. You were wise last night to let it in without struggling."

"Was I really a wolf?"

"Weren't you?"

"I think so."

"That's all you can know, then."

"Did you see me?"

Béres just smiled. "How's that shoulder?"

"Asleep, I guess," Lazaro said, rubbing it, then noticed it was not sleep which made it numb. On his shoulder was a bandage, bloodied. He felt a far-off throb of pain.

Béres nodded at the shoulder. "It will hurt later, but it won't cause you any trouble. Those Turkish blades are sharp and clean. I cleaned the wound, seared it, and left you to sleep, you looked so peaceful." He handed him some dried leaves. "If the pain becomes great, just chew these." Together they walked through the gore of the battle.

Lazaro kicked the hand of a Turk, then picked it up and threw it onto the cart being wheeled past toward the fires.

"*Aut deus aut lupus*," Lazaro said.

Béres looked up. "What?"

Lazaro shook his head. "Nothing."

By eight o'clock it was known that the Order had lost 180 men, and burials were being arranged in all available places. There was no point in counting the wounded, for they were all wounded and if they were living at all they would be expected to fight. And it was little comfort that the Turks had lost perhaps five thousand men — thousands more waited outside the walls. With no supplies, no possibility of reinforcements, and all of the open spots in the city turned into graveyards, morale plummeted. From all corners came talk of surrender. Though the Knights had resolved to die rather than allow the infidels to take their city from them, the natives of Rhodes petitioned the Grand Master to treaty with Suleiman and the Chapter finally agreed that at least the terms should be heard.

On the tenth a white flag was raised over St. John's Gate and the Turkish emissary brought Suleiman's brief message. The Knights could leave with their belongings, excepting their brass cannons, and all people who wished to accompany them were free to go, even Tadini. All who remained of their own free will would be allowed the privileges normally granted to those who lived with the Realm of Peace — freedom of religion, freedom to trade, in return for modest taxes and a promise to abide by the Sultan's laws. However, if the Knights refused to leave, Suleiman would not turn away until the city had been leveled and every living thing within it was dead. A five-day truce was declared but the Knights could not bring themselves to agree before it had run its course, and so Suleiman ordered his gunners to resume their barrage.

In the midst of this darkest moment it seemed that perhaps God had decided to send salvation after all. Nicholas Fairfax broke through the Turkish blockade the next day, but the joy was short-lived. Except for Vom Scheidt and most of the crew he had departed with, he brought no reinforcements. Venice had closed the port at Candia. By subterfuge he had escaped the port authorities and had been able to bring along a full load of wine which, given the spirits of the men and the quality of the city's water, was perhaps the best donation to the cause. It had become clear to everyone that Rhodes was lost, but the arrival of wine allowed them some respite from this thought.

Lazaro saw the Grand Master immediately, but De L'Isle Adam was not anxious to keep his promise to allow the rest of Fugger's payment out. De L'Isle Adam knew that it was over and he had to hold on to everything he had. Lazaro saw that he could get nowhere with things the way they were and so he negotiated for a contract which would indebt the Order for the remainder of Fugger's payment, at some undetermined point in the future. Given all that had transpired, Lazaro was confident that this would not be seen as failure by Fugger and that their arrangement would stand. As he left the audience, he was oddly happy, for he knew that soon he would be free of Rhodes and on his way to Candia either through terms of surrender or, if need be, by running the blockade with whoever had more stomach for that than for remaining to the bitter end. The end was approaching, the waiting was over.

Returning from the meeting, Lazaro found Vom Scheidt in their burned and wet quarters, unpacking his load.

"What in hell happened here?" Vom Scheidt asked after greeting Lazaro.

"It was Béres and his cooking," Lazaro said with a grin, then could contain himself no longer. "So, how is Margoleit?" He saw the disquiet in Vom Scheidt's eyes and the bundle of letters which he took from his sack. Lazaro recognized them as the letters he had sent to her at the end of August.

"She's gone, Lazaro," Vom Scheidt said as he handed the packet to Lazaro.

"What do you mean, gone?"

Vom Scheidt sat on the edge of his cot. "Gone. When I got there I went to Lucrezia's but the old woman said Margoleit had left two months before, saying she had to leave, that she was returning to her family in Venice. Lucrezia was to tell no one. When Lomann delivered your letters, she was already gone. Lucrezia didn't want anyone to know, so she kept them and gave them to me. She left a letter for you. Lucrezia didn't want to give it to me at first. She had been told to put it in your hands. When I explained what was going on here she decided to send it with me." Vom Scheidt now held in his hand a single letter. Lazaro made no movement to take it, and so Vom Scheidt pushed it into his hands. "It may be a good thing. It may have been getting dangerous for her to stay there. You didn't tell me there was a child on its way."

Lazaro stood staring at Vom Scheidt. At that moment Béres returned with loud guffaws; Vom Scheidt caught him and led him outside, leaving Lazaro alone with his letter.

"My dearest Lazaro," it began. Lazaro immediately felt the need for wine and lifted a flask to his lips.

> Writing this is so difficult when I have no way of knowing if you'll ever read it. I've spent most of my days waiting by the harbor. I watch, hoping that I will see you, and I listen, hoping that I will not hear you've been killed. But I have to believe. And I'm sure God will watch over you.
>
> This is also hard because what I have to say should be said to you, but it's too late. I must leave. Please don't blame yourself for not being here. It's what I have to do. Even if we were together, it would still have to be this way. I am returning to my home. There was a voice inside me from the beginning saying what we were trying to do could never work. Fear and love made me believe that it could. But when I felt my child quicken in me, I knew that this couldn't be. I can't live apart from who I am and I don't want my child to either.
>
> There was a story my father told me once. Maybe it will help explain what I'm doing. It's a parable of the dove and the hawk. A dove escaped from the dovecote and flew free. A hawk chased the dove, and she took shelter in a cleft in the rock. But a snake had curled up in the cleft. The dove couldn't enter the cleft and couldn't go back out with the hawk circling. So she clapped her wings and cried out so that the owner of the dovecote would hear her and take her back.

> I have to go back. I don't regret anything we have done. In fact I'm glad for everything, because it showed me that I had to come back to who I am.

Lazaro sat as if he had been hit with a lance through the chest. In the shock, there was no air to breathe, no feeling. It seemed that small stars rained inside his eyes. He turned to the wine and emptied the remaining contents of the flask down his throat. He knew that the pain would come later, as the shock wore off, and as a man knowledgeable in wounds, he sought anesthetic. The waiting was over, the end had come.

At dusk the next day a more complete anesthetic became available to Lazaro. A Turkish assault was launched on the Posts of Aragon and England, and before the battle was a quarter of an hour old it was clear that only by throwing caution to the wind, pulling all of their troops from other stations, and expending nearly all of their powder and other resources could the Order hold the day.

Béres had seen the massing of the Azabs and Janissaries beyond the walls and knew before it started what was to come. In his chambers he gathered his small band of berserkers and offered the bowl to Vom Scheidt and Lazaro, but they declined and moved out into the streets.

Darkness was not a problem for those fighting at Aragon and elsewhere around the city, for there were enough fires in and around the fighting that it was easy enough to make out the faces of the attackers and defenders alike. And here and there along the walls, boiling oil and Greek fire turned men into torches, to run screaming through the mass and eventually tumble, providing yet another bizarre marker in the field of battle.

Time and time again waves of Janissaries would break through the defenses or spring out of the ground. Before the night was over there was fighting in every quarter and the size of the piles of bodies began to rival imagination. Lazaro wondered when it would stop or when he would drop from exhaustion, but there was no respite. He could see from Vom Scheidt's face that he was experiencing the same thing. After a time, for Lazaro, it was as if he was already dead, and the small wounds which he took from time to time ceased to have any noticeable effect. Though he had none, he sensed that the *bolond gomba* had somehow come back into him, like a familiar spirit. He was possessed with the battle and assumed, in his mind, the countenance of the wolf.

Before dawn the Turks suddenly began to pull back and the Knights had no energy to pursue them. The pressure eased where Lazaro and Vom Scheidt had been fighting long enough for Lazaro to turn to his comrade with a smile and ask him if he wished a glass of wine. Vom Scheidt, leaning against the stone wall, made no answer. When Lazaro came closer to him he saw that his sword, though still in his hand, had its tip resting on the ground in an odd fashion. He knew then that he was dead.

Through the smoke and the crowd of friend helping friend off the battlefield, Lazaro carried Vom Scheidt over his shoulder until he made his way to the ruined room which had served as their quarters. He laid Vom Scheidt down on what remained of his bed and put his sword by his side. On a first examination Lazaro could not find the fatal wound. There were many gashes, but none which could have accounted for his death. Then he noticed a small wound in his side, a red hole in his jacket. Opening the jacket and pulling back his shirt Lazaro could see a small wound on Vom Scheidt's side. Lazaro pressed the wound and felt within it something that made his blood begin to seethe in anger. He pressed his finger against the wound and felt a sharp prick on his fingertip. It was a shard of glass.

"Glass?" a voice asked.

Lazaro wheeled around, his stiletto drawn, and saw Tadini. He didn't lower his blade.

Tadini looked at the blade with his one eye then stepped through what was left of the doorway, brushed some rubble off a low table, and sat. "Was it him they wanted? Or you?" Tadini waited for a response but Lazaro simply stood there, his blade still pointing in Tadini's direction. "You, then. And you think perhaps I had something to do with it?"

Suddenly Lazaro's arm felt very tired. He sheathed his stiletto and pulled a blanket over Vom Scheidt's corpse. "I don't know. I didn't suspect them here."

"It's unlikely he was here long."

"Or maybe he just found out about me."

"From me?"

"No," Lazaro said finally. "No, not from you."

Tadini seemed pleased. "It's better when you say it. I could say it too easily. What do they want you for?"

"Glass."

With a flick of his wrist Tadini dismissed the word. "There's little point to that at the moment." He dusted himself off and set to tightening the leather patch which was strapped across the right half of his face. "More likely an assassin came in on the last boat and recognized you. But even if the Secretariat has found you here, it is unlikely that any other boats will get through, or that we will be alive much longer for that matter. The assassins can wait and let Suleiman do their work for them."

Lazaro looked out the window and saw Knights milling about, beginning to gather the wounded and the dead. "He may still be out there."

"Bets would be on him being dead, seeing that you're still alive. But I'd watch my back if I were you." Tadini stood and headed out the door.

"Where're you going now?"

"I want to talk to De L'Isle Adam. We can't sit here on our asses. And I'd advise you to go help with the burying. It may satisfy your curiosity."

Each side began to gather its wounded from the field and to count its dead. Lazaro looked where he could but there was no white mask, no Venetian cape or hat. It would require a trip to Venice to settle this matter. He did find Béres, spread on the ground, his head half severed from his body, surrounded by dead Janissaries. The great warrior, assassin of Kaziklu Bey, had finally been bested. He lay now in state with what appeared to be the last three of his berserkers, including Locsi, kneeling beside him, drinking and talking. They greeted Lazaro as he passed and told him of Béres's last fight, of how he had received so many wounds that he had been unable to stand, and how the Janissaries had paused in their attack long enough for him to tie himself up to a post so that he might face his end standing. In honor of Béres, Lazaro took a drink of the Tokay which Locsi offered, but the taste had left the wine.

It was clear now that the Knights had had enough. There were few in the city with any sense left who wished to continue the fight. Word was sent out and Suleiman's emissary again rode to St. John's Gate. By the twenty-fourth of December the terms of surrender were settled and at noon the gates of the city were opened. The Grand Master had ordered all of those who would be leaving to gather in the buildings still standing near his headquarters. Arrangements had been made for an early Mass to be said for the Feast of the Nativity and then the churches were to be locked and guarded by the Janissaries, in preparation for their conversion into mosques.

Lazaro stayed in what remained of his rooms during the evening and had the suite to himself. As the restrictions against the use of fuel had been lifted, he stoked his brazier and felt warm for the first time since the onset of winter. Throughout the city Christians were giving thanks that the siege had ended and were preparing to celebrate the feast of the birth of their Lord. For Lazaro there was only the thought of death. There was nothing for which he wished to be thankful. The fact that he had come out of all of this alive was nothing to him. Like Lazarus before him, he had been called from death only to be left with the knowledge that the horror would come again. What kindness was there in calling a man back from the grave but leaving him mortal?

But Lazaro paused and unclenched his fist. Sitting close to the brazier, he was reminded of the nights he had spent in Venice with Margoleit. It seemed now that all that was dead. But Venice still figured in his plans. Regardless of the risk, he had to return there. He had to find Margoleit, to see if she and the child to be were safe, to see — and here he allowed himself a moment of flight before crashing to the cold ground — to see if there was a chance that she might change her mind now and go away with him. Warming his fingers before the brazier, he counted out the months from May. There was a confused excitement as he realized that his child might be born by the time he got back to Venice. If Margoleit was still alive.

And there was also Angelo. Given the relative success of Lazaro's mission, Fugger would honor his promise of providing Angelo with everything he needed in Augsburg. Perhaps Lazaro would finally be in a position to convince the old man to leave Venice. Lazaro didn't think now of profit, but of gathering together those for whom he cared in a safer place.

But out of the darkness came the face of Beccaria. The mask was now a mask of death, a death which had been visited on his father and brother, on Vom Scheidt and perhaps, though he tried to push the thought from his mind, on Margoleit. Now that the battle was finished and the graves had been dug and filled, he found it more difficult to keep these thoughts from his mind. Comfort, true comfort, came only when he thought of how he would kill Beccaria.

The transition which took place in Rhodes over the next week was surprisingly smooth after such a prolonged battle, thanks more to Suleiman's power over his Janissaries than to De L'Isle Adam's hold on his Knights. As dusk gathered on the evening of the first of January, 1523, the Hospitallers of St. John of Jerusalem, bound for Candia, sailed from the harbor at Rhodes for the last time.

XXIV

Candia cradled the broken Knights with arms that could have saved them but preferred to comfort them once defeated. The Governor, the Duke of Trevisiano, made De L'Isle Adam and his fellow refugees welcome and even acted in a brotherly fashion toward Tadini. He was less friendly when it came to Lazaro. Expecting that his life might be the subject of a fee, due to the appearance of Beccaria's assassin in Rhodes, Lazaro slipped over the side of the ship as it gained harbor at dusk, with assistance from Locsi, the Magyar who was taking Béres's bones back to Krakoi Boros, and from Tadini. Tadini agreed to search for a ship to carry him out of Candia and to meet him two nights later at a waterfront inn. When the Duke got around to questioning Tadini and De L'Isle Adam, they both expressed surprise — one honestly — at his disappearance. The Duke let it be known that there would be many ducats for information which would allow the "renegade Turk," as he called him, to be brought to justice. However, among the battle-weary Knights there was little interest.

Lazaro's first effort was to speak with Lucrezia. This might have posed some difficulty, as her house was clearly being watched by a *bravo* who, though he was unmasked, was nevertheless one of Beccaria's men. At least he was not one of Beccaria's more intelligent *bravi*. As the moon rose he wandered off to one of the many establishments catering to soldiers who had been long without the comfort of alcohol and women.

Lucrezia was surprised by the appearance of Lazaro and at first did not recognize him.

"Fighting must do that," she said as she brought him something to eat, though he protested he was not hungry. "It's more than losing weight. It changes your eyes, and the set of your mouth."

Though it was a pleasant meal, his mother's old nurse could tell him little more than he already knew. "I told her it would be dangerous to travel, but she said it was more dangerous to stay. She wasn't far enough along that it would have done the baby any damage. I suppose she wanted to have the child among her own. It's understandable. She left that letter I gave to your friend. Did he make it out?"

Lazaro shook his head.

"Oh well," she said, then paused as if she was searching for something else to say. When she realized there was nothing, she continued. "There was a trader, a Jew. I think she met him in the market. She spent a lot of time there, watching for you. Anyway, she said he would take her back to Venice. She was a nice girl, strong-minded, but a nice girl. So you can find her in Venice, then?"

Lazaro didn't wish to share his doubts with her, and so he just agreed. Then, thinking of the man who had been watching the house, he asked, "Did any men come looking for her?"

"After she left. About two, maybe three weeks. Two of them, from Venice by their accent and their clothes." Lucrezia laughed. "I told them a good lie, that she had paid me to hide her from her father, that she had told me her name was Ruth, like in the Bible, and that she had run off in the night and left me without a month's pay. They may not have believed me, but they left me alone."

Lazaro thought there was no need to tell her of the man who was watching her house. In all likelihood he had been placed there as a last precaution. But how had they found the house? It might have been nothing more than some stalwart citizen reporting a strange face that could have been a Turkish agent. Or it might have been Fugger's agent, Lomann. Believing the former rather than the latter, Lazaro also reasoned that if Lomann had turned her in, there was no point in visiting him. Fugger's establishment would be much better guarded and there was no point in alerting anyone to the fact that he was alive and looking for Margoleit.

He thanked Lucrezia and slipped off into the night. All that mattered now was getting back to Venice. He had to find Margoleit, to see if there was any way she might change her mind. And he had to settle his score with Beccaria. However, it was clear to Lazaro that even getting to Venice would prove difficult. Aside from the effect which the Turks still had on shipping, the winter winds which blew down the Gulf made travel direct to Venice next to impossible. He hoped Tadini would be able to bring him good news but, except for safe lodgings, Tadini could do little.

"The Knights are going nowhere until spring; even Bosio is waiting out the winter," Tadini said as they shared a jug of wine in a dark waterfront tavern. "But in the spring we'll head for Messina where we've been promised temporary quarters."

"Not much chance for piracy in Messina," Lazaro said cynically.

Tadini agreed. "But there's talk of one likely spot, a strategic island belonging to Emperor Charles. And word was waiting for the Grand Master when he arrived that Fugger would assist in the negotiations."

Lazaro raised his mug. "To Fugger. The merchant always wins." Fugger would be happy, Lazaro thought. He had managed to rescue almost all of his collateral from Rhodes and now had the Knights and the emperor asking for his assistance. For Fugger, each day meant more profit. Placing his mug back on the table, Lazaro leaned to Tadini. "So, will you help me get to Venice?"

"Of course I will, if that's what you want. There's a ship, if I can call it that, leaving next week for Ragusa, though there will be many stops along the Dalmatian coast. The captain wishes to avoid paying any exit duties and is also interested in high-profit cargo. I assured him that you were such a cargo." Tadini smiled and refilled Lazaro's mug. "He's an old friend, Constantine. Ugly as sin, but he can be trusted. He's agreed to carry you to Ragusa, though it's likely to be slow going. And from there you'll have to go overland and up the coast until you can find a local trading boat to take you across. There're lots of them in the north this time of year carrying firewood. And you needn't travel alone. That Hungarian friend of yours, Locsi, he wants to head for home as well."

Lazaro nodded. "He wants to get Béres's bones back to Boros Krakoi. So, I leave with Constantine, then?"

"If you must." Tadini put his hand on top of Lazaro's. "If they were expecting you here, they'll be expecting you there. It might be better to ride with Locsi. In the spring you could make for Augsburg."

"If she's still alive, she'll have my child soon, if she hasn't had it already. I can't leave her there with Beccaria. Eventually he'll tire of using her for bait."

"And what will you do when you find her?" Tadini asked as they huddled over the small table. "She may not want to see you."

Lazaro said nothing.

Tadini shrugged. "They say the storms of winter are worse this year. They say it's the Turk." Still Lazaro said nothing, and so Tadini finished the wine in his mug. "I'll take you to meet Constantine. And by the way, you're traveling under the name of Conversalo again."

XXV

Lazaro stood on the deck of the cog settling into its anchor in the Bacino and listened as the *mattutin* sounded, as it did each morning in Venice, signaling that dawn was now less than an hour away. The city had not changed. A year had passed, but it was nothing. *Rii* had been dredged, *calli* had been paved, people had died. The meanderings of the group might have arrived at some new fashions, but it was all superficial, a mask. Venice had not changed.

He had been fortunate to arrange for this transportation, though the price had been tantamount to extortion. However, as Tadini had warned him and as Constantine had reminded him all the way to Ragusa, the storms of winter were worse this year than ever in men's memories. Much of the overlong journey with Constantine had been spent just keeping the leaky ship afloat and getting in and out of the small ports without losing their heads or their keel. And when they finally made Ragusa, Lazaro had been glad for the company of Locsi, and Béres's bones. The winter snows had made traveling difficult to the point of danger, and beyond that point there were still a few Akinji roaming through the mountains. They were able to avoid them, but everywhere the talk in the small villages was the same: a change was coming, heralded by the Turk. He stood ready to fulfill the prophecies of St. John the Divine. Even in the smallest villages there were those who wandered about, tempting reason with talk of the demon wind which would blow through Europe and bring with it a flood of death. And from the bones of the old order would come a new order, from destruction would come salvation, but only for the initiated.

However, for Lazaro the time had been occupied wondering about Margoleit — and their child. Her letter had dismissed any possibility of their being together, but Lazaro clung to a belief that if he could see her face to face he might find some way to persuade her to try once more. And when he wasn't thinking of her he was thinking of Beccaria. But at the moment Murano and Angelo were uppermost in his mind. It would be foolish to go directly to Margoleit. If Beccaria were watching for him he would expect that. He might well expect that Lazaro would also seek out Angelo, but that was a chance Lazaro would have to take. Angelo was the only one in Venice he could go to now, and Lazaro needed to find out what had happened in Venice during his absence. Like a wolf he would have to circle Venice, test the air for scent, and move at the right moment.

A raft of gondolas and topos approached and Lazaro descended with the other men to the decks of the stabilizing *camels* where they arranged for transport to the Piazzetta. However, Lazaro directed his gondolier to a different route, past the Molo and in through the watery paths of the city, the Rio della Pietà, the Rio di Santa Giustina, emerging on the north in the Laguna Morta and from there crossing the dark waters past San Michele to Murano.

Dawn was breaking as Lazaro arrived at the wharf nearest Angelo's factory on the Rio dei Vetrai. Across the lagoon he could hear the pealing of the *mezza terza*. Paying off the gondolier, he headed through the alley to the side door. It was bolted and locked from the outside which meant that Domenico, the porter, was not at his post. He hurried around to the other side of the building and, checking that no one was about to see him, quickly scaled the side to the balcony. In a moment he was inside. The room which had been his was now taken over by more of the old man's creations. The brightening sky gave little light and he was unsure of anything in the room. He noticed a full-length mirror with an eerie skeleton figure imbedded in it and moved to one side. Twice he felt his face push against clear glass and had to move around it. Finally he found the door and was out in the hallway which led to Angelo's room.

The door opened slowly and with less creaking than Lazaro had expected. Inside he saw Angelo, resting on his cot, asleep. Beside him on the table a candle still burned over the book which the old man had been consulting. The candle's light seemed to spread out and warmly fill the room with its soft glow, lighting the books and papers which were crammed on the shelves covering the walls of the room. The light shone through the dust in the air to highlight the folds in Angelo's face in humble chiaroscuro. Again he reminded Lazaro of the prophets, their faces weathered by the dry wind of the Levant. Small wonder, for the artists of Italy used men such as these for models, old worn men whose hides had been tanned not by the rigors of following God in a bleak and desolate place but by the machinery of the state.

Lazaro put his pack on the floor, then reached out his hand to the old man's face, afraid for a moment that he was dead. The bright eyes opened.

"Lazaro. You're back."

Lazaro laughed and hugged the old man as he sat up. "Only for a little while."

The old man pushed him back the length of his arms. "Let me look at you in the light," he said, then reached for the candle. He was silent for a moment, then asked, "What has happened?"

Lazaro laughed and shook his head. "Nothing, old man. I've been out to the world and now I have come back to see you."

"And to kill?"

"Ah," Lazaro said in a friendly but dismissive tone. He noticed that light was beginning to come in through the skylight. "How have you been? Is your health still good?"

Angelo's eyes lit up. "My health is fine. And there's more." He jumped out of bed and almost tripped on his long nightshirt before he was able to straighten it. "I have something you must see."

Lazaro was taken aback by the old man's activity. "Can't it wait?"

Angelo turned with a devilish grin. "No," he said, pulling on his boots, and headed out and down the stairs. Lazaro followed the old man as he went outside and ran across the cold, dark paving stones to the entrance to the factory. It was an odd sight to see Angelo run in his boots and nightshirt, his skinny legs bright white in the early-morning light. He unbolted the door and pulled Lazaro inside, pausing to push the door shut, then dragged him on, through the porter's room and into the factory. It was warm inside, though Lazaro could see that the furnaces had been allowed to burn down to coals. There were pieces everywhere and more mirrors than Lazaro had ever seen in Angelo's factory.

Angelo saw him looking at the mirrors. "We've been busy. I've had some large orders and we just finished this week. The men have a few days off to enjoy Carnevale. I thought I'd give Domenico a rest as well." He headed to the back of the chamber. "We won't be disturbed." There was a creaking sound as he opened the door to his private workroom and entered. Lazaro waited for what seemed to be a long time and was ready to call out to Angelo when the old man reappeared with cobwebs in his hair. He dragged something bundled in cloth and with the shape and size of a wall mirror. "I haven't shown anyone," he said, smiling. "I've been waiting for you. I knew you'd be back." He stopped in the middle of the floor and pulled open the bundle. The brown cloth dropped about his feet and he held against his legs a square piece of clear glass which reached to midthigh.

Lazaro came over to him and looked at the glass. It was finely made, a bit thick, but a fine piece of glass, clear, smooth, with no apparent flaws.

Angelo placed it on the floor between them. "Break it."

Lazaro looked at the glass and began to protest but Angelo held his hand up then motioned toward the glass and moved his lips, silently repeating his request, then chuckled and stepped back.

Lazaro decided to do just as he'd been asked. He lifted his foot and stomped on the glass. Nothing happened. He shoved it with his foot so that it rested on an uneven bit of floor and stomped again. The glass remained intact.

The old man was smiling and offered him a *punti* stick. "Here," he said with a grin, "maybe this will help."

Lazaro dropped the metal rod on the center of the glass. He couldn't believe his eyes. The glass was unharmed. He lifted the rod again and again but still the glass would not break.

Angelo began to chuckle in his mad fashion and pushed Lazaro out of the way, then grabbed the piece of glass and threw it against the wall of the furnace. There was a loud clanging and the glass slid to the floor, unbroken. The old man grinned proudly. "I've found the formula," he said, then walked back to the glass, squatted, and began polishing it.

Lazaro began to follow, but noticed across the factory a woman standing by the entrance. She waved at him and he walked over, but it wasn't until he was very close that he saw that it was Renata. He wondered for a moment how much she had seen, but when his eyes met hers he saw that she was interested in him rather than in anything the old man had been displaying. She pulled him by the hand back into the porter's room, and, with a glance back for Angelo, who was still occupied with the glass, Lazaro went.

Renata didn't stop until she had pulled him back into the street and then she hugged him tightly and kissed him. "At first I thought I'd seen a ghost. I just happened to glance out my window and there you were," she said, waving her hand in the direction of the tavern. "But you're back. I knew you wouldn't leave for good."

He pulled himself free and they stood in the cold air, their breath white in the early morning. As he looked at her he noticed that her skin had changed, taken on the hue of the rash of those infected with the French pox, though she had covered it with powder. And the color of her hair was different. The blonde had given way to a deep red. Her body was the same, though the pox marks could be seen on her exposed chest and the curves of her breasts which pushed out of her dress. She pulled her cloak tighter, not as a result of his gaze but from the cold. Lazaro noticed that the cape was of very fine cloth. Renata had been doing well.

"Still the barbarian," she said, slapping his leather jacket with the flat of her hand. "Well, on you it looks good."

"Come in from the cold," he offered.

She smiled and stepped back. "No, I can't. That old fart doesn't like me." She smiled and raised her eyebrows. "His workmen seem to have too strong an interest in me."

Lazaro chuckled and Renata laughed as well. "You look well," he said.

"I'm doing fine," she said, nodding. "I've got a half interest in the tavern here now. And Mother is dead, finally," she said with a crooked smile, "so I have the Dancing Mouse as well, but I let Father run that. It's become a popular place. I just got back from there a little while ago."

"Well," Lazaro said, not sure what to do.

"They're still looking for you," Renata said, looking a little more serious.

"Who?"

"You know," she said and held up her hands to mask her face then poked her finger into his side, laughing. "You made a lot of people very angry, running off with that Jew. Is she still with you?"

Lazaro wondered how much she knew but just shrugged and gave an appropriate smile. "She left for Bruges, for family. I ended up in Rhodes. Just got back from there. I'm passing through."

"I've heard about that," Renata said. "It must have been horrible."

"There are worse things," Lazaro said. "Anyway, it's finished. There'll be lots of work in the spring, in Hungary." He could see that she was only vaguely aware of where Hungary was.

"Came by to see old friends, then," she said, nodding back to Angelo. Lazaro bent over and, through the doorways, could see that he was now dragging the piece of glass from the center of the floor back to his workroom.

Lazaro began to feel the hairs rise on the back of his neck. "The only ship I could get was coming here so I thought I might as well see him. He barely remembers me."

"And do you remember that Zorzi woman?"

"I remember the trouble," Lazaro said honestly. "Is she still in Rome?"

Renata nodded. "The convent's a good place for her. I hear her mother's settled in to a long illness and will require a nurse for some time."

The hairs on Lazaro's neck were now fully erect. "You're well informed."

"You come by a lot of information in my business." Renata poked him in the side again. "Don't worry about me. I'm not going to tell anyone you're here. I'd like to see you too. Come over once I've had a chance to rest," she said, then yawned long and hard. "I really have to get some sleep. You know how busy it is in Carnevale. But I can find some time." She began to head up the *calle* toward her tavern, then stopped and hurried back to him. "Tonight isn't a good night, though," she said in a conspiratorial whisper. "Some of my guests will be *bravi* from the Secretariat." She smiled. "They are so eager. But you be careful," she said, then scuttled off.

Lazaro waved after her, shut the door and bolted it, then went into the factory and stood by the furnace to warm up. But there was another chill which the fire did not drive away. Renata had never been friendly and forgiving without a purpose. And that fine cloak was an assassin's cloak. "Still the barbarian" she had said. Had she meant a Barbarian at law who would fetch a good price? Her mention of Margoleit meant she had some information but she didn't seem at all surprised when he said she had gone to Bruges. Perhaps Margoleit had been able to return to the ghetto in secrecy. It seemed so unlikely for Venice. And he wondered again how much Renata had seen of Angelo's demonstration.

Lazaro found Angelo inside his workroom, the plate of unbreakable glass resting on a workbench in front of him. The old man seemed to be a bit disoriented. Lazaro saw now that the mercury was taking its toll physically as well as mentally. It would not be long before he would need a great deal of care. Fugger had promised a place for the old man and now with this latest discovery it was important that he get out of Venice. The Secretariat would not take kindly to this new glass. Fugger would, and he would reward Angelo accordingly.

Lazaro stood beside him and ran his hand along the edge of the glass. "That's incredible. But the Secretariat won't like it. Or the guild."

"A pox on the Secretariat," Angelo said and spit against the hot side of his small furnace.

"Were they hard on you after I left?" Lazaro asked as the spittle hissed.

A smile spread over Angelo's face. "Not really. I warranted questioning by Beccaria about a week after you were gone, but when I was finished with them they left me alone."

"You may not be as lucky this time," Lazaro started, "and I could find you a safe place . . ."

Angelo's shoulders sagged a bit. "I've thought of that myself, but I know I can't leave. This is my home. Where else would I find such light?" he said, pointing to the window.

For Lazaro there was only darkness in Venice but he could think of nothing to say which might convince Angelo to leave, and he could see that the old man was too weak for a conversation.

Angelo looked up at him. "I'm tired. Will you stay with me for a while?"

"We'll see," Lazaro said and helped him back upstairs to bed, then set about making him some soup. When the old man had been fed they visited for most of the afternoon, and though Angelo was quite useful in bringing Lazaro up to date on the goings-on in Venice over the last year, it was clear to Lazaro that at times the old man was slipping through the mirror. By dusk he had drifted off to sleep and so Lazaro changed his clothes, found a mask among the refuse in the storeroom, and set off for Venice.

The calendar allowed Martedi Grosso to occur earlier this year, and so Carnevale took place while winter still held sway. It seemed as if the Piazza and the streets he had been gone from for almost a year had not changed at all. Everywhere people in costume and masks celebrated the season, trying desperately to banish the dreariness of a winter which seemed uninterested in ending. But if it was a bit colder this year than last, it didn't really change anything. Here and there were people and costumes which he knew he had seen before. Near the Orologio he even thought he spied the beggar he had known as the wolfman but a crowd shoved by and when it had passed, the beggar was nowhere to be seen. Still, he was sure that the beggar would still be in Venice, somewhere.

Lazaro had decided that before he contacted Margoleit, he would first check at the Fondaco, to see what plans might be made to get out of Venice. He pushed his way along the Mercerie then paused by the Rialto Bridge, between Pander's and the Fondaco, half expecting to see Béres and Vom Scheidt. He had expected as well to catch sight of one of Beccaria's men, but none of his *bravi* were in sight. When he finally got inside he went immediately to the rooms where Fugger's agents could be found. However, when he asked for Gottfried, he was told abruptly that Gottfried would not be in until the next day.

Back outside he moved across the Rialto Bridge and stopped in the Campo Rialto, buying some food from a street vendor, and wondered how he might find Margoleit. The ghetto would already be locked up for the night and so he would have to wait until the next day to look for her there or in the markets near the ghetto. But that seemed so long away, especially when he was so close. He had been proceeding on the assumption that she really was back in Venice, that their child had been born, and these assumptions had been sufficient when he was on his way to Venice. But now that he was here he needed something more definite. Remembering Francesca, he made his way to her house, thinking that at least she might have some news of Margoleit and the child. He waited outside the house for about half an hour but the woman he saw through the window was not Francesca, and there was a man, and children. Finally he spotted a young boy coming out of the next house and caught him as he ran past.

"I'm looking for Francesca. She used to live there," he said, pointing to the house.

The young boy pulled his hand free of Lazaro's. "Not since last spring. The men in the masks took her away and then she moved, to Mestre, I think." He waited for a coin but when one didn't come he kicked Lazaro in the shin and ran off into the crowd.

"Mestre at best," Lazaro thought. She had not been as lucky as Angelo during the questioning, but there was nothing he could do about it now. He thought of going to Bomberg's printing shop but decided against it. It was better not to involve anyone else. And for a moment he wondered if he should find some way into the ghetto, but he dismissed that as foolishness. Though he didn't relish the thought, he would have to spend one more night wondering. He made his way back to the Rialto Bridge and found a gondola to take him to Murano. The night was clear and cold and as soon as they were free of the city he moved out from under the *felze* and enjoyed the dark quiet. He had known that Rhodes had changed him but somehow it had become more apparent this evening as he had found himself in the noisy frivolity of Carnevale. He would be glad when he was finished with Venice.

Murano was much quieter than Venice, so quiet in fact that he found himself wanting some form of company. He drifted past Angelo's dark factory and made his way to Renata's tavern. With his mask on, he entered and took a seat by the door with his back to the wall. The place was smoky and filled with revelers, but through the crowd he saw Renata and it appeared that she saw him as well, though she didn't display it. She had been right about the *bravi*. There were at least eight of them seated at a large table on the other side of the room, enjoying the company of Renata and her girls. Lazaro felt the urge. It was *bravi* such as these who had stalked him and Margoleit as they fled Venice, killed Vom Scheidt in Rhodes, searched for Margoleit on Crete. But they were just instruments of the one at the center. As thoughts of Beccaria filled his mind he realized that Renata had extracted herself from the party and had come to his table with a mug of wine.

She leaned over and kissed him on the cheek, then planted herself on his lap, acting as if he was an old customer. "You are a fool to come here tonight. Even if they can't recognize you, they are always suspicious of strangers."

Lazaro smiled beneath his mask. "I felt the need of drink."

"And company," she said with a smile.

Lazaro took a drink of wine and shook his head. "Not tonight. It's better for me to just sit here and watch others."

One of the *bravi* called out for Renata and she yelled back at him through the crowd that she would be there in a moment. "I'll keep them busy but you really shouldn't stay. Not tonight. Tomorrow?" she asked as she stood.

"Maybe," Lazaro answered and took another drink of wine.

Renata walked back across the room and into the waiting arms of the *bravo* who had called to her. There she began to do her best to distract him and the others. For Lazaro, it had been enough company, and, with Margoleit on his mind, he drank the last of his wine, then left for the peace and quiet of Angelo's factory.

Before dawn he awoke and the thoughts which had plagued him as he fell into sleep were gone, or dulled so that they caused him no pain. There was a brief moment between sleep and wakefulness when he thought of Margoleit and expected her beside him, but it vanished as he opened his eyes.

Angelo was overjoyed to see that Lazaro was still there, as if he had feared he had only dreamed of his return. As Lazaro prepared him some breakfast, he brought up again the question of Angelo leaving Venice, but Angelo dismissed it as quickly as he had the day before. Lazaro realized that there would be no point in pursuing it. Angelo would live out his life in Venice, and for him there was a life here.

With dawn lighting the sky Lazaro was back in Venice and heading along the Mercerie once again. It was thronged now with people looking for bargains in the fish and meat markets, preparing for the last supper before Lent. There were plenty of masked revelers as well and Lazaro, in the mask he had worn the night before, blended in with them as he jostled over bridge after bridge until finally he was in the street leading to the ghetto.

He had seen Margoleit many times in his dreams, wondered if she had survived, if their child had been born, whether he would ever see them, what he would say to her if he did? Now, in sight of the gates, he could think of nothing to say. He paused by the side of the crowded *calle*, but as he stood there he thought of her smile, her laughter, the warm caress of her hands on his body. Those days had been few in number, but they were days of Heaven. "God is love, and Heaven is where God is." He had no wish to remain in this Hell which was where God was not.

He looked down along the *rio* and saw the place where they had escaped almost a year before, remembered how he had come back to the *riva* and had seen her standing there, wet and naked, shivering, trying to save her father's life. And then, as clear as a bell across still water, he saw her face in the crowd, staring at him. He stared back for a moment, sure that it was not her, that it was perhaps a mirage, or the face of a relative of hers, but it was neither. It was Margoleit. He remembered that he had a mask on and wondered how she could be looking so intently at a stranger in a mask. But she continued to stare. Then she shifted her gaze and suddenly it was not her, just someone similar. He watched as she walked along the *calle*, a woman carrying a child. Distance seemed to collapse and light drained out of everything but her face. He watched her walk the slow dance of a madonna. And then when she was very close he smelled a gentle scent which reminded him of her, and again she was Margoleit.

When he spoke her name she had already passed him. She stopped but didn't turn, then began to walk on. Again he spoke her name, again she stopped. This time she turned and he lowered his mask. It was truly Margoleit. She didn't say anything, but a smile broke through her clouded face. Then, as quickly as it had appeared, it disappeared. He stood and she looked about nervously, then signaled for him to follow her into a nearby alleyway.

"You're alive," she said with a smile, as he reached her, but made no move to touch him. "I was sure you were dead. I waited so long."

"The Turks were not interested in letting us wander about. And I was under contract. For us, I thought." He could see that his last comment had made her more uncomfortable and immediately regretted it.

"I tried to explain in the letter I left for you. You did get it?"

"Yes. I got it in December, and I went to Candia as soon as we left Rhodes. Lucrezia explained things to me, as much as she could."

"What about Vom Scheidt?" Margoleit asked, changing the subject.

Lazaro shook his head. "Béres ended up there as well, but he didn't make it out either."

Margoleit nodded. "The news was horrible all along. And they're saying that when the city fell the Turks tore it apart."

"They did no more than the Knights would have done. But it's over now. And Fugger got everything he wanted. He owes me. He owes us." Lazaro waited for some indication from Margoleit, but she said nothing. "There's no need to remain here. We can go to Augsburg now."

"I can't," Margoleit said without looking up. She busied herself adjusting the shawl which covered the baby.

The words stung him.

She paced back to the opening of the narrow alley and checked the street.

"You seemed glad to see me," he said finally.

"I was. I am. But you shouldn't have come here." She was silent and they stood, looking at each other's face. He realized that the mask was dangling about his ears, pulled it backward off his head, and straightened his hair. Then he looked at the small face of the child which she held, swaddled, in her arms.

She caught his glance and pulled the baby closer to her breast, checking through the folds of the dark cloth to see that the child was still sleeping, then looked up at him.

He leaned forward and looked at the young child sleeping in Margoleit's arms, a girl, beautiful, with dark hair and a face which reminded him of his mother. He felt things stir inside him which he could not express, and so leaned farther and kissed the child in her sleep. She stirred briefly, making her small hands into fists, then settled.

"Her name is Rebecca. Do you mind?"

Lazaro shook his head and looked at his daughter. In the quiet he felt reluctant to speak, but finally he felt the words well up inside of him. "She's beautiful." He looked into Margoleit's eyes and saw them soften a bit. "For what we had together, there must be a way. I want to be who I am when I am with you."

"And the part of you that was there the rest of the time?" Margoleit asked.

"I'll banish it forever," Lazaro said with a smile.

There was silence. Margoleit looked at him with dark, moist eyes, and for a moment he felt they were reunited. Then she smiled and the smile had a measure of sadness within it that clarified his error, even before she spoke.

"I've been through this many times in my mind. Even after I believed I would never see you again. It didn't always end the same. But in reality it must. Even before it happened, I think I knew what I would do, from the first moment I felt attracted to you, even though I had doubts about my own strength." She took his hand and pulled him close to her. "Even when I first thought I was pregnant and wanted to run from here, there was a part of me that knew I shouldn't involve you. If you believe I was somehow dishonest I'm sorry." She didn't take her eyes from his. "My child is a Jew, and we will live here. I am accepted. After you left, I had plenty of time to think. It wasn't the fear of the assassins that made me come back here. It was her. I didn't want either of us to be cut off from who we are. When I returned I explained to the rabbis that I had run away to find an uncle I have in France but that I had been raped by the man I had hired to take me to my uncle and was carried off to Crete."

"You told them that I raped you?"

"Not you. I said it was a man named Conversalo. I explained that he was killed in Rhodes and so I was able to get free."

Lazaro smiled. "Unfortunately I used that name to come here. I'll certainly stop now."

"I'm sorry, but it was all I could do."

There was silence.

"You planned this before you left Venice?" he asked.

"No. I loved you." She paused and looked away from Lazaro. "I still love you. I know this isn't the way you see things, so it's hard for you to understand. You may be able to be someone other than who you are. I tried to forget who I was, to be someone different, but it is impossible. As Rebecca came closer, she reminded me. And then it became clear that I had to return. It isn't planning, it's just knowing what must be done, regardless of consequences."

She turned her head toward Lazaro and he stared into her eyes.

"You don't understand," Margoleit said after a moment's pause. "You remember the parable of the dove and the hawk. I clapped my wings so many times in Crete. Even before, when I ran from here, I was clapping my wings, calling to the owner to bring the dovecote, and I didn't even know it. Everything I did just made it clearer to me that I had to come back."

There was an uncomfortable pause interrupted by Rebecca stirring. Margoleit quieted her, then reached into her shawl and took out a small piece of canvas. It was the miniature of Lazaro's mother. "You're asking us to be outsiders. Look what that has done to you." She pressed the miniature into Lazaro's hand. "I've held this for you, fearing I might never be able to return it."

He held it out. "Keep it for Rebecca; a gift from her father."

Margoleit didn't take the miniature back, but instead pulled her shawl up over her head and wiped tears from her face. "Rebecca's father is dead. And for my daughter's sake, and mine, I hope the Master of the Assassins never believes anything else." She looked into his eyes long enough to know that she had secured consent, then turned and walked back into the street.

Lazaro stuffed the miniature inside his vest and stood in the alley, feeling the mist on his face. It was as if he was underground again in Rhodes and a low rumble was racing toward him. It overtook him and he felt as if the air had been pushed away and everything had gone black. The mist turned to rain and he leaned against the wall.

When Lazaro came out of the alley Margoleit was nowhere to be seen. However, as he turned the corner he saw, on the other side of the street, a familiar shape. For a moment it made him feel that he had returned home: the beggar he had thought of as the wolfman sat in the rain, his begging bowl in front of him, hair disheveled and covering his face, tattered clothing barely covering his shivering body. Lazaro crossed over and dropped a ducat in the man's bowl. In his blue eyes he could see that the wolfman recognized him.

It was a struggle to move back through the crowded *calli* to the Fondaco dei Tedeschi, partly because of the crowd and partly because he wanted to go back to Margoleit. But he knew he had to make contact with Fugger's agent and arrange for transport; he had to leave. Gottfried had not yet arrived, but Lazaro was assured he would be there that day, and so Lazaro left word that he would wait for him at Pander's.

The tavern was crowded, but he found a table near a shuttered window and sat with a cold draft blowing over him as he drank the best beer Pander had. The sound of people carousing all around was difficult to take. A thousand times he wanted to run back to the ghetto and find Margoleit and Rebecca. As many times he realized she was right. If he was near them it would only bring them trouble. There was nothing for him in this city and the sooner he left, the better. He repeated this over and over in his mind until the beer he had been drinking allowed him to begin to accept it.

Gottfried did not arrive until very late in the afternoon. After brief greetings he confirmed that a group was heading to Augsburg in two days and that arrangements could be made for him to travel along, and that if there was another, that would be fine. The agent indicated that he had been advised by Fugger to expect three, but Lazaro just shook his head and no more questions were asked.

As Lazaro stepped back into Carnevale he realized he was glad there would be a slight delay. Two days would give him just enough time to deal with Beccaria. Neither Margoleit nor Rebecca would have anything to fear from the Master of the Assassins.

XXVI

As he sat in the gondola winding through the *rii* of Venice, heading back to Murano, a light snow mist began to fall. Night had come, and with it the Carnevale was in full swing. In some other frame of mind he might have found in the snow delicate patterns which might appear enshrined in glass or used to decorate some holy work. But now it was just the dust of death which hung over all things. The thought twisted in him like a waking nightmare and he could not set it right. Images filled his mind, and he saw in his waking nightmare the four horsemen of the Apocalypse. They did not ride with wild abandon through the countryside, but cantered comfortably for they reigned supreme. War, starvation, and pestilence rode with the figure which held scales in his hands. It was clear to him. Those were not the scales of justice and the final judgment. Those were the scales of the merchant.

Lazaro admitted to himself now that he had not expected to find Margoleit again. Somehow the grave in which he had placed her in his imagination was easier to take than the grave to which she had relegated their relationship. Seeing Rebecca had made it even more difficult. Worst of all, his return had placed them in danger. He could not clap his wings and cry out. He had to attack the hawk. There was nothing else for him to do but gather his weapons from the old man's factory and find Beccaria.

A feeling of emptiness and dread came over him. Night was again closing over his soul. He had allowed himself to think it might be otherwise but it was not to be. As a child he had believed in beauty but he had soon learned that the belief was misguided. With Margoleit there would have been a chance for him to find that beauty but now it would never be. He knew how Lucifer must have felt, to be banished from the presence of God. Little wonder he was the way he was.

It was as Lazaro stood on the *fondamenta* in front of Angelo's factory that he first felt something was wrong. There was an emptiness within him as he looked up at the dark building, and it increased as he mounted the stairs. He drew his stiletto and entered the laboratory. At first he saw strange reflections everywhere and felt dizzy, as if all that he knew to be real was somehow rearranged. Then he realized that there were broken mirrors everywhere. The small amount of light in the room, which came from a smoldering brazier, was reflected in each shard and he felt in that moment that he was somehow walking among the stars or in some other world. The feeling passed as he began to search for the old man. He moved slowly, unsure of who or what might still be lurking somewhere in the dark room. He was also afraid that he would find, among the broken mirrors, a broken man. As he approached the bedroom he was startled by a man lurking off to the side. No sooner did he freeze than he realized that it was his reflection in a half-silvered piece of glass which had somehow been missed by the intruders. He continued and moved past the half-open door and into Angelo's bedroom. There was some light coming from the window and in that half light he could see Angelo's empty bed. He had felt within him some weak hope that, somehow, everything was all right, that the old man had had a seizure and had broken his mirrors before collapsing in exhaustion on the bed. But Angelo was not there. He wondered then if perhaps the old man was out somewhere and burglars had broken in searching for gold or alchemical secrets, but he knew this was no closer to the truth. Without looking closely he could see that the papers and books which had lined the shelves were gone, each and every one of them. The Secretariat had struck.

It was in his old room that Lazaro found Angelo, lying amid the broken glass and mirrors. As he stood over Angelo he saw on the windowsill a goblet, much like the one which Beccaria had broken so long ago in this room. It had been left for him to see. He picked up the broken body and carried it back out to the laboratory, laying it on the floor. There must have been many men for the mess in the workroom was considerable and the shelves were bare. Nothing remained of the books which the old man had studied and in which he had written his secrets. They had wanted to be sure that nothing would remain. And the old man's death was the final security.

Lazaro didn't look for a candle. There was nothing more for him to see. He knelt for a moment beside the old man's body and searched for the anger and pain which he knew was inside him, but it refused to come and kept back, in the dark corners, mute. He closed the old man's eyes, smoothed his beard, and placed his hands together on his chest, the right over the left.

Going back to the bedroom, he retrieved his bag, then came back and stood for a moment in the dark and mirror-speckled workroom. The mysteries which had furnished the room were shattered and with them everything which had defined Angelo. There was nothing left for him here. But still the picture was incomplete. As he headed for the door he tipped the brazier over, spilling its coals among the broken bottles of chemicals and pieces of wood which littered the floor. Even as he shut the door the flames began to dance.

Back in the *calle* he walked to the small side door which led to the factory. Inside, the furnaces were burning, unattended. Someone had stoked them, perhaps to burn some of Angelo's records, though others would no doubt be locked away within the Secretariat. The holes were open and the dancing flames lit the entire area. He walked slowly about the room. There was less evidence of intrusion here, but a stool was overturned, and the drawings which normally remained here and there on the floor had been washed off. Near the back, the floor was covered with shattered glass.

It was in behind the tables, to the side of the larger furnace, that he found her, though he had truly hoped that he would not. In the light which was always kind to scarred and pitted flesh, she looked beautiful now. They had taken the time to close her eyes, but even then had left their mark; he could see a faint smear of blood across her face. Perhaps she had gone back into the corner expecting some less violent reward for her services. Perhaps Renata had known what would befall her. Whatever had happened, he had no interest in laying out the choreography. It had happened. Beccaria, accompanied, had quieted the old man and the informer. The Secretariat was safe. There was nothing to be learned from further analysis.

Lazaro pulled stools and tables together and threw a torch into their midst. With successive torches, he sowed fire in each nook and cranny of the building. Angelo would have a fiery pyre to signal his exit, and Renata would be swept up into the afterlife in the glow of flames.

The heat finally drove him from the building. As he stood outside he could see the fire spreading throughout, casting shadows in the courtyard and the *calle*. Lazaro prayed that the fire would spread and engulf all of Murano and what it had come to mean to him. But he knew that the God he prayed to had no power here. The God of commerce would join with the men of Murano and they would contain the fire, securing their livelihood from harm. In a little while it would be as if nothing had happened. The carboned bones of the building would be pulled down and a new factory would rise from the ashes. But as Lazaro watched the flames dance higher he knew he had one more thing to do that night. He would act and his act would not be swept away like so much sand before the changing tide.

People were gathering now, preparing to fight the fire which had already begun to lick at the roof. Lazaro glanced up the *calle* and saw that Renata's tavern was dark, shuttered. He would have to seek out his quarry in Venice. Silently, he stepped back into the shadows to find a boat which would take him there.

Carnevale had reached its zenith and the brief snowfall had turned the paving stones to slippery mirrored surfaces as Lazaro walked through the Piazza. All about him revelers abounded, drinking, squeezing, leering, slipping. He knew that he had walked these streets before, but he could not picture himself in them. The place appeared now as a dream and it was as if he was being led, yet he knew where it would end. It reminded him of hunting strange game in a strange land. But he knew the name of his quarry, and he could feel him.

He headed for the gate under the huge clock and walked along the winding street lined with merchants. The Rialto Bridge appeared to him and he turned to the right for Pander's Inn where he was given a small room, the only one left, little more than a bed, a window, and a door. But it was all that he needed. He opened his sack and removed the clothes he had not worn since Rhodes: his long leather shirt studded with metal rings, his pantaloons, wristbands studded with metal to fend off the odd blow, his sword, his stiletto. In his mind it should have taken longer, but it was over so quickly that he was out in the *calli* again before he was truly prepared for the crush of people. They were everywhere. The bowels of Venice had opened up and let forth with their best.

As he turned a corner heading for a tavern that was clear in his memory, a crush of people threw him against the railing beside a *rio*. Two of the people fell over the railings and into the water. Their friends laughed and tossed insults their way as the poor unfortunates tried to make for the side without swallowing any of the filthy water. Lazaro pushed his way through the laughing crowd and bumped into a mask vendor.

"*Signore*, hide your face," the vendor said, holding forth a silly mask.

Lazaro looked at his pocked face, his toothless grin, the bald spots showing through his greasy hair.

"I have all kinds, *signore*. All manner of man and beast."

Lazaro looked at his tray and found a mask to his liking. Tossing a coin to the vendor, he walked away, stuffing the mask in his belt. He didn't feel like wearing it just yet.

The tavern he was looking for suddenly appeared in front of him. He entered the Dancing Mouse and walked past the man who had once been his landlord. In a room in the back he found the young men he knew would be here; two *bravi*, alone, talking quietly. They wore the insignia of the Secretariat and had masks propped against their wine flask on the table. Before they could move Lazaro had drawn his sword and held it to one man's neck. "Put your weapons on the table." They did not respond immediately; he pushed the point slightly, and a trickle of blood dripped from the wound in the man's neck. His eyes widened, and he cried to his friend, "Do it!" They quickly but carefully put their swords and stilettos on the table. He signaled for them to move away from the table and they obeyed, standing with their backs to the wall as Lazaro sat on the edge of the table, his sword still pointing toward them. "You know who I am?"

They both shook their heads that they did not.

"Your master wants me. I believe he wants me to himself. Go and find him and tell him that Lazarus has returned from the dead and will meet him in the Basilica." He dismissed them with a flick of his sword, and they hurried out of the room and into the street. After finishing their wine, he gathered their swords and stilettos and took them outside, dumping them in the *rio*, then headed for the Piazza.

When the doors to the Basilica closed, the raucous sounds of Carnevale died abruptly. The church was silent, dark, cavernous. As Lazaro walked, his footsteps echoing, he felt like Jonah in the belly of the monster. Something from his youth stirred in his memory and he thought of the tale of Sinbad. Sinbad and his men had come aground on a small island to rest, had built a fire to warm themselves, had cooked their meat. Then the earth had shifted and in a moment the dry, secure island had become a writhing sea monster, a great fish, a spouting angry whale. Venice was like that for him. After the ruination of the wars in Terraferma, Venice had appeared to him as some calm island retreat, lying in the shallows of the Adriatic, a refuge from the furious storm of war raging all about him. And yet Venice had writhed and tossed him. But now he had returned to Venice and the womb of Mother Church. He would not clap his wings and cry out.

Under the central dome Lazaro stopped and looked up into the darkness where he knew Christ sat. Listening but hearing nothing, he moved over to the south nave aisle and sat on a rough bench with his back resting against the cold marble.

Tadini had said that Beccaria had been there when his father had been killed. Lazaro scanned the faces embedded in his memory, searching their eyes. There had been four young men, unmasked, bold, armed. They had come in the night and invaded the peace of that first home. His father had fought and died. They had grabbed his mother and him. And young Nicolo — Lazaro had heard only the frightened screams, then silence. As his father had warned him, Kaziklu Bey had come to eat his brother. And he had not been there to save him. He and his mother had been spirited away in pain, and for his omission they had both suffered.

Now the turmoil would end. Beccaria would come and he would make that demon answer before his death. In his mind he rehearsed the pain that he would inflict upon him, for the family he had once had, for the family he would never have, for all the evils real and imagined which had resulted from the intrusion of this Venetian.

There was a sound, perhaps a pigeon somewhere high above, perhaps a rat. And then, like some clear bell far off through the fog, he knew it was Beccaria. He could feel the presence.

He pulled the small convex mirror from his breast and held it up so he could see his face. Strangely, he felt no more of the fear of the beast within him. He felt totally human. The eyes which looked back at him were not the eyes of an animal but of a man. He felt the peace of knowing that he was simply himself.

He saw in the mirror that Beccaria was standing behind him, silently, his hands folded in front of him, his cape and hat, his white mask. And in the dark those eyes shone across and lost themselves in the mirror. There was the beast.

Beccaria stood amid the columns, quiet, relaxed, ready. Lazaro stood and took one step toward him then waited. For an eternity there was no sound. The silence swelled in his ears. His hand rested on the pommel of his sword, and Beccaria watched. A smile crossed Beccaria's face, twisting his lips in a friendly grin.

"You look well. Rhodes was kind to you."

"But not to your *bravi.*"

Beccaria shrugged. "That was their job. The ones you met tonight were most taken with your skill, and most embarrassed."

"I'm glad you could come," Lazaro said.

Beccaria leaned against a column and rested his hand on his sword. "It isn't often that Lazarus returns from the dead. So what is it that you want?"

"I want to see your face."

"Which one?"

"You. The real you."

"This is the real me," Beccaria said and turned around slowly, stopping when he again faced Lazaro. "You've seen my other faces, whether you realize it or not. I go by many names. I think most of all you accepted me as a beggar."

Beccaria grunted and Lazaro stumbled in reaction, recognizing the sound as the grunt of the wolfman, the beggar he had seen so many times, the last as he was leaving Margoleit that morning.

Beccaria laughed. "And you were so generous. I find that when I am masked, people are more generous, even more honest. They respond to the mask and don't think of the human underneath."

"And you need to hide beneath those masks."

"Wake up, Lazaro. We all hide. We hide from those who would know us too closely and divine our weaknesses, and from those who would weaken our self-proclaimed divinity. We hide from the priest, from the mistress, from the parent, from the tax collector, we would hide from God if God existed, and if we believe God does exist we hide from him. It's in our blood. Adam's first action when he became a man was to hide."

"And we hide from the past."

Beccaria's shoulders seemed to droop and his eyes looked to the ceiling. "Yes. We hide most from our past. But I have something to offer you. A chance to change that, to leave the past behind. You have talent, and you have a mind which does not hamper your talent. You're worth ten of my *bravi*. Come and work with me. Together this city can be ours. I have no interest in the Jew. She's safe. And she had no interest in you, so you are free."

"And Angelo?"

Beccaria shook his head. "That old man threatened a way of life. He had the glory of discovery. What we did after was necessary."

"And the girl? Renata?"

There was a chuckle in Beccaria's voice. "The whore? Don't sound so concerned now. You cared nothing for her while she was alive. Given the blemishes on her skin she wasn't long for this world anyway." Beccaria turned and took a couple of steps, moving into a shadow. "Loyalty is such a strange thing. She discovered that we were coming to Murano to look for you and she tried to buy your safety by offering us information about Angelo's discovery. I expected her to be better at bargaining, but when she told us what she knew it was clear that they both would have to die." Beccaria leaned forward slightly and the light caught his mask. His face seemed to float, disembodied, in the surrounding dark. "Small loss, though, wouldn't you agree, when there is so much at stake?" Then Beccaria stepped back into the light. "There is an opportunity here Lazarus, and you must seize it or it will be lost to you, and you to me. I'm offering you a chance to work with me."

Lazaro felt his blood rushing. "You're mad. My only reason for being here is to kill you."

Beccaria smiled. "For those people? That was business. You can understand that. It's not much different than any business you've ever engaged in. And it's not worth your life."

"And my family," Lazaro said, staring at Beccaria. "That was your business, wasn't it?"

Beccaria's head swung up and he stared toward the darkness where Christ sat.

Lazaro could feel his heart beating faster in his chest. "You were there, weren't you."

Beccaria sighed, then he lowered his gaze and his eyes struck Lazaro's with leaden resolve. "I was there."

Lazaro felt his legs soften. He was aware of the moisture between his palm and the pommel of his sword. "You killed my father." Lazaro's voice echoed.

The echo linked with Beccaria's voice as he spoke. "You don't know what you're talking about. I saw him die. Where were you?" Beccaria's eyes flashed accusingly beneath his mask.

As if a parent's hand struck his face, Lazaro recoiled from the statement. "I was outside."

Beccaria now took a step forward. "You didn't see the Turk fall to his knees, paying for what he had done."

Sweat formed beads on Lazaro's forehead. He wanted to reach for his sword, to draw it and run it through Beccaria. But he couldn't. He stood there, frozen with the frozen faces of Christ and the Saints looking down at him.

As Beccaria stepped forward again his lips moved beneath the mask though the eyes, like glass balls of deep blue, moved not one iota. "You were taken away with her."

Lazaro felt powerless in the exchange. He wanted to scream outrage at this assassin who spoke of his mother this way but the echo of Beccaria's voice rang in his ears.

"Did you see her die?" Beccaria asked.

Beccaria was close now, so close that Lazaro could see the red in his eyes, the anger, the pain. "I saw her die," Lazaro answered.

A smile spread over Beccaria's face. He stopped, so close to Lazaro that his breath moved the hair hanging by Lazaro's neck. "You don't know me, do you?"

Lazaro stared into his dark eyes, deep pools filled with death, filled with death and a strange longing.

Beccaria spoke in a near whisper. "From the moment I saw you, I have known who you are and known the talent you must carry within you. Too many times I let you get away with things that should not have gone unpunished. But I had a purpose. Together we would have had the run of this city. We could have recovered things which were lost to us. But if you are not with me then you are against me, and if I have learned one thing, it is to trust my own judgment, and to follow it."

Lazaro could only stare into those blue eyes. They trapped him. Like some forest beast, he was transfixed. He could not stir. The eyes behind the white mask had bewitched him. He saw a wet pain grow like some flower of death in the pupils of Beccaria's eyes.

"I sought you, but I found you not," Beccaria said and, as he spoke, there was a rustle of cloth and Beccaria's left hand moved from under his cloak. Lazaro saw the glint on the metal stiletto and pushed his right hand out fast and hard. The blade collided with the small mirror which Lazaro had held in his hand and there was the sound of breaking glass as it shattered into a thousand pieces and fell by their feet. The stiletto fell too. Their eyes were locked together. In a single movement, Beccaria drew another blade, this one of glass, with his right hand and moved it up with force toward Lazaro's belly. Lazaro grasped Beccaria's wrist as he had done to so many adversaries so many times before but never with so much reluctance. It was nearly instinctual. Had he thought about it more he might not have done what he now did. The blade moved not to him but, bent with force, pierced Beccaria's gut. Lazaro jerked his hand and the blade broke off. Beccaria's hand went limp, yet his eyes stayed hard, locked in a cold embrace with Lazaro's. Beccaria raised his hands and put them around Lazaro's neck. He pulled Lazaro's face to his, turned his head slightly, and kissed him full on the lips.

"I would have killed you, Brother," he said, then his legs went limp. As he slid to the floor, the mask came off, and Lazaro saw the face which had plagued him in his darkest dreams. It was not the face of one of the men who had come to kill his father and steal his mother away. It was the face he had carried with him all these years — the face of his brother.

Lazaro stood as Nicolo settled on the floor, the red seeping from the wound in his stomach. As he glanced down he saw himself, holding the white mask of the assassin in his hand. He placed it over Nicolo's face.

There was a sound from above and Lazaro looked up. In the walkway above was Tagliapietro. He placed his hands on the railing and leaned forward, calling down to Lazaro, "These things happen, young captain: an accident of birth, and now an accidental death. The leader of the assassins who went after your father was named Beccaria, a young man who served Venice faithfully. But who among us is without weakness? And in his weakness he did not kill the young boy who stayed by his dead father's side. Instead he brought him back — a *devshurmeh*, if you will. They stole one of ours, we took one of theirs. He raised him as his own and never hid the truth from his new son. The truth isn't hidden from the Janissaries and look what strength they have. The truth always makes us strong, Lazaro. And his new son grew to love him, to respect him, to follow in his profession. And when the elder died, the junior took his new father's place."

Lazaro stood beside his dead brother, looking up at Tagliapietro. It seemed as if the darkness in which Tagliapietro stood was spreading out, extinguishing the little light there had been in the Basilica.

Tagliapietro's black silks rustled as he took a couple of steps on the walkway, then stopped. "What would you have wanted for your brother? To die in Rhodes? To live as you have lived? He had someone to watch over him, to train him as he grew into a man. And he had a city which needed him. He would have had you work with him but he would not allow you to live and be against him. Who can fault such judgment? It's just good business. But that is finished. Best not to let your mind dwell on it. There is work to be done. Soon there will be a new Doge, even a new Pope. It appears I am in need of a Master of the Assassins and you seem well qualified."

It felt to Lazaro as if all about him doors were slamming shut. He stumbled away from Nicolo, heading for the door which opened onto the Piazza. Above him he could hear the sounds of Tagliapietro's robes rustling in the darkness. Then there was only the tomb-like silence of the Basilica, and a low murmur from beyond its walls. His hands found the doors and he pushed them open, stepping out into the Piazza, hoping against all hope that there would be fresh air outside. There was none; only the stale air of Venice. Revelers raced past masked. He turned and looked up at the Basilica and saw Tagliapietro appear above him on the balcony, standing to the side of the four horses.

"Your answer?" Tagliapietro called as he leaned over the railing.

Another crowd of masked revelers bumped into Lazaro, then pulled him into the human stream as the Marangona began to peal midnight. Lazaro looked back at Tagliapietro but the crowd pulled him on and he couldn't hear what was being yelled at him. His hand dropped to his belt and he felt the mask which he had slung there. Taking it, he moved out into the Piazza and pulled it over his face.

It was the mask of the wolf.